The Best Horror Stories

The Best Horror Stories

Authors Include

ROBERT BLOCH

RAY BRADBURY

ROALD DAHL

WILLIAM FAULKNER

PATRICIA HIGHSMITH

DOROTHY L. SAYERS

IVY LEAF

This volume first published in Great Britain in 1990 by The
Octopus Group Limited

This edition published in 1990 by
Ivy Leaf
Michelin House
81 Fulham Road
London SW3 6RB

Reprinted 1990

This edition produced exclusively in Great Britain for Bookmart
Limited

ISBN 0 86363 002 2

Printed in Great Britain at The Bath Press, Avon

CONTENTS

Edgar Allan Poe

The Black Cat

For the most wild, yet most homely narrative which I am about to pen, I neither expect nor solicit belief. Mad indeed would I be to expect it, in a case where my very senses reject their own evidence. Yet, mad am I not – and very surely do I not dream. But tomorrow I die, and today I would unburden my soul. My immediate purpose is to place before the world, plainly, succinctly, and without comment, a series of mere household events. In their consequences, these events have terrified – have tortured – have destroyed me. Yet I will not attempt to expound them. To me, they have presented little but horror – to many they will seem less terrible than *baroques*. Hereafter, perhaps, some intellect may be found which will reduce my phantasm to the commonplace – some intellect more calm, more logical, and far less excitable than my own, which will perceive, in the circumstances I detail with awe, nothing more than an ordinary succession of very natural causes and effects.

From my infancy I was noted for the docility and humanity of my disposition. My tenderness of heart was even so conspicuous as to make me the jest of my companions. I was especially fond of animals, and was indulged by my parents with a great variety of pets. With these I spent most of my time, and never was so happy as when feeding and caressing them. This peculiarity of character grew with my growth, and, in my manhood, I derived from it one of my principal sources of pleasure. To those who have cherished an affection for a faithful and sagacious dog, I need hardly be at the trouble of explaining the nature or the intensity of the gratification thus derivable. There is something in the unselfish and self-sacrificing love of a brute, which goes directly to the heart of him who has had frequent occasion to test the paltry friendship and gossamer fidelity of mere *Man*.

I married early, and was happy to find in my wife a disposition not uncongenial with my own. Observing my partiality for domestic pets, she lost no opportunity of procuring those of the most agreeable kind. We had birds, goldfish, a fine dog, rabbits, a small monkey, and *a cat*.

This latter was a remarkably large and beautiful animal, entirely black, and sagacious to an astonishing degree. In speaking of his intelligence, my wife, who at heart was not a little tinctured with superstition, made frequent allusion to the ancient popular notion, which regarded all black cats as witches in disguise. Not that she was ever *serious* upon this point – and I mention the matter at all for no better reason than that it happens, just now, to be remembered.

Pluto – this was the cat's name – was my favourite pet and playmate. I alone fed him, and he attended me wherever I went about the house. It was even with difficulty that I could prevent him from following me through the streets.

Our friendship lasted, in this manner, for several years, during which my general temperament and character – through the instrumentality of the fiend Intemperance – had (I blush to confess it) experienced a radical alteration for the worse. I grew, day by day, more moody, more irritable, more regardless of the feelings of others. I suffered myself to use intemperate language to my wife. At length, I even offered her personal violence. My pets, of course, were made to feel the change in my disposition. I not only neglected, but ill-used them. For Pluto, however, I still retained sufficient regard to restrain me from maltreating him, as I made no scruple of maltreating the rabbits, the monkey, or even the dog, when by accident, or through affection, they came in my way. But my disease grew upon me – for what disease is like alcohol? – and at length even Pluto, who was now becoming old, and consequently somewhat peevish – even Pluto began to experience the effects of my ill temper.

One night, returning home, much intoxicated, from one of my haunts about town, I fancied that the cat avoided my presence. I seized him; when, in his fright at my violence, he inflicted a slight wound upon my hand with his teeth. The fury of a demon instantly possessed me. I knew myself no longer. My original soul seemed, at once, to take its flight from my body; and a more than fiendish malevolence, gin-nurtured, thrilled every fibre of my frame. I took from my waistcoat pocket a pen-knife, opened it, grasped the poor beast by the throat, and deliberately cut one of its eyes from the socket! I blush, I burn, I shudder, while I pen the damnable atrocity.

When reason returned with the morning – when I had slept off the fumes of the night's debauch – I experienced a sentiment half of horror, half of remorse, for the crime of which I had been guilty; but it was, at best, a feeble and equivocal feeling, and the soul remained untouched.

THE BLACK CAT

I again plunged into excess, and soon drowned in wine all memory of the deed.

In the meantime the cat slowly recovered. The socket of the lost eye presented, it is true, a frightful appearance, but he no longer appeared to suffer any pain. He went about the house as usual, but, as might be expected, fled in extreme terror at my approach. I had so much of my old heart left, as to be at first grieved by this evident dislike on the part of a creature which had once so loved me. But this feeling soon gave place to irritation. And then came, as if to my final and irrevocable overthrow, the spirit of PERVERSENESS. Of this spirit philosophy takes no account. Yet I am not more sure that my soul lives, than I am that perverseness is one of the primitive impulses of the human heart – one of the indivisible primary faculties, or sentiments, which give direction to the character of man. Who has not, a hundred times, found himself committing a vile or a silly action, for no other reason than because he knows he should *not*? Have we not a perpetual inclination, in the teeth of our best judgment, to violate that which is *Law*, merely because we understand it to be such? This spirit of perverseness, I say, came to my final overthrow. It was this unfathomable longing of the soul *to vex itself* – to offer violence to its own nature – to do wrong for the wrong's sake only – that urged me to continue and finally to consummate the injury I had inflicted upon the unoffending brute. One morning, in cool blood, I slipped a noose about its neck and hung it to the limb of a tree – hung it with the tears streaming from my eyes, and with the bitterest remorse at my heart – hung it *because* I knew that it had loved me, and *because* I felt it had give me no reason of offence – hung it *because* I knew that in so doing I was committing a sin – a deadly sin that would so jeopardise my immortal soul as to place it – if such a thing were possible – even beyond the reach of the infinite mercy of the Most Merciful and Most Terrible God.

On the night of the day on which this cruel deed was done, I was aroused from sleep by the cry of 'Fire!' The curtains of my bed were in flames. The whole house was blazing. It was with great difficulty that my wife, a servant, and myself, made our escape from the conflagration. The destruction was complete. My entire worldly wealth was swallowed up, and I resigned myself thenceforward to despair.

I am above the weakness of seeking to establish a sequence of cause and effect between the disaster and the atrocity. But I am detailing a chain of facts, and wish not to leave even a possible link imperfect. On the day succeeding the fire, I visited the ruins. The walls, with one exception, had fallen in. This exception was found in a compartment wall, not very thick, which stood about the middle of the house, and against which had rested the head of my bed. The plastering had here, in great measure,

resisted the action of the fire – a fact which I attributed to its having been
recently spread. About this wall a dense crowd were collected, and many
persons seemed to be examining a particular portion of it with very
minute and eager attention. The words 'strange!' 'singular!' and other
similar expressions, excited my curiosity. I approached and saw, as if
graven in bas-relief upon the white surface, the figure of a gigantic *cat*.
The impression was given with an accuracy truly marvellous. There was
a rope about the animal's neck.

When I first beheld this apparition – for I could scarcely regard it as
less – my wonder and my terror were extreme. But at length reflection
came to my aid. The cat, I remembered, had been hung in a garden
adjacent to the house. Upon the alarm of fire, this garden had been immediately filled by the crowd – by some one of whom the animal must
have been cut from the tree and thrown, through an open window, into
my chamber. This had probably been done with the view of arousing me
from sleep. The falling of other walls had compressed the victim of my
cruelty into the substance of the freshly-spread plaster; the lime of which,
with the flames and the *ammonia* from the carcass, had then accomplished
the portraiture as I saw it.

Although I thus readily accounted to my reason, if not altogether to
my conscience, for the startling fact just detailed, it did not the less fail
to make a deep impression upon my fancy. For months I could not rid
myself of the phantasm of the cat; and, during this period, there came
back into my spirit a half-sentiment that seemed, but was not, remorse.
I went so far as to regret the loss of the animal, and to look about me,
among the vile haunts which I now habitually frequented, for another
pet of the same species, and of somewhat similar appearance, with which
to supply its place.

One night as I sat, half stupefied, in a den of more than infamy, my
attention was suddenly drawn to some black object, reposing upon the
head of one of the immense hogsheads of gin, or of rum, which constituted
the chief furniture of the apartment. I had been looking steadily at the
top of this hogshead for some minutes, and what now caused me surprise
was the fact that I had not sooner perceived the object thereupon. I
approached it, and touched it with my hand. It was a black cat – a very
large one – fully as large as Pluto, and closely resembling him in every
respect but one. Pluto had not a white hair upon any portion of his body;
but this cat had a large, although indefinite, splotch of white, covering
nearly the whole region of the breast.

Upon my touching him, he immediately arose, purred loudly, rubbed
against my hand, and appeared delighted with my notice. This, then,
was the very creature of which I was in search. I at once offered to purchase it of the landlord; but this person made no claim to it – knew

nothing of it – had never seen it before.

I continued my caresses, and when I prepared to go home, the animal evinced a disposition to accompany me. I permitted it to do so; occasionally stooping and patting it as I proceeded. When it reached the house it domesticated itself at once, and became immediately a great favourite with my wife.

For my own part, I soon found a dislike to it arising within me. This was just the reverse of what I had anticipated; but – I know not how or why it was – its evident fondness for myself rather disgusted and annoyed me. By slow degrees, these feelings of disgust and annoyance rose into the bitterness of hatred. I avoided the creature; a certain sense of shame, and the remembrance of my former deed of cruelty, preventing me from physically abusing it. I did not, for some weeks, strike, or otherwise violently ill-use it; but gradually – very gradually – I came to look upon it with unutterable loathing, and to flee silently from its odious presence, as from the breath of a pestilence.

What added, no doubt, to my hatred of the beast, was the discovery, on the morning after I brought it home, that, like Pluto, it also had been deprived of one of its eyes. The circumstance, however, only endeared it to my wife, who, as I have already said, possessed, in a high degree, that humanity of feeling which had once been my distinguishing trait, and the source of many of my simplest and purest pleasures.

With my aversion to this cat, however, its partiality for myself seemed to increase. It followed my footsteps with a pertinacity which it would be difficult to make the reader comprehend. Whenever I sat, it would crouch beneath my chair, or spring upon my knees, covering me with its loathsome caresses. If I arose to walk, it would get between my feet, and thus nearly throw me down, or, fastening its long and sharp claws in my dress, clamber, in this manner, to my breast. At such times, although I longed to destroy it with a blow, I was yet withheld from so doing, partly by a memory of my former crime, but chiefly – let me confess it at once – by absolute *dread* of the beast.

This dread was not exactly a dread of physical evil – and yet I should be at a loss how otherwise to define it. I am almost ashamed to own – yes, even in this felon's cell, I am almost ashamed to own – that the terror and horror with which the animal inspired me, had been heightened by one of the merest chimeras it would be possible to conceive. My wife had called my attention, more than once, to the character of the mark of white hair, of which I have spoken, and which constituted the sole visible difference between the strange beast and the one I had destroyed. The reader will remember that this mark, although large, had been originally very indefinite; but, by slow degrees – degrees nearly imperceptible, and which for a long time my reason struggled to reject as fanciful – it had, at length, assumed a rigorous distinctness of outline. It was now the representation of an object that I shudder to name – and for this, above all, I loathed, and dreaded, and would have rid myself of the monster *had I dared* – it was now, I say, the image of a hideous – of a ghastly thing – of the GALLOWS! – oh, mournful and terrible engine of horror and of crime – of agony and of death!

And now was I indeed wretched beyond the wretchedness of mere humanity. And *a brute beast* – whose fellow I had contemptuously destroyed – *a brute beast* to work out for *me* – for me, a man, fashioned in the image of the High God – so much of insufferable woe! Alas! neither by day nor by night knew I the blessing of rest any more! During the former the creature left me no moment alone; and, in the latter, I started, hourly, from dreams of unutterable fear, to find the hot breath of *the thing* upon my face, and its vast weight – an incarnate nightmare that I had no power to shake off – incumbent eternally upon my *heart*!

Beneath the pressure of torments such as these, the feeble remnant of the good within me succumbed. Evil thoughts became my sole intimates – the darkest and most evil of thoughts. The moodiness of my usual temper increased to hatred of all things and of all mankind; while, from the sudden, frequent, and ungovernable outbursts of a fury to which I now blindly abandoned myself, my uncomplaining wife, alas! was the most usual and the most patient of sufferers.

One day she accompanied me, upon some household errand, into the cellar of the old building which our poverty compelled us to inhabit. The cat followed me down the steep stairs, and, nearly throwing me headlong, exasperated me to madness. Uplifting an axe, and forgetting, in my wrath, the childish dread which had hitherto stayed my hand, I aimed a blow at the animal which, of course, would have proved instantly fatal had it descended as I wished. But this blow was arrested by the hand of my wife. Goaded, by the interference, into a rage more than demoniacal, I withdrew my arm from her grasp, and buried the axe in her brain. She fell dead upon the spot, without a groan.

This hideous murder accomplished, I set myself forthwith, and with entire deliberation, to the task of concealing the body. I knew that I could not remove it from the house, either by day or by night, without the risk of being observed by the neighbours. Many projects entered my mind. At one period I thought of cutting the corpse into minute fragments, and destroying them by fire. At another, I resolved to dig a grave for it in the floor of the cellar. Again, I deliberated about casting it into the well in the yard – about packing it in a box, as if merchandise, with the usual arrangements, and so getting a porter to take it from the house. Finally I hit upon what I considered a far better expedient than either of these. I determined to wall it up in the cellar – as the monks of the

Middle Ages are recorded to have walled up their victims.

For a purpose such as this the cellar was well adapted. Its walls were loosely constructed, and had lately been plastered throughout with a rough plaster, which the dampness of the atmosphere had prevented from hardening. Moreover, in one of the walls was a projection, caused by a false chimney, or fireplace, that had been filled up, and made to resemble the rest of the cellar. I made no doubt that I could readily displace the bricks at this point, insert the corpse, and wall the whole up as before, so that no eye could detect anything suspicious.

And in this calculation I was not deceived. By means of a crowbar I easily dislodged the bricks, and, having carefully deposited the body against the inner wall, I propped it in that position, while, with little trouble, I relaid the whole structure as it originally stood. Having procured mortar, sand, and hair, with every possible precaution, I prepared a plaster which could not be distinguished from the old, and with this I very carefully went over the new brickwork. When I had finished, I felt satisfied that all was right. The wall did not present the slightest appearance of having been disturbed. The rubbish on the floor was picked up with the minutest care. I looked around triumphantly, and said to myself, 'Here at least, then, my labour has not been in vain.'

My next step was to look for the beast which had been the cause of so much wretchedness; for I had, at length, firmly resolved to put it to death. Had I been able to meet with it, at the moment, there could have been no doubt of its fate; but it appeared that the crafty animal had been alarmed at the violence of my previous anger, and forebore to present itself in my present mood. It is impossible to describe, or to imagine, the deep, the blissful sense of relief which the absence of the detested creature occasioned in my bosom. It did not make its appearance during the night – and thus for one night at least, since its introduction into the house, I soundly and tranquilly slept; aye, *slept* even with the burden of murder upon my soul!

The second and the third day passed, and still my tormentor came not. Once again I breathed as a free man. The monster, in terror, had fled the premises for ever! I should behold it no more! My happiness was supreme! The guilt of my dark deed disturbed me but little. Some few inquiries had been made, but these had been readily answered. Even a search had been instituted – but of course nothing was to be discovered. I looked upon my future felicity as secured.

Upon the fourth day of the assassination, a party of the police came, very unexpectedly, into the house, and proceeded again to make rigorous investigation of the premises. Secure, however, in the inscrutability of my place of concealment, I felt no embarrassment whatever. The officers bade me accompany them in their search. They left no nook or corner unexplored. At length, for the third or fourth time, they descended into the cellar. I quivered not in a muscle. My heart beat calmly as that of one who slumbers in innocence. I walked the cellar from end to end. I folded my arms upon my bosom, and roamed easily to and fro. The police were thoroughly satisfied, and prepared to depart. The glee at my heart was too strong to be restrained. I burned to say if but one word, by way of triumph, and to render doubly sure their assurance of my guiltlessness.

'Gentlemen,' I said at last, as the party ascended the steps, 'I delight to have allayed your suspicions. I wish you all health, and a little more courtesy. By-the-bye, gentlemen, this – this is a very well-constructed house.' (In the rabid desire to say something easily, I scarcely knew what I uttered at all.) 'I may say an *excellently* well-constructed house. These walls – are you going, gentlemen? – these walls are solidly put together;' and here, through the mere frenzy of bravado, I rapped heavily, with a cane which I held in my hand, upon that very portion of the brickwork behind which stood the corpse of the wife of my bosom.

But may God shield and deliver me from the fangs of the Arch-Fiend! No sooner had the reverberation of my blows sunk into silence, than I was answered by a voice from within the tomb! – by a cry, at first muffled and broken, like the sobbing of a child, and then quickly swelling into one long, loud, and continuous scream, utterly anomalous and in-human – a howl – a wailing shriek, half of horror and half of triumph, such as might have arisen only out of hell, conjointly from the throats of the damned in their agony and of the demons that exult in the damnation.

Of my own thoughts it is folly to speak. Swooning, I staggered to the opposite wall. For one instant the party upon the stairs remained motion-less, through extremity of terror and of awe. In the next, a dozen stout arms were toiling at the wall. It fell bodily. The corpse, already greatly decayed and clotted with gore, stood erect before the eyes of the specta-tors. Upon its head, with red extended mouth and solitary eye of fire, sat the hideous beast whose craft had seduced me into murder, and whose informing voice had consigned me to the hangman. I had walled the monster up within the tomb!

Edgar Allan Poe

The Tell-Tale Heart

True! – nervous – very, very dreadfully nervous I had been and am;
but why *will* you say that I am mad? The disease had sharpened my
senses – not destroyed – not dulled them. Above all was the sense of
hearing acute. I heard all things in the heaven and in the earth. I heard
many things in hell. How, then, am I mad? Hearken! and observe how
healthily – how calmly I can tell you the whole story.

It is impossible to say how first the idea entered my brain; but onec
conceived, it haunted me day and night. Object there was none. Passion
there was none. I loved the old man. He had never wronged me. He
had never given me insult. For his gold I had no desire. I think it was
his eye! yes, it was this! One of his eyes resembled that of a vulture – a
pale blue eye, with a film over it. Whenever it fell upon me, my blood
ran cold; and so by degrees – very gradually – I made up my mind to
take the life of the old man, and thus rid myself of the eye for ever.

Now this is the point. You fancy me mad. Madmen know nothing.
But you should have seen *me*. You should have seen how wisely I proceeded – with what caution – with what foresight – with what dissimula-
tion I went to work! I was never kinder to the old man than during the
whole week before I killed him. And every night, about midnight, I
turned the latch of his door and opened it – oh, so gently! And then,
when I had made an opening sufficient for my head, I put in a dark
lantern, all closed, closed, so that no light shone out, and then I thrust
in my head. Oh, you would have laughed to see how cunningly I thrust
it in! I moved it slowly – very, very slowly, so that I might not disturb
the old man's sleep. It took me an hour to place my whole head within
the opening so far that I could see him as he lay upon his bed. Ha! –
would a madman have been so wise as this? And then, when my head

was well in the room, I undid the lantern, cautiously – oh, so cautiously – cautiously (for the hinges creaked) I undid it just so much that a single thin ray fell upon the vulture eye. And this I did for seven long nights – every night just at midnight – but I found the eye always closed; and so it was impossible to do the work; for it was not the old man who vexed me, but his Evil Eye. And every morning, when the day broke, I went boldly into the chamber, and spoke courageously to him, calling him by name in a hearty tone, and inquiring how he had passed the night. So you see he would have been a very profound old man, indeed, to suspect that every night, just at twelve, I looked in upon him while he slept.

Upon the eighth night I was more than usually cautious in opening the door. A watch's minute hand moves more quickly than did mine. Never before that night had I *felt* the extent of my own powers – of my sagacity. I could scarcely contain my feelings of triumph. To think that there I was, opening the door, little by little, and he not even to dream of my secret deeds or thoughts. I fairly chuckled at the idea; and perhaps he heard me – for he moved on the bed suddenly, as if startled. Now you may think that I drew back – but no. His room was as black as pitch with the thick darkness (for the shutters were close-fastened, through fear of robbers), and so I knew that he could not see the opening of the door, and I kept pushing it on steadily, steadily.

I had my head in, and was about to open the lantern, when my thumb slipped upon the tin fastening, and the old man sprang up in the bed, crying out, 'Who's there?'

I kept quite still and said nothing. For a whole hour I did not move a muscle, and in the meantime I did not hear him lie down. He was sitting up in the bed, listening – just as I have done, night after night, hearkening to the death-watches in the wall.

Presently I heard a groan, and I knew it was the groan of mortal terror. It was not a groan of pain or grief – oh, no! – it was the low stifled sound that arises from the bottom of the soul when overcharged with awe. I knew the sound well. Many a night, just at midnight, when all the world slept, it has welled up from my own bosom, deepening, with its dreadful echo, the terrors that distracted me. I say I knew it well. I knew what the old man felt, and pitied him, although I chuckled at heart. I knew that he had been lying awake ever since the first slight noise, when he had turned in the bed. His fears had been ever since growing upon him. He had been trying to fancy them causeless, but could not. He had been saying to himself, 'It is nothing but the wind in the chimney – it is only a mouse crossing the floor,' or, 'It is merely a cricket which has made a single chirp.' Yes, he had been trying to comfort himself with these suppositions; but he had found all in vain. *All in vain;* because Death, in approaching him, had stalked with his black shadow before him, and enveloped the victim. And it was the mournful influence of the unperceived shadow that caused him to feel – although he neither saw nor heard – to *feel* the presence of my head within the room.

When I had waited a long time, very patiently, without hearing him lie down, I resolved to open a little – a very, very little crevice in the lantern. So I opened it – you cannot imagine how stealthily, stealthily – until, at length, a single dim ray, like the thread of the spider, shot from out the crevice and fell upon the vulture eye.

It was open – wide, wide open – and I grew furious as I gazed upon it. I saw it with perfect distinctness – all a dull blue, with a hideous veil over it that chilled the very marrow in my bones; but I could see nothing else of the old man's face or person, for I had directed the ray, as if by instinct, precisely upon the damned spot.

And now have I not told you what you mistake for madness is but over-acuteness of the senses? – now, I say, there came to my ears a low, dull, quick sound, such as a watch makes when enveloped in cotton. I knew *that* sound well, too. It was the beating of the old man's heart. It increased my fury, as the beating of a drum stimulates the soldier into courage.

But even yet I refrained and kept still. I scarcely breathed. I held the lantern motionless. I tried how steadily I could maintain the ray upon the eye. Meantime the hellish tattoo of the heart increased. It grew quicker and quicker, and louder and louder every instant. The old man's terror *must* have been extreme! It grew louder, I say, louder every moment! – do you mark me well? I have told you that I am nervous: so I am. And now, at the dead hour of the night, amid the dreadful silence of that old house, so strange a noise as this excited me to uncontrollable terror. Yet, for some minutes longer, I refrained and stood still. But the beating grew louder, louder! I thought the heart must burst. And now a new anxiety seized me – the sound would be heard by a neighbour! The old man's hour had come! With a loud yell I threw open the lantern and leaped into the room. He shrieked once – once only. In an instant I dragged him to the floor, and pulled the heavy bed over him. I then smiled gaily, to find the deed so far done. But, for many minutes, the heart beat on with a muffled sound. This, however, did not vex me; it would not be heard through the wall. At length it ceased. The old man was dead. I removed the bed and examined the corpse. Yes, he was stone, stone dead. I placed my hand upon the heart and held it there many minutes. There was no pulsation. He was stone dead. His eye would trouble me no more.

If you still think me mad, you will think so no longer when I describe the wise precautions I took for the concealment of the body. The night waned, and I worked hastily, but in silence. First of all I dismembered the corpse. I cut off the head and the arms and the legs.

I then took up three planks from the flooring of the chamber and deposited all between the scantlings. I then replaced the boards so cleverly, so cunningly, that no human eye – not even *his* – could have detected anything wrong. There was nothing to wash out – no stain of any kind – no blood-spot whatever. I had been too wary for that. A tub had caught all – ha! ha!

When I had made an end of these labours, it was four o'clock – still dark as midnight. As the bell sounded the hour, there came a knocking at the street door. I went down to open it with a light heart – for what had I *now* to fear? There entered three men, who introduced themselves, with perfect suavity, as officers of the police. A shriek had been heard by a neighbour during the night; suspicion of foul play had been aroused; information had been lodged at the police office, and they (the officers) had been deputed to search the premises.

I smiled – for *what* had I to fear? I bade the gentlemen welcome. The shriek, I said, was my own in a dream. The old man, I mentioned, was absent in the country. I took my visitors all over the house. I bade them search – search *well*. I led them, at length, to *his* chamber. I showed them his treasures, secure, undisturbed. In the enthusiasm of my confidence, I brought chairs into the room, and desired them *here* to rest from their fatigues, while I myself, in the wild audacity of my perfect triumph, placed my own seat upon the very spot beneath which reposed the corpse of the victim.

The officers were satisfied. My manner had convinced them. I was singularly at ease. They sat, and while I answered cheerily, they chatted of familiar things. But, ere long, I felt myself getting pale and wished them gone. My head ached, and I fancied a ringing in my ears; but still they sat and chatted. The ringing became more distinct – it continued and became more distinct. I talked more freely to get rid of the feeling; but it continued and gained definitiveness – until, at length, I found that the noise was *not* within my ears.

No doubt I now grew very pale; but I talked more fluently, and with a heightened voice. Yet the sound increased – and what could I do? It was *a low, dull, quick sound – much such a sound as a watch makes when enveloped in cotton*. I gasped for breath – and yet the officers heard it not. I talked more quickly – more vehemently; but the noise steadily increased. I arose and argued about trifles, in a high key and with violent gesticulations; but the noise steadily increased. Why *would* they not be gone? I paced the floor to and fro with heavy strides, as if excited to fury by the observations of the men – but the noise steadily increased. O God! what *could* I do? I foamed – I raved – I swore! I swung the chair upon which I had been sitting, and grated it upon the boards, but the noise arose over all and continually increased. It grew louder – louder – *louder!* And still the men chatted pleasantly, and smiled. Was it possible they heard not? Almighty God! – no, no! They heard! – they suspected! – they *knew!* – they were making a mockery of my horror! – this I thought and this I think. But anything was better than this agony! Anything was more tolerable than this derision! I could bear those hypocritical smiles no longer! I felt that I must scream or die! – and now – again! hark! louder! louder! louder! *louder!*——

'Villains!' I shrieked, 'dissemble no more! I admit the deed! – tear up the planks! – here, here! – it is the beating of his hideous heart!'

Edgar Allan Poe

The Premature Burial

There are certain themes of which the interest is all-absorbing, but which are too entirely horrible for the purposes of legitimate fiction. These the mere romanticist must eschew, if he do not wish to offend, or to disgust. They are with propriety handled only when the severity and majesty of truth sanctify and sustain them. We thrill, for example, with the most intense of 'pleasurable pain', over the accounts of the Passage of the Beresina, of the Earthquake at Lisbon, of the Plague at London, of the Massacre of St Bartholomew, or of the stifling of the hundred and twenty-three prisoners in the Black Hole at Calcutta. But, in these accounts, it is the fact – it is the reality – it is the history which excites. As inventions, we should regard them with simple abhorrence.

I have mentioned some few of the more prominent and august calamities on record; but in these it is the extent, not less than the character of the calamity, which so vividly impresses the fancy. I need not remind the reader that, from the long and weird catalogue of human miseries, I might have selected many individual instances more replete with essential suffering than any of these vast generalities of disaster. The true wretchedness, indeed – the ultimate woe – is particular, not diffuse. That the ghastly extremes of agony are endured by man the unit, and never by man the mass – for this let us thank a merciful God!

To be buried while alive is, beyond question, the most terrific of these extremes which has ever fallen to the lot of mere mortality. That it has frequently, very frequently, so fallen, will scarcely be denied by those who think. The boundaries which divide Life from Death are at best shadowy and vague. Who shall say where the one ends, and where the other begins? We know that there are diseases in which occur total cessations of all the apparent functions of vitality, and yet in which these cessations are merely suspensions, properly so called. They are only temporary pauses in the incomprehensible mechanism. A certain period elapses, and some unseen mysterious principle again sets in motion the magic pinions and the wizard wheels. The silver cord was not for ever loosed, nor the golden bowl irreparably broken. But where, meantime, was the soil?

Apart, however, from the inevitable conclusion, *a priori*, that such causes must produce such effects – that the well-known occurrence of such cases of suspended animation must naturally give rise, now and then, to premature interments – apart from this consideration, we have the direct testimony of medical and ordinary experience, to prove that a vast number of such interments have actually taken place. I might refer at once, if necessary, to a hundred well-authenticated instances. One of very remarkable character, and of which the circumstances may be fresh in the memory of some of my readers, occurred, not very long ago, in the neighbouring city of Baltimore, where it occasioned a painful, intense, and widely extended excitement. The wife of one of the most respectable citizens – a lawyer of eminence and a member of Congress – was seized with a sudden and unaccountable illness, which completely baffled the skill of her physicians. After much suffering, she died, or was supposed to die. No one suspected, indeed, or had reason to suspect, that she was not actually dead. She presented all the ordinary appearances of death. The face assumed the usual pinched and sunken outline. The lips were of the usual marble pallor. The eyes were lustreless. There was no warmth. Pulsation had ceased. For three days the body was preserved unburied, during which it had acquired a stony rigidity. The funeral, in short, was hastened, on account of the rapid advance of what was supposed to be decomposition.

The lady was deposited in her family vault, which, for three subsequent years, was undisturbed. At the expiration of this term, it was opened for the reception of a sarcophagus – but, alas! how fearful a shock awaited the husband, who, personally, threw open the door. As its portals swung outwardly back, some white-apparelled object fell rattling within his arms. It was the skeleton of his wife in her yet unmouldered shroud.

A careful investigation rendered it evident that she had revived within two days after her entombment – that her struggles within the coffin had caused it to fall from a ledge, or shelf, to the floor, where it was so broken as to permit her escape. A lamp which had been accidentally left, full of oil, within the tomb, was found empty; it might have been exhausted, however, by evaporation. On the uppermost of the steps which led down into the dread chamber, was a large fragment of the coffin, with which it seemed that she had endeavoured to arrest attention, by striking the iron door. While thus occupied, she probably swooned, or possibly died, through sheer terror; and, in falling, her shroud became entangled in some ironwork which projected interiorly. Thus she remained, and thus she rotted, erect.

In the year 1810, a case of living inhumation happened in France, attended with circumstances which go far to warrant the assertion that truth is, indeed, stranger than fiction. The heroine of the story was a Mademoiselle Victorine Lafourcade, a young girl of illustrious family, of wealth, and of great personal beauty. Among her numerous suitors was Julien Bossuet, a poor *litterateur*, or journalist, of Paris. His talents and general amiability had recommended him to the notice of the heiress, by whom he seems to have been truly beloved; but her pride of birth decided her, finally, to reject him, and to wed a Monsieur Renelle, banker, and a diplomatist of some eminence. After marriage, however, this gentleman neglected, and, perhaps, even more positively ill-treated her. Having passed with him some wretched years, she died – at least her condition so closely resembled death as to deceive every one who saw her. She was buried – not in a vault – but in an ordinary grave in the village of her nativity. Filled with despair, and still inflamed by the memory of a profound attachment, the lover journeys from the capital to the remote province in which the village lies, with the romantic purpose of disinterring the corpse, and possessing himself of its luxuriant tresses. He reaches the grave. At midnight he unearths the coffin, opens it, and is in the act of detaching the hair, when he is arrested by the unclosing of the beloved eyes. In fact, the lady had been buried alive. Vitality had not altogether departed; and she was aroused, by the caresses of her lover, from the lethargy which had been mistaken for death. He bore her frantically to his lodgings in the village. He employed certain powerful restoratives suggested by no little medical learning. In fine, she revived. She recognised her preserver. She remained with him until, by slow degrees, she fully recovered her original health. Her woman's heart was not adamant, and this last lesson of love sufficed to soften it. She bestowed it upon Bossuet. She returned no more to her husband, but concealing from him her resurrection, fled with her lover to America. Twenty years afterwards, the two returned to France, in the persuasion that time had so greatly altered the lady's appearance, that her friends would be unable to recognise her. They were mistaken, however; for, at the first meeting, Monsieur Renelle did actually recognise and make claim to his wife. This claim she resisted; and a judicial tribunal sustained her in her resistance; deciding that the peculiar circumstances, with the long lapse of years, had extinguished, not only equitably, but legally, the authority of the husband.

The *Chirurgical Journal* of Leipsic – a periodical of high authority and

THE PREMATURE BURIAL

merit, which some American bookseller would do well to translate and republish – records, in a late number, a very distressing event of the character in question.

An officer of artillery, a man of gigantic stature and of robust health, being thrown from an unmanageable horse, received a very severe contusion upon the head, which rendered him insensible at once; the skull was slightly fractured; but no immediate danger was apprehended. Trepanning was accomplished successfully. He was bled, and many other of the ordinary means of relief were adopted. Gradually, however, he fell into a more and more hopeless state of stupor; and, finally, it was thought that he died.

The weather was warm; and he was buried, with indecent haste, in one of the public cemeteries. His funeral took place on Thursday. On the Sunday following, the grounds of the cemetery were, as usual, much thronged with visitors; and about noon, an intense excitement was created by the declaration of a peasant, that, while sitting upon the grave of the officer, he had distinctly felt a commotion of the earth, as if occasioned by some one struggling beneath. At first, little attention was paid to the man's asseveration; but his evident terror, and the dogged obstinacy with which he persisted in his story, had at length their natural effect upon the crowd. Spades were hurriedly procured, and the grave, which was shamefully shallow, was, in a few minutes, so far thrown open that the head of its occupant appeared. He was then, seemingly, dead; but he sat nearly erect within his coffin, the lid of which, in his furious struggles, he had partially uplifted.

He was forthwith conveyed to the nearest hospital and, there pronounced to be still living, although in an asphytic condition. After some hours he revived, recognised individuals of his acquaintance, and, in broken sentences, spoke of his agonies in the grave.

From what he related, it was clear that he must have been conscious of life for more than an hour, while inhumed, before lapsing into insensibility. The grave was carelessly and loosely filled with an exceedingly porous soil; and thus some air was necessarily admitted. He heard the footsteps of the crowd overhead, and endeavoured to make himself heard in turn. It was the tumult within the grounds of the cemetery, he said, which appeared to awaken him from a deep sleep – but no sooner was he awake than he became fully aware of the awful horrors of his position.

This patient, it is recorded, was doing well, and seemed to be in a fair way of ultimate recovery, but fell a victim to the quackeries of medical experiment. The galvanic battery was applied, and he suddenly expired in one of those ecstatic paroxysms which, occasionally, it superinduces.

The mention of the galvanic battery, nevertheless, recalls to my memory a well-known and very extraordinary case in point, where its action proved the means of restoring to animation a young attorney of London, who had been interred for two days. This occurred in 1831, and created, at the time, a very profound sensation wherever it was made the subject of converse.

The patient, Mr Edward Stapleton, had died, apparently, of typhus fever, accompanied with some anomalous symptoms which had excited the curiosity of his medical attendants. Upon his seeming decease, his friends were requested to sanction a *post-mortem* examination, but declined to permit it. As often happens, when such refusals are made, the practitioners resolved to disinter the body and dissect it at leisure, in private. Arrangements were easily effected with some of the numerous corps of body-snatchers with which London abounds; and, upon the third night after the funeral, the supposed corpse was unearthed from a grave eight feet deep, and deposited in the operating chamber of one of the private hospitals.

An incision of some extent had been actually made in the abdomen, when the fresh and undecayed appearance of the subject suggested an application of the battery. One experiment succeeded another, and the customary effects supervened, with nothing to characterise them in any respect, except, upon one or two occasions, a more than ordinary degree of life-likeness in the convulsive action.

It grew late. The day was about to dawn; and it was thought expedient, at length, to proceed at once to the dissection. A student, however, was especially desirous of testing a theory of his own, and insisted upon applying the battery to one of the pectoral muscles. A rough gash was made, and a wire hastily brought in contact; when the patient, with a hurried, but quite unconvulsive movement, arose from the table, stepped into the middle of the floor, gazed about him uneasily for a few seconds, and then – spoke. What he said was unintelligible; but the words were uttered; the syllabification was distinct. Having spoken, he fell heavily to the floor.

For some moments all were paralysed with awe – but the urgency of the case soon restored them their presence of mind. It was seen that Mr Stapleton was alive, although in a swoon. Upon exhibition of ether he revived and was rapidly restored to health, and to the society of his friends – from whom, however, all knowledge of his resuscitation was withheld, until a relapse was no longer to be apprehended. Their wonder – their rapturous astonishment – may be conceived.

The most thrilling peculiarity of this incident, nevertheless, is involved in what Mr S. himself asserts. He declares that at no period was he altogether insensible – that, dully and confusedly, he was aware of everything which happened to him, from the moment in which he was pronounced *dead* by his physicians, to that in which he fell swooning to the floor of the hospital. 'I am alive,' were the uncomprehended words which, upon recognising the locality of the dissecting-room, he had endeavoured, in his extremity, to utter.

It were an easy matter to multiply such histories as these – but I forbear – for, indeed, we have no need of such to establish the fact that premature interments occur. When we reflect how very rarely, from the nature of the case, we have it in our power to detect them, we must admit that they may *frequently* occur without our cognisance. Scarcely, in truth, is a graveyard ever encroached upon, for any purpose, to any great extent, that skeletons are not found in postures which suggest the most fearful of suspicions.

Fearful indeed the suspicion – but more fearful the doom! It may be asserted, without hesitation, that *no* event is so terribly well adapted to inspire the supremeness of bodily and of mental distress, as is burial before death. The unendurable oppression of the lungs – the stifling fumes of the damp earth – the clinging to the death garments – the rigid embrace of the narrow house – the blackness of the absolute Night – the silence like a sea that overwhelms – the unseen but palpable presence of the Conqueror Worm – these things, with thoughts of the air and grass above, with memory of dear friends who would fly to save us if but informed of our fate, and with consciousness that of this fate they can *never* be informed – that our hopeless portion is that of the really dead – these considerations, I say, carry into the heart, which still palpitates, a degree of appalling and intolerable horror from which the most daring imagination must recoil. We know of nothing so agonising upon Earth – we can dream of nothing half so hideous in the realms of the nethermost Hell. And thus all narratives upon this topic have an interest profound; an interest, nevertheless, which, through the sacred awe of the topic itself, very properly and very peculiarly depends upon our conviction of the *truth* of the matter narrated. What I have now to tell, is of my own actual knowledge – of my own positive and personal experience.

For several years I had been subject to attacks of the singular disorder which physicians have agreed to term catalepsy, in default of a more definite title. Although both the immediate and the predisposing causes, and even the actual diagnosis of this disease, are still mysteries, its obvious and apparent character is sufficiently well understood. Its variations seem to be chiefly of degree. Sometimes the patient lies, for a day only, or even for a shorter period, in a species of exaggerated lethargy. He is senseless and externally motionless; but the pulsation of the heart is still faintly perceptible; some traces of warmth remain; a slight colour lingers within the centre of the cheek; and, upon application of a mirror to the lips, we can detect a torpid, unequal, and vacillating action of the lungs. Then, again, the duration of the trance is for weeks – even for months; while the closest scrutiny, and the most rigorous medical tests, fail to establish any material distinction between the state of the sufferer and what we conceive of absolute death. Very usually, he is saved from premature interment solely by the knowledge of his friends that he has been previously subject to catalepsy, by the consequent suspicion excited, and, above all, by the non-appearance of decay. The advances of the malady are, luckily, gradual. The first manifestations, although marked, are unequivocal. The fits grow successively more and more distinctive, and endure each for a longer term than the preceding. In this lies the principal security from inhumation. The unfortunate whose *first* attack should be of the extreme character which is occasionally seen, would almost inevitably be consigned alive to the tomb.

My own case differed in no important particular from those mentioned in medical books. Sometimes, without any apparent cause, I sank, little by little, into a condition of semi-syncope, or half swoon; and, in this condition, without pain, without ability to stir, or strictly speaking, to think, but with a dull lethargic consciousness of life and of the presence of those who surrounded my bed, I remained, until the crisis of the disease restored me, suddenly, to perfect sensation. At other times I was quickly and impetuously smitten. I grew sick, and numb, and chilly, and dizzy, and so fell prostate at once. Then, for weeks, all was void, and black, and silent, and Nothing became the universe. Total annihilation could be no more. From these latter attacks I awoke, however, with a gradation slow in proportion to the suddenness of the seizure. Just as the day dawns to the friendless and houseless beggar who roams the streets throughout the long desolate winter night – just so tardily – just so wearily – just so cheerily came back the light of the Soul to me.

Apart from the tendency to trance, however, my general health appeared to be good; nor could I perceive that it was at all affected by the one prevalent malady – unless, indeed, an idiosyncrasy in an ordinary *sleep* may be looked upon as superinduced. Upon awaking from slumber, I could never gain, at once, thorough possession of my senses, and always remained, for many minutes, in much bewilderment and perplexity – the mental faculties in general, but the memory in especial, being in a condition of absolute abeyance.

In all that I endured there was no physical suffering, but of moral distress an infinitude. My fancy grew charnel. I talked 'of worms, of tombs and epitaphs'. I was lost in reveries of death, and the idea of premature burial held continual possession of my brain. The ghastly danger to which I was subjected haunted me day and night. In the former, the torture of meditation was excessive – in the latter, supreme. When the grim darkness overspread the earth, then, with very horror of thought, I shook – shook as the quivering plumes upon the hearse. When nature could endure wakefulness no longer, it was with a struggle that I consented to sleep – for I shuddered to reflect that, upon awaking, I might find myself the tenant of a grave. And when, finally, I sank into slumber, it was only to rush at once into a world of phantasms, above which, with vast, sable, overshadowing wings, however, predominant, the one sepulchral Idea.

From the innumerable images of gloom which thus oppressed me in dreams, I select for record but a solitary vision. Methought I was immersed in a cataleptic trance of more than usual duration and profundity. Suddenly there came an icy hand upon my forehead, and an impatient, gibbering voice whispered the word 'Arise!' within my ear.

I sat erect. The darkness was total. I could not see the figure of him who had aroused me. I could call to mind neither the period at which I had fallen into the trance, nor the locality in which I then lay. While I remained motionless, and busied in endeavours to collect my thoughts, the cold hand grasped me fiercely by the wrist, shaking it petulantly, while the gibbering voice said again –

'Arise! did I not bid thee arise?'

'And who,' I demanded, 'art thou?'

'I have no name in the regions which I inhabit,' replied the voice mournfully; 'I was mortal, but am fiend. I was merciless, but am pitiful. Thou dost feel that I shudder. My teeth chatter as I speak, yet it is not with the chilliness of the night – of the night without end. But this hideousness is insufferable. How canst *thou* tranquilly sleep? I cannot rest for the cry of these great agonies. These sights are more than I can bear. Get thee up! Come with me into the outer Night, and let me unfold to thee the graves. Is not this a spectacle of woe? Behold!'

I looked; and the unseen figure, which still grasped me by the wrist, had caused to be thrown open the graves of all mankind; and from each issued the faint phosphoric radiance of decay, so that I could see into the innermost recesses, and there view the shrouded bodies in their sad and solemn slumbers with the worm. But, alas! the real sleepers were fewer, by many millions, than those who slumbered not at all; and there was a feeble struggling; and there was a general sad unrest; and from out the depths of the countless pits there came a melancholy rustling from the garments of the buried. And, of those who seemed tranquilly to repose I saw that a vast number had changed, in a greater or less degree, the rigid and uneasy position in which they had originally been entombed. And the voice again said to me, as I gazed –

'Is it not – oh, is it *not* a pitiful sight?' But, before I could find words to reply, the figure had ceased to grasp my wrist, the phosphoric lights expired, and the graves were closed with a sudden violence, while from out them arose a tumult of despairing cries, saying again, 'Is it not – O

God! is it *not* a very pitiful sight?'

Phantasies such as these, presenting themselves at night, extended their terrific influence far into my waking hours. My nerves became thoroughly unstrung, and I fell a prey to perpetual horror. I hesitated to ride, or to walk, or to indulge in any exercise that would carry me from home. In fact, I no longer dared trust myself out of the immediate presence of those who were aware of my proneness to catalepsy, lest, falling into one of my usual fits, I should be buried before my real condition could be ascertained. I doubted the care, the fidelity of my dearest friends. I dreaded that, in some trance of more than customary duration, they might be prevailed upon to regard me as irrecoverable. I even went so far as to fear that, as I occasioned much trouble, they might be glad to consider any very protracted attack as sufficient excuse for getting rid of me altogether. It was in vain they endeavoured to reassure me by the most solemn promises. I exacted the most sacred oaths, that under no circumstances they would bury me until decomposition had so materially advanced as to render further preservation impossible. And, even then, my mortal terrors would listen to no reason – would accept no consolation. I entered into a series of elaborate precautions. Among other things, I had the family vault so remodelled as to admit of being readily opened from within. The slightest pressure upon a long lever that extended far into the tomb would cause the iron portals to fly back. There were arrangements also for the free admission of air and light, and convenient receptacles for food and water, within immediate reach of the coffin intended for my reception. This coffin was warmly and softly padded, and was provided with a lid, fashioned upon the principle of the vault-door, with the addition of springs so contrived that the feeblest movement of the body would be sufficient to set it at liberty. Besides all this, there was suspended from the roof of the tomb a large bell, the rope of which, it was designed, should extend through a hole in the coffin, and so be fastened to one of the hands of the corpse. But, alas! what avails the vigilance against the Destiny of man? Not even these well-contrived securities sufficed to save from the uttermost agonies of living inhumation a wretch to these agonies foredoomed!

There arrived an epoch – as often before there had arrived – in which I found myself emerging from total unconsciousness into the first feeble and indefinite sense of existence. Slowly – with a tortoise gradation – approached the faint grey dawn of the psychal day. A torpid uneasiness. An apathetic endurance of dull pain. No care – no hope – no effort. Then, after long interval, a ringing in the ears; then, after a lapse still longer, a prickling or tingling sensation in the extremities; then a seemingly eternal period of pleasurable quiescence, during which the awakening feelings are struggling into thought; then a brief resinking into nonentity; then a sudden recovery. At length the slight quivering of an eyelid, and immediately thereupon an electric shock of a terror, deadly and indefinite, which sends the blood in torrents from the temples to the heart. And now the first positive effort to think. And now the first endeavour to remember. And now a partial and evanescent success. And now the memory has so far regained its dominion, that, in some measure, I am cognisant of my state. I feel that I am not awaking from ordinary sleep. I recollect that I have been subject to catalepsy. And now, at last, as if by the rush of an ocean, my shuddering spirit is overwhelmed by the one grim Danger – by the one spectral and ever-prevalent Idea.

For some minutes after this fancy possessed me, I remained without motion. And why? I could not summon courage to move. I dared not make the effort which was to satisfy me of my fate – and yet there was something at my heart which whispered me *it was sure*. Despair – such as no other species of wretchedness ever calls into being – despair alone urged me, after long irresolution, to uplift the heavy lids of my eyes. I uplifted them. It was dark – all dark. I knew that the fit was over. I knew that the crisis of my disorder had long passed. I knew that I had now fully recovered the use of my visual faculties – and yet it was dark – all dark – the intense and utter raylessness of the Night that endureth for evermore.

I endeavoured to shriek; and my lips and my parched tongue moved convulsively together in the attempt – but no voice issued from the cavernous lungs, which, oppressed as if by the weight of some incumbent mountain, gasped and palpitated, with the heart, at every elaborate and struggling inspiration.

The movement of the jaws, in this effort to cry aloud, showed me that they were bound up, as is usual with the dead. I felt, too, that I lay upon some hard substance; and by something similar my sides were, also, closely compressed. So far, I had not ventured to stir any of my limbs – but now I violently threw up my arms, which had been lying at length, with the wrists crossed. They struck a solid wooden substance, which extended above my person at an elevation of not more than six inches from my face. I could no longer doubt that I reposed within a coffin at last.

And now, amid all my infinite miseries, came sweetly the cherub Hope – for I thought of my precautions. I writhed, and made spasmodic exertions to force open the lid; it would not move. I felt my wrists for the bell-rope; it was not to be found. And now the Comforter fled for ever, and a still sterner Despair reigned triumphant; for I could not help perceiving the absence of the paddings which I had so carefully prepared – and then, too, there came suddenly to my nostrils the strong peculiar odour of moist earth. The conclusion was irresistible. I was *not* within the vault. I had fallen into a trance while absent from home – while among strangers – when, or how, I could not remember – and it was they who had buried me as a dog – nailed up in some common coffin – and thrust, deep, deep, and for ever, into some ordinary and nameless *grave*.

As this awful conviction forced itself, thus, into the innermost chambers of my soul, I once again struggled to cry aloud. And in this second endeavour I succeeded. A long, wild, and continuous shriek, or yell, of agony, resounded through the realms of the subterrene Night.

'Hillo! hillo, there!' said a gruff voice, in reply.

'What the devil's the matter now?' said a second.

'Get out o' that!' said a third.

'What do you mean by yowling in that ere kind of style, like a catty-mount?' said a fourth; and hereupon I was seized and shaken without ceremony, for several minutes, by a junto of very rough-looking individuals. They did not arouse me from my slumber – for I was wide awake when I screamed – but they restored me to full possession of my memory.

This adventure occurred near Richmond, in Virginia. Accompanied by a friend, I had proceeded, upon a gunning expedition, some miles down the banks of James River. Night approached, and we were over-taken by a storm. The cabin of a small sloop lying at anchor in the stream, and laden with garden mould, afforded us the only available shelter. We made the best of it, and passed the night on board. I slept in one of the only two berths in the vessel – and the berths of a sloop of sixty or seventy tons need scarcely be described. That which I occupied had no bedding of any kind. Its extreme width was eighteen inches. The distance of its bottom from the deck overhead was precisely the same. I found it a matter of exceeding difficulty to squeeze myself in. Nevertheless, I slept soundly; and the whole of my vision – for it was no dream, and no night-mare – arose naturally from the circumstances of my position – from my ordinary bias of thought – and from the difficulty, to which I have alluded, of collecting my senses, and especially of regaining my memory, for a long time after awaking from slumber. The men who shook me were the crew of the sloop, and some labourers engaged to unload it. From the load itself came the earthy smell. The bandage about the jaws was a silk handkerchief in which I bound up my head, in default of my customary nightcap.

The tortures endured, however, were indubitably quite equal, for the time, to those of actual sepulture. They were fearfully – they were in-conceivably hideous; but out of evil proceeded good; for their very excess wrought in my spirit an inevitable revulsion. My soul acquired tone – acquired temper. I went abroad. I took vigorous exercise. I breathed the free air of heaven. I thought upon other subjects than death. I discarded my medical books. 'Buchan' I burned. I read no

'Night Thoughts' – no fustian about churchyards – no bugaboo tales – *such as this*. In short I became a new man, and lived a man's life. From that memorable night I dismissed for ever my charnel apprehensions, and with them vanished the cataleptic disorder, of which, perhaps, they had been less the consequence than the cause.

There are moments when, even to the sober eye of Reason, the world of our sad Humanity may assume the semblance of a Hell – but the imagination of man is no Carathis, to explore with impunity its every cavern. Alas! the grim legion of sepulchral terrors cannot be regarded as altogether fanciful – but, like the Demons in whose company Afrasiab made his voyage down the Oxus, they must sleep, or they will devour us – they must be suffered to slumber, or we perish.

Villiers de l'Isle Adam

The Torture of Hope

Many years ago, as evening was closing in, the venerable Pedro Arbuez d'Espila, sixth prior of the Dominicans of Segovia, and third Grand Inquisitor of Spain, followed by a *fra redemptor*, and preceded by two familiars of the Holy Office, the latter carrying lanterns, made their way to a subterranean dungeon. The bolt of a massive door creaked, and they entered a mephitic *in pace*, where the dim light revealed between rings fastened to the wall a bloodstained rack, a brazier and a jug. On a pile of straw, loaded with fetters and his neck encircled by an iron carcan, sat a haggard man, of uncertain age, clothed in rags.

This prisoner was no other than Rabbi Aser Abarbanel, a Jew of Aragon, who – accused of usury and pitiless scorn for the poor – had been daily subjected to torture for more than a year. Yet 'his blindness was as dense as his hide', and he had refused to abjure his faith.

Proud of a filiation dating back thousands of years, proud of his ancestors – for all Jews worthy of the name are vain of their blood – he descended Talmudically from Othoniel and consequently from Ipsiboa, the wife of the last judge of Israel, a circumstance which had sustained his courage amid incessant torture. With tears in his eyes at the thought of this resolute soul rejecting salvation, the venerable Pedro Arbuez d'Espila, approaching the shuddering rabbi, addressed him as follows:

'My son, rejoice: your trials here below are about to end. If in the presence of such obstinacy I was forced to permit, with deep regret, the use of great severity, my task of fraternal correction has its limits. You are the fig tree which, having failed so many times to bear fruit, at last withered, but God alone can judge your soul. Perhaps Infinite Mercy will shine upon you at the last moment! We must hope so. There are examples. So sleep in peace tonight. Tomorrow you will be included in the *auto da fé*: that is, you will be exposed to the *quémadero*, the symbolical flames of the Everlasting Fire: it burns, as you know, only at a distance, my son; and Death is at least two hours (often three) in coming, on account of the wet, iced bandages with which we protect the heads and hearts of the condemned. There will be forty-three of you. Placed in the last row, you will have time to invoke God and offer to Him this baptism of fire, which is of the Holy Spirit. Hope in the Light, and rest.'

With these words, having signed to his companions to unchain the prisoner, the prior tenderly embraced him. Then came the turn of the *fra redemptor*, who, in a low tone, entreated the Jew's forgiveness for what he had made him suffer for the purpose of redeeming him; then the two familiars silently kissed him. This ceremony over, the captive was left, solitary and bewildered, in the darkness.

Rabbi Aser Abarbanel, with parched lips and visage worn by suffering, at first gazed at the closed door with vacant eyes. Closed? The word unconsciously roused a vague fancy in his mind, the fancy that he had seen for an instant the light of the lanterns through a chink between the door and the wall. A morbid idea of hope, due to the weakness of his brain, stirred his whole being. He dragged himself toward the strange *appearance*. Then, very gently and cautiously, slipping one finger into the crevice, he drew the door toward him. Marvellous! By an extraordinary accident the familiar who closed it had turned the huge key an instant before it struck the stone casing, so that the rusty bolt not having entered the hole, the door again rolled on its hinges.

The rabbi ventured to glance outside. By the aid of a sort of luminous dusk he distinguished at first a semicircle of walls indented by winding stairs; and opposite to him, at the top of five or six stone steps, a sort of black portal, opening into an immense corridor, whose first arches only were visible from below.

Stretching himself flat he crept to the threshold. Yes, it was really a corridor, but endless in length. A wan light illumined it: lamps suspended from the vaulted ceiling lightened at intervals the dull hue of the atmosphere – the distance was veiled in shadow. Not a single door appeared in the whole extent! Only on one side, the left, heavily grated loopholes, sunk in the walls, admitted a light which must be that of evening, for crimson bars at intervals rested on the flags of the pavement. What a terrible silence! Yet, yonder, at the far end of that passage there might be a doorway of escape! The Jew's vacillating hope was tenacious, for it was *the last*.

Without hesitating, he ventured on the flags, keeping close under the loopholes, trying to make himself part of the blackness of the long walls. He advanced slowly, dragging himself along on his breast, forcing back the cry of pain when some raw wound sent a keen pang through his whole body.

Suddenly the sound of a sandalled foot approaching reached his ears. He trembled violently, fear stifled him, his sight grew dim. Well, it was over, no doubt. He pressed himself into a niche and, half lifeless with terror, waited.

It was a familiar hurrying along. He passed swiftly by, holding in his clenched hand an instrument of torture – a frightful figure – and vanished. The suspense which the rabbi had endured seemed to have suspended the functions of life, and he lay nearly an hour unable to move. Fearing an increase of tortures if he were captured, he thought of returning to his dungeon. But the old hope whispered in his soul that divine *perhaps*, which comforts us in our sorest trials. A miracle had happened. He could doubt no longer. He began to crawl toward the chance of escape. Exhausted by suffering and hunger, trembling with pain, he pressed onward. The sepulchral corridor seemed to lengthen mysteriously, while he, still advancing, gazed into the gloom where there *must* be some avenue of escape.

Oh! oh! He again heard footsteps, but this time they were slower, more heavy. The white and black forms of two inquisitors appeared, emerging from the obscurity beyond. They were conversing in low tones, and seemed to be discussing some important subject, for they were gesticulating vehemently.

At this spectacle Rabbi Aser Abarbanel closed his eyes: his heart beat so violently that it almost suffocated him; his rags were damp with the cold sweat of agony; he lay motionless by the wall, his mouth wide open, under the rays of a lamp, praying to the God of David.

Just opposite to him the two inquisitors paused under the light of the lamp – doubtless owing to some accident due to the course of their argument. One, while listening to his companion, gazed at the rabbi! And, beneath the look – whose absence of expression the hapless man did not at first notice – he fancied he again felt the burning pincers scorch his flesh, he was to be once more a living wound. Fainting, breathless, with fluttering eyelids, he shivered at the touch of the monk's floating robe. But – strange yet natural fact – the inquisitor's gaze was evidently that of a man deeply absorbed in his intended reply, engrossed by what he was hearing; his eyes were fixed – and seemed to look at the Jew *without seeing him*.

In fact, after the lapse of a few minutes, the two gloomy figures slowly pursued their way, still conversing in low tones, toward the place whence the prisoner had come; HE HAD NOT BEEN SEEN! Amid the horrible confusion of the rabbi's thoughts, the idea darted through his brain: 'Can I be already dead that they did not see me?' A hideous impression roused him from his lethargy: in looking at the wall against which his face was pressed, he imagined he beheld two fierce eyes watching him! He flung his head back in a sudden frenzy of fright, his hair fairly bristling! Yet, no! No. His hand groped over the stones: it was the *reflection* of the inquisitor's eyes, still retained in his own, which had been refracted from two spots on the wall.

Forward! He must hasten toward that goal which he fancied (absurdly, no doubt) to be deliverance, toward the darkness from which he was now barely thirty paces distant. He pressed forward faster on his knees, his hands, at full length, dragging himself painfully along, and soon entered the dark portion of this terrible corridor.

Suddenly the poor wretch felt a gust of cold air on the hands resting upon the flags; it came from under the little door to which the two walls led.

Oh, Heaven, if that door should open outward. Every nerve in the miserable fugitive's body thrilled with hope. He examined it from top to bottom, though scarcely able to distinguish its outlines in the surrounding darkness. He passed his hand over it: no bolt, no lock! A latch! He started up, the latch yielded to the pressure of his thumb: the door silently swung open before him.

'Halleluia!' murmured the rabbi in a transport of gratitude as, standing on the threshold, he beheld the scene before him.

The door had opened into the gardens, above which arched a starlit sky, into spring, liberty, life! It revealed the neighbouring fields, stretching toward the sierras, whose sinuous blue lines were relieved against the horizon. Yonder lay freedom! Oh, to escape! He would journey all night through the lemon groves, whose fragrance reached him. Once in the mountains and he was safe! He inhaled the delicious air; the breeze revived him, his lungs expanded! He felt in his swelling heart the *Veni foràs* of Lazarus! And to thank once more the God who had bestowed this mercy upon him, he extended his arms, raising his eyes toward Heaven. It was an ecstasy of joy!

Then he fancied he saw the shadow of his arms approach him – fancied that he felt those shadowy arms inclose, embrace him – and that he was pressed tenderly to someone's breast. A tall figure actually did stand directly before him. He lowered his eyes – and remained motionless, gasping for breath, dazed, with fixed eyes, fairly drivelling with terror.

Horror! He was in the clasp of the Grand Inquisitor himself, the venerable Pedro Arbuez d'Espila, who gazed at him with tearful eyes, like a good shepherd who had found his stray lamb.

The dark-robed priest pressed the hapless Jew to his heart with so fervent an outburst of love, that the edges of the monachal haircloth rubbed the Dominican's breast. And while Aser Abarbanel with protruding eyes gasped in agony in the ascetic's embrace, vaguely comprehending that *all the phases of this fatal evening were only a prearranged torture, that of* Hope, the Grand Inquisitor, with an accent of touching reproach and a look of consternation, murmured in his ear, his breath parched and burning from long fasting:

'What, my son! On the eve, perchance, of salvation – you wished to leave us?'

Honoré de Balzac

An Episode of the Terror

On the 22nd of January, 1793, toward eight o'clock in the evening, an old lady came down the steep street that comes to an end opposite the Church of Saint Laurent in the Faubourg Saint Martin. It had snowed so heavily all day long that the lady's footsteps were scarcely audible; the streets were deserted, and a feeling of dread, not unnatural amid the silence, was further increased by the whole extent of the Terror beneath which France was groaning in those days; what was more, the old lady so far had met no one by the way. Her sight had long been failing, so that the few foot passengers dispersed like shadows in the distance over the wide thoroughfare through the faubourg were quite invisible to her by the light of the lanterns.

She passed the end of the Rue des Morts, when she fancied that she could hear the firm, heavy tread of a man walking behind her. Then it seemed to her that she had heard that sound before, and dismayed by the idea of being followed, she tried to walk faster toward a brightly lit shop window, in the hope of verifying the suspicions which had taken hold of her mind.

So soon as she stood in the shaft of light that streamed out across the road, she turned her head suddenly, and caught sight of a human figure looming through the fog. The dim vision was enough for her. For one moment she reeled beneath an overpowering weight of dread, for she could not doubt any longer that the man had followed her the whole way from her own door; then the desire to escape from the spy gave her strength. Unable to think clearly, she walked twice as fast as before, as if it were possible to escape from a man who of course could move much faster; and for some minutes she fled on, till, reaching a pastry-cook's shop, she entered and sank rather than sat down upon a chair by the counter.

A young woman busy with embroidery looked up from her work at the rattling of the door-latch, and looked out through the square window panes. She seemed to recognize the old-fashioned violet silk mantle, for she went at once to a drawer as if in search of something put aside for the newcomer. Not only did this movement and the expression of the woman's face show a very evident desire to be rid as soon as possible of an unwelcome visitor, but she even permitted herself an impatient exclamation when the drawer proved to be empty. Without looking at the lady, she hurried from her desk into the back shop and called to her husband who appeared at once.

'Wherever have you put . . . ?' she began mysteriously, glancing at the customer by way of finishing her question.

The pastry-cook could only see the old lady's head-dress, a huge black-silk bonnet with knots of violet ribbon around it, but he looked at his wife as who should say, 'Did you think I should leave such a thing as that lying about in your drawer?' and then vanished.

The old lady kept so still and silent that the shopkeeper's wife was surprised. She went back to her, and on a nearer view a sudden impulse of pity, blended perhaps with curiosity, got the better of her. The old lady's face was naturally pale; she looked as though she secretly practiced austerities; but it was easy to see that she was paler than usual from recent agitation of some kind. Her head-dress was so arranged as almost to hide hair that was white, no doubt with age, for there was not a trace of powder on the collar of her dress. The extreme plainness of her dress lent an air of austerity to her face, and her features were proud and grave. The manner and habits of people of condition were so different from those of other classes in former times that a noble was easily known, and the shopkeeper's wife felt persuaded that her customer was a *ci-devant*, and that she had been about the Court.

'Madame?' she began with involuntary respect, forgetting that the title was proscribed.

But the old lady made no answer. She was staring fixedly at the shop window as though some dreadful thing had taken shape against the panes. The pastry-cook came at that moment, and drew the lady from her musings, by holding out a little cardboard box wrapped in blue paper.

'What is the matter, *citoyenne?*' he asked.

'Nothing, nothing, my friends,' she answered, in a gentle voice. She looked up at the man as she spoke, as if to thank him by a glance; but she saw the red cap on his head, and a cry broke from her. 'Ah! *You* have betrayed me!'

The man and his young wife replied by an indignant gesture that brought the colour to the old lady's face; perhaps she felt relief, she blushed for her suspicions.

'Forgive me!' she said, with a childlike sweetness in her tones. Then, drawing a gold louis from her pocket, she held it out to the pastry-cook. 'That is the price agreed upon,' she added.

There is a kind of want that is felt instinctively by those who know want. The man and his wife looked at one another, then at the elderly woman before them, and read the same thoughts in each other's eyes. That bit of gold was so plainly the last. Her hands shook a little as she held it out, looking at it sadly but ungrudgingly, as one who knows the full extent of the sacrifice. Hunger and penury had carved lines as easy to read in her face as the traces of asceticism and fear. There were vestiges of by-gone splendour in her clothes. She was dressed in thread-bare silk, a neat but well-worn mantle, and daintily mended lace – in the rags of former grandeur, in short. The shopkeeper and his wife, drawn two ways by pity and self-interest, began by lulling their consciences with words.

'You seem very poorly, *citoyenne* . . .'

'Perhaps Madame might like to take something,' the wife broke in.

'We have some very nice broth,' added the pastry-cook.

'And it is so cold,' continued his wife. 'Perhaps you have caught a chill, Madame, on your way here. But you can rest and warm yourself a bit.'

'We are not so black as the devil!' cried the man.

The kindly intention in the words and tones of the charitable couple won the old lady's confidence. She said that a strange man had been following her, and she was afraid to go home alone.

'Is that all?' returned he of the red bonnet. 'Wait for me, *citoyenne*.'

He handed the gold coin to his wife, and then went out to put on his National Guard's uniform, impelled, thereto, by the idea of making some adequate return for the money; an idea that sometimes slips into a tradesman's head when he has been prodigiously overpaid for goods of no great value. He took up his cap, buckled on his sabre, and came out in full dress. But his wife had had time to reflect, and reflection, as not unfrequently happens, closed the hand that kindly intentions had opened. Feeling frightened and uneasy lest her husband might be drawn into something unpleasant, she tried to catch the skirt of his coat, to hold him back, but he, good soul, obeying his charitable first thought, brought out his offer to see the lady home, before his wife could stop him.

'The man of whom the *citoyenne* is afraid is still prowling about the shop, it seems,' she said sharply.

'I am afraid so,' the lady said innocently.

'How if it is a spy? A plot? Don't go. And take the box away from her . . .'

The words whispered in the pastry-cook's ear cooled his hot fit of courage down to zero.

'Oh! I will just go out and say a word or two. I will rid you of him soon enough,' he exclaimed, as he bounced out of the shop.

The old lady meanwhile, passive as a child and almost dazed, sat down on her chair again. But the honest pastry-cook came back directly. A countenance red enough to begin with, and further flushed by the bake-house fire, was suddenly blanched; such terror perturbed him that he reeled as he walked, and stared about him like a drunken man.

'Miserable aristocrat! Do you want to have our heads cut off?' he shouted furiously. 'You just take to your heels and never show yourself here again. Don't come to me for materials for your plots.'

He tried, as he spoke, to take away the little box which she had slipped into one of her pockets. But at the touch of a profane hand on her clothes, the stranger recovered youth and activity for a moment, preferring to face the dangers of the street with no protector save God, to the loss of the thing that she had just paid for. She sprang to the door, flung it open, and disappeared, leaving the husband and wife dumfounded and quaking with fright.

Once outside in the street, she started away at a quick walk; but her strength soon failed her. She heard the sound of the snow crunching under a heavy step, and knew that the pitiless spy was on her track. She was obliged to stop. He stopped likewise. From sheer terror, or lack of intelligence, she did not dare to speak or to look at him. She went slowly on; the man slackened his pace and fell behind so that he could still keep her in sight. He might have been her very shadow.

Nine o'clock struck as the silent man and woman passed again by the Church of Saint Laurent. It is in the nature of things that calm must succeed to violent agitation, even in the weakest soul; for if feeling is infinite, our capacity to feel is limited. So, as the strange lady met with no harm from her supposed persecutor, she tried to look upon him as an unknown friend anxious to protect her. She thought of all the circumstances in which the stranger had appeared, and put them together, as if to find some ground for this comforting theory, and felt inclined to credit him with good intentions rather than bad. Forgetting the fright that he had given the pastry-cook, she walked on with a firmer step through the upper end of the Faubourg Saint Martin; and another half hour's walk brought her to a house at the corner where the road to the Barrière de Pantin turns off from the main thoroughfare. Even at this day, the place is one of the least frequented parts of Paris. The north wind sweeps over the Buttes-Chaumont and Belleville, and whistles through the houses (the hovels rather) scattered over an almost uninhabited low-lying waste, where the fences are heaps of earth and bones.

AN EPISODE OF THE TERROR

It was a desolate-looking place, a fitting refuge for despair and misery.

The sight of it appeared to make an impression upon the relentless pursuer of a poor creature so daring as to walk alone at night through the silent streets. He stood in thought, and seemed by his attitude to hesitate. She could see him dimly now, under the street lamp that sent a faint, flickering light through the fog. Fear gave her eyes. She saw, or thought she saw, something sinister about the stranger's features. Her old terrors awoke; she took advantage of a kind of hesitation on his part, slipped through the shadows to the door of the solitary house, pressed a spring, and vanished swiftly as a phantom.

For a while the stranger stood motionless, gazing up at the house. It was in some sort a type of the wretched dwellings in the suburb; a tumble-down hovel, built of rough stones, daubed over with a coat of yellowish stucco, and so riven with great cracks that there seemed to be danger lest the slightest puff of wind might blow it down. The roof, covered with brown moss-grown tiles, had given way in several places, and looked as though it might break down altogether under the weight of the snow. The frames of the three windows on each story were rotten with damp and warped by the sun; evidently the cold must find its way inside. The house standing thus quite by itself looked like some old tower that Time had forgotten to destroy. A faint light shone from the attic windows pierced at irregular distances in the roof; otherwise the whole building was in total darkness.

Meanwhile the old lady climbed not without difficulty up the rough, clumsily built staircase, with a rope by way of a hand-rail. At the door of the lodging in the attic she stopped and tapped mysteriously; an old man brought forward a chair for her. She dropped into it at once.

'Hide! Hide!' she exclaimed, looking up at him. 'Seldom as we leave the house everything that we do is known, and every step is watched...'

'What is it now?' asked another elderly woman, sitting by the fire.

'The man that has been prowling about the house yesterday and today, followed me tonight...'

At those words all three dwellers in the wretched den looked in each other's faces and did not try to dissimulate the profound dread that they felt. The old priest was the least overcome, probably because he ran the greatest danger. If a brave man is weighed down by great calamities or the yoke of persecution, he begins, as it were, by making the sacrifice of himself; and thereafter every day of his life becomes one more victory snatched from fate. But from the way in which the women looked at him it was easy to see that their intense anxiety was on his account.

'Why should our faith in God fail us, my sisters?' he said, in low but fervent tones. 'We sang His praises through the shrieks of murderers and their victims at the Carmelites. If it was His will that I should come alive out of that butchery, it was, no doubt, because I was reserved for some fate which I am bound to endure without murmuring. God will protect His own; He can do with them according to His will. It is for you, not for me that we must think.'

'No,' answered one of the women. 'What is our life compared with a priest's life?'

'Once outside the Abbaye de Chelles, I look upon myself as dead,' added the nun who had not left the house, while the Sister that had just returned held out the little box to the priest.

'Here are the wafers . . . But I can hear someone coming up the stairs!' At this, the three began to listen. The sound ceased.

'Do not be alarmed if somebody tries to come in,' said the priest. 'Somebody on whom we could depend was to make all necessary arrangements for crossing the frontier. He is to come for the letters that I have written to the Duc de Langeais and the Marquis de Beauséant, asking them to find some way of taking you out of this dreadful country, and away from the death or the misery that waits for you here.'

'But you are not going to follow us?' the nuns cried under their breath, almost despairingly.

'My post is here where the sufferers are,' the priest said simply, and the women said no more, but looked at their guest in reverent admiration. He turned to the nun with the wafers.

'Sister Marthe,' he said, 'the messenger will say *Fiat Voluntas* in answer to the word *Hosanna*.'

'There is someone on the stairs!' cried the other nun, opening a hiding-place contrived in the roof.

This time it was easy to hear, amid the deepest silence, a sound echoing up the staircase: it was a man's tread on the steps covered with dried lumps of mud. With some difficulty the priest slipped into a kind of cupboard, and the nun flung some clothes over him.

'You can shut the door, Sister Agathe,' he said in a muffled voice.

He was scarcely hidden before three raps sounded on the door. The holy women looked into each other's eyes for counsel, and dared not say a single word.

They seemed to be about sixty years of age. They had lived out of the world for forty years, and had grown so accustomed to the life of the convent that they could scarcely imagine any other. To them, as to plants kept in a hot-house, a change of air meant death. And so, when the grating was broken down one morning, they knew with a shudder that they were free. The effect produced by the Revolution upon their simple souls is easy to imagine; it produced a temporary imbecility not natural to them. They could not bring the ideas learned in the convent into harmony with life and its difficulties; they could not even understand their own position. They were like children whom others have always cared for, deserted by their maternal providence. And as a child cries, they betook themselves to prayer. Now, in the presence of imminent danger, they were mute and passive, knowing no defence save Christian resignation.

The man at the door, taking silence for consent, presented himself, and the women shuddered. This was the prowler that had been making inquiries about them for some time past. But they looked at him with frightened curiosity, much as shy children stare silently at a stranger; and neither of them moved.

The newcomer was a tall, burly man. Nothing in his behaviour, bearing or expression suggested malignity as, following the example set by the nuns, he stood motionless, while his eyes travelled around the room.

Two straw mats laid upon planks did duty as beds. On the one table, placed in the middle of the room, stood a brass candlestick, several plates, three knives and a round loaf. A small fire burned in the grate. A few bits of wood in a heap in a corner bore further witness to the poverty of the recluses. You had only to look at the coating of paint on the walls to discover the bad condition of the roof, and the ceiling was a perfect network of brown stains made by rain water. A relic, saved no doubt from the wreck of the Abbaye de Chelles, stood like an ornament on the chimney piece. Three chairs, two boxes, and a rickety chest of drawers completed the list of the furniture, but a door beside the fireplace suggested an inner room beyond.

The brief inventory was soon made by the personage introduced into their midst under such terrible auspices. It was with a compassionate expression that he turned to the two women; he looked benevolently at them, and seemed, at least, as much embarrassed as they. But the strange silence did not last long, for presently the stranger began to understand. He saw how inexperienced, how helpless (mentally speaking), the two poor creatures were, and he tried to speak gently.

'I am far from coming as an enemy, *citoyennes* . . .' he began. Then he suddenly broke off and went on, 'Sisters, if anything should happen to you, believe me, I shall have no share in it. I have come to ask a favour of you.'

Still the women were silent.

'If I am annoying you – if – if I am intruding, speak freely, and I will go; but you must understand that I am entirely at your service; that if I can do anything for you, you need not fear to make use of me. I, and I only, perhaps, am above the law, since there is no King now.'

There was such a ring of sincerity in the words that Sister Agathe hastily pointed to a chair as if to bid their guest be seated. Sister Agathe came of the house of Langeais; her manner seemed to indicate that once she had been familiar with brilliant scenes, and had breathed the air of courts. The stranger seemed half pleased, half distressed when he understood her invitation; he waited to sit down until the women were seated.

'You are giving shelter to a reverend father who refused to take the oath, and escaped the massacres at the Carmelites by a miracle . . .'

'*Hosanna!*' Sister Agathe exclaimed eagerly, interrupting the stranger, while she watched him with curious eyes.

'That is not the name, I think,' he said.

'But, Monsieur,' Sister Marthe broke in quickly, 'we have no priest here, and . . .'

'In that case you should be more careful and on your guard,' he answered gently, stretching out his hand for a breviary that lay on the table. 'I do not think that you know Latin, and . . .'

He stopped; for, at the sight of the great emotion in the faces of the two poor nuns, he was afraid that he had gone too far. They were trembling, and the tears stood in their eyes.

'Do not fear,' he said frankly. 'I know your names and the name of your guest. Three days ago I heard of your distress and devotion to the venerable Abbé de—'

'Hush!' Sister Agathe cried, in the simplicity of her heart, as she laid her finger on her lips.

'You see, Sisters, that if I had conceived the horrible idea of betraying you, I could have given you up already, more than once . . .'

At the words the priest came out of his hiding-place and stood in their midst.

'I cannot believe, Monsieur, that you can be one of our persecutors,' he said, addressing the stranger, 'and I trust you. What do you want with me?'

The priest's holy confidence, the nobleness expressed in every line in his face, would have disarmed a murderer. For a moment the mysterious stranger, who had brought an element of excitement into lives of misery and resignation, gazed at the little group; then he turned to the priest and said, as if making a confidence, 'Father, I came to beg you to celebrate a mass for the repose of – of – of an august personage whose body will never rest in consecrated earth . . .'

Involuntarily the abbé shivered. As yet, neither of the Sisters understood of whom the stranger was speaking; they sat with their heads stretched out and faces turned toward the speaker, curiosity in their whole attitude. The priest, meanwhile, was scrutinizing the stranger; there was no mistaking the anxiety in the man's face, the ardent entreaty in his eyes.

'Very well,' returned the abbé. 'Come back at midnight. I shall be ready to celebrate the only funeral service that it is in our power to offer in expiation of the crime of which you speak.'

A quiver ran through the stranger, but a sweet yet sober satisfaction seemed to prevail over a hidden anguish. He took his leave respectfully, and the three generous souls felt his unspoken gratitude.

Two hours later, he came back and tapped at the garret door. Mademoiselle de Beauséant showed the way into the second room in their humble lodging. Everything had been made ready. The Sisters had moved the old chest of drawers between the two chimneys, and covered its quaint outlines over with a splendid altar cloth of green watered silk.

The bare walls looked all the barer, because the one thing that hung there was the great ivory and ebony crucifix, which of necessity attracted the eyes. Four slender little altar candles, which the Sisters had contrived to fasten into their places with sealing-wax, gave a faint pale light, almost absorbed by the walls; the rest of the room lay well-nigh in the dark. But the dim brightness, concentrated upon the holy things, looked like a ray from Heaven shining down upon the unadorned shrine. The floor was reeking with damp. An icy wind swept in through the chinks here and there, in a roof that rose sharply on either side, after the fashion of attic roofs. Nothing could be less imposing; yet perhaps, too, nothing could be more solemn than this mournful ceremony. A silence so deep that they could have heard the faintest sound of a voice on the Route d'Allemagne, invested the night-piece with a kind of sombre majesty; while the grandeur of the service – all the grander for the strong contrast with the poor surroundings – produced a feeling of reverent awe.

The Sisters kneeling on either side of the altar, regardless of the deadly chill from the wet brick floor, were engaged in prayer, while the priest, arrayed in pontifical vestments, brought out a golden chalice set with gems; doubtless one of the sacred vessels saved from the pillage of the Abbaye de Chelles. Beside a ciborium, the gift of royal munificence, the wine and water for the holy sacrifice of the mass, stood ready in two glasses such as could scarcely be found in the meanest tavern. For want of a missal, the priest had laid his breviary on the altar, and a common earthenware plate was set for the washing of hands that were pure and undefiled with blood. It was all so infinitely great, yet so little, poverty-stricken yet noble, a mingling of sacred and profane.

The stranger came forward reverently to kneel between the two nuns. But the priest had tied crape around the chalice of the crucifix, having no other way of marking the mass as a funeral service; it was as if God himself had been in mourning. The man suddenly noticed this, and the sight appeared to call up some overwhelming memory, for great drops of sweat stood out on his broad forehead.

Then the four silent actors in the scene looked mysteriously at one another; and their souls in emulation seemed to stir and communicate the thoughts within them until all were melted into one feeling of awe and pity. It seemed to them that the royal martyr whose remains had been consumed with quicklime, had been called up by their yearning and now stood, a shadow in their midst, in all the majesty of a king. They were celebrating an anniversary service for the dead whose body lay elsewhere. Under the disjointed laths and tiles, four Christians were holding a funeral service without a coffin, and putting up prayers to God for the soul of a King of France. No devotion could be purer than this. It was a wonderful act of faith achieved without an afterthought. Surely in the sight of God it was like the cup of cold water which counterbalances the loftiest virtues. The prayers put up by two feeble nuns and a priest representing the whole Monarchy, and possibly at the same time, the Revolution found expression in the stranger, for the remorse in his face was so great that it was impossible not to think that he was fulfilling the vows of a boundless repentance.

When the priest came to the Latin words, *Introibo ad altare Dei* a sudden divine inspiration flashed upon him; he looked at the three kneeling figures, the representatives of Christian France, and said instead, as though to blot out the poverty of the garret, 'We are about to enter the Sanctuary of God!'

Those words, uttered with thrilling earnestness, struck reverent awe into the nuns and the stranger. Under the vaulted roof of St Peter's in Rome, God would not have revealed Himself in greater majesty than here for the eyes of the Christians in that poor refuge; so true is it that all intermediaries between God and the soul of man are superfluous and all the grandeur of God proceeds from Himself alone.

The stranger's fervour was sincere. One emotion blended the prayers of the four servants of God and the King in a single supplication. The holy words rang like the music of heaven through the silence. At one moment, tears gathered in the stranger's eyes. This was during the *Pater Noster;* for the priest added a petition in Latin, and his audience doubtless understood him when he said: '*Et remitte scelus regicidis sicut Ludovicus eis remisit semetipse* . . .' Forgive the regicides as Louis himself forgave them.

The Sisters saw two great tears trace a channel down the stranger's manly cheeks and fall to the floor. Then the office for the dead was recited; the *Domine salvum fac regem* chanted in an undertone that went to the hearts of the faithful Royalists, for they thought how the child-King for whom they were praying was even then a captive in the hands of his enemies; and a shudder ran through the stranger, as he thought that a new crime might be committed, and that he could not choose but take his part in it.

The service came to an end. The priest made a sign to the Sisters, and they withdrew. As soon as he was left alone with the stranger, he went toward him with a grave, gentle face, and said, in fatherly tones: 'My son, if your hands are stained with the blood of the royal martyr, confide in me. There is no sin may not be blotted out in the sight of God by penitence as sincere and touching as yours appears to be.'

At the first words, the man stared with terror, in spite of himself. Then he recovered composure, and looked quietly at the astonished priest.

'Father,' he said, and the other could not miss the tremor in his voice, 'no one is more guiltless than I of the blood shed . . .'

'I am bound to believe you,' said the priest. He paused a moment, and again he scrutinized his penitent. But, persisting in the idea that the man before him was one of the members of the Convention, one of the timorous voters who betrayed an inviolable and anointed head to save their own, he began again gravely:

'Remember, my son, that it is not enough to have taken no active part in the great crime; that fact does not absolve you. The men who might have defended the King and left their swords in their scabbards will have a very heavy account to render to the King of Heaven . . . Ah! yes,' he added, with an eloquent shake of the head, 'heavy indeed! For by doing nothing they became accomplices in the awful wickedness . . .'

'But do you think that an indirect participation will be punished?' the stranger asked with a bewildered look. 'There is the private soldier commanded to fall into line – is he actually responsible?'

The priest hesitated. The stranger was glad; he had put the Royalist precisian in a dilemma, between the dogma of passive obedience on the one hand (for the upholders of the Monarchy maintained that obedience was the first principle of military law), and the equally important dogma which turns respect for the person of a king into a matter of religion. In the priest's indecision he was eager to see a favourable solution of the doubts which seemed to torment him. To prevent too prolonged reflection on the part of the reverend Jansenist, he added:

'I should blush to offer remuneration of any kind for the funeral service which you have just performed for the repose of the King's soul and the relief of my conscience. The only possible return for something of inestimable value is an offering likewise beyond price. Will you deign, Monsieur, to take my gift of a holy relic? A day will perhaps come when you will understand its value.'

As he spoke the stranger held out a box; it was very small and exceedingly light. The priest took it mechanically, as it were, so astonished was he by the man's solemn words, the tones of his voice, and the reverence with which he held out the gift.

The two men went back together into the first room. The Sisters were
waiting for them.

'This house that you are living in belongs to Mucius Scaevola, the
plasterer on the first floor,' he said. 'He is well known in the section for
his patriotism, but in reality he is an adherent of the Bourbons. He used
to be a huntsman in the service of His Highness, the Prince de Conti,
and he owes everything to him. So long as you stay in the house, you
are safer here than anywhere else in France. Do not go out. Pious souls
will minister your necessities, and you can wait in safety for better
times. Next year, on the 21st of January' – he could not hide an involuntary shudder as he spoke – 'next year, if you are still in this dreary refuge.
I will come back again to celebrate the expiatory mass with you ...'

He broke off, bowed to the three, who answered not a word, gave a
last look at the garret with its signs of poverty, and vanished.

Such an adventure possessed all the interest of a romance in the lives
of the innocent nuns. So, as soon as the venerable abbé told them the
story of the mysterious gift, it was placed upon the table, and by the
feeble light of the tallow dip an indescribable curiosity appeared in the
three anxious faces. Mademoiselle de Langeais opened the box, and
found a very fine lawn handkerchief, soiled with sweat; darker stains
appeared as they unfolded it.

'That is blood!' exclaimed the priest.

'It is marked with a royal crown!' cried Sister Agathe.

The women, aghast, allowed the precious relic to fall. For their
simple souls the mystery that hung about the stranger grew inexplicable:
as for the priest, from that day forth he did not even try to understand it,

Before very long the prisoners knew that, in spite of the Terror, some
powerful hand was extended over them. It began when they received
firewood and provisions; and next the Sisters knew that a woman had
lent counsel to their protector, for linen was sent to them, and clothes
in which they could leave the house without causing remark upon the
aristocrat's dress that they had been forced to wear. After a while Mucius
Scaevola gave them two civic cards; and often tidings necessary for the
priest's safety came to them in roundabout ways. Warnings and advice
reached them so opportunely that they could only have been sent by
some person in the possession of state secrets. And, at a time when famine
threatened Paris, invisible hands brought rations of white bread for the
proscribed women in the wretched garret. Still they fancied that Citizen
Mucius Scaevola was only the mysterious instrument of a kindness always ingenious, and no less intelligent.

The noble ladies in the garret could no longer doubt that their protector was the stranger of the expiatory mass on the night of the 22nd of January, 1793; and a kind of cult of him sprang up among them. Their one hope was in him; they lived through him. They added special petitions for him to their prayers; night and morning the pious souls prayed for his happiness, his prosperity, his safety; entreating God to remove all snares far from his path; to deliver him from his enemies, to grant him a long and peaceful life. And with this daily renewed gratitude, as it may be called, there blended a feeling of curiosity which grew more lively day by day. They talked over the circumstances of his first sudden appearance, their conjectures were endless; the stranger had conferred one more benefit upon them by diverting their minds. Again, and again, they said, when he next came to see them as he promised, to celebrate the sad anniversary of the death of Louis XVI, he should not escape their friendship.

The night so impatiently awaited came at last. At midnight the old wooden staircase echoed with the stranger's heavy footsteps. They had made the best of their room for his coming; the altar was ready, and this time the door stood open, and the two Sisters were out at the stairhead, eager to light the way. Mademoiselle de Langeais even came down a few steps, to meet their benefactor the sooner.

'Come,' she said, with a quaver in the affectionate tones. 'Come in, we are expecting you.'

He raised his face, gave her a dark look, and made no answer. The Sister felt as if an icy mantle had fallen over her, and said no more. At the sight of him, the glow of gratitude and curiosity died away in their hearts. Perhaps he was not so cold, not so taciturn, not so stern as he seemed to them, for in their highly wrought mood they were ready to pour out their feeling of friendship. But the three poor prisoners understood that he wished to be a stranger to them – and submitted. The priest fancied that he saw a smile on the man's lips as he saw their preparations for his visit, but it was at once repressed. He heard mass, said his prayer, and then disappeared, declining, with a few polite words, Mademoiselle de Langeais's invitation to partake of the little collation made ready for him.

After the 9th Thermidor, the Sisters and the Abbé de Marolles could go about Paris without the least danger. The first time that the abbé went out he walked to a perfumer's shop at the sign of the Queen of Roses, kept by the Citizen Ragon and his wife, court perfumers. The Ragons had been faithful adherents of the Royalist cause; it was through their means that the Vendéen leaders kept up a correspondence with the Princes and the Royalist Committee in Paris. The abbé, in the ordinary dress of the time, was standing on the threshold of the shop, which stood between Saint Roch and the Rue des Frondeurs, when he saw that the Rue Saint Honoré was filled with a crowd and he could not go out.

'What is the matter?' he asked Madame Ragon.

'Nothing,' she said. 'It is only the tumbril cart and the executioner going to the Place Louis XV. Ah! We used to see it often enough last year; but today, four days after the anniversary of the 21st of January, one does not feel sorry to see the ghastly procession.'

'Why not?' asked the abbé. 'That is not said like a Christian.'

'Eh! But it is the execution of Robespierre's accomplices. They defended themselves as long as they could, but now it is their turn to go where they sent so many innocent people.'

The crowd poured by like a flood. The abbé, yielding to an impulse of curiosity, looked up above the heads, and there in the tumbril stood the man who had heard mass in the garret three days ago.

'Who is it?' he asked. 'Who is the man with . . . ?'

'That is the headsman,' answered M. Ragon, calling the executioner – the *exécuteur des hautes oeuvres* – by the name he had borne under the Monarchy.

'Oh! My dear, my dear! M. l'abbé is dying!' cried out old Madame Ragon. She caught up a flask of vinegar, and tried to restore the old priest to consciousness.

'He must have given me the handkerchief that the King used to wipe his brow on the way to his martyrdom,' murmered he. 'Poor man! There was a heart in the steel blade, when none was found in all France . . .'

The perfumers thought that the poor abbé was raving.

Guy de Maupassant

The Hand

We were all seated round Monsieur Bermutier, the magistrate, who was giving us his opinion on the affair at St Cloud. The inexplicable crime had convulsed Paris for a whole month, yet no single being had solved the mystery.

Upright, with his back to the fireplace, Monsieur Bermutier held forth, marshalled proofs, and discussed divers opinions, but he came to no conclusion.

Several of the women present had risen from their seats to be nearer to him; and they remained standing, their eyes fixed on the clean-shaven lips whence issued such words of grave import. They thrilled and shuddered, devoured with curiosity and with that avid and insatiable love of the horrible that haunts their souls and tortures them like hunger.

One, paler than the others, broke the silence:

'It is terrible! It is almost supernatural! We shall never know anything about it.'

The magistrate turned to her:

'You are right, madame; it is quite probable we shall never know anything about it. But the word "supernatural" that you used a moment ago has no meaning in this case. We have before us a crime very ably conceived and very ably carried out, so wrapped in mystery that we are unable to dissociate it from the impenetrable circumstances surrounding it. But in times gone by I had to follow up a case where the fantastic element was really intermingled. We had to abandon it, however, as no one was able to throw any light on it.'

Breathlessly, and as if with one voice, several of the ladies exclaimed:

'Oh, do tell us about it!'

Monsieur Bermutier smiled gravely, as befits a magistrate, and continued:

You must not think for a moment that I fancied there was any element of the supernatural in this case. I am no believer in the abnormal. But if, instead of using the word 'supernatural' to explain what we do not understand, we were to use the word 'inexplicable', it would be far better. At any rate, in the tale I am about to relate to you it was mainly the surrounding circumstances, the preparatory circumstances, so to speak, which affected me. Briefly, these are the facts:

In those days I was resident magistrate at Ajaccio, a little white town nestled on the borders of a beautiful gulf, and surrounded by high mountains.

What I had principally to deal with were cases of vendetta. There were some that were really magnificent, others excessively dramatic, savage, and again heroic. The most splendid subjects of revenge that a man may dream of – time-honoured hatreds momentarily appeased, perhaps, but never really extinguished – abominably cunning tricks, murder swelling into massacre, and actions almost noble.

For two years I heard of nothing but the price of blood, of the terrible Corsican law which enforces vengeance on the evil-doer to be borne by his descendents and near relations. I had seen old men, children, and cousins with their throats cut. My brain teemed with such happenings.

One day I heard that an Englishman had rented a little villa on the edge of the gulf for several years. He had brought a French manservant with him, picked up on the way at Marseilles. Soon everyone was talking of this queer foreigner, who lived alone in his house; leaving it only to hunt and fish. He never spoke to anyone, never entered the town, and practised shooting every morning for two or three hours with pistol and rifle.

Stories were rife about him. Some made out he was a great personage who had fled his country for political reasons, others affirmed that he was in hiding for having committed a terrible crime. They even cited the particularly horrible details.

In my position as magistrate I wanted to gain some information about this man, but I failed to learn anything at all. He gave his name as Sir John Rowell.

So I had to be content to watch him closely, but, to speak candidly, my attention was called to nothing suspicious about him. However, as the rumours about him continued, swelled, and became common talk, I resolved to see him for myself; and I set about shooting regularly in his neighbourhood.

For a long while I awaited an opportunity. At last it came, in the shape of a partridge which I shot and killed under the Englishman's nose. My dog brought it to me. Taking the bird, I went and excused myself for my want of manners, and begged Sir John Rowell to accept the dead bird.

He was a huge man, red-haired and red-bearded, very tall, very big, a placid and polite Hercules. He had none of that so-called British stiffness; and he thanked me warmly for my small civility in French with an accent from over the water. After a month had gone by we had spoken five or six times together.

At length one evening as I passed his door and I saw him sitting in his garden, astride a chair, smoking a pipe. I bowed, and he invited me to come in and drink a glass of beer. I did not wait to be asked twice.

He received me with the meticulous courtesy of an Englishman, spoke warmly of France and Corsica, declaring that he liked both country and seashore extremely.

Then cautiously I put to him some leading questions under the guise of a lively interest in his life and doings. He answered without any embarrassment, told me that he had travelled much in Africa, India, and America, and added, laughing:

'Oh, I had many adventures!'

Then I talked sport, and he gave me some exceedingly curious details gathered in pursuit of the hippopotamus, the tiger, the elephant, and even the gorilla.

'Those are all formidable beasts?' said I.

He smiled and replied:

'Oh, no; man was the worst!'

And he laughed outright, with the hearty laugh of a satisfied Englishman.

'Man was often my game,' he added.

Then he spoke of arms, and invited me to come in and look at some rifles of different makes. His sitting-room was hung with black – black silk embroidered with gold. Large yellow flowers sprawled over the dark stuff, and shone like fire. The stuff was Japanese, he told me.

In the centre of the largest panel something extraordinary caught my eye. A black object stood out in relief against a square of red velvet. I went up to it. It was a hand – a man's hand! No bleached and well-cleaned skeleton hand, but a dried-up black hand, with its yellow nails, its bared muscles, and traces of dried blood – blood smeared like mud on the bones – cut off cleanly as if by a hatchet in the middle of the forearm.

Round the wrist a heavy iron chain was riveted, welded to this unclean member, and holding it fast to the wall with a ring strong enough to hold an elephant in leash.

'What is that?' I asked:

'He was my deadliest foe,' replied the Englishman quietly. 'It came from America. It was cut off with a sword, the skin torn away with a flint, and then dried in the sun for a week. A good stroke of work on my part.'

I touched this remnant of humanity; it must have belonged to a colossus. The exaggeratedly long fingers were attached by tremendous tendons, which bore scraps of skin here and there. The hand was horrible to look at, skinned thus; it made one's thoughts turn instinctively to some savage and ferocious form of revenge.

'He must have been a very strong man,' said I.

'Yes,' answered the Englishman calmly; 'but I proved the stronger. I put on that chain to hold him fast.'

Thinking he was speaking in fun, I said:

'But that chain is of no use now: the hand will not try and escape.'

'It has always wanted to go; that chain was necessary,' gravely replied Sir John Rowell.

I looked at him with a rapid glance. Had I to deal with a madman, or did he but joke in very bad taste?

His face remained impenetrable, tranquil, and good-natured. I spoke of other things. I admired his guns. I observed, however, that three loaded revolvers lay about the room, as if this man lived in constant dread of being attacked.

I went to see him several times again; then I went no more. We had become used to his presence; he had become a matter of indifference to all.

A whole year slipped by. Then one morning towards the end of November my servant woke me, telling me that Sir John Rowell had been murdered during the night.

Half an hour later I entered the Englishman's house, accompanied by the Commissioner and the Chief Inspector of Police. Overcome with grief, and half distracted, the manservant stood crying in the doorway. At first I suspected the man, but he was innocent. We were never able to find the murderer.

The first thing I saw on entering Sir John's sitting-room was the body lying on its back in the middle of the room. The waistcoat was torn; one sleeve hung in ribbons; there was every sign that a terrible struggle had taken place.

The Englishman had died of strangulation. His black and swollen face, terrifying, seemed to wear an expression of awful fear. He held something between his clenched teeth; and the throat, pierced with five holes that might have been made with fangs of iron, was covered with blood.

THE HAND

A doctor had joined us. Lengthily he examined the marks of fingers on the flesh, and then queerly remarked:

'One might think he had been strangled by a skeleton.'

A shudder ran down my spine, and I looked towards the wall at the spot where I had seen the horrible skinned hand. It was no longer there. The chain hung down, broken.

Then I stooped over the dead man, and found between the tense jaws a finger from the hand that had disappeared, cut, or rather sawn, by the teeth just at the second joint.

Inquiries were instituted. Nothing was discovered. Neither door, window, nor furniture had been tampered with. The two watchdogs had not been aroused.

Here, briefly, is the manservant's testimony. For a month past his master had appeared restless. He had received many letters, burnt as soon as received.

In a rage which approached madness he would often take up his whip and furiously beat the shrivelled hand chained to the wall, and which had been removed, no one knew how, at the hour of the crime.

He went to bed very late, and locked himself in with care. He always had firearms within reach of his hand. Often in the night he was heard speaking with raised voice, as if he were quarrelling with someone.

That night, by chance, he had made no sound; and it was only on coming to open the windows that the servant had discovered Sir John lying murdered. He suspected no one.

I told the officers of the law all I knew of the dead man, and a minute inquiry was instituted all over the island. They discovered nothing.

Now, it happened one night three months after the crime had taken place I had a most horrible nightmare. I thought I saw the hand, the sinister hand, run like a scorpion or a spider along my curtains and walls. Three times did I wake, three times did I fall asleep; three times did I see the hideous thing gallop round my room, moving its fingers like feet.

The following day they brought it to me, found in the cemetery on the grave of Sir John Rowell, who had been laid there as we failed to discover his family. The first finger was missing. That, ladies, is my story. I know no more.

The women were all shuddering, terror-struck, and pale.

'But,' exclaimed one, 'that cannot be the end; that is no explanation! We shall none of us close our eyes tonight if you do not tell us what you think occurred.'

The magistrate smiled as he answered reprovingly:

'For my part, madame, I shall certainly spoil your horror-filled dreams, for I merely think that the rightful owner of the hand was not dead, and that he came to seek it with the one left to him. But I was unable to find out how he went about it. That was a kind of vendetta.'

One of the women murmured:

'No; it could not have been that!'

'I told you my explanation would not satisfy you,' said the magistrate, still smiling.

Thomas Hardy

The Withered Arm

I. *A Lorn Milkmaid*

It was an eighty-cow dairy, and the troop of milkers, regular and super-numerary, were all at work; for, though the time of year was as yet but early April, the feed lay entirely in water-meadows, and the cows were 'in full pail'. The hour was about six in the evening, and three-fourths of the large, red, rectangular animals having been finished off, there was opportunity for a little conversation.

'He do bring home his bride tomorrow, I hear. They've come as far as Anglebury today.'

The voice seemed to proceed from the belly of the cow called Cherry, but the speaker was a milking-woman, whose face was buried in the flank of that motionless beast.

'Hav' anybody seen her?' said another.

There was a negative response from the first. 'Though they say she's a rosy-cheeked, tisty-tosty little body enough,' she added; and as the milkmaid spoke she turned her face so that she could glance past her cow's tail to the other side of the barton, where a thin, fading woman of thirty milked somewhat apart from the rest.

'Years younger than he, they say,' continued the second, with also a glance of reflectiveness in the same direction.

'How old do you call him, then?'

'Thirty or so.'

'More like forty,' broke in an old milkman near, in a long white pina-fore or 'wropper', and with the brim of his hat tied down, so that he looked like a woman. ''A was born before our Great Weir was builded, and I hadn't man's wages when I laved water there.'

The discussion waxed so warm that the purr of the milk streams became jerky, till a voice from another cow's belly cried with authority, 'Now then, what the Turk do it matter to us about Farmer Lodge's age, or Farmer Lodge's new mis'ess? I shall have to pay him nine pound a year for the rent of every one of these milchers, whatever his age or hers. Get on with your work, or 'twill be dark afore we have done. The evening is pinking in a'ready.' This speaker was the dairyman himself, by whom the milkmaids and men were employed.

Nothing more was said publicly about Farmer Lodge's wedding, but the first woman murmured under her cow to her next neighbour, ' 'Tis hard for *she*,' signifying the thin worn milkmaid aforesaid.

'O no,' said the second. 'He ha'n't spoke to Rhoda Brook for years.'

When the milking was done they washed their pails and hung them on a many-forked stand made as usual of the peeled limb of an oak-tree, set upright in the earth, and resembling a colossal antlered horn. The majority then dispersed in various directions homeward. The thin woman who had not spoken was joined by a boy of twelve or thereabout, and the twain went away up the field also.

Their course lay apart from that of the others, to a lonely spot high above the water-meads, and not far from the border of Egdon Heath, whose dark countenance was visible in the distance as they drew nigh to their home.

'They've just been saying down in barton that your father brings his young wife home from Anglebury tomorrow,' the woman observed. 'I shall want to send you for a few things to market, and you'll be pretty sure to meet 'em.'

'Yes, mother,' said the boy. 'Is father married then?'

'Yes. . . . You can give her a look, and tell me what she's like, if you do see her.'

'Yes, mother.'

'If she's dark or fair, and if she's tall – as tall as I. And if she seems like a woman who has ever worked for a living, or one that has been always well off, and has never done anything, and shows marks of the lady on her, as I expect she do.'

'Yes.'

They crept up the hill in the twilight and entered the cottage. It was built of mud-walls, the surface of which had been washed by many rains into channels and depressions that left none of the original flat face visible; while here and there in the thatch above a rafter showed like a bone protruding through the skin.

She was kneeling down in the chimney-corner, before two pieces of turf laid together with the heather inwards, blowing at the red-hot ashes with her breath till the turves flamed. The radiance lit her pale cheek, and made her dark eyes, that had once been handsome, seem handsome anew. 'Yes,' she resumed, 'see if she is dark or fair, and if you can, notice if her hands be white; if not, see if they look as though she had ever done housework, or are milker's hands like mine.'

The boy again promised, inattentively this time, his mother not observing that he was cutting a notch with his pocket-knife in the beech-backed chair.

II. *The Young Wife*

The road from Anglebury to Holmstoke is in general level; but there is one place where a sharp ascent breaks its monotony. Farmers homeward-bound from the former market-town, who trot all the rest of the way, walk their horses up this short incline.

The next evening while the sun was yet bright a handsome new gig, with a lemon-coloured body and red wheels, was spinning westward along the level highway at the heels of a powerful mare. The driver was a yeoman in the prime of life, cleanly shaven like an actor, his face being toned to that bluish-vermilion hue which so often graces a thriving farmer's features when returning home after successful dealings in the town. Beside him sat a woman, many years his junior – almost, indeed, a girl. Her face too was fresh in colour, but it was of a totally different quality – soft and evanescent, like the light under a heap of rose-petals.

Few people travelled this way, for it was not a main road; and the long white riband of gravel that stretched before them was empty, save of one small scarce-moving speck, which presently resolved itself into the figure of a boy, who was creeping on at a snail's pace, and continually looking behind him – the heavy bundle he carried being some excuse for, if not the reason of, his dilatoriness. When the bouncing gig-party slowed at the bottom of the incline above mentioned, the pedestrian was only a few yards in front. Supporting the large bundle by putting one hand on his hip, he turned and looked straight at the farmer's wife as though he would read her through and through, pacing along abreast of the horse.

The low sun was full in her face, rendering every feature, shade, and contour distinct, from the curve of her little nostril to the colour of her eyes. The farmer, though he seemed annoyed at the boy's persistent presence, did not order him to get out of the way; and thus the lad preceded them, his hard gaze never leaving her, till they reached the top of the ascent, when the farmer trotted on with relief in his lineaments – having taken no outward notice of the boy whatever.

'How that poor lad stared at me!' said the young wife.

'Yes, dear; I saw that he did.'

'He is one of the village, I suppose?'

'One of the neighbourhood. I think he lives with his mother a mile or two off.'

'He knows who we are, no doubt?'

'O yes. You must expect to be stared at just at first, my pretty Gertrude.'

'I do – though I think the poor boy may have looked at us in the hope we might relieve him of his heavy load, rather than from curiosity.'

'O no,' said her husband off-handedly. 'These country lads will carry a hundredweight once they get it on their backs; besides his pack had more size than weight in it. Now, then, another mile and I shall be able to show you our house in the distance – if it is not too dark before we get there.' The wheels spun round, and particles flew from their periphery as before, till a white house of ample dimensions revealed itself, with farm-buildings and ricks at the back.

Meanwhile the boy had quickened his pace, and turning up a by-lane some mile and half short of the white farmstead, ascended towards the leaner pastures, and so on to the cottage of his mother.

She had reached home after her day's milking at the outlying dairy, and was washing cabbage at the doorway in the declining light. 'Hold up the net a moment,' she said, without preface, as the boy came up.

He flung down his bundle, held the edge of the cabbage-net, and as she filled its meshes with the dripping leaves she went on, 'Well, did you see her?'

'Yes; quite plain.'

'Is she ladylike?'

'Yes; and more. A lady complete.'

'Is she young?'

'Well, she's growed up, and her ways be quite a woman's.'

'Of course. What colour is her hair and face?'

'Her hair is lightish, and her face as comely as a live doll's.'

'Her eyes, then, are not dark like mine?'

'No – of a bluish turn, and her mouth is very nice and red; and when she smiles, her teeth show white.'

'Is she tall?' said the woman sharply.

'I couldn't see. She was sitting down.'

'Then do you go to Holmstoke church tomorrow morning: she's sure to be there. Go early and notice her walking in, and come home and tell me if she's taller than I.'

'Very well, mother. But why don't you go and see for yourself?'

'*I* go to see her! I wouldn't look up at her if she were to pass my window this instant. She was with Mr Lodge, of course. What did he say or do?'

'Just the same as usual.'

'Took no notice of you?'

'None.'

Next day the mother put a clean shirt on the boy, and started him off for Holmstoke church. He reached the ancient little pile when the door was just being opened, and he was the first to enter. Taking his seat by the font, he watched all the parishioners file in. The well-to-do Farmer Lodge came nearly last; and his young wife, who accompanied him, walked up the aisle with the shyness natural to a modest woman who had appeared thus for the first time. As all other eyes were fixed upon her, the youth's stare was not noticed now.

When he reached home his mother said, 'Well?' before he had entered the room.

'She is not tall. She is rather short,' he replied.

'Ah!' said his mother, with satisfaction.

'But she's very pretty – very. In fact, she's lovely.' The youthful freshness of the yeoman's wife had evidently made an impression even on the somewhat hard nature of the boy.

'That's all I want to hear,' said his mother quickly. 'Now, spread the table-cloth. The hare you wired is very tender; but mind that nobody catches you. – You've never told me what sort of hands she had.'

'I have never seen 'em. She never took off her gloves.'

'What did she wear this morning?'

'A white bonnet and a silver-coloured gownd. It whewed and whistled so loud when it rubbed against the pews that the lady coloured up more than ever for very shame at the noise, and pulled it in to keep it from touching; but when she pushed into her seat, it whewed more than ever. Mr Lodge, he seemed pleased, and his waistcoat stuck out, and his great golden seals hung like a lord's; but she seemed to wish her noisy gownd anywhere but on her.'

'Not she! However, that will do now.'

These descriptions of the newly-married couple were continued from time to time by the boy at his mother's request, after any chance encounter he had had with them. But Rhoda Brook, though she might easily have seen young Mrs Lodge for herself by walking a couple of miles, would never attempt an excursion towards the quarter where the farmhouse lay. Neither did she, at the daily milking in the dairyman's yard on Lodge's outlying second farm, ever speak on the subject of the recent marriage. The dairyman, who rented the cows of Lodge, and knew perfectly the tall milkmaid's history, with manly kindliness always kept the gossip in the cow-barton from annoying Rhoda. But the atmosphere thereabout was full of the subject during the first days of Mrs Lodge's arrival; and from her boy's description and the casual words of the other milkers, Rhoda Brook could raise a mental image of the unconscious Mrs Lodge that was realistic as a photograph.

III. *A Vision*

One night, two or three weeks after the bridal return, when the boy was gone to bed, Rhoda sat a long time over the turf ashes that she had raked out in front of her to extinguish them. She contemplated so intently the new wife, as presented to her in her mind's eye over the embers, that she forgot the lapse of time. At last, wearied with her day's work, she too retired.

But the figure which had occupied her so much during this and the previous days was not to be banished at night. For the first time Gertrude Lodge visited the supplanted woman in her dreams. Rhoda Brook dreamed – since her assertion that she really saw, before falling asleep, was not to be believed – that the young wife, in the pale silk dress and white bonnet, but with features shockingly distorted, and wrinkled as by age, was sitting upon her chest as she lay. The pressure of Mrs Lodge's person grew heavier; the blue eyes peered cruelly into her face; and then the figure thrust forward its left hand mockingly, so as to make the wedding-ring it wore glitter in Rhoda's eyes. Maddened mentally, and nearly suffocated by pressure, the sleeper struggled; the incubus, still regarding her, withdrew to the foot of the bed, only, however, to come forward by degrees, resume her seat, and flash her left hand as before.

Gasping for breath, Rhoda, in a last desperate effort, swung out her right hand, seized the confronting spectre by its obtrusive left arm, and whirled it backward to the floor, starting up herself as she did so with a low cry.

'O, merciful heaven!' she cried, sitting on the edge of the bed in a cold sweat; 'that was not a dream – she was here!'

She could feel her antagonist's arm within her grasp even now – the very flesh and bone of it, as it seemed. She looked on the floor whither she had whirled the spectre, but there was nothing to be seen.

Rhoda Brook slept no more that night, and when she went milking at the next dawn they noticed how pale and haggard she looked. The milk that she drew quivered into the pail; her hand not calmed even yet, and still retained the feel of the arm. She came home to breakfast as wearily as if it had been supper-time.

'What was that noise in your chimmer, mother, last night?' said her son. 'You fell off the bed, surely?'

'Did you hear anything fall? At what time?'

'Just when the clock struck two.'

She could not explain, and when the meal was done went silently about her household work, the boy assisting her, for he hated going afield on the farms, and she indulged his reluctance. Between eleven and twelve the garden-gate clicked, and she lifted her eyes to the window. At the bottom of the garden, within the gate, stood the woman of her vision. Rhoda seemed transfixed.

'Ah, she said she would come!' exclaimed the boy, also observing her.

'Said so – when? How does she know us?'

'I have seen and spoken to her. I talked to her yesterday.'

'I told you,' said the mother, flushing indignantly, 'never to speak to anybody in that house, or go near the place.'

'I did not speak to her till she spoke to me. And I did not go near the place. I met her in the road.'

'What did you tell her?'

'Nothing. She said, "Are you the poor boy who had to bring the heavy load from market?" And she looked at my boots, and said they would not keep my feet dry if it came on wet, because they were so cracked. I told her I lived with my mother, and we had enough to do to keep ourselves; and that's how it was; and she said then, "I'll come and bring you some better boots, and see your mother." She gives away things to other folks in the meads besides us.'

Mrs Lodge was by this time close to the door – not in her silk, as Rhoda had dreamt of in the bed-chamber, but in a morning hat, and gown of common light material, which became her better than silk. On her arm she carried a basket.

The impression remaining from the night's experience was still strong. Brook had almost expected to see the wrinkles, the scorn, and the cruelty on her visitor's face. She would have escaped an interview, had escape been possible. There was, however, no backdoor to the cottage, and in an instant the boy had lifted the latch to Mrs Lodge's gentle knock.

'I see I have come to the right house,' said she, glancing at the lad, and smiling. 'But I was not sure till you opened the door.'

The figure and action were those of the phantom; but her voice was so indescribably sweet, her glance so winning, her smile so tender, so unlike that of Rhoda's midnight visitant, that the latter could hardly believe the evidence of her senses. She was truly glad that she had not hidden away in sheer aversion, as she had been inclined to do. In her basket Mrs Lodge brought the pair of boots that she had promised to the boy, and other useful articles.

At these proofs of a kindly feeling towards her and hers Rhoda's heart reproached her bitterly. This innocent young thing should have her blessing and not her curse. When she left them a light seemed gone from the dwelling. Two days later she came again to know if the boots fitted; and less than a fortnight after that paid Rhoda another call. On this occasion the boy was absent.

'I walk a good deal,' said Mrs Lodge, 'and your house is the nearest outside our own parish. I hope you are well. You don't look quite well.'

Rhoda said she was well enough; and, indeed, though the paler of the two, there was more of the strength that endures in her well-defined features and large frame than in the soft-cheeked young woman before her. The conversation became quite confidential as regarded their powers and weaknesses; and when Mrs Lodge was leaving, Rhoda said, 'I hope you will find this air agree with you, ma'am, and not suffer from the damp of the water meads.'

The younger one replied that there was not much doubt of it, her general health being usually good. 'Though, now you remind me,' she added, 'I have one little ailment which puzzles me. It is nothing serious, but I cannot make it out.'

She uncovered her left hand and arm; and their outline confronted Rhoda's gaze as the exact original of the limb she had beheld and seized in her dream. Upon the pink round surface of the arm were faint marks of an unhealthy colour, as if produced by a rough grasp. Rhoda's eyes became riveted on the discolorations; she fancied that she discerned in them the shape of her own four fingers.

'How did it happen?' she said mechanically.

'I cannot tell,' replied Mrs Lodge, shaking her head. 'One night when I was sound asleep, dreaming I was away in some strange place, a pain suddenly shot into my arm there, and was so keen as to awaken me. I must have struck it in the daytime, I suppose, though I don't remember doing so.' She added, laughing, 'I tell my dear husband that it looks just as if he had flown into a rage and struck me there. O, I daresay it will soon disappear.'

'Ha, ha! Yes. . . . On what night did it come?'

Mrs Lodge considered, and said it would be a fortnight ago on the morrow. 'When I awoke I could not remember where I was,' she added, 'till the clock striking two reminded me.'

She had named the night and the hour of Rhoda's spectral encounter, and Brook felt like a guilty thing. The artless disclosure startled her; she did not reason on the freaks of coincidence; and all the scenery of that ghastly night returned with double vividness to her mind.

'O, can it be,' she said to herself, when her visitor had departed, 'that I exercise a malignant power over people against my own will?' She knew that she had been slyly called a witch since her fall; but never having understood why that particular stigma had been attached to her, it had passed disregarded. Could this be the explanation, and had such things as this ever happened before?

IV. *A Suggestion*

The summer drew on, and Rhoda Brook almost dreaded to meet Mrs Lodge again, notwithstanding that her feeling for the young wife amounted well-nigh to affection. Something in her own individuality seemed to convict Rhoda of crime. Yet a fatality sometimes would direct the steps of the latter to the outskirts of Holmstoke whenever she left her house for any other purpose than her daily work; and hence it happened that their next encounter was out of doors. Rhoda could not avoid the subject which had so mystified her, and after the first few words she stammered, 'I hope your – arm is well again, ma'am?' She had perceived with consternation that Gertrude Lodge carried her left arm stiffly.

'No; it is not quite well. Indeed it is no better at all; it is rather worse. It pains me dreadfully sometimes.'

'Perhaps you had better go to a doctor, ma'am.'

She replied that she had already seen a doctor. Her husband had insisted upon her going to one. But the surgeon had not seemed to understand the afflicted limb at all; he had told her to bathe it in hot water, and she had bathed it, but the treatment had done no good.

'Will you let me see it?' said the milkwoman.

Mrs Lodge pushed up her sleeve and disclosed the place, which was a few inches above the wrist. As soon as Rhoda Brook saw it, she could hardly preserve her composure. There was nothing of the nature of a wound, but the arm at that point had a shrivelled look, and the outline of the four fingers appeared more distinct than at the former time. Moreover, she fancied that they were imprinted in precisely the relative position of her clutch upon the arm in the trance; the first finger towards Gertrude's wrist, and the fourth towards her elbow.

What the impress resembled seemed to have struck Gertrude herself since their last meeting. 'It looks almost like finger-marks,' she said; adding with a faint laugh, 'my husband says it is as if some witch, or the devil himself, had taken hold of me there, and blasted the flesh.'

Rhoda shivered. 'That's fancy,' she said hurriedly. 'I wouldn't mind it, if I were you.'

'I shouldn't so much mind it,' said the younger, with hesitation, 'if – if I hadn't a notion that it makes my husband – dislike me – no, love me less. Men think so much of personal appearance.'

'Some do – he for one.'

'Yes; and he was very proud of mine, at first.'

'Keep your arm covered from his sight.'

'Ah – he knows the disfigurement is there!' She tried to hide the tears that filled her eyes.

'Well, ma'am, I earnestly hope it will go away soon.'

And so the milkwoman's mind was chained anew to the subject by a horrid sort of spell as she returned home. The sense of having been guilty of an act of malignity increased, affect as she might to ridicule her superstition. In her secret heart Rhoda did not altogether object to a slight diminution of her successor's beauty, by whatever means it had come about; but she did not wish to inflict upon her physical pain. For though this pretty young woman had rendered impossible any reparation which Lodge might have made Rhoda for his past conduct, everything like resentment at the unconscious usurpation had quite passed away from the elder's mind.

If the sweet and kindly Gertrude Lodge only knew of the dream-scene in the bed-chamber, what would she think? Not to inform her of it seemed treachery in the presence of her friendliness; but tell she could not of her own accord – neither could she devise a remedy.

She mused upon the matter the greater part of the night; and the next day, after the morning milking, set out to obtain another glimpse of Gertrude Lodge if she could, being held to her by a gruesome fascination. By watching the house from a distance the milkmaid was presently able to discern the farmer's wife in a ride she was taking alone – probably to join her husband in some distant field. Mrs Lodge perceived her, and cantered in her direction.

'Good morning, Rhoda!' Gertrude said, when she had come up. 'I was going to call.'

Rhoda noticed that Mrs Lodge held the reins with some difficulty.

'I hope – the bad arm,' said Rhoda.

'They tell me there is possibly one way by which I might be able to find out the cause, and so perhaps the cure, of it,' replied the other anxiously. 'It is by going to some clever man over in Egdon Heath. They did not know if he was still alive – and I cannot remember his name at this moment; but they said that you knew more of his movements than anybody else hereabout, and could tell me if he were still to be consulted. Dear me – what was his name? But you know.'

'Not Conjuror Trendle?' said her thin companion, turning pale.

'Trendle – yes. Is he alive?'

'I believe so,' said Rhoda, with reluctance.

'Why do you call him conjuror?'

'Well – they say – they used to say he was a – he had powers other folks have not.'

'O, how could my people be so superstitious as to recommend a man of that sort! I thought they meant some medical man. I shall think no more of him.'

Rhoda looked relieved, and Mrs Lodge rode on. The milkwoman had inwardly seen, from the moment she heard of her having been mentioned as a reference for this man, that there must exist a sarcastic feeling among the work-folk that a sorceress would know the whereabouts of the exorcist. They suspected her, then. A short time ago this would have

THE WITHERED ARM

given no concern to a woman of her common-sense. But she had a haunting reason to be superstitious now; and she had been seized with sudden dread that this Conjuror Trendle might name her as the malignant influence which was blasting the fair person of Gertrude, and so lead her friend to hate her for ever, and to treat her as some fiend in human shape.

But all was not over. Two days after, a shadow intruded into the window-pattern thrown on Rhoda Brook's floor by the afternoon sun. The woman opened the door at once, almost breathlessly.

'Are you alone?' said Gertrude. She seemed to be no less harassed and anxious than Brook herself.

'Yes,' said Rhoda.

'The place on my arm seems worse, and troubles me!' the young farmer's wife went on. 'It is so mysterious! I do hope it will not be an incurable wound. I have again been thinking of what they said about Conjuror Trendle. I don't really believe in such men, but I should not mind just visiting him, from curiosity – though on no account must my husband know. Is it far to where he lives?'

'Yes – five miles,' said Rhoda backwardly. 'In the heart of Egdon.'

'Well, I should have to walk. Could not you go with me to show me the way – say to-morrow afternoon?'

'O, not I; that is——,' the milkwoman murmured, with a start of dismay. Again the dread seized her that something to do with her fierce act in the dream might be revealed, and her character in the eyes of the most useful friend she had ever had be ruined irretrievably.

Mrs Lodge urged, and Rhoda finally assented, though with much misgiving. Sad as the journey would be to her, she could not conscientiously stand in the way of a possible remedy for her patron's strange affliction. It was agreed that, to escape suspicion of their mystic intent, they should meet at the edge of the heath at the corner of a plantation which was visible from the spot where they now stood.

V. *Conjuror Trendle*

By the next afternoon Rhoda would have done anything to escape this inquiry. But she had promised to go. Moreover, there was a horrid fascination at times in becoming instrumental in throwing such possible light on her own character as would reveal her to be something greater in the occult world than she had ever herself suspected.

She started just before the time of day mentioned between them, and half-an-hour's brisk walking brought her to the south-eastern extension of the Egdon tract of country, where the fir plantation was. A slight figure, cloaked and veiled, was already there. Rhoda recognized, almost with a shudder, that Mrs Lodge bore her left arm in a sling.

They hardly spoke to each other, and immediately set out on their climb into the interior of this solemn country, which stood high above the rich alluvial soil they had left half-an-hour before. It was a long walk; thick clouds made the atmosphere dark, though it was as yet only early afternoon; and the wind howled dismally over the slopes of the heath – not improbably the same heath which had witnessed the agony of the Wessex King Ina, presented to after-ages as Lear. Gertrude Lodge talked most, Rhoda replying with monosyllabic preoccupation. She had a strange dislike to walking on the side of her companion where hung the afflicted arm, moving round to the other when inadvertently near it. Much heather had been brushed by their feet when they descended upon a cart-track, beside which stood the house of the man they sought.

He did not profess his remedial practices openly, or care anything about their continuance, his direct interests being those of a dealer in furze, turf, 'sharp sand', and other local products. Indeed, he affected not to believe largely in his own powers, and when warts that had been shown him for cure miraculously disappeared – which it must be owned they infallibly did – he would say lightly, 'O, I only drink a glass of grog upon 'em at your expense – perhaps it's all chance,' and immediately turn the subject.

He was at home when they arrived, having in fact seen them descending into his valley. He was a grey-bearded man, with a reddish face, and he looked singularly at Rhoda the first moment he beheld her. Mrs Lodge told him her errand; and then with words of self-disparagement he examined her arm.

'Medicine can't cure it,' he said promptly. ' 'Tis the work of an enemy.'

Rhoda shrank into herself, and drew back.

'An enemy? What enemy?' asked Mrs Lodge.

He shook his head. 'That's best known to yourself,' he said. 'If you like, I can show the person to you, though I shall not myself know who it is. I can do no more; and don't wish to do that.'

She pressed him; on which he told Rhoda to wait outside where she stood, and took Mrs Lodge into the room. It opened immediately from the door; and, as the latter remained ajar, Rhoda Brook could see the proceedings without taking part in them. He brought a tumbler from the dresser, nearly filled it with water, and fetching an egg, prepared it in some private way; after which he broke it on the edge of the glass, so that the white went in and the yolk remained. As it was getting gloomy, he took the glass and its contents to the window, and told Gertrude to watch the mixture closely. They leant over the table together, and the milkwoman could see the opaline hue of the egg-fluid changing form as it sank in the water, but she was not near enough to define the shape that it assumed.

'Do you catch the likeness of any face or figure as you look?' demanded the conjuror of the young woman.

She murmured a reply, in tones so low as to be inaudible to Rhoda, and continued to gaze intently into the glass. Rhoda turned, and walked a few steps away.

When Mrs Lodge came out, and her face was met by the light, it appeared exceedingly pale – as pale as Rhoda's – against the sad dun shades of the upland's garniture. Trendle shut the door behind her, and they at once started homeward together. But Rhoda perceived that her companion had quite changed.

'Did he charge much?' she asked tentatively.

'O no – nothing. He would not take a farthing,' said Gertrude.

'And what did you see?' inquired Rhoda.

'Nothing I – care to speak of.' The constraint in her manner was remarkable; her face was so rigid as to wear an oldened aspect, faintly suggestive of the face in Rhoda's bed-chamber.

'Was it you who first proposed coming here?' Mrs Lodge suddenly inquired, after a long pause. 'How very odd, if you did!'

'No. But I am not sorry we have come, all things considered,' she replied. For the first time a sense of triumph possessed her, and she did not altogether deplore that the young thing at her side should learn that their lives had been antagonized by other influences than their own.

The subject was no more alluded to during the long and dreary walk home. But in some way or other a story was whispered about the many-dairied lowland that winter that Mrs Lodge's gradual loss of the use of her left arm was owing to her being 'overlooked' by Rhoda Brook. The latter kept her own counsel about the incubus, but her face grew sadder and thinner; and in the spring she and her boy disappeared from the neighbourhood of Holmstoke.

VI. *A Second Attempt*

Half a dozen years passed away, and Mr and Mrs Lodge's married experience sank into prosiness, and worse. The farmer was usually gloomy and silent: the woman whom he had wooed for her grace and beauty was contorted and disfigured in the left limb; moreover, she had brought him no child, which rendered it likely that he would be the last of a family who had occupied that valley for some two hundred years. He thought of Rhoda Brook and her son; and feared this might be a judgment from heaven upon him.

The once blithe-hearted and enlightened Gertrude was changing into an irritable, superstitious woman, whose whole time was given to experimenting upon her ailment with every quack remedy she came across. She was honestly attached to her husband, and was ever secretly hoping against hope to win back his heart again by regaining some at least of her personal beauty. Hence it arose that her closet was lined with bottles, packets, and ointment-pots of every description – nay, bunches of mystic herbs, charms, and books of necromancy, which in her schoolgirl time she would have ridiculed as folly.

'Damned if you won't poison yourself with these apothecary messes and witch mixtures some time or other,' said her husband, when his eye chanced to fall upon the multitudinous array.

She did not reply, but turned her sad, soft glance upon him in such heart-swollen reproach that he looked sorry for his words, and added, 'I only meant it for your good, you know, Gertrude.'

'I'll clear out the whole lot, and destroy them,' said she huskily, 'and try such remedies no more!'

'You want somebody to cheer you,' he observed. 'I once thought of adopting a boy; but he is too old now. And he is gone away I don't know where.'

She guessed to whom he alluded; for Rhoda Brook's story had in the course of years become known to her; though not a word had ever passed between her husband and herself on the subject. Neither had she ever spoken to him of her visit to Conjuror Trendle, and of what was revealed to her, or she thought was revealed to her, by that solitary heathman.

She was now five-and-twenty; but she seemed older. 'Six years of marriage, and only a few months of love,' she sometimes whispered to herself. And then she thought of the apparent cause, and said, with a tragic glance at her withering limb, 'If I could only again be as I was when he first saw me!'

She obediently destroyed her nostrums and charms; but there remained a hankering wish to try something else – some other sort of cure altogether. She had never revisited Trendle since she had been conducted to the house of the solitary by Rhoda against her will; but it now suddenly occurred to Gertrude that she would, in a last desperate effort at deliverance from this seeming curse, again seek out the man, if he yet lived. He was entitled to a certain credence, for the indistinct form he had raised in the glass had undoubtedly resembled the only woman in the world who – as she now knew, though not then – could have a reason for bearing her ill-will. The visit should be paid.

This time she went alone, though she nearly got lost on the heath, and roamed a considerable distance out of her way. Trendle's house was reached at last, however: he was not indoors, and instead of waiting at the cottage, she went to where his bent figure was pointed out to her at work a long way off. Trendle remembered her, and laying down the handful of furze-roots which he was gathering and throwing into a heap, he offered to accompany her in her homeward direction, as the distance was considerable and the days were short. So they walked together, his head bowed nearly to the earth, and his form of a colour with it.

'You can send away warts and other excrescences, I know,' she said; 'why can't you send away this?' And the arm was uncovered.

'You think too much of my powers!' said Trendle; 'and I am old and weak now, too. No, no; it is too much for me to attempt in my own person. What have ye tried?'

She named to him some of the hundred medicaments and counter-spells which she had adopted from time to time. He shook his head.

'Some were good enough,' he said approvingly; 'but not many of them for such as this. This is of the nature of a blight, not of the nature of a wound; and if you ever do throw it off, it will be all at once.'

'If I only could!'

'There is only one chance of doing it known to me. It has never failed in kindred afflictions – that I can declare. But it is hard to carry out, and especially for a woman.'

'Tell me!' said she.

'You must touch with the limb the neck of a man who's been hanged.'

She started a little at the image he had raised.

'Before he's cold – just after he's cut down,' continued the conjuror impassively.

'How can that do good?'

'It will turn the blood and change the constitution. But, as I say, to do it is hard. You must go to the jail when there's a hanging, and wait for him when he's brought off the gallows. Lots have done it, though per-haps not such pretty women as you. I used to send dozens for skin complaints. But that was in former times. The last I sent was in '13 – near twelve years ago.'

He had no more to tell her; and, when he had put her into a straight track homeward, turned and left her, refusing all money as at first.

VII. *A Ride*

The communication sank deep into Gertrude's mind. Her nature was rather a timid one; and probably of all remedies that the white wizard could have suggested there was not one which would have filled her with so much aversion as this, not to speak of the immense obstacles in the way of its adoption.

Casterbridge, the county-town, was a dozen or fifteen miles off; and though in those days, when men were executed for horse-stealing, arson, and burglary, an assize seldom passed without a hanging, it was not likely that she could get access to the body of the criminal unaided. And the fear of her husband's anger made her reluctant to breathe a word of Trendle's suggestion to him or to anybody about him.

She did nothing for months, and patiently bore her disfigurement as before. But her woman's nature, craving for renewed love, through the medium of renewed beauty (she was but twenty-five), was ever stimulating her to try what, at any rate, could hardly do her any harm. 'What came by a spell will go by a spell surely,' she would say. Whenever her imagination pictured the act she shrank in terror from the possibility of it: then the words of the conjuror, 'It will turn your blood,' were seen to be capable of a scientific no less than a ghastly interpretation; the mastering desire returned, and urged her on again.

There was at this time but one county paper, and that her husband only occasionally borrowed. But old-fashioned days had old-fashioned means, and news was extensively conveyed by word of mouth from market to market, or from fair to fair, so that, whenever such an event as an execution was about to take place, few within a radius of twenty miles were ignorant of the coming sight; and, so far as Holmstoke was concerned, some enthusiasts had been known to walk all the way to Casterbridge and back in one day, solely to witness the spectacle. The next assizes were in March; and when Gertrude Lodge heard that they had been held, she inquired stealthily at the inn as to the result, as soon as she could find opportunity.

She was, however, too late. The time at which the sentences were to be carried out had arrived, and to make the journey and obtain admission at such short notice required at least her husband's assistance. She dared not tell him, for she had found by delicate experiment that these smouldering village beliefs made him furious if mentioned, partly because he half entertained them himself. It was therefore necessary to wait for another opportunity.

Her determination received a fillip from learning that two epileptic children had attended from this very village of Holmstoke many years before with beneficial results, though the experiment had been strongly condemned by the neighbouring clergy. April, May, June, passed; and it is no overstatement to say that by the end of the last-named month Gertrude well-nigh longed for the death of a fellow-creature. Instead of her formal prayers each night, her unconscious prayer was, 'O Lord, hang some guilty or innocent person soon!'

This time she made earlier inquiries, and was altogether more systematic in her proceedings. Moreover, the season was summer, between the haymaking and the harvest, and in the leisure thus afforded him her husband had been holiday-taking away from home.

The assizes were in July, and she went to the inn as before. There was to be one execution – only one – for arson.

Her greatest problem was not how to get to Casterbridge, but what means she should adopt for obtaining admission to the jail. Though

THE WITHERED ARM

access for such purposes had formerly never been denied, the custom had fallen into desuetude; and in contemplating her possible difficulties, she was again almost driven to fall back upon her husband. But, on sounding him about the assizes, he was so uncommunicative, so more than usually cold, that she did not proceed, and decided that whatever she did she would do alone.

Fortune, obdurate hitherto, showed her unexpected favour. On the Thursday before the Saturday fixed for the execution, Lodge remarked to her that he was going away from home for another day or two on business at a fair, and that he was sorry he could not take her with him.

She exhibited on this occasion so much readiness to stay at home that he looked at her in surprise. Time had been when she would have shown deep disappointment at the loss of such a jaunt. However, he lapsed into his usual taciturnity, and on the day named left Holmstoke.

It was now her turn. She at first had thought of driving, but on reflection held that driving would not do, since it would necessitate her keeping to the turnpike-road, and so increase by tenfold the risk of her ghastly errand being found out. She decided to ride, and avoid the beaten track, notwithstanding that in her husband's stables there was no animal just at present which by any stretch of imagination could be considered a lady's mount, in spite of his promise before marriage to always keep a mare for her. He had, however, many cart-horses, fine ones of their kind; and among the rest was a serviceable creature, an equine Amazon, with a back as broad as a sofa, on which Gertrude had occasionally taken an airing when unwell. This horse she chose.

On Friday afternoon one of the men brought it round. She was dressed, and before going down looked at her shrivelled arm. 'Ah!' she said to it, 'if it had not been for you this terrible ordeal would have been saved me!'

When strapping up the bundle in which she carried a few articles of clothing, she took occasion to say to the servant, 'I take these in case I should not get back tonight from the person I am going to visit. Don't be alarmed if I am not in by ten, and close up the house as usual. I shall be at home tomorrow for certain.' She meant then to tell her husband privately: the deed accomplished was not like the deed projected. He would almost certainly forgive her.

And then the pretty palpitating Gertrude Lodge went from her husband's homestead; but though her goal was Casterbridge she did not take the direct route thither through Stickleford. Her cunning course at first was in precisely the opposite direction. As soon as she was out of sight, however, she turned to the left, by a road which led into Egdon, and on entering the heath wheeled round, and set out in the true course, due westerly. A more private way down the county could not be imagined; and as to direction, she had merely to keep her horse's head to a point a little to the right of the sun. She knew that she would light upon a furze-cutter or cottager of some sort from time to time, from whom she might correct her bearing.

Though the date was comparatively recent, Egdon was much less fragmentary in character than now. The attempts – successful and otherwise – at cultivation on the lower slopes, which intrude and break up the original heath into small detached heaths, had not been carried far; Enclosure Acts had not taken effect, and the banks and fences which now exclude the cattle of those villagers who formerly enjoyed rights of commonage thereon, and the carts of those who had turbary privileges which kept them in firing all the year round, were not erected. Gertrude, therefore, rode along with no other obstacles than the prickly furze-bushes, the mats of heather, the white water-courses, and the natural steeps and declivities of the ground.

Her horse was sure, if heavy-footed and slow, and though a draught animal, was easy-paced; had it been otherwise, she was not a woman who could have ventured to ride over such a bit of country with a half-dead arm. It was therefore nearly eight o'clock when she drew rein to breathe her bearer on the last outlying high point of heath-land towards Casterbridge, previous to leaving Egdon for the cultivated valleys.

She halted before a pool called Rushy-pond, flanked by the ends of two hedges; a railing ran through the centre of the pond, dividing it in half. Over the railing she saw the low green country; over the green trees the roofs of the town; over the roofs a white flat façade, denoting the entrance to the county jail. On the roof of this front specks were moving about; they seemed to be workmen erecting something. Her flesh crept. She descended slowly, and was soon amid corn-fields and pastures. In another half-hour, when it was almost dusk, Gertrude reached the White Hart, the first inn of the town on that side.

Little surprise was excited by her arrival; farmers' wives rode on horseback then more than they do now; though, for that matter, Mrs Lodge was not imagined to be a wife at all; the innkeeper supposed her some harum-skarum young woman who had come to attend 'hang-fair' next day. Neither her husband nor herself ever dealt in Casterbridge market, so that she was unknown. While dismounting she beheld a crowd of boys standing at the door of a harness-maker's shop just above the inn, looking inside it with deep interest.

'What is going on there?' she asked of the ostler.

'Making the rope for tomorrow.'

She throbbed responsively, and contracted her arm.

' 'Tis sold by the inch afterwards,' the man continued. 'I could get you a bit, miss, for nothing, if you'd like?'

She hastily repudiated any such wish, all the more from a curious creeping feeling that the condemned wretch's destiny was becoming interwoven with her own; and having engaged a room for the night, sat down to think.

Up to this time she had formed but the vaguest notions about her means of obtaining access to the prison. The words of the cunning-man returned to her mind. He had implied that she should use her beauty, impaired though it was, as a pass-key. In her inexperience she knew little about jail functionaries; she had heard of a high-sheriff and an under-sheriff, but dimly only. She knew, however, that there must be a hangman, and to the hangman she determined to apply.

VIII. *A Water-side Hermit*

At this date, and for several years after, there was a hangman to almost every jail. Gertrude found, on inquiry, that the Casterbridge official dwelt in a lonely cottage by a deep slow river flowing under the cliff on which the prison buildings were situate – the stream being the self-same one, though she did not know it, which watered the Stickleford and Holmstoke meads lower down in its course.

Having changed her dress, and before she had eaten or drunk – for she could not take her ease till she had ascertained some particulars – Gertrude pursued her way by a path along the water-side to the cottage indicated. Passing thus the outskirts of the jail, she discerned on the level roof over the gateway three rectangular lines against the sky, where the specks had been moving in her distant view; she recognized what the erection was, and passed quickly on. Another hundred yards brought her to the executioner's house, which a boy pointed out. It stood close to the same stream, and was hard by a weir, the waters of which emitted a steady roar.

While she stood hesitating the door opened, and an old man came forth shading a candle with one hand. Locking the door on the outside, he turned to a flight of wooden steps fixed against the end of the cottage, and began to ascend them, this being evidently the staircase to his bed-room. Gertrude hastened forward, but by the time she reached the foot of the ladder he was at the top. She called to him loudly enough to be heard above the roar of the weir; he looked down and said, 'What d'ye want here?'

'To speak to you a minute.'

The candle-light, such as it was, fell upon her imploring, pale, up-turned face, and Davies (as the hangman was called) backed down the ladder. 'I was just going to bed,' he said; ' "Early to bed and early to rise," but I don't mind stopping a minute for such a one as you. Come into the house.' He reopened the door, and preceded her to the room within.

The implements of his daily work, which was that of a jobbing gardener, stood in a corner, and seeing probably that she looked rural, he said, 'If you want me to undertake country work I can't come, for I never leave Casterbridge for gentle nor simple – not I. My real calling is officer of justice,' he added formally.

'Yes, yes! That's it. Tomorrow!'

'Ah! I thought so. Well, what's the matter about that? 'Tis no use to come here about the knot – folks do come continually, but I tell 'em one knot is as merciful as another if ye keep it under the ear. Is the unfortunate man a relation; or, I should say, perhaps' (looking at her dress) 'a person who's been in your employ?'

'No. What time is the execution?'

'The same as usual – twelve o'clock, or as soon after as the London mail-coach gets in. We always wait for that, in case of a reprieve.'

'O – a reprieve – I hope not!' she said involuntarily.

'Well – hee, hee! – as a matter of business, so do I! But still if ever a young fellow deserved to be let off, this one does; only just turned eighteen, and only present by chance when the rick was fired. Howsomever, there's not much risk of it, as they are obliged to make an example of him, there having been so much destruction of property that way lately.'

'I mean,' she explained, 'that I want to touch him for a charm, a cure of an affliction, by the advice of a man who has proved the virtue of the remedy.'

'O yes, miss! Now I understand. I've had such people come in past years. But it didn't strike me that you looked of a sort to require blood-turning. What's the complaint? The wrong kind for this, I'll be bound.'

'My arm.' She reluctantly showed the withered skin.

'Ah! – 'tis all a-scram!' said the hangman, examining it.

'Yes,' said she.

'Well,' he continued, with interest, 'that *is* the class o' subject, I'm bound to admit! I like the look of the wownd; it is truly as suitable for the cure as any I ever saw. 'Twas a knowing-man that sent 'ee, whoever he was.'

'You can contrive for me all that's necessary?' she said breathlessly.

'You should really have gone to the governor of the jail, and your doctor with 'ee, and given your name and address – that's how it used to be done, if I recollect. Still, perhaps, I can manage it for a trifling fee.'

'O, thank you! I would rather do it this way, as I should like it kept private.'

'Lover not to know, eh?'

'No – husband.'

'Aha! Very well. I'll get 'ee a touch of the corpse.'

'Where is it now?' she said, shuddering.

'It? – *he*, you mean; he's living yet. Just inside that little small winder up there in the glum.' He signified the jail on the cliff above.

She thought of her husband and her friends. 'Yes, of course,' she said; 'and how am I to proceed?'

He took her to the door. 'Now, do you be waiting at the little wicket in the wall, that you'll find up there in the lane, not later than one o'clock. I will open it from the inside, as I shan't come home to dinner till he's cut down. Good-night. Be punctual; and if you don't want anybody to know 'ee, wear a veil. Ah – once I had such a daughter as you!'

She went away, and climbed the path above, to assure herself that she would be able to find the wicket next day. Its outline was soon visible to her – a narrow opening in the outer wall of the prison precincts. The steep was so great that, having reached the wicket, she stopped a moment to breathe; and, looking back upon the water-side cot, saw the hangman again ascending his outdoor staircase. He entered the loft or chamber to which it led, and in a few minutes extinguished his light.

The town clock struck ten, and she returned to the White Hart as she had come.

IX. *A Rencounter*

It was one o'clock on Saturday. Gertrude Lodge, having been admitted to the jail as above described, was sitting in a waiting-room within the second gate, which stood under a classic archway of ashlar, then comparatively modern, and bearing the inscription, 'COVNTY JAIL: 1793'. This had been the façade she saw from the heath the day before. Near at hand was a passage to the roof on which the gallows stood.

The town was thronged, and the market suspended; but Gertrude had seen scarcely a soul. Having kept her room till the hour of the appointment, she had proceeded to the spot by a way which avoided the open space below the cliff where the spectators had gathered; but she could, even now, hear the multitudinous babble of their voices, out of which rose at intervals the hoarse croak of a single voice uttering the words, 'Last dying speech and confession!' There had been no reprieve, and the execution was over; but the crowd still waited to see the body taken down.

Soon the persistent woman heard a trampling overhead, then a hand beckoned to her, and, following directions, she went out and crossed the inner paved court beyond the gatehouse, her knees trembling so that she could scarcely walk. One of her arms was out of its sleeve, and only covered by her shawl.

On the spot at which she had now arrived were two trestles, and before she could think of their purpose she heard heavy feet descending stairs somewhere at her back. Turn her head she would not, or could not, and, rigid in this position, she was conscious of a rough coffin passing her shoulder, borne by four men. It was open, and in it lay the body of a young man, wearing the smockfrock of a rustic, and fustian breeches. The corpse had been thrown into the coffin so hastily that the skirt of the smockfrock was hanging over. The burden was temporarily deposited on the trestles.

By this time the young woman's state was such that a grey mist seemed to float before her eyes, on account of which, and the veil she wore, she could scarcely discern anything: it was as though she had nearly died, but was held up by a sort of galvanism.

'Now!' said a voice close at hand, and she was just conscious that the word had been addressed to her.

By a last strenuous effort she advanced, at the same time hearing persons approaching behind her. She bared her poor curst arm; and Davies, uncovering the face of the corpse, took Gertrude's hand, and held it so that her arm lay across the dead man's neck, upon a line the colour of an unripe blackberry, which surrounded it.

Gertrude shrieked: 'the turn o' the blood,' predicted by the conjuror, had taken place. But at that moment a second shriek rent the air of the enclosure: it was not Gertrude's, and its effect upon her was to make her start round.

Immediately behind her stood Rhoda Brook, her face drawn, and her eyes red with weeping. Behind Rhoda stood Gertrude's own husband; his countenance lined, his eyes dim, but without a tear.

'D—n you! what are you doing here?' he said hoarsely.

'Hussy – to come between us and our child now!' cried Rhoda. 'This is the meaning of what Satan showed me in the vision! You are like her at last!' And clutching the bare arm of the younger woman, she pulled her unresistingly back against the wall. Immediately Brook had loosened her hold the fragile young Gertrude slid down against the feet of her husband. When he lifted her up she was unconscious.

The mere sight of the twain had been enough to suggest to her that the dead young man was Rhoda's son. At that time the relatives of an executed convict had the privilege of claiming the body for burial, if they chose to do so; and it was for this purpose that Lodge was awaiting the inquest with Rhoda. He had been summoned by her as soon as the young man was taken in the crime, and at different times since; and he had attended in court during the trial. This was the 'holiday' he had been indulging in of late. The two wretched parents had wished to avoid exposure; and hence had come themselves for the body, a waggon and sheet for its conveyance and covering being in waiting outside.

Gertrude's case was so serious that it was deemed advisable to call to her the surgeon who was at hand. She was taken out of the jail into the town; but she never reached home alive. Her delicate vitality, sapped perhaps by the paralyzed arm, collapsed under the double shock that followed the severe strain, physical and mental, to which she had subjected herself during the previous twenty-four hours. Her blood had been 'turned' indeed – too far. Her death took place in the town three days after.

Her husband was never seen in Casterbridge again; once only in the old market-place at Anglebury, which he had so much frequented, and very seldom in public anywhere. Burdened at first with moodiness and remorse, he eventually changed for the better, and appeared as a chastened and thoughtful man. Soon after attending the funeral of his poor young wife he took steps towards giving up the farms in Holmstoke and the adjoining parish, and, having sold every head of his stock, he went away to Port-Bredy, at the other end of the county, living there in solitary lodgings till his death two years later of a painless decline. It was then found that he had bequeathed the whole of his not inconsiderable property to a reformatory for boys, subject to the payment of a small annuity to Rhoda Brook, if she could be found to claim it.

For some time she could not be found; but eventually she reappeared in her old parish – absolutely refusing, however, to have anything to do with the provision made for her. Her monotonous milking at the dairy was resumed, and followed for many long years, till her form became bent, and her once abundant dark hair white and worn away at the forehead – perhaps by long pressure against the cows. Here, sometimes, those who knew her experiences would stand and observe her, and wonder what sombre thoughts were beating inside that impassive, wrinkled brow, to the rhythm of the alternating milk-streams.

'Blackwood's Magazine,'
    January 1888.

Joseph Conrad

The Idiots

We were driving along the road from Treguier to Kervanda. We passed at a smart trot between the hedges topping an earth wall on each side of the road; then at the foot of the steep ascent before Ploumar the horse dropped into a walk, and the driver jumped down heavily from the box. He flicked his whip and climbed the incline, stepping clumsily uphill by the side of the carriage, one hand on the footboard, his eyes on the ground. After a while he lifted his head, pointed up the road with the end of the whip, and said—

'The idiot!'

The sun was shining violently upon the undulating surface of the land. The rises were topped by clumps of meagre trees, with their branches showing high on the sky as if they had been perched upon stilts. The small fields, cut up by hedges and stone walls that zigzagged over the slopes, lay in rectangular patches of vivid greens and yellows, resembling the unskilful daubs of a naive picture. And the landscape was divided in two by the white streak of a road stretching in long loops far away, like a river of dust crawling out of the hills on its way to the sea.

'Here he is,' said the driver, again.

In the long grass bordering the road a face glided past the carriage at the level of the wheels as we drove slowly by. The imbecile face was red, and the bullet head with close-cropped hair seemed to lie alone, its chin in the dust. The body was lost in the bushes growing thick along the bottom of the deep ditch.

It was a boy's face. He might have been sixteen, judging from the size – perhaps less, perhaps more. Such creatures are forgotten by time, and live untouched by years till death gathers them up into its compassionate bosom; the faithful death that never forgets in the press of work the most insignificant of its children.

'Ah! there's another,' said the man; with a certain satisfaction in his tone, as if he had caught sight of something expected.

There was another. That one stood nearly in the middle of the road in the blaze of sunshine at the end of his own short shadow. And he stood with his hands pushed into the opposite sleeves of his long coat, his head sunk between the shoulders, all hunched up in the flood of heat. From a distance he had the aspect of one suffering from intense cold.

'Those are twins,' explained the driver.

The idiot shuffled two paces out of the way and looked at us over his shoulder when we brushed past him. The glance was unseeing and staring, a fascinated glance; but he did not turn to look after us. Probably the image passed before the eyes without leaving any trace on the misshapen brain of the creature. When we had topped the ascent I looked over the hood. He stood in the road just where we had left him.

The driver clambered into his seat, clicked his tongue, and we went down hill. The brake squeaked horribly from time to time. At the foot he eased off the noisy mechanism and said, turning half round on his box—

'We shall see some more of them by-and-by.'

'More idiots? How many of them are there, then?' I asked.

'There's four of them – children of a farmer near Ploumar here ... The parents are dead now,' he added, after a while. 'The grandmother lives on the farm. In the daytime they knock about on this road, and they come home at dusk along with the cattle ... It's a good farm.'

We saw the other two: a boy and a girl, as the driver said. They were dressed exactly alike, in shapeless garments with petticoat-like skirts. The imperfect thing that lived within them moved those beings to howl at us from the top of the bank, where they sprawled amongst the tough stalks of furze. Their cropped black heads stuck out from the bright yellow wall of countless small blossoms. The faces were purple with the strain of yelling; the voices sounded blank and cracked like a mechanical imitation of old people's voices; and suddenly ceased when we turned into a lane.

I saw them many times in my wandering about the country. They lived on that road, drifting along its length here and there, according to the inexplicable impulses of their monstrous darkness. They were an offence to the sunshine, a reproach to empty heaven, a blight on the concentrated and purposeful vigour of the wild landscape. In time the story of their parents shaped itself before me out of the listless answers to my questions, out of the indifferent words heard in wayside inns or on the very road those idiots haunted. Some of it was told by an emaciated and sceptical old fellow with a tremendous whip, while we trudged together over the sands by the side of a two-wheeled cart loaded with dripping seaweed. Then at other times other people confirmed and completed the story: till it stood at last before me, a tale formidable and simple, as they always are, those disclosures of obscure trials endured by ignorant hearts.

When he returned from his military service Jean-Pierre Bacadou found the old people very much aged. He remarked with pain that the work of the farm was not satisfactorily done. The father had not the energy of old days. The hands did not feel over them the eye of the master. Jean-Pierre noted with sorrow that the heap of manure in the courtyard before the only entrance to the house was not so large as it should have been. The fences were out of repair, and the cattle suffered from neglect. At home the mother was practically bedridden, and the girls chattered loudly in the big kitchen, unrebuked, from morning to night. He said to himself: 'We must change all this.' He talked the matter over with his father one evening when the rays of the setting sun entering the yard between the outhouses ruled the heavy shadows with luminous streaks. Over the manure heap floated a mist, opal-tinted and odorous, and the marauding hens would stop in their scratching to examine with a sudden glance of their round eye the two men, both lean and tall, talking in hoarse tones. The old man, all twisted with rheumatism and bowed with years of work, the younger bony and straight, spoke without gestures in the indifferent manner of peasants, grave and slow. But before the sun had set the father had submitted to the sensible arguments of the son. 'It is not for me that I am speaking,' insisted Jean-Pierre. 'It is for the land. It's a pity to see it badly used. I am not impatient for myself.' The old fellow nodded over his stick. 'I dare say; I dare say,' he muttered. 'You may be right. Do what you like. It's the mother that will be pleased.'

The mother was pleased with her daughter-in-law. Jean-Pierre brought the two-wheeled spring-cart with a rush into the yard. The grey horse galloped clumsily, and the bride and bridegroom, sitting side by side, were jerked backwards and forwards by the up and down motion of the shafts, in a manner regular and brusque. On the road the distanced wedding guests straggled in pairs and groups. The men advanced with heavy steps, swinging their idle arms. They were clad in town clothes: jackets cut with clumsy smartness, hard black hats, immense boots polished highly. Their women all in simple black, with white caps and shawls of faded tints folded triangularly on the back, strolled lightly by their side. In front the violin sang a strident tune, and the biniou snored and hummed, while the player capered solemnly, lifting high his heavy clogs. The sombre procession drifted in and out of the narrow lanes, through sunshine and through shade, between fields and hedgerows, scaring the little birds that darted away in troops right and left. In the yard of Bacadou's farm the dark ribbon wound itself up into a mass of men and women pushing at the door with cries and greetings. The wedding dinner was remembered for months. It was a splendid feast in the orchard. Farmers of considerable means and excellent repute were to be found sleeping in ditches, all along the road to Treguier, even as late as the afternoon of the next day. All the countryside participated in the happiness of Jean-Pierre. He remained sober, and, together with his quiet wife, kept out of the way, letting father and mother reap their due of honour and thanks. But the next day he took hold strongly, and the old folks felt a shadow – precursor of the grave – fall upon them finally. The world is to the young.

When the twins were born there was plenty of room in the house, for the mother of Jean-Pierre had gone away to dwell under a heavy stone in the cemetery of Ploumar. On that day, for the first time since his son's marriage, the elder Bacadou, neglected by the cackling lot of strange women who thronged the kitchen, left in the morning his seat under the mantel of the fireplace, and went into the empty cow-house, shaking his white locks dismally. Grandsons were all very well, but he wanted his soup at midday. When shown the babies, he stared at them with a fixed gaze, and muttered something like: 'It's too much.' Whether he meant too much happiness, or simply commented upon the number of his descendants, it is impossible to say. He looked offended – as far as his old wooden face could express anything; and for days afterwards could be seen, almost any time of the day, sitting at the gate, with his nose over his knees, a pipe between his gums, and gathered up into a kind of raging concentrated sulkiness. Once he spoke to his son, alluding to the newcomers with a groan: 'They will quarrel over the land.' 'Don't bother about that, father,' answered Jean-Pierre, stolidly, and passed, bent double, towing a recalcitrant cow over his shoulder.

He was happy, and so was Susan, his wife. It was not an ethereal joy welcoming new souls to struggle, perchance to victory. In fourteen years both boys would be a help; and, later on, Jean-Pierre pictured two big sons striding over the land from patch to patch, wringing tribute from the earth beloved and fruitful. Susan was happy too, for she did not want to be spoken of as the unfortunate woman, and now she had children no one could call her that. Both herself and her husband had seen something of the larger world – he during the time of his service; while she had spent a year or so in Paris with a Breton family; but had been too home-sick to remain longer away from the hilly and green country, set in a barren circle of rocks and sands, where she had been born. She thought that one of the boys ought perhaps to be a priest, but said nothing to her husband, who was a republican, and hated the 'crows,' as he called the ministers of religion. The christening was a splendid affair. All the commune came to it, for the Bacadous were rich and influential, and, now and then, did not mind the expense. The grandfather had a new coat.

Some months afterwards, one evening when the kitchen had been swept, and the door locked, Jean-Pierre, looking at the cot, asked his wife: 'What's the matter with those children?' And, as if these words, spoken calmly, had been the portent of misfortune, she answered with a loud wail that must have been heard across the yard in the pig-sty; for the pigs (the Bacadous had the finest pigs in the country) stirred and grunted complainingly in the night. The husband went on grinding his bread and butter slowly, gazing at the wall, the soup-plate smoking under his chin. He had returned late from the market, where he had overheard (not for the first time) whispers behind his back. He revolved the words in his mind as he drove back. 'Simple! Both of them . . . Never any use! . . . Well! May be, may be. One must see. Would ask his wife.' This was her answer. He felt like a blow on his chest, but said only: 'Go, draw me some cider. I am thirsty!'

She went out moaning, an empty jug in her hand. Then he arose, took up the light, and moved slowly towards the cradle. They slept. He looked at them sideways, finished his mouthful there, went back, heavily, and sat down before his plate. When his wife returned he never looked up, but swallowed a couple of spoonfuls noisily, and remarked, in a dull manner—

'When they sleep they are like other people's children.'

She sat down suddenly on a stool near by, and shook with a silent tempest of sobs, unable to speak. He finished his meal, and remained idly thrown back in his chair, his eyes lost amongst the black rafters of the ceiling. Before him the tallow candle flared red and straight, sending up a slender thread of smoke. The light lay on the rough, sunburnt skin of his throat; the sunk cheeks were like patches of darkness, and his aspect was mournfully stolid, as if he had ruminated with difficulty endless ideas. Then he said, deliberately—

'We must see . . . consult people. Don't cry . . . They won't be all like that . . . surely! We must sleep now.'

After the third child, also a boy, was born, Jean-Pierre went about his work with tense hopefulness. His lips seemed more narrow, more tightly compressed than before; as if for fear of letting the earth he tilled hear the voice of hope that murmured within his breast. He watched the child, stepping up to the cot with a heavy clang of sabots on the stone floor, and glanced in, along his shoulder, with that indifference which is like a deformity of peasant humanity. Like the earth they master and serve, those men, slow of eye and speech, do not show the inner fire;

so that, at last, it becomes a question with them as with the earth, what there is in the core: heat, violence, a force mysterious and terrible – or nothing but a clod, a mass fertile and inert, cold and unfeeling, ready to bear a crop of plants that sustain life or give death.

The mother watched with other eyes; listened with otherwise expectant ears. Under the high hanging shelves supporting great sides of bacon overhead, her body was busy by the great fireplace, attentive to the pot swinging on iron gallows, scrubbing the long table where the field hands would sit down directly to their evening meal. Her mind remained by the cradle, night and day on the watch, to hope and suffer. That child, like the other two, never smiled, never stretched its hands to her, never spoke; never had a glance of recognition for her in its big black eyes, which could only stare fixedly at any glitter, but failed hopelessly to follow the brilliance of a sun-ray slipping slowly along the floor. When the men were at work she spent long days between her three idiot children and the childish grandfather, who sat grim, angular, and immovable, with his feet near the warm ashes of the fire. The feeble old fellow seemed to suspect that there was something wrong with his grandsons. Only once, moved either by affection or by the sense of proprieties, he attempted to nurse the youngest. He took the boy up from the floor, clicked his tongue at him, and essayed a shaky gallop of his bony knees. Then he looked closely with his misty eyes at the child's face and deposited him down gently on the floor again. And he sat, his lean shanks crossed, nodding at the steam escaping from the cooking-pot with a gaze senile and worried.

Then mute affliction dwelt in Bacadou's farmhouse, sharing the breath and the bread of its inhabitants; and the priest of the Ploumar parish had great cause for congratulation. He called upon the rich landowner, the Marquis de Chavanes, on purpose to deliver himself with joyful unction of solemn platitudes about the inscrutable ways of Providence. In the vast dimness of the curtained drawing-room, the little man, resembling a black bolster, leaned towards a couch, his hat on his knees, and gesticulated with a fat hand at the elongated, gracefully-flowing lines of the clear Parisian toilette from within which the half-amused, half-bored marquise listened with gracious languor. He was exulting and humble, proud and awed. The impossible had come to pass. Jean-Pierre Bacadou, the enraged republican farmer, had been to mass last Sunday – had proposed to entertain the visiting priests at the next festival of Ploumar! It was a triumph for the Church and for the good cause. 'I thought I would come at once to tell Monsieur le Marquis. I know how anxious he is for the welfare of our country,' declared the priest, wiping his face. He was asked to stay to dinner.

The Chavanes returning that evening, after seeing their guest to the main gate of the park, discussed the matter while they strolled in the moonlight, trailing their long shadows up the straight avenue of chestnuts. The marquis, a royalist of course, had been mayor of the commune which includes Ploumar, the scattered hamlets of the coast, and the stony islands that fringe the yellow flatness of the sands. He had felt his position insecure, for there was a strong republican element in that part of the country; but now the conversion of Jean-Pierre made him safe. He was very pleased 'You have no idea how influential those people are,' he explained to his wife. 'Now, I am sure, the next communal election will go all right. I shall be re-elected,' 'Your ambition is perfectly insatiable, Charles,' exclaimed the marquise, gaily. 'But, ma chère amie,' argued the husband, seriously, 'it's most important that the right man should be mayor this year, because of the elections to the Chamber. If you think it amuses me . . .'

Jean-Pierre had surrendered to his wife's mother. Madame Levaille was a woman of business, known and respected within a radius of at least fifteen miles. Thick-set and stout, she was seen about the country, on foot or in an acquaintance's cart, perpetually moving, in spite of her fifty-eight years, in steady pursuit of business. She had houses in all the hamlets, she worked quarries of granite, she freighted coasters with stone – even traded with the Channel Islands. She was broad-cheeked, wide-eyed, persuasive in speech: carrying her point with the placid and invincible obstinacy of an old woman who knows her own mind. She very seldom slept for two nights together in the same house; and the wayside inns were the best places to inquire in as to her whereabouts. She had either passed, or was expected to pass there at six; or somebody, coming in, had seen her in the morning, or expected to meet her that evening. After the inns that command the roads, the churches were the buildings she frequented most. Men of liberal opinions would induce small children to run into sacred edifices to see whether Madame Levaille was there, and to tell her that so-and-so was in the road waiting to speak to her – about potatoes, or flour, or stones, or houses; and she would curtail her devotions, come out blinking and crossing herself into the sunshine; ready to discuss business matters in a calm, sensible way across the table in the kitchen of the inn opposite. Latterly she had stayed for a few days several times with her son-in-law, arguing against sorrow and misfortune with composed face and gentle tones. Jean-Pierre felt the convictions imbibed in the regiment torn out of his breast – not by arguments, but by facts. Striding over his fields he thought it over. There were three of them. Three! All alike! Why? Such things did not happen to everybody – to nobody he ever heard of. One yet – it might pass. But three! All three. For ever useless, to be fed while he lived and . . . What would become of the land when he died? This must be

seen to. He would sacrifice his convictions. One day he told his wife—
'See what your God will do for us. Pay for some masses.'

Susan embraced her man. He stood unbending, then turned on his heels and went out. But afterwards, when a black *soutane* darkened his doorway, he did not object; even offered some cider himself to the priest. He listened to the talk meekly; went to mass between the two women; accomplished what the priest called 'his religious duties' at Easter. That morning he felt like a man who had sold his soul. In the afternoon he fought ferociously with an old friend and neighbour who had remarked that the priests had the best of it and were now going to eat the priest-eater. He came home dishevelled and bleeding, and happening to catch sight of his children (they were kept generally out of the way), cursed and swore incoherently, banging the table. Susan wept. Madame Levaille sat serenely unmoved. She assured her daughter that 'It will pass'; and taking up her thick umbrella, departed in haste to see after a schooner she was going to load with granite from her quarry.

A year or so afterwards the girl was born. A girl. Jean-Pierre heard of it in the fields, and was so upset by the news that he sat down on the boundary wall and remained there till the evening, instead of going home as he was urged to do. A girl! He felt half cheated. However, when he got home he was partly reconciled to his fate. One could marry her to a good fellow – not to a good for nothing, but to a fellow with some under-standing and a good pair of arms. Besides, the next may be a boy, he thought. Of course they would be all right. His new credulity knew of no doubt. The ill luck was broken. He spoke cheerily to his wife. She was also hopeful. Three priests came to that christening, and Madame Levaille was godmother. The child turned out an idiot too.

Then on market days Jean-Pierre was seen bargaining bitterly, quarrel-some and greedy; then getting drunk with taciturn earnestness; then driving home in the dusk at a rate fit for a wedding, but with a face gloomy enough for a funeral. Sometimes he would insist for his wife to come with him; and they would drive in the early morning, shaking side by side on the narrow seat above the helpless pig, that, with tied legs, grunted a melancholy sigh at every rut. The morning drives were silent; but in the evening, coming home, Jean-Pierre, tipsy, was viciously muttering, and growled at the confounded woman who could not rear children that were like anybody else's. Susan, holding on against the erratic swayings of the cart, pretended not to hear. Once, as they were driving through Ploumar, some obscure and drunken impulse caused him to pull up sharply opposite the church. The moon swam amongst light white clouds. The tombstones gleamed pale under the fretted shadows of the trees in the churchyard. Even the village dogs slept. Only the nightingales, awake, spun out the thrill of their song above the silence of graves. Jean-Pierre said thickly to his wife—

'What do you think is there?'

He pointed his whip at the tower – in which the big dial of the clock appeared high in the moonlight like a pallid face without eyes – and getting out carefully, fell down at once by the wheel. He picked himself up and climbed one by one the few steps to the iron gate of the church-yard. He put his face to the bars and called out indistinctly—

'Hey there! Come out!'

'Jean! Return! Return!' entreated his wife in low tones.

He took no notice, and seemed to wait there. The song of nightingales beat on all sides against the high walls of the church, and flowed back between stone crosses and flat grey slabs, engraved with words of hope and sorrow.

'Hey! Come out!' shouted Jean-Pierre loudly.

The nightingales ceased to sing.

'Nobody?' went on Jean-Pierre. 'Nobody there. A swindle of the crows. That's what this is. Nobody anywhere. I despise it. Allez! Houp!'

He shook the gate with all his strength, and the iron bars rattled with a frightful clanging, like a chain dragged over stone steps. A dog near-by barked hurriedly. Jean-Pierre staggered back, and after three successive dashes got into his cart. Susan sat very quiet and still. He said to her with drunken severity—

'See? Nobody. I've been made a fool! Malheur! Somebody will pay for it. The next one I see near the house I will lay my whip on . . . on the black spine . . . I will. I don't want him in there . . . he only helps the carrion crows to rob poor folk. I am a man . . . We will see if I can't have children like anybody else . . . now you mind . . . They won't be all . . . all . . . we see . . .'

She burst out through the fingers that hid her face—

'Don't say that, Jean; don't say that, my man!'

He struck her a swinging blow on the head with the back of his hand and knocked her into the bottom of the cart, where she crouched, thrown about lamentably by every jolt. He drove furiously, standing up, brandishing his whip, shaking the reins over the grey horse that galloped ponderously, making the heavy harness leap upon his broad quarters. The country rang clamorous in the night with the irritated barking of farm dogs, that followed the rattle of wheels all along the road. A couple of belated wayfarers had only just time to step into the ditch. At his own gate he caught the post and was shot out of the cart head first. The horse went on slowly to the door. At Susan's piercing cries the farm hands rushed out. She thought him dead, but he was only sleeping where he fell, and cursed his men, who hastened to him, for disturbing his slumbers.

THE IDIOTS

Autumn came. The clouded sky descended low upon the black contours of the hills; and the dead leaves danced in spiral whirls under naked trees, till the wind, sighing profoundly, laid them to rest in the hollows of bare valleys. And from morning till night one could see all over the land black denuded boughs, the boughs gnarled and twisted, as if contorted with pain, swaying sadly between the wet clouds and the soaked earth. The clear and gentle streams of summer days rushed discoloured and raging at the stones that barred the way to the sea, with the fury of madness bent upon suicide. From horizon to horizon the great road to the sands lay between the hills in a dull glitter of empty curves, resembling an unnavigable river of mud.

Jean-Pierre went from field to field, moving blurred and tall in the drizzle, or striding on the crests of rises, lonely and high upon the grey curtain of drifting clouds, as if he had been pacing along the very edge of the universe. He looked at the black earth, at the earth mute and promising, at the mysterious earth doing its work of life in death-like stillness under the veiled sorrow of the sky. And it seemed to him that to a man worse than childless there was no promise in the fertility of fields, that from him the earth escaped, defied him, frowned at him like the clouds, sombre and hurried above his head. Having to face alone his own fields, he felt the inferiority of man who passes away before the clod that remains. Must he give up the hope of having by his side a son who would look at the turned-up sods with a master's eye? A man that would think as he thought, that would feel as he felt; a man who would be part of himself, and yet remain to trample masterfully on that earth when he was gone! He thought of some distant relations, and felt savage enough to curse them aloud. They! Never! He turned homewards, going straight at the roof of his dwelling visible between the enlaced skeletons of trees. As he swung his legs over the stile a cawing flock of birds settled slowly on the field; dropped down behind his back, noiseless and fluttering, like flakes of soot.

That day Madame Levaille had gone early in the afternoon to the house she had near Kervanion. She had to pay some of the men who worked in her granite quarry there, and she went in good time because her little house contained a shop where the workmen could spend their wages without the trouble of going to town. The house stood alone amongst rocks. A lane of mud and stones ended at the door. The sea-winds coming ashore on Stonecutter's point, fresh from the fierce turmoil of the waves, howled violently at the unmoved heaps of black boulders holding up steadily short-armed, high crosses against the tremendous rush of the invisible. In the sweep of gales the sheltered dwelling stood in a calm resonant and disquieting, like the calm in the centre of a hurricane. On stormy nights, when the tide was out, the bay of Fougère, fifty feet below the house, resembled an immense black pit, from which ascended mutterings and sighs as if the sands down there had been alive and complaining. At high tide the returning water assaulted the ledges of rock in short rushes, ending in bursts of livid light and columns of spray, that flew inland, stinging to death the grass of pastures.

The darkness came from the hills, flowed over the coast, put out the red fires of sunset, and went on to seaward pursuing the retiring tide. The wind dropped with the sun, leaving a maddened sea and a devastated sky. The heavens above the house seemed to be draped in black rags, held up here and there by pins of fire. Madame Levaille, for this evening the servant of her own workmen, tried to induce them to depart. 'An old woman like me ought to be in bed at this late hour,' she good-humouredly repeated. The quarrymen drank, asked for more. They shouted over the table as if they had been talking across a field. At one end four of them played cards, banging the wood with their hard knuckles, and swearing at every lead. One sat with a lost gaze, humming a bar of some song, which he repeated endlessly. Two others, in a corner, were quarrelling confidentially and fiercely over some woman, looking close into one another's eyes as if they had wanted to tear them out, but speaking in whispers that promised violence and murder discreetly, in a venomous sibillation of subdued words. The atmosphere in there was thick enough to slice with a knife. Three candles burning about the long room glowed red and dull like sparks expiring in ashes.

The slight click of the iron latch was at that late hour as unexpected and startling as a thunder-clap. Madame Levaille put down a bottle she held above a liqueur glass; the players turned their heads; the whispered quarrel ceased; only the singer, after darting a glance at the door, went on humming with a stolid face. Susan appeared in the doorway, stepped in, flung the door to, and put her back against it, saying, half aloud—

'Mother!'

Madame Levaille, taking up the bottle again, said calmly: 'Here you are, my girl. What a state you are in!' The neck of the bottle rang on the rim of the glass, for the old woman was startled, and the idea that the farm had caught fire had entered her head. She could think of no other cause for her daughter's appearance.

Susan, soaked and muddy, stared the whole length of the room towards the men at the far end. Her mother asked—

'What has happened? God guard us from misfortune!'

Susan moved her lips. No sound came. Madame Levaille stepped up to her daughter, took her by the arm, looked into her face.

'In God's name,' she said shakily, 'what's the matter? You have been rolling in mud . . . Why did you come? . . . Where's Jean?'

THE IDIOTS

The men had all got up and approached slowly, staring with dull surprise. Madame Levaille jerked her daughter away from the door, swung her round upon a seat close to the wall. Then she turned fiercely to the men—

'Enough of this! Out you go – you others! I close.'

One of them observed, looking down at Susan collapsed on the seat: 'She is – one may say – half dead.'

Madame Levaille flung the door open.

'Get out! March!' she cried, shaking nervously.

They dropped out into the night, laughing stupidly. Outside, the two Lotharios broke out into loud shouts. The others tried to soothe them, all talking at once. The noise went away up the lane with the men, who staggered together in a tight knot, remonstrating with one another foolishly.

'Speak, Susan. What is it? Speak!' entreated Madame Levaille, as soon as the door was shut.

Susan pronounced some incomprehensible words, glaring at the table. The old woman clapped her hands above her head, let them drop, and stood looking at her daughter with disconsolate eyes. Her husband had been 'deranged in his head' for a few years before he died, and now she began to suspect her daughter was going mad. She asked, pressingly—

'Does Jean know where you are? Where is Jean?'

Susan pronounced with difficulty—

'He knows . . . he is dead.'

'What!' cried the old woman. She came up near, and peering at her daughter, repeated three times: 'What do you say? What do you say? What do you say?'

Susan sat dry-eyed and stony before Madame Levaille, who contemplated her, feeling a strange sense of inexplicable horror creep into the silence of the house. She had hardly realised the news, further than to understand that she had been brought in one short moment face to face with something unexpected and final. It did not even occur to her to ask for any explanation. She thought: accident – terrible accident – blood to the head – fell down a trap door in the loft . . . She remained there, distracted and mute, blinking her old eyes.

Suddenly, Susan said—

'I have killed him.'

For a moment the mother stood still, almost unbreathing, but with composed face. The next second she burst out into a shout—

'You miserable madwoman . . . they will cut your neck . . .'

She fancied the gendarmes entering the house, saying to her: 'We want your daughter; give her up:' the gendarmes with the severe, hard faces of men on duty. She knew the brigadier well – an old friend, familiar and respectful, saying heartily, 'To your good health, madame!'

before lifting to his lips the small glass of cognac – out of the special bottle she kept for friends. And now! . . . She was losing her head. She rushed here and there, as if looking for something urgently needed – gave that up, stood stock still in the middle of the room, and screamed at her daughter—

'Why? Say! Say! Why?'

The other seemed to leap out of her strange apathy.

'Do you think I am made of stone?' she shouted back, striding towards her mother.

'No! It's impossible . . .' said Madame Levaille, in a convinced tone.

'You go and see, mother,' retorted Susan, looking at her with blazing eyes. 'There's no mercy in heaven – no justice. No! . . . I did not know . . . Do you think I have no heart? Do you think I have never heard people jeering at me, pitying me, wondering at me? Do you know how some of them were calling me? The mother of idiots – that was my nickname! And my children never would know me, never speak to me. They would know nothing; neither men – nor God. Haven't I prayed! But the Mother of God herself would not hear me. A mother! . . . Who is accursed – I, or the man who is dead? Eh? Tell me. I took care of myself. Do you think I would defy the anger of God and have my house full of those things – that are worse than animals who know the hand that feeds them? Who blasphemed in the night at the very church door? Was it I? . . . I only wept and prayed for mercy . . . and I feel the curse at every moment of the day – I see it round me from morning to night . . . I've got to keep them alive – to take care of my misfortune and shame. And he would come. I begged him and Heaven for mercy . . . No! . . . Then we shall see . . . He came this evening. I thought to myself: 'Ah! again!' . . . I had my long scissors. I heard him shouting . . . I saw him near . . . I must – must I? . . . Then take! . . . And I struck him in the throat above the breastbone. . . . I never heard him even sigh. . . . I left him standing. . . . It was a minute ago. How did I come here?'

Madame Levaille shivered. A wave of cold ran down her back, down her fat arms under her tight sleeves, made her stamp gently where she stood. Quivers ran over the broad cheeks, across the thin lips, ran amongst the wrinkles at the corners of her steady old eyes. She stammered—

'You wicked woman – you disgrace me. But there! You always resembled your father. What do you think will become of you . . . in the other world? In this . . . Oh misery!'

She was very hot now. She felt burning inside. She wrung her perspiring hands – and suddenly, starting in great haste, began to look for her big shawl and umbrella, feverishly, never once glancing at her daughter, who stood in the middle of the room following her with a gaze distracted and cold.

'Nothing worse than in this,' said Susan.

Her mother, umbrella in hand and trailing the shawl over the floor, groaned profoundly.

'I must go to the priest,' she burst out passionately. 'I do not know whether you even speak the truth! You are a horrible woman. They will find you anywhere. You may stay here – or go. There is no room for you in this world.'

Ready now to depart, she yet wandered aimlessly about the room, putting the bottles on the shelf, trying to fit with trembling hands the covers on cardboard boxes. Whenever the real sense of what she had heard emerged for a second from the haze of her thoughts she would fancy that something had exploded in her brain without, unfortunately, bursting her head to pieces – which would have been a relief. She blew the candles out one by one without knowing it, and was horribly startled by the darkness. She fell on a bench and began to whimper. After a while she ceased, and sat listening to the breathing of her daughter, whom she could hardly see, still and upright, giving no other sign of life. She was becoming old rapidly at last, during those minutes. She spoke in tones unsteady, cut about by the rattle of teeth, like one shaken by a deadly cold fit of ague.

'I wish you had died little. I will never dare to show my old head in the sunshine again. There are worse misfortunes than idiot children. I wish you had been born to me simple – like your own . . .'

She saw the figure of her daughter pass before the faint and livid clearness of a window. Then it appeared in the doorway for a second, and the door swung to with a clang. Madame Levaille, as if awakened by the noise from a long nightmare, rushed out.

'Susan!' she shouted from the doorstep.

She heard a stone roll a long time down the declivity of the rocky beach above the sands. She stepped forward cautiously, one hand on the wall of the house, and peered down into the smooth darkness of the empty bay. Once again she cried—

'Susan! You will kill yourself there.'

The stone had taken its last leap in the dark, and she heard nothing now. A sudden thought seemed to strangle her, and she called no more. She turned her back upon the black silence of the pit and went up the lane towards Ploumar, stumbling along with sombre determination, as if she had started on a desperate journey that would last, perhaps, to the end of her life. A sullen and periodic clamour of waves rolling over reefs followed her far inland between the high hedges sheltering the gloomy solitude of the fields.

Susan had run out, swerving sharp to the left at the door, and on the

edge of the slope crouched down behind a boulder. A dislodged stone
went on downwards, rattling as it leaped. When Madame Levaille called
out, Susan could have, by stretching her hand, touched her mother's
skirt, had she had the courage to move a limb. She saw the old woman
go away, and she remained still, closing her eyes and pressing her side
to the hard and rugged surface of the rock. After a while a familiar face
with fixed eyes and an open mouth became visible in the intense obscurity amongst the boulders. She uttered a low cry and stood up. The
face vanished, leaving her to gasp and shiver alone in the wilderness of
stone heaps. But as soon as she had crouched down again to rest, with her
head against the rock, the face returned, came very near, appeared eager
to finish the speech that had been cut short by death, only a moment
ago. She scrambled quickly to her feet and said: 'Go away, or I will do
it again.' The thing wavered, swung to the right, to the left. She moved
this way and that, stepped back, fancied herself screaming at it, and was
appalled by the unbroken stillness of the night. She tottered on the
brink, felt the steep declivity under her feet, and rushed down blindly
to save herself from a headlong fall. The shingle seemed to wake up; the
pebbles began to roll before her, pursued her from above, raced down
with her on both sides, rolling past with an increasing clatter. In the
peace of the night the noise grew, deepening to a rumour, continuous
and violent, as if the whole semicircle of the stony beach had started to
tumble down into the bay. Susan's feet hardly touched the slope that
seemed to run down with her. At the bottom she stumbled, shot forward,
throwing her arms out, and fell heavily. She jumped up at once and
turned swiftly to look back, her clenched hands full of sand she had
clutched in her fall. The face was there, keeping its distance, visible
in its own sheen that made a pale stain in the night. She shouted, 'Go
away' – she shouted at it with pain, with fear, with all the rage of that
useless stab that could not keep him quiet, keep him out of her sight. What
did he want now? He was dead. Dead men have no children. Would
he never leave her alone? She shrieked at it – waved her outstretched
hands. She seemed to feel the breath of parted lips, and, with a long cry
of discouragement, fled across the level bottom of the bay.

She ran lightly, unaware of any effort of her body. High sharp rocks
that, when the bay is full, show above the glittering plain of blue water
like pointed towers of submerged churches, glided past her, rushing to
the land at tremendous pace. To the left, in the distance, she could see
something shining: a broad disc of light in which narrow shadows
pivoted round the centre like the spokes of a wheel. She heard a voice
calling, 'Hey! There!' and answered with a wild scream. So, he could
call yet! He was calling after her to stop. Never! . . . She tore through
the night, past the startled group of seaweed-gatherers who stood round

their lantern paralysed with fear at the unearthly screech coming from that fleeing shadow. The men leaned on their pitchforks staring fearfully. A woman fell on her knees, and, crossing herself, began to pray aloud. A little girl with her ragged skirt full of slimy seaweed began to sob despairingly, lugging her soaked burden close to the man who carried the light. Somebody said: 'The thing ran out towards the sea.' Another voice exclaimed: 'And the sea is coming back! Look at the spreading puddles. Do you hear – you woman – there! Get up!' Several voices cried together. 'Yes, let us be off! Let the accursed thing go to the sea!' They moved on, keeping close round the light. Suddenly a man swore loudly. He would go and see what was the matter. It had been a woman's voice. He would go. There were shrill protests from women – but his high form detached itself from the group and went off running. They sent a unanimous call of scared voices after him. A word, insulting and mocking, came back, thrown at them through darkness. A woman moaned. An old man said gravely: 'Such things ought to be left alone.' They went on slower, shuffling in the yielding sand and whispering to one another that Millot feared nothing, having no religion, but that it would end badly some day.

Susan met the incoming tide by the Raven islet and stopped, panting, with her feet in the water. She heard the murmur and felt the cold caress of the sea, and, calmer now, could see the sombre and confused mass of the Raven on one side and on the other the long white streak of Molène sands that are left high above the dry bottom of Fougère Bay at every ebb. She turned round and saw far away, along the starred background of the sky, the ragged outline of the coast. Above it, nearly facing her, appeared the tower of Ploumar church; a slender and tall pyramid shooting up dark and pointed into the clustered glitter of the stars. She felt strangely calm. She knew where she was, and began to remember how she came there – and why. She peered into the smooth obscurity near her. She was alone. There was nothing there; nothing near her, either living or dead.

The tide was creeping in quietly, putting out long impatient arms of strange rivulets that ran towards the land between ridges of sand. Under the night the pools grew bigger with mysterious rapidity, while the great sea, yet far off, thundered in a regular rhythm along the indistinct line of the horizon. Susan splashed her way back for a few yards without being able to get clear of the water that murmured tenderly all around and, suddenly, with a spiteful gurgle, nearly took her off her feet. Her heart thumped with fear. This place was too big and too empty to die in. To-morrow they would do with her what they liked. But before she died she must tell them – tell the gentlemen in black clothes that there are things no woman can bear. She must explain how it happened . . .

She splashed through a pool, getting wet to the waist, too pre-occupied to care ... She must explain. 'He came in the same way as ever and said, just so: "Do you think I am going to leave the land to those people from Morbihan that I do not know? Do you? We shall see! Come along, you creature of mischance!" And he put his arms out. Then, Messieurs, I said: "Before God – never!" And he said, striding at me with open palms: "There is no God to hold me! Do you understand, you useless carcass. I will do what I like." And he took me by the shoulders. Then I, Messieurs, called to God for help, and next minute, while he was shaking me, I felt my long scissors in my hand. His shirt was unbuttoned, and, by the candle-light, I saw the hollow of his throat. I cried: "Let go!" He was crushing my shoulders. He was strong, my man was! Then I thought: No! ... Must I? ... Then take! – and I struck in the hollow place. I never saw him fall. Never! Never! ... Never saw him fall ... The old father never turned his head. He is deaf and childish, gentlemen ... Nobody saw him fall. I ran out ... Nobody saw ...'

She had been scrambling amongst the boulders of the Raven and now found herself, all out of breath, standing amongst the heavy shadows of the rocky islet. The Raven is connected with the main land by a natural pier of immense and slippery stones. She intended to return home that way. Was he still standing there? At home. Home! Four idiots and a corpse. She must go back and explain. Anybody would understand ...

Below her the night or the sea seemed to pronounce distinctly —

'Aha! I see you at last!'

She started, slipped, fell; and without attempting to rise, listened, terrified. She heard heavy breathing, a clatter of wooden clogs. It stopped.

'Where the devil did you pass?' said an invisible man, hoarsely.

She held her breath. She recognised the voice. She had not seen him fall. Was he pursuing her there dead, or perhaps ... alive?

She lost her head. She cried from the crevice where she lay huddled, 'Never, never!'

'Ah! You are still there. You led me a fine dance. Wait, my beauty, I must see how you look after all this. You wait ...'

Millot was stumbling, laughing, swearing meaninglessly out of pure satisfaction, pleased with himself for having run down that fly-by-night. 'As if there were such things as ghosts! Bah! It took an old African soldier to show those clodhoppers ... But it was curious. Who the devil was she?'

Susan listened, crouching. He was coming for her, this dead man. There was no escape. What a noise he made amongst the stones ... She saw his head rise up, then the shoulders. He was tall – her own man! His long arms waved about, and it was his own voice sounding a little strange . . . because of the scissors. She scrambled out quickly, rushed to the edge of the causeway, and turned round. The man stood still on a high stone, detaching himself in dead black on the glitter of the sky.

'Where are you going to?' he called roughly.

She answered, 'Home!' and watched him intensely. He made a striding, clumsy leap on to another boulder, and stopped again, balancing himself, then said—

'Ha! ha! Well, I am going with you. It's the least I can do. Ha! ha! ha!'

She stared at him till her eyes seemed to become glowing coals that burned deep into her brain, and yet she was in mortal fear of making out the well-known features. Below her the sea lapped softly against the rock with a splash, continuous and gentle.

The man said, advancing another step—

'I am coming for you. What do you think?'

She trembled. Coming for her! There was no escape, no peace, no hope. She looked round despairingly. Suddenly the whole shadowy coast, the blurred islets, the heaven itself, swayed about twice, then came to a rest. She closed her eyes and shouted—

'Can't you wait till I am dead!'

She was shaken by a furious hate for that shade that pursued her in this world, unappeased even by death in its longing for an heir that would be like other people's children.

'Hey! What?' said Millot, keeping his distance prudently. He was saying to himself: 'Look out! Some lunatic. An accident happens soon.'

She went on, wildly—

'I want to live. To live alone – for a week – for a day. I must explain to them . . . I would tear you to pieces, I would kill you twenty times over rather than let you touch me while I live. How many times must I kill you – you blasphemer! Satan sends you here. I am damned too!'

'Come,' said Millot, alarmed and conciliating. 'I am perfectly alive! .. Oh, my God!'

She had screamed, 'Alive!' and at once vanished before his eyes, as if the islet itself had swerved aside from under her feet. Millot rushed forward, and fell flat with his chin over the edge. Far below he saw the water whitened by her struggles, and heard one shrill cry for help that seemed to dart upwards along the perpendicular face of the rock, and soar past, straight into the high and impassive heaven.

Madame Levaille sat, dry-eyed, on the short grass of the hill side, with her thick legs stretched out, and her old feet turned up in their black cloth shoes. Her clogs stood near by, and further off the umbrella lay on the withered sward like a weapon dropped from the grasp of a vanquished warrior. The Marquis of Chavanes, on horseback, one gloved hand on thigh, looked down at her as she got up laboriously, with groans. On the narrow track of the seaweed-carts four men were carrying inland Susan's body on a hand barrow, while several others straggled listlessly behind. Madame Levaille looked after the procession. 'Yes, Monsieur le Marquis,' she said dispassionately, in her usual calm tone of a reasonable old woman. 'There are unfortunate people on this earth. I had only one child. Only one! And they won't bury her in consecrated ground!'

Her eyes filled suddenly, and a short shower of tears rolled down the broad cheeks. She pulled the shawl close about her. The Marquis leaned slightly over in his saddle, and said—

'It is very sad. You have all my sympathy. I shall speak to the Curé. She was unquestionably insane, and the fall was accidental. Millot says so distinctly. Good-day, Madame.'

And he trotted off, thinking to himself: I must get this old woman appointed guardian of those idiots, and administrator of the farm. It would be much better than having here one of those other Bacadous, probably a red republican, corrupting my commune.

Thomas Burke

The Bird

It is a tale that they tell softly in Pennyfields, when the curtains are drawn and the shapes of the night are shut out. . . .

Those who held that Captain Chudder, s.s. *Peacock*, owners, Peter Dubbin & Co., had a devil in him, were justified. But they were nearer the truth who held that his devil was not within him, but at his side, perching at his elbow, dropping sardonic utterance in his ear; moving with him day and night and prompting him – so it was held – to frightful excesses. His devil wore the shape of a white parrot, a bird of lusty wings and the cruellest of beaks. There were those who whispered that the old man had not always been the man that his crew knew him to be: that he had been a normal, kindly fellow until he acquired his strange companion from a native dealer in the malevolent Solomons. Certainly his maniac moods dated from its purchase; and there was truth in the dark hints of his men that there was something wrong with that damned bird . . . a kind of . . . something you sort of felt when it looked at you or answered you back. For one thing, it had a diabolical knack of mimicry, and many a chap would cry: 'Yes, George!' or 'Right, sir!' in answer to a commanding voice which chuckled with glee as he came smartly to order. They invariably referred to it as 'that bloody bird', though actually it had done nothing to merit such opprobrium. When they thought it over calmly, they could think of no harm that it had done to them: nothing to arouse such loathing as every man on the boat felt towards it. It was not spiteful; it was not bad-tempered. Mostly, it was in cheery mood and would chuckle deep in the throat, like the Captain, and echo or answer, quite pleasantly, such remarks, usually rude, as were addressed to it.

And yet . . . Somehow. . . .

There it was. It was always there – everywhere; and in its speech they seemed to find a sinister tone which left them guessing at the meaning of its words. On one occasion, the cook, in the seclusion of the fo'c'sle, had remarked that he would like to wring its neck if he could get hold of it; but old grizzled Snorter had replied that that bird couldn't be killed. There was something about that bird that . . . well, he betted no one wouldn't touch that bird without trouble. And a moment of panic stabbed the crowd as a voice leapt from the sombre shadows of the corner.

'That's the style, me old brown son. Don't try to come it with me – what?' and ceased in a spasmodic flutter of wicked white wings.

That night, as the cook was ascending the companion, he was caught by a huge sea, which swept across the boat from nowhere and dashed him, head-on, below. For a week he was sick with a broken head, and throughout that week the bird would thrust its beak to the berth where he lay, and chortle to him:

'Yep, me old brown son. Wring his bleeding neck – what? Waltz me around again, Willie, round and round and round!'

That is the seamen's story and, as the air of Limehouse is thick with seamen's stories, it is not always good to believe them. But it is a widely known fact that on the last voyage the Captain did have a devil with him, the foulest of all devils that possess mortal men, not the devil of slaughter, but the devil of cruelty. They were from Swatow to London, and it was noted that he was drinking heavily ashore, and he continued the game throughout the voyage. He came aboard from Swatow, drunk, bringing with him a Chinese boy, also drunk. The greaser, being a big man, kicked him below, otherwise, the boat in his charge would have gone there, and so he sat or sprawled in his cabin, with a rum-bottle before him and, on the corner of his chair, the white parrot, which conversed with him and sometimes fluttered on deck to shout orders in the frightful voice of his master and chuckle to see them momentarily obeyed.

'Yes,' repeated old man Snorter, sententiously, 'I'd run a hundred miles 'fore I'd try to monkey with the old man or his bloody bird. There's something about that bird . . . I said so before. I 'eard a story once about a bird. Out in T'ai-ping I 'eard it. It'll make yeh sick if I tell it. . . .'

Now while the Captain remained drunk in his cabin, he kept with him for company the miserable, half-starved Chinky boy whom he had brought aboard. And it would make others sick if the full dark tale were told here of what the master of the *Peacock* did to that boy. You may read of monstrosities in police reports of cruelty cases, you may read old records of the Middle Ages, but the bestialities of Captain Chudder could not be told in words.

His orgy of drink and delicious torture lasted till they were berthed in the Thames, and the details remain sharp and clear in the memories of those who witnessed it. At all the ceremonial horrors which were wrought in that wretched cabin, the parrot was present. It jabbered to the old man, the old man jabbered back, and gave it an occasional sip of rum from his glass, and the parrot would mimic the Chink's entreaties, and wag a grave claw at him as he writhed under the ritual of punishment, and when that day's ceremony was finished it would flutter from bow to stern of the boat, its cadaverous figure stinging the shadows with shapes of fear for all aboard, perching here, perching there, simpering and whining in tune with the Chink's placid moaning.

Placid; yes, outwardly. But the old man's wickedness had lighted a flame beneath that yellow skin which nothing could quench, nothing but the floods of vengeance. Had the old man been a little more cute and a little less drunk, he might have remembered that a Chinaman does not forget. He would have read danger in the face that was so submissive under his devilries. Perhaps he did see it, but, because of the rum that was in him, felt himself secure from the hate of any outcast Chink; knew that his victim would never once get the chance to repay him, Captain Chudder, master of the *Peacock*, and one of the very smartest. The Chink was alone and weaponless, and dare not come aft without orders. He was master of the boat, he had a crew to help him, and knives and guns, and he had his faithful white bird to warn him. Too, as soon as they docked at Limehouse, he would sling him off or arrange quick transfer to an outward boat, since he had no further use for him.

But it happened that he made no attempt to transfer. He had forgotten that idea. He just sat below, finished his last two bottles, paid off his men, and then, after a sleep, went ashore to report. Having done that, he forgot all trivial affairs, such as business, and set himself seriously to search for amusement. He climbed St George's, planning a real good booze-up, and the prospect that spread itself before his mind was so compelling that he did not notice a lurking yellow phantom that hung on his shadow. He visited the Baltic on the chance of finding an old pal or so, and, meeting none, he called at a shipping office in Fenchurch Street, where he picked up an acquaintance, and the two returned eastward to Poplar, and the Phantom feet *sup-supped* after them. Through the maze and glamour of the London streets and traffic the shadow slid; it dodged and danced about the Captain's little cottage in Gill Street, and when he, and others, came out and strolled to a bar, and, later, to a music-hall, it flitted, moth-like, around them.

Surely since there is no step in the world that has just the obvious stealth of the Chinaman's, he must have heard those whispering feet?

Surely his path was darkened by that shadow? But no. After the music-hall he drifted to a water-side wine-shop and then, with a bunch of the others, went wandering.

It was late. Eleven notes straggled across the waters from many grey towers. Sirens were screeching their derisive song, and names of various Scotch whiskies spelt themselves in letters of yellow flame along the night. Far in the darkness a voice was giving the chanty:

'What shall we do with a drunken sailor?'

The Captain braced himself up and promised himself a real glittering night of good-fellowship, and from gin-warmed bar to gin-warmed bar he roved, meeting the lurid girls of the places and taking one of them upstairs. At the last bar his friends, too, went upstairs with their ladies, and, it being then one o'clock in the morning, he brought a pleasant evening to a close at a certain house in Poplar High Street, where he took an hour's amusement by flinging half-crowns over the fan-tan table.

But always the yellow moth was near, and when, at half past two, he came, with uncertain steps, into the sad street, now darkened and loud only with the drunken, who found unfamiliar turnings in familiar streets, and the old landmarks many yards away from their rightful places, the moth buzzed closer and closer.

The Captain talked as he went. He talked of the night he had had, and the girls his hands had touched. His hard face was cracked to a meaningless smile, and he spat words at obstructive lamp posts and kerbstones, and swears dropped like toads from his lips. But at last he found his haven in Gill Street, and his hefty brother, with whom he lived when ashore, shoved him upstairs to his bedroom. He fell across the bed, and the sleep of the swinish held him fast.

The grey towers were rolling three o'clock, and the thick darkness of the water-side covered the night like a blanket. The lamps were pale and few. The waters sucked miserably at the staples of the wharves. One heard the measured beat of a constable's boot, sometimes the rattle of chains and blocks, mournful hooters, shudders of noise as engines butted lines of trucks at the shunting station.

Captain Chudder slept, breathing stertorously, mouth open, limbs heavy and nerveless. His room was deeply dark, and so little light shone on the back reaches of the Gill Street cottages that the soft raising of the window made no visible aperture. Into this blank space something rose from below, and soon it took the shape of a flat, yellow face which hung motionless, peering into the room. Then a yellow hand came through, the aperture was widened, and swiftly and silently a lithe, yellow body hauled itself up and slipped over the sill.

It glided, with outstretched hand, from the window and, the moment it touched the bed, its feeling fingers went here and there, and it stood still, gazing upon the sleep of drunkenness. Calmly and methodically a yellow hand moved to its waist and withdrew a kris. The same hand raised the kris and held it poised. It was long, keen, and beautifully curved, but not a ray of light was in the room to fall upon it, and the yellow hand had to feel its bright blade to find whether the curve ran from or towards it.

Then, with terrific force and speed, it came down, one – two – three. The last breath rushed from the open lips. Captain Chudder was out.

The strong yellow hand withdrew the kris for the last time, wiped it on the coverlet of the bed, and replaced it in its home. The figure turned, like a wraith, for the window, turned for the window and found, in a moment of panic, that it knew not which way to turn. It hesitated for a moment. It thought it heard a sound at the bed. It touched the coverlet and the boots of the Captain; all was still. Stretching a hand to the wall, Sung Dee began to creep and to feel his way along. Dark as the room was, he had found his way in, without matches or illuminant. Why could he not find his way out? Why was he afraid of something?

Blank wall was all he found at first. Then his hand touched what seemed to be a picture frame. It swung and clicked and the noise seemed to echo through the still house. He moved farther, and a sharp rattle told him that he had struck the loose handle of the door. But that was of little help. He could not use the door, he knew not what perils lay behind it. It was the window he wanted – the window.

Again he heard that sound from the bed. He stepped boldly and judged that he was standing in the middle of the room. Momentarily a sharp shock surged over him. He prayed for matches, and something in his throat was almost crying, 'The window! The window!' He seemed like an island in a sea of darkness, one man surrounded by legions of immortal intangible enemies. His cold Chinese heart went hot with fear.

The middle of the room he judged, and took another step forward, a step which landed his chin sharply against the jutting edge of the mantel-shelf over the fireplace. He jumped like a cat and his limbs shook, for now he had lost the door and the bed, as well as the window, and had made terrible noises which might bring disaster. All sense of direction was gone. He knew not whether to go forward or backwards, to right or left. He heard the tinkle of the shunting trains, and he heard a rich voice crying something in his own tongue. But he was lapped around by darkness and terror, and a cruel fancy came to him that he was imprisoned here for ever and for ever, and that he would never escape from this enveloping, suffocating room. He began to think that—

And then a hot iron of agony rushed down his back as, sharp and clear, at his elbow came the Captain's voice:

'Get forrard, you damn lousy Chink – get forrard. Lively there! Get out of my room!'

He sprang madly aside from the voice that had been the terror of his life for so many weeks, and collided with the door; realised that he had made further fearful noises; dashed away from it and crashed into the bed; fell across it and across the warm, wet body that lay there. Every nerve in every limb of him was seared with horror at the contact, and he leapt off, kicking, biting, writhing. He leapt off, and fell against a table, which tottered, and at last fell with a stupendous crash into the fender.

'Lively, you damn Chink!' said the Captain. 'Lively, I tell yeh. Dance, d'yeh hear? I'll have yeh for this. I'll learn you something. I'll give you something with a sharp knife and bit of hot iron, my cocky. I'll make yer yellow skin crackle, yeh damn lousy chopstick. I'll have yeh in a minute. And when I get yeh, orf with yeh clothes. I'll cut yeh to pieces I will.'

Sung Dee shrieked. He ran round and round, beating the wall with his hands, laughing, crying, jumping, while all manner of shapes arose in his path, lit by the grey light of fear. He realised that it was all up now. He cared not how much noise he made. He hadn't killed the old man; only wounded him. And now all he desired was to find the door and any human creatures who might save him from the Captain. He met the bed again, suddenly, and the tormentor who lay there. He met the upturned table and fell upon it, and he met the fireplace and the blank wall; but never, never the window or the door. They had vanished. There was no way out. He was caught in that dark room, and the Captain would do as he liked with him. . . . He heard footsteps in the passage and sounds of menace and alarm below. But to him they were friendly sounds, and he screamed loudly towards them.

He cried to the Captain, in his pidgin, for mercy.

'Oh, Captain – no burn me today, Captain. Sung Dee be heap good sailor, heap good servant, all same slave. Sung Dee heap plenty solly hurt Captain. Sung Dee be good boy. No do feller bad lings no feller more. O Captain. Let Sung Dee go lis time. Let Sung Dee go. O Captain!'

But 'Oh, my Gawd!' answered the Captain. 'Bless your yellow heart. Wait till I get you trussed up. Wait till I get you below. I'll learn yeh.'

And now those below came upstairs, and they listened in the passage, and for the space of a minute they were hesitant. For they heard all manner of terrible noises, and by the noises there might have been half a dozen fellows in the Captain's room. But very soon the screaming and

THE BIRD

the pattering feet were still, and they heard nothing but low moans; and at last the bravest of them, the Captain's brother, swung the door open and flashed a large lantern.

And those who were with him fell back in dumb horror, while the brother cried harshly: 'Oh! . . . my . . . God!' For the lantern shone on a Chinaman seated on the edge of the bed. Across his knees lay the dead body of the Captain, and the Chink was fondling his damp, dead face, talking baby talk to him, dancing him on his knee, and now and then making idiot moans. But what sent the crowd back in horror was that a great death-white Thing was flapping about the yellow face of the Chink, cackling: 'I'll learn yeh! I'll learn yeh!' and dragging strips of flesh away with every movement of the beak.

Arthur Conan Doyle

Lot No. 249

Of the dealings of Edward Bellingham with William Monkhouse Lee, and of the cause of the great terror of Abercrombie Smith, it may be that no absolute and final judgment will ever be delivered. It is true that we have the full and clear narrative of Smith himself, and such corroboration as he could look for from Thomas Styles the servant, from the Reverend Plumptree Peterson, Fellow of Old's, and from such other people as chanced to gain some passing glance at this or that incident in a singular chain of events. Yet, in the main, the story must rest upon Smith alone, and the most will think that it is more likely that one brain, however outwardly sane, has some subtle warp in its texture, some strange flaw in its workings, than that the path of Nature has been overstepped in open day in so famed a centre of learning and light as the University of Oxford. Yet when we think how narrow and how devious this path of Nature is, how dimly we can trace it, for all our lamps of science, and how from the darkness which girds it round great and terrible possibilities loom ever shadowly upwards, it is a bold and confident man who will put a limit to the strange by-paths into which the human spirit may wander.

In a certain wing of what we will call Old College in Oxford there is a corner turret of an exceeding great age. The heavy arch which spans the open door has bent downwards in the centre under the weight of its years, and the grey, lichen-blotched blocks of stone are bound and knitted together with withes and strands of ivy, as though the old mother had set herself to brace them up against wind and weather. From the door a stone stair curves upward spirally, passing two landings, and terminating in a third one, its steps all shapeless and hollowed by the tread of so many generations of the seekers after knowledge. Life has flowed

LOT NO. 249

like water down this winding stair, and, waterlike, has left these smooth-worn grooves behind it. From the long-gowned, pedantic scholars of Plantagenet days down to the young bloods of a later age, how full and strong had been that tide of young, English life. And what was left now of all those hopes, those strivings, those fiery energies, save here and there in some old-world churchyard a few scratches upon a stone, and perchance a handful of dust in a mouldering coffin? Yet here were the silent stair and the grey, old wall, with bend and saltire and many another heraldic device still to be read upon its surface, like grotesque shadows thrown back from the days that had passed.

In the month of May, in the year 1884, three young men occupied the sets of rooms which opened on to the separate landings of the old stair. Each set consisted simply of a sitting-room and of a bedroom, while the two corresponding rooms upon the ground-floor were used, the one as a coal-cellar, and the other as the living-room of the servant, or scout, Thomas Styles, whose duty it was to wait upon the three men above him. To right and to left was a line of lecture-rooms and of offices, so that the dwellers in the old turret enjoyed a certain seclusion, which made the chambers popular among the more studious undergraduates. Such were the three who occupied them now – Abercombie Smith above, Edward Bellingham beneath him, and William Monkhouse Lee upon the lowest storey.

It was ten o'clock on a bright, spring night, and Abercombie Smith lay back in his arm-chair, his feet upon the fender, and his briar-root pipe between his lips. In a similar chair, and equally at his ease, there lounged on the other side of the fireplace his old school friend Jephro Hastie. Both men were in flannels, for they had spent their evening upon the river, but apart from their dress no one could look at their hard-cut, alert faces without seeing that they were open-air men – men whose minds and tastes turned naturally to all that was manly and robust. Hastie, indeed, was stroke of his college boat, and Smith was an even better oar, but a coming examination had already cast its shadow over him and held him to his work, save for the few hours a week which health demanded. A litter of medical books upon the table, with scattered bones, models, and anatomical plates, pointed to the extent as well as the nature of his studies, while a couple of single-sticks and a set of boxing-gloves above the mantelpiece hinted at the means by which, with Hastie's help, he might take his exercise in its most compressed and least-distant form. They knew each other very well – so well that they could sit now in that soothing silence which is the very highest development of companionship.

'Have some whisky,' said Abercombie Smith at last between two cloudbursts. 'Scotch in the jug and Irish in the bottle.'

'No, thanks. I'm in for the sculls. I don't liquor when I'm training.

How about you?'

'I'm reading hard. I think it best to leave it alone.'

Hastie nodded, and they relapsed into a contented silence.

'By the way, Smith,' asked Hastie, presently, 'have you made the acquaintance of either of the fellows on your stair yet?'

'Just a nod when we pass. Nothing more.'

'Hum! I should be inclined to let it stand at that. I know something of them both. Not much, but as much as I want. I don't think I should take them to my bosom if I were you. Not that there's much amiss with Monkhouse Lee.'

'Meaning the thin one?'

'Precisely. He is a gentlemanly little fellow. I don't think there is any vice in him. But then you can't know him without knowing Bellingham.'

'Meaning the fat one?'

'Yes, the fat one. And he's a man whom I, for one, would rather not know.'

Abercombie Smith raised his eyebrows and glanced across at his companion.

'What's up, then?' he asked. 'Drink? Cards? Cad? You used not to be censorious.'

'Ah! you evidently don't know the man, or you wouldn't ask. There's something damnable about him – something reptilian. My gorge always rises at him. I should put him down as a man with secret vices – an evil liver. He's no fool, though. They say that he is one of the best men in his line that they have ever had in the college.'

'Medicine or classics?'

'Eastern languages. He's demon at them. Chillingworth met him somewhere above the second cataract last long, and he told me that he just prattled to the Arabs as if he had been born and nursed and weaned among them. He talked Coptic to the Copts, and Hebrew to the Jews, and Arabic to the Bedouins, and they were all ready to kiss the hem of his frock-coat. There are some old hermit Johnnies up in those parts who sit on rocks and scowl and spit at the casual stranger. Well, when they saw this chap Bellingham, before he had said five words they just lay down on their bellies and wriggled. Chillingworth said that he never saw anything like it. Bellingham seemed to take it as his right, too, and strutted about among them and talked down to them like a Dutch uncle. Pretty good for an undergrad. of Old's, wasn't it?'

'Why do you say you can't know Lee without knowing Bellingham?'

'Because Bellingham is engaged to his sister Eveline. Such a bright little girl, Smith! I know the whole family well. It's disgusting to see that brute with her. A toad and a dove, that's what they always remind me of.'

LOT NO. 249

Abercombie Smith grinned and knocked his ashes out against the side of the grate.

'You show every card in your hand, old chap,' said he. 'What a prejudiced, green-eyed, evil-thinking old man it is! You have really nothing against the fellow except that.'

'Well, I've known her ever since she was as long as that cherry-wood pipe, and I don't like to see her taking risks. And it is a risk. He looks beastly. And he has a beastly temper, a venomous temper. You remember his row with Long Norton?'

'No; you always forget that I am a freshman.'

'Ah, it was last winter. Of course. Well, you know the towpath along by the river. There were several fellows going along it, Bellingham in front, when they came on an old market-woman coming the other way. It had been raining – you know what those fields are like when it has rained – and the path ran between the river and a great puddle that was nearly as broad. Well, what does this swine do but keep the path, and push the old girl into the mud, where she and her marketings came to terrible grief. It was a blackguard thing to do, and Long Norton, who is as gentle a fellow as ever stepped, told him what he thought of it. One word led to another, and it ended in Norton laying his stick across the fellow's shoulders. There was the deuce of a fuss about it, and it's a treat to see the way in which Bellingham looks at Norton when they meet now. By Jove, Smith, it's nearly eleven o'clock!'

'No hurry. Light your pipe again.'

'Not I. I'm supposed to be in training. Here I've been sitting gossiping when I ought to have been safely tucked up. I'll borrow your skull, if you can spare it. Williams has had mine for a month. I'll take the little bones of your ear, too, if you are sure you won't need them. Thanks very much. Never mind a bag, I can carry them very well under my arm. Good night, my son, and take my tip as to your neighbour.'

When Hastie, bearing his anatomical plunder, had clattered off down the winding stair, Abercombie Smith hurled his pipe into the wastepaper basket, and drawing his chair nearer to the lamp, plunged into a formidable, green-covered volume, adorned with great, coloured maps of that strange, internal kingdom of which we are the hapless and helpless monarchs. Though a freshman at Oxford, the student was not so in medicine, for he had worked for four years at Glasgow and at Berlin, and this coming examination would place him finally as a member of his profession. With his firm mouth, broad forehead, and clear-cut, somewhat hard-featured face, he was a man who, if he had no brilliant talent, was yet so dogged, so patient, and so strong that he might in the end overtop a more showy genius. A man who can hold his own among Scotchmen and North Germans is not a man to be easily set back. Smith had left a name at Glasgow and at Berlin, and he was bent now upon doing as much at Oxford, if hard work and devotion could accomplish it.

He had sat reading for about an hour, and the hands of the noisy carriage clock upon the side-table were rapidly closing together upon the twelve, when a sudden sound fell upon the student's ear – a sharp, rather shrill sound, like the hissing intake of a man's breath who gasps under some strong emotion. Smith laid down his book and slanted his ear to listen. There was no one on either side or above him, so that the interruption came certainly from the neighbour beneath – the same neighbour of whom Hastie had given so unsavoury an account. Smith knew him only as a flabby, pale-faced man of silent and studious habits, a man whose lamp threw a golden bar from the old turret even after he had extinguished his own. This community in lateness had formed a certain silent bond between them. It was soothing to Smith when the hours stole on towards dawning to feel that there was another so close who set as small a value upon his sleep as he did. Even now, as his thoughts turned towards him, Smith's feelings were kindly. Hastie was a good fellow, but he was rough, strong-fibred, with no imagination or sympathy. He could not tolerate departures from what he looked upon as the model type of manliness. If a man could not be measured by a public-school standard, then he was beyond the pale with Hastie. Like so many who are themselves robust, he was apt to confuse the constitution with the character, to ascribe to want of principle what was really a want of circulation. Smith, with his stronger mind, knew his friend's habit, and made allowance for it now as his thoughts turned towards the man beneath him.

There was no return of the singular sound, and Smith was about to turn to his work once more, when suddenly there broke out in the silence of the night a hoarse cry, a positive scream – the call of a man who is moved and shaken beyond all control. Smith sprang out of his chair and dropped his book. He was a man of fairly firm fibre, but there was something in this sudden, uncontrollable shriek of horror which chilled his blood and pringled in his skin. Coming in such a place and at such an hour, it brought a thousand fantastic possibilities into his head. Should he rush down, or was it better to wait? He had all the national hatred of making a scene, and he knew so little of his neighbour that he would not lightly intrude upon his affairs. For a moment he stood in doubt and even as he balanced the matter there was a quick rattle of footsteps upon the stairs, and young Monkhouse Lee, half-dressed and as white as ashes, burst into his room.

'Come down!' he gasped. 'Bellingham's ill.'

Abercrombie Smith followed him closely downstairs into the sitting-room which was beneath his own, and intent as he was upon the matter in hand, he could not but take an amazed glance around him as he crossed the threshold. It was such a chamber as he had never seen before – a museum rather than a study. Walls and ceiling were thickly covered with a thousand strange relics from Egypt and the East. Tall, angular figures bearing burdens or weapons stalked in an uncouth frieze round the apartments. Above were bull-headed, stork-headed, cat-headed, owl-headed statues, with viper-crowned, almond-eyed monarchs, and strange, beetle-like deities cut out of the blue Egyptian lapis lazuli. Horus and Isis and Osiris peeped down from every niche and shelf, while across the ceiling a true son of Old Nile, a great, hanging-jawed crocodile, was slung in a double noose.

In the centre of this singular chamber was a large, square table, littered with papers, bottles, and the dried leaves of some graceful, palm-like plant. These varied objects had all been heaped together in order to make room for a mummy case, which had been conveyed from the wall, as was evident from the gap there, and laid across the front of the table. The mummy itself, a horrid, black, withered thing, like a charred head on a gnarled bush, was lying half out of the case, with its claw-like hand and bony forearm resting upon the table. Propped up against the sarcophagus was an old, yellow scroll of papyrus, and in front of it, in a wooden arm-chair, sat the owner of the room, his head thrown back, his widely opened eyes directed in a horrified stare to the crocodile above him, and his blue, thick lips puffing loudly with every expiration.

'My God! he's dying!' cried Monkhouse Lee, distractedly.

He was a slim, handsome young fellow, olive-skinned and dark-eyed, of a Spanish rather than of an English type, with a Celtic intensity of manner which contrasted with the Saxon phlegm of Abercrombie Smith.

'Only a faint, I think,' said the medical student. 'Just give me a hand with him. You take his feet. Now on to the sofa. Can you kick all those little wooden devils off? What a litter it is! Now he will be all right if we undo his collar and give him some water. What has he been up to at all?'

'I don't know. I heard him cry out. I ran up. I know him pretty well, you know. It is very good of you to come down.'

'His heart is going like a pair of castanets,' said Smith, laying his hand on the breast of the unconscious man. 'He seems to me to be frightened all to pieces. Chuck the water over him! What a face he has got on him!'

It was indeed a strange and most repellent face, for colour and outline were equally unnatural. It was white, not with the ordinary pallor of fear, but with an absolutely bloodless white, like the under side of a sole. He was very fat, but gave the impression of having at some time been considerably fatter, for his skin hung loosely in creases and folds, and was shot with a meshwork of wrinkles. Short, stubbly brown hair bristled

THE BEST HORROR STORIES

up from his scalp, with a pair of thick, wrinkled ears protruding at the sides. His light-grey eyes were still open, the pupils dilated and the balls projecting in a fixed and horrid stare. It seemed to Smith as he looked down upon him that he had never seen Nature's danger signals flying so plainly upon a man's countenance, and his thoughts turned more seriously to the warning which Hastie had given him an hour before.

'What the deuce can have frightened him so?' he asked.

'It's the mummy.'

'The mummy? How, then?'

'I don't know. It's beastly and morbid. I wish he would drop it. It's the second fright he has given me. It was the same last winter. I found him just like this, with that horrid thing in front of him.'

'What does he want with the mummy, then?'

'Oh, he's a crank, you know. It's his hobby. He knows more about these things than any man in England. But I wish he wouldn't! Ah, he's beginning to come to.'

A faint tinge of colour had begun to steal back into Bellingham's ghastly cheeks, and his eyelids shivered like a sail after a calm. He clasped and unclasped his hands, drew a long, thin breath between his teeth, and suddenly jerking up his head, threw a glance of recognition around him. As his eyes fell upon the mummy, he sprang off the sofa, seized the roll of papyrus, thrust it into a drawer, turned the key, and then staggered back on to the sofa.

'What's up?' he asked. 'What do you chaps want?'

'You've been shrieking out and making no end of a fuss,' said Monkhouse Lee. 'If our neighbour here from above hadn't come down, I'm sure I don't know what I should have done with you.'

'Ah, it's Abercrombie Smith,' said Bellingham, glancing up at him. 'How very good of you to come in! What a fool I am! Oh, my God, what a fool I am!'

He sank his head on to his hands, and burst into peal after peal of hysterical laughter.

'Look here! Drop it!' cried Smith, shaking him roughly by the shoulder.

'Your nerves are all in a jangle. You must drop these little midnight games with mummies, or you'll be going off your chump. You're all on wires now.'

'I wonder,' said Bellingham, 'whether you would be as cool as I am if you had seen——'

'What then?'

'Oh, nothing. I meant that I wonder if you could sit up at night with a mummy without trying your nerves. I have no doubt that you are quite right. I dare say that I have been taking it out of myself too much lately.

LOT NO. 249

But I am all right now. Please don't go, though. Just wait for a few minutes until I am quite myself.'

'The room is very close,' remarked Lee, throwing open the window and letting in the cool night air.

'It's balsamic resin,' said Bellingham. He lifted up one of the dried palmate leaves from the table and frizzled it over the chimney of the lamp. It broke away into heavy smoke wreaths, and a pungent, biting odour filled the chamber. 'It's the sacred plant – the plant of the priests,' he remarked. 'Do you know anything of Eastern languages, Smith?'

'Nothing at all. Not a word.'

The answer seemed to lift a weight from the Egyptologist's mind.

'By the way,' he continued, 'how long was it from the time that you ran down, until I came to my senses?'

'Not long. Some four or five minutes.'

'I thought it could not be very long,' said he, drawing a long breath. 'But what a strange thing unconsciousness is! There is no measurement to it. I could not tell from my own sensations if it were seconds or weeks. Now that gentleman on the table was packed up in the days of the eleventh dynasty, some forty centuries ago, and yet if he could find his tongue, he would tell us that this lapse of time has been but a closing of the eyes and a reopening of them. He is a singularly fine mummy, Smith.'

Smith stepped over to the table and looked down with a professional eye at the black and twisted form in front of him. The features, though horribly discoloured, were perfect, and two little nut-like eyes still lurked in the depths of the black, hollow sockets. The blotched skin was drawn tightly from bone to bone, and a tangled wrap of black, coarse hair fell over the ears. Two thin teeth, like those a of rat, overlay the shrivelled lower lip. In its crouching position, with bent joints and craned head, there was a suggestion of energy about the horrid thing which made Smith's gorge rise. The gaunt ribs, with their parchment-like covering, were exposed, and the sunken, leaden-hued abdomen, with the long slit where the embalmer had left his mark; but the lower limbs were wrapped round with coarse, yellow bandages. A number of little clove-like pieces of myrrh and of cassia were sprinkled over the body, and lay scattered on the inside of the case.

'I don't know his name,' said Bellingham, passing his hand over the shrivelled head. 'You see the outer sarcophagus with the inscriptions is missing. Lot 249 is all the title he has now. You see it printed on his case. That was his number in the auction at which I picked him up.'

'He has been a very pretty sort of fellow in his day,' remarked Abercrombie Smith.

'He has been a giant. His mummy is six feet seven in length, and that would be a giant over there, for they were never a very robust race. Feel these great, knotted bones, too. He would be a nasty fellow to tackle.'

'Perhaps these very hands helped to build the stones into the pyramids,' suggested Monkhouse Lee, looking down with disgust in his eyes at the crooked, unclean talons.

'No fear. This fellow has been pickled in natron, and looked after in the most approved style. They did not serve hodsmen in that fashion. Salt or bitumen was enough for them. It has been calculated that this sort of thing cost about seven hundred and thirty pounds in our money. Our friend was a noble at the least. What do you make of that small inscription near his feet, Smith?'

'I told you that I know no Eastern tongue.'

'Ah, so you did. It is the name of the embalmer, I take it. A very conscientious worker he must have been. I wonder how many modern works will survive four thousand years?'

He kept on speaking lightly and rapidly, but it was evident to Abercrombie Smith that he was still palpitating with fear. His hands shook, his lower lip trembled, and look where he would, his eye always came sliding round to his gruesome companion. Through all his fear, however, there was a suspicion of triumph in his tone and manner. His eyes shone, and his footstep, as he paced the room, was brisk and jaunty. He gave the impression of a man who has gone through an ordeal, the marks of which he still bears upon him, but which has helped him to his end.

'You're not going yet?' he cried, as Smith rose from the sofa. At the prospect of solitude, his fears seemed to crowd back upon him, and he stretched out a hand to detain him.

'Yes, I must go. I have my work to do. You are all right now. I think that with your nervous system you should take up some less morbid study.'

'Oh, I am not nervous as a rule; and I have unwrapped mummies before.'

'You fainted last time,' observed Monkhouse Lee.

'Ah, yes, so I did. Well, I must have a nerve tonic or a course of electricity. You are not going, Lee?'

'I'll do whatever you wish, Ned.'

'Then I'll come down with you and have a shakedown on your sofa. Good night, Smith. I am so sorry to have disturbed you with my foolishness.'

They shook hands, and as the medical student stumbled up the spiral and irregular stair he heard a key turn in a door, and the steps of his two new acquaintances as they descended to the lower floor.

In this strange way began the acquaintance between Edward Bellingham and Abercrombie Smith, an acquaintance which the latter, at least, had no desire to push further. Bellingham, however, appeared to have taken a fancy to his rough-spoken neighbour, and made his advances in such a way that he could hardly be repulsed without absolute brutality. Twice he called to thank Smith for his assistance, and many times afterwards he looked in with books, papers and such other civilities as two bachelor neighbours can offer each other. He was, as Smith soon found, a man of wide reading, with catholic tastes and an extraordinary memory. His manner, too, was so pleasing and suave that one came, after a time, to overlook his repellent appearance. For a jaded and wearied man he was no unpleasant companion, and Smith found himself, after a time, looking forward to his visits, and even returning them.

Clever as he undoubtedly was, however, the medical student seemed to detect a dash of insanity in the man. He broke out at times into a high, inflated style of talk which was in contrast with the simplicity of his life.

'It is a wonderful thing,' he cried, 'to feel that one can command powers of good and of evil – a ministering angel or a demon of vengeance.' And again, of Monkhouse Lee, he said, – 'Lee is a good fellow, an honest fellow, but he is without strength or ambition. He would not make a fit partner for a man with a great enterprise. He would not make a fit partner for me.'

At such hints and innuendoes stolid Smith, puffing solemnly at his pipe, would simply raise his eyebrows and shake his head, with little interjections of medical wisdom as to earlier hours and fresher air.

One habit Bellingham had developed of late which Smith knew to be a frequent herald of a weakening mind. He appeared to be for ever talking to himself. At late hours of the night, when there could be no visitor with him, Smith could still hear his voice beneath him in a low, muffled monologue, sunk almost to a whisper, and yet very audible in the silence. This solitary babbling annoyed and distracted the student, so that he spoke more than once to his neighbour about it. Bellingham, however, flushed up at the charge, and denied curtly that he had uttered a sound; indeed, he showed more annoyance over the matter than the occasion seemed to demand.

Had Abercrombie Smith had any doubts as to his own ears he had not to go far to find corroboration. Tom Styles, the little wrinkled man-servant who had attended to the wants of the lodgers in the turret for a longer time than any man's memory could carry him, was sorely put to it over the same matter.

'If you please, sir,' said he, as he tidied down the top chamber one morning, 'do you think Mr Bellingham is all right, sir?'

'All right, Styles?'

'Yes, sir. Right in his head, sir.'

'Why should he not be, then?'

'Well, I don't know, sir. His habits has changed of late. He's not the same man he used to be, though I make free to say that he was never quite one of my gentlemen, like Mr Hastie or yourself, sir. He's took to talkin' to himself something awful. I wonder it don't disturb you. I don't know what to make of him, sir.'

'I don't know what business it is of yours, Styles.'

'Well, I takes an interest, Mr Smith. It may be forward of me, but I can't help it. I feel sometimes as if I was mother and father to my young gentlemen. It all falls on me when things go wrong and the relations come. But Mr Bellingham, sir. I want to know what it is that walks about his room sometimes when he's out and when the door's locked on the outside.'

'Eh? you're talking nonsense, Styles.'

'Maybe so, sir; but I heard it more'n once with my own ears.'

'Rubbish, Styles.'

'Very good, sir. You'll ring the bell if you want me.'

Abercrombie Smith gave little heed to the gossip of the old man-servant, but a small incident occurred a few days later which left an unpleasant effect upon his mind, and brought the words of Styles forcibly to his memory.

Bellingham had come up to see him late one night, and was entertaining him with an interesting account of the rock tombs of Beni Hassan in Upper Egypt, when Smith, whose hearing was remarkably acute, distinctly heard the sound of a door opening on the landing below.

'There's some fellow gone in or out of your room,' he remarked.

Bellingham sprang up and stood helpless for a moment, with the expression of a man who is half-incredulous and half-afraid.

'I surely locked it. I am almost positive that I locked it,' he stammered. 'No one could have opened it.'

'Why, I hear someone coming up the steps now,' said Smith.

Bellingham rushed out through the door, slammed it loudly behind him, and hurried down the stairs. About half-way down Smith heard him stop, and thought he caught the sound of whispering. A moment later the door beneath him shut, a key creaked in a lock, and Bellingham, with beads of moisture upon his pale face, ascended the stairs once more, and re-entered the room.

'It's all right,' he said, throwing himself down in a chair. 'It was that fool of a dog. He had pushed the door open. I don't know how I came to forget to lock it.'

'I didn't know you kept a dog,' said Smith, looking very thoughtfully at the disturbed face of his companion.

'Yes, I haven't had him long. I must get rid of him. He's a great nuisance.'

'He must be, if you find it so hard to shut him up. I should have thought that shutting the door would have been enough, without locking it.'

'I want to prevent old Styles from letting him out. He's of some value, you know, and it would be awkward to lose him.'

'I am a bit of a dog-fancier myself,' said Smith, still gazing hard at his companion from the corner of his eyes. 'Perhaps you'll let me have a look at it.'

'Certainly. But I am afraid it cannot be to-night; I have an appointment. Is that clock right? Then I am a quarter of an hour late already. You'll excuse me, I am sure.'

He picked up his cap and hurried from the room. In spite of his appointment, Smith heard him re-enter his own chamber and lock his door upon the inside.

This interview left a disagreeable impression upon the medical student's mind. Bellingham had lied to him, and lied so clumsily that it looked as if he had desperate reasons for concealing the truth. Smith knew that his neighbour had no dog. He knew, also, that the step which he had heard upon the stairs was not the step of an animal. But if it were not, then what could it be? There was old Style's statement about the something which used to pace the room at times when the owner was absent. Could it be a woman? Smith rather inclined to the view. If so, it would mean disgrace and expulsion to Bellingham if it were discovered by the authorities, so that his anxiety and falsehoods might be accounted for. And yet it was inconceivable that an undergraduate could keep a woman in his rooms without being instantly detected. Be the explanation what it might, there was something ugly about it, and Smith determined, as he turned to his books, to discourage all further attempts at intimacy on the part of his soft-spoken and ill-favoured neighbour.

But his work was destined to interruption that night. He had hardly caught up the broken threads when a firm, heavy footfall came three steps at a time from below, and Hastie, in blazer and flannels, burst into the room.

'Still at it!' said he, plumping down into his wonted arm-chair. 'What a chap you are to stew! I believe an earthquake might come and knock Oxford into a cocked hat, and you would sit perfectly placid with your books among the ruins. However, I won't bore you long. Three whiffs of baccy, and I am off.'

'What's the news, then?' asked Smith, cramming a plug of bird's-eye into his briar with his forefinger.

'Nothing very much. Wilson made 70 for the freshmen against the eleven. They say that they will play him instead of Buddicomb, for Buddicomb is clean off colour. He used to be able to bowl a little, but it's nothing but half-volleys and long hops now.'

'Medium right,' suggested Smith, with the intense gravity which comes upon a 'varsity man when he speaks of athletics.

'Inclining to fast, with a work from leg. Comes with the arm about three inches or so. He used to be nasty on a wet wicket. Oh, by the way, have you heard about Long Norton?'

'What's that?'

'He's been attacked.'

'Attacked?'

'Yes, just as he was turning out of the High Street, and within a hundred yards of the gate of Old's.'

'But who——'

'Ah, that's the rub! If you said "what," you would be more grammatical. Norton swears that it was not human, and, indeed, from the scratches on his throat, I should be inclined to agree with him.'

'What, then? Have we come down to spooks?'

Abercrombie Smith puffed his scientific contempt.

'Well, no; I don't think that is quite the idea, either. I am inclined to think that if any showman has lost a great ape lately, and the brute is in these parts, a jury would find a true bill against it. Norton passes that way every night, you know, about the same hour. There's a tree that hangs low over the path – the big elm from Rainy's garden. Norton thinks the thing dropped on him out of the tree. Anyhow, he was nearly strangled by two arms, which, he says, were as strong and as thin as steel bands. He saw nothing; only those beastly arms that tightened and tightened on him. He yelled his head nearly off, and a couple of chaps came running, and the thing went over the wall like a cat. He never got a fair sight of it the whole time. It gave Norton a shake up, I can tell you. I tell him it has been as good as a change at the seaside for him.'

'A garrotter, most likely,' said Smith.

'Very possibly. Norton says not; but we don't mind what he says. The garrotter had long nails, and was pretty smart at swinging himself over walls. By the way, your beautiful neighbour would be pleased if he heard about it. He had a grudge against Norton, and he's not a man, from what I know of him, to forget his little debts. But hallo, old chap, what have you got in your noddle?'

'Nothing,' Smith answered curtly.

He had started in his chair, and the look had flashed over his face which comes upon a man who is struck suddenly by some unpleasant idea.

'You looked as if something I had said had taken you on the raw. By the way, you have made the acquaintance of Master B. since I looked in

LOT NO. 249

last, have you not? Young Monkhouse Lee told me something to that effect.'

'Yes; I know him slightly. He has been up here once or twice.'

'Well, you're big enough and ugly enough to take care of yourself. He's not what I should call exactly a healthy sort of Johnny, though, no doubt, he's very clever, and all that. But you'll soon find out for yourself. Lee is all right; he's a very decent little fellow. Well, so long, old chap! I row Mullins for the Vice-Chancellor's pot on Wednesday week, so mind you come down, in case I don't see you before.'

Bovine Smith laid down his pipe and turned stolidly to his books once more. But with all the will in the world, he found it very hard to keep his mind upon his work. It would slip away to brood upon the man beneath him, and upon the little mystery which hung round his chambers. Then his thoughts turned to this singular attack of which Hastie had spoken, and to the grudge which Bellingham was said to owe the object of it. The two ideas would persist in rising together in his mind, as though there were some close and intimate connection between them. And yet the suspicion was so dim and vague that it could not be put down in words.

'Confound the chap!' cried Smith, as he shied his book on pathology across the room. 'He has spoiled my night's reading, and that's reason enough, if there were no other, why I should steer clear of him in the future.'

For ten days the medical student confined himself so closely to his studies that he neither saw nor heard anything of either of the men beneath him. At the hours when Bellingham had been accustomed to visit him, he took care to sport his oak, and though he more than once heard a knocking at his outer door, he resolutely refused to answer it. One afternoon, however, he was descending the stairs when, just as he was passing it, Bellingham's door flew open, and young Monkhouse Lee came out with his eyes sparkling and a dark flush of anger upon his olive cheeks. Close at his heels followed Bellingham, his fat, unhealthy face all quivering with malignant passion.

'You fool!' he hissed. 'You'll be sorry.'

'Very likely,' cried the other. 'Mind what I say. It's off! I won't hear of it!'

'You've promised, anyhow.'

'Oh, I'll keep that! I won't speak. But I'd rather little Eva was in her grave. Once for all, it's off. She'll do what I say. We don't want to see you again.'

So much Smith could not avoid hearing, but he hurried on, for he had no wish to be involved in their dispute. There had been a serious breach between them, that was clear enough, and Lee was going to cause the engagement with his sister to be broken off. Smith thought of Hastie's comparison of the toad and the dove, and was glad to think that the matter was at an end. Bellingham's face when he was in a passion was not pleasant to look upon. He was not a man to whom an innocent girl could be trusted for life. As he walked, Smith wondered languidly what could have caused the quarrel, and what the promise might be which Bellingham had been so anxious that Monkhouse Lee should keep.

It was the day of the sculling match between Hastie and Mullins, and a stream of men were making their way down to the banks of the Isis. A May sun was shining brightly, and the yellow path was barred with the black shadows of the tall elm-trees. On either side the grey colleges lay back from the road, and hoary old mothers of minds looking out from their high, mullioned windows at the tide of young life which swept so merrily past them. Black-clad tutors, prim officials, pale, reading men, brown-faced, straw-hatted young athletes in white sweaters or many-coloured blazers, all were hurrying towards the blue, winding river which curves through the Oxford meadows.

Abercrombie Smith, with the intuition of an old oarsman, chose his position at the point where he knew that the struggle, if there were a struggle, would come. Far off he heard the hum which announced the start, the gathering roar of the approach, the thunder of running feet, and the shouts of the men in the boats beneath him. A spray of half-clad, deep-breathing runners shot past him, and craning over their shoulders, he saw Hastie pulling a steady thirty-six, while his opponent, with a jerky forty, was a good boat's length behind him. Smith gave a cheer for his friend, and pulling out his watch, was starting off again for his chambers, when he felt a touch upon his shoulder, and found that young Monkhouse Lee was beside him.

'I saw you there,' he said, in a timid, deprecating way. 'I wanted to speak to you, if you could spare me a half-hour. This cottage is mine. I share it with Harrington of King's. Come in and have a cup of tea.'

'I must be back presently,' said Smith. 'I am hard on the grind at present. But I'll come in for a few minutes with pleasure. I wouldn't have come out only Hastie is a friend of mine.'

'So he is of mine. Hasn't he a beautiful style? Mullins wasn't in it. But come into the cottage. It's a little den of a place, but it is pleasant to work in during the summer months.'

It was a small, square, white building, with green doors and shutters, and a rustic trellis-work porch, standing back some fifty yards from the river's bank. Inside, the main room was roughly fitted up as a study – deal table, unpainted shelves with books, and a few cheap oleographs upon the wall. A kettle sang upon a spirit-stove, and there were tea things upon a tray on the table.

'Try that chair and have a cigarette,' said Lee. 'Let me pour you out a cup of tea. It's so good of you to come in, for I know that your time if a good deal taken up. I wanted to say to you that, if I were you, I should change my rooms at once.'

'Eh?'

Smith sat staring with a lighted match in one hand and his unlit cigarette in the other.

'Yes; it must seem very extraordinary, and the worst of it is that I cannot give any reasons, for I am under a solemn promise – a very solemn promise. But I may go so far as to say that I don't think Bellingham is a very safe man to live near. I intend to camp out here as much as I can for a time.'

'Not safe! What do you mean?'

'Ah, that's what I mustn't say. But do take my advice and move your rooms. We had a grand row to-day. You must have heard us, for you came down the stairs.'

'I saw that you had fallen out.'

'He's a horrible chap, Smith. That is the only word for him. I have had doubts about him ever since that night when he fainted – you remember, when you came down. I taxed him to-day, and he told me things that made my hair rise, and wanted me to stand in with him. I'm not straight-laced, but I am a clergyman's son, you know, and I think there are some things which are quite beyond the pale. I only thank God that I found him out before it was too late, for he was to have married into my family.'

'This is all very fine, Lee,' said Abercrombie Smith curtly. 'But either you are saying a great deal too much or a great deal too little.'

'I give you a warning.'

'If there is real reason for warning, no promise can bind you. If I see a rascal about to blow a place up with dynamite no pledge will stand in my way of preventing him.'

'Ah, but I cannot prevent him, and I can do nothing but warn you.'

'Without saying what you warn me against.'

'Against Bellingham.'

'But that is childish. Why should I fear him, or any man?'

'I can't tell you. I can only entreat you to change your rooms. You are in danger where you are. I don't even say that Bellingham would wish to injure you. But it might happen, for he is a dangerous neighbour just now.'

'Perhaps I know more than you think,' said Smith, looking keenly at the young man's boyish, earnest face. 'Suppose I tell you that someone else shares Bellingham's rooms.'

Monkhouse Lee sprang from his chair in uncontrollable excitement.

'You know, then?' he gasped.

'A woman.'

Lee dropped back again with a groan.

'My lips are sealed,' he said. 'I must not speak.'

'Well, anyhow,' said Smith, rising, 'it is not likely that I should allow myself to be frightened out of rooms which suit me very nicely. It would be a little too feeble for me to move out all my goods and chattels because you say that Bellingham might in some unexplained way do me an injury. I think that I'll just take my chance, and stay where I am, and as I see that it's nearly five o'clock, I must ask you to excuse me.'

He bade the young student adieu in a few curt words, and made his way homeward through the sweet spring evening, feeling half-ruffled, half-amused, as any other strong, unimaginative man might who has been menaced by a vague and shadowy danger.

There was one little indulgence which Abercrombie Smith always allowed himself, however closely his work might press upon him. Twice a week, on the Tuesday and the Friday, it was his invariable custom to walk over to Farlingford, the residence of Doctor Plumptree Peterson, situated about a mile and a half out of Oxford. Peterson had been a close friend of Smith's elder brother, Francis, and as he was a bachelor, fairly well-to-do, with a good cellar and a better library, his house was a pleasant goal for a man who was in need of a brisk walk. Twice a week, then, the medical student would swing out there along the dark country roads and spend a pleasant hour in Peterson's comfortable study, discussing, over a glass of old port, the gossip of the 'varsity or the latest developments of medicine or of surgery.

On the day which followed his interview with Monkhouse Lee, Smith shut up his books at a quarter past eight, the hour when he usually started for his friend's house. As he was leaving his room, however, his eyes chanced to fall upon one of the books which Bellingham had lent him, and his conscience pricked him for not having returned it. However repellent the man might be, he should not be treated with discourtesy. Taking the book, he walked downstairs and knocked at his neighbour's door. There was no answer; but on turning the handle he found that it was unlocked. Pleased at the thought of avoiding an interview, he stepped inside, and placed the book with his card upon the table.

The lamp was turned half down, but Smith could see the details of the room plainly enough. It was all much as he had seen it before – the frieze, and animal-headed gods, the hanging crocodile, and the table littered over with papers and dried leaves. The mummy case stood upright against the wall, but the mummy itself was missing. There was no sign of any second occupant of the room, and he felt as he withdrew that he had probably done Bellingham an injustice. Had he a guilty secret to preserve, he would hardly leave his door open so that all the world might enter.

The spiral stair was a black as pitch, and Smith was slowly making his way down its irregular steps, when he was suddenly conscious that something had passed him in the darkness. There was a faint sound a whiff of air, a light brushing past his elbow, but so slight that he could scarcely be certain of it. He stopped and listened, but the wind was rustling among the ivy outside, and he could hear nothing else.

'Is that you, Styles?' he shouted.

There was no answer, and all was still behind him. It must have been a sudden gust of air, for there were crannies and cracks in the old turret. And yet he could almost have sworn that he heard a footfall by his very side. He had emerged into the quadrangle, still turning the matter over in his head, when a man came running swiftly across the smooth-cropped lawn.

'Is that you, Smith?'

'Hullo, Hastie!'

'For God's sake come at once! Young Lee is drowned! Here's Harrington of King's with the news. The doctor is out. You'll do, but come along at once. There may be life in him.'

'Have you brandy?'

'No.'

'I'll bring some. There's a flask on my table.'

Smith bounded up the stairs, taking three at a time, seized the flask, and was rushing down with it, when, as he passed Bellingham's room, his eyes fell upon something which left him gasping and staring upon the landing.

The door, which he had closed behind him, was now open, and right in front of him, with the lamp-light shining upon it, was the mummy case. Three minutes ago it had been empty. He could swear to that. Now it framed the lank body of its horrible occupant, who stood, grim and stark, with his black, shrivelled face towards the door. The form was lifeless and inert, but it seemed to Smith as he gazed that there still lingered a lurid spark of vitality, some faint sign of consciousness in the little eyes which lurked in the depths of the hollow sockets. So astounded and shaken was he that he had forgotten his errand, and was still staring at the lean, sunken figure when the voice of his friend below recalled him to himself.

'Come on, Smith!' he shouted. 'It's life and death, you know. Hurry up! Now, then,' he added, as the medical student reappeared, 'let us do a sprint. It is well under a mile, and we should do it in five minutes. A human life is better worth running for than a pot.'

Neck and neck they dashed through the darkness, and did not pull up until panting and spent, they had reached the little cottage by the river. Young Lee, limp and dripping like a broken water-plant, was stretched upon the sofa, the green scum of the river upon his black hair, and a fringe of white foam upon his leaden-hued lips. Beside him knelt his fellow-student, Harrington, endeavouring to chafe some warmth back into his rigid limbs.

'I think there's life in him,' said Smith, with his hand to the lad's side. 'Put your watch glass to his lips. Yes, there's dimming on it. You take one arm, Hastie. Now work it as I do, and we'll soon pull him round.'

For ten minutes they worked in silence, inflating and depressing the chest of the unconscious man. At the end of that time a shiver ran through his body, his lips trembled, and he opened his eyes. The three students burst out into an irrepressible cheer.

'Wake up, old chap. You've frightened us quite enough.'

'Have some brandy. Take a sip from the flask.'

'He's all right now,' said his companion Harrington. 'Heavens, what a fright I got! I was reading here, and he had gone out for a stroll as far as the river, when I heard a scream and a splash. Out I ran, and by the time I could find him and fish him out, all life seemed to have gone. Then Simpson couldn't get a doctor, for he has a game-leg, and I had to run, and I don't know what I'd have done without you fellows. That's right, old chap. Sit up.'

Monkhouse Lee had raised himself on his hands, and looked wildly about him.

'What's up?' he asked. 'I've been in the water. Ah, yes; I remember.'

A look of fear came into his eyes, and he sank his face into his hands.

'How did you fall in?'

'I didn't fall in.'

'How then?'

'I was thrown in. I was standing by the bank, and something from behind picked me up like a feather and hurled me in. I heard nothing, and I saw nothing. But I know what it was, for all that.'

'And so do I,' whispered Smith.

Lee looked up with a quick glance of surprise.

'You've learned, then?' he said. 'You remember the advice I gave you?'

'Yes, and I begin to think that I shall take it.'

'I don't know what the deuce you fellows are talking about,' said Hastie, 'but I think, if I were you, Harrington, I should get Lee to bed at once. It will be time enough to discuss the why and the wherefore when he is a little stronger. I think, Smith, you and I can leave him alone now. I am walking back to college; if you are coming in that direction, we can have a chat.'

But it was little chat that they had upon their homeward path. Smith's mind was too full of the incidents of the evening, the absence of the mummy from his neighbour's rooms, the step that passed him on the stair, the reappearance – the extraordinary, inexplicable reappearance of the grisly thing – and then this attack upon Lee, corresponding so closely to the previous outrage upon another man against whom Bellingham bore a grudge. All this settled in his thoughts, together with the many little incidents which had previously turned him against his neighbour, and the singular circumstances under which he was first called in to him. What had been a dim suspicion, a vague, fantastic conjecture, had suddenly taken form, and stood out in his mind as a grim fact, a thing not to be denied. And yet, how monstrous it was! how unheard of! how entirely beyond all bounds of human experience. An impartial judge, or even the friend who walked by his side, would simply tell him that his eyes had deceived him, that the mummy had been there all the time, that young Lee had tumbled into the river as any other man tumbles into a river, and the blue pill was the best thing for a disordered liver. He felt that he would have said as much if the positions had been reversed. And yet he could swear that Bellingham was a murderer at heart, and that he wielded a weapon such as no man had ever used in all the grim history of crime.

Hastie had branched off to his rooms with a few crisp and emphatic comments upon his friend's unsociability, and Abercrombie Smith crossed the quadrangle to his corner turret with a strong feeling of repulsion for his chambers and their associations. He would take Lee's advice, and move his quarters as soon as possible, for how could a man study when his ear was ever straining for every murmur or footstep in the room below? He observed, as he crossed over the lawn, that the light was still shining in Bellingham's window, and as he passed up the staircase the door opened, and the man himself looked out at him. With his fat, evil face he was like some bloated spider fresh from the weaving of his poisonous web.

'Good evening,' said he. 'Won't you come in?'

'No,' cried Smith fiercely.

'No? You are as busy as ever? I wanted to ask you about Lee. I was sorry to hear that there was a rumour that something was amiss with him.'

His features were grave, but there was the gleam of a hidden laugh in his eyes as he spoke. Smith saw it, and he could have knocked him down for it.

'You'll be sorrier still to hear that Monkhouse Lee is doing very well, and is out of all danger,' he answered. 'Your hellish tricks have not come off this time. Oh, you needn't try to brazen it out. I know all about it.'

Bellingham took a step back from the angry student, and half-closed the door as if to protect himself.

'You are mad,' he said. 'What do you mean? Do you assert that I had anything to do with Lee's accident?'

'Yes,' thundered Smith. 'You and that bag of bones behind you; you worked it between you. I tell you what it is, Master B., they have given up burning folk like you, but we still keep a hangman, and, by George! if any man in this college meets his death while you are here, I'll have you up, and if you don't swing for it, it won't be my fault. You'll find that your filthy Egyptian tricks won't answer in England.'

'You're a raving lunatic,' said Bellingham.

'All right. You just remember what I say, for you'll find that I'll be better than my word.'

The door slammed, and Smith went fuming up to his chamber, where he locked the door upon the inside, and spent half the night in smoking his old briar and brooding over the strange events of the evening.

Next morning Abercrombie Smith heard nothing of his neighbour, but Harrington called upon him in the afternoon to say that Lee was almost himself again. All day Smith stuck fast to his work, but in the evening he determined to pay the visit to his friend Doctor Peterson upon which he had started the night before. A good walk and a friendly chat would be welcome to his jangled nerves.

Bellingham's door was shut as he passed, but glancing back when he was some distance from the turret, he saw his neighbour's head at the window outlined against the lamp-light, his face pressed apparently against the glass as he gazed out into the darkness. It was a blessing to be away from all contact with him, if but for a few hours, and Smith stepped out briskly, and breathed the soft spring air into his lungs. The half-moon lay in the west between two Gothic pinnacles, and threw upon the silvered street a dark tracery from the stonework above. There was a brisk breeze, and light, fleecy clouds drifted swiftly across the sky. Old's was on the very border of the town, and in five minutes Smith found himself beyond the houses and between the hedges of a May-scented, Oxfordshire lane.

It was a lonely and little-frequented road which led to his friend's house. Early as it was, Smith did not meet a single soul upon his way. He walked briskly along until he came to the avenue gate, which opened into the long, gravel drive leading up to Farlingford. In front of him he could see the cosy, red light of the windows glimmering through the foliage. He stood with his hand upon the iron latch of the swinging gate, and he glanced back at the road along which he had come. Something was coming swiftly down it.

It moved in the shadow of the hedge, silently and furtively, a dark, crouching figure, dimly visible against the black background. Even as he gazed back at it, it had lessened its distance by twenty paces, and was fast closing upon him. Out of the darkness he had a glimpse of a scraggy neck, and of two eyes that will ever haunt him in his dreams. He turned, and with a cry of terror he ran for his life up the avenue. There were the red lights, the signals of safety, almost within a stone's-throw of him. He was a famous runner, but never had he run as he ran that night.

The heavy gate had swung into the place behind him but he heard it dash open again before his pursuer. As he rushed madly and wildly through the night, he could hear a swift, dry patter behind him, and could see, as he threw back a glance, that this horror was bounding like a tiger at his heels, with blazing eyes and one stringy arm out-thrown. Thank God, the door was ajar. He could see the thin bar of light which shot from the lamp in the hall. Nearer yet sounded the clatter from behind. He heard a hoarse gurgling at his very shoulder. With a shriek he flung himself against the door, slammed and bolted it behind him, and sank half-fainting on to the hall chair.

'My goodness, Smith, what's the matter?' asked Peterson, appearing at the door of his study.

'Give me some brandy.'

Peterson disappeared, and came rushing out again with a glass and a decanter.

'You need it,' he said, as his visitor drank off what he poured out for him. 'Why, man, you are as white as a cheese.'

Smith laid down his glass, rose up, and took a deep breath.

'I am my own man again now,' said he. 'I was never so unmanned before. But, with your leave, Peterson, I will sleep here to-night, for I don't think I could face that road again except by daylight. It's weak, I know, but I can't help it.'

Peterson looked at his visitor with a very questioning eye.

'Of course you shall sleep here if you wish. I'll tell Mrs Burney to make up the spare bed. Where are you off to now?'

'Come up with me to the window that overlooks the door. I want you to see what I have seen.'

They went up to the window of the upper hall whence they could look upon the approach to the house. The drive and the fields on either side lay quiet and still, bathed in the peaceful moonlight.

'Well, really, Smith,' remarked Peterson, 'it is well that I know you to be an abstemious man. What in the world can have frightened you?'

'I'll tell you presently. But where can it have gone? Ah, now, look,

look! See the curve of the road just beyond your gate.'

'Yes, I see; you needn't pinch my arm off. I saw someone pass. I should say a man, rather thin, apparently, and tall, very tall. But what of him? And what of yourself? You are still shaking like an aspen leaf.'

'I have been within hand-grip of the devil, that's all. But come down to your study, and I shall tell you the whole story.'

He did so. Under the cheery lamp-light with a glass of wine on the table beside him, and the portly form and florid face of his friend in front, he narrated, in their order, all the events, great and small, which had formed so singular a chain, from the night on which he had found Bellingham fainting in front of the mummy case until this horrid experience of an hour ago.

'There now,' he said as he concluded, 'that's the whole, black business. It is monstrous and incredible, but it is true.'

Doctor Plumptree Peterson sat for some time in silence with a very puzzled expression upon his face.

'I never heard of such a thing in my life, never!' he said at last. 'You have told me the facts. Now tell me your inferences.'

'You can draw your own.'

'But I should like to hear yours. You have thought over the matter, and I have not.'

'Well, it must be a little vague in detail, but the main points seem to me to be clear enough. This fellow Bellingham, in his Eastern studies, has got hold of some infernal secret by which a mummy – or possibly only this particular mummy – can be temporarily brought to life. He was trying this disgusting business on the night when he fainted. No doubt the sight of the creature moving had shaken his nerve, even though he had expected it. You remember that almost the first words he said were to call out upon himself as a fool. Well, he got more hardened afterwards, and carried the matter through without fainting. The vitality which he could put into it was evidently only a passing thing, for I have seen it continually in its case as dead as this table. He has some elaborate process, I fancy, by which he brings the thing to pass. Having done it, he naturally bethought him that he might use the creature as an agent. It has intelligence and it has strength. For some purpose he took Lee into his confidence; but Lee, like a decent Christian, would have nothing to do with such a business. Then they had a row, and Lee vowed that he would tell his sister of Bellingham's true character. Bellingham's game was to prevent him, and he nearly managed it, by setting this creature of his on his track. He had already tried its powers upon another man – Norton – towards whom he had a grudge. It is the merest chance that he has not two murders upon his soul. Then, when I taxed him with the matter, he had the strongest reasons for wishing to get me out of the way before I could convey my knowledge to anyone else. He got his chance when I went out, for he knew my habits and where I was bound for. I have had a narrow shave, Peterson, and it is mere luck you didn't find me on your doorstep in the morning. I'm not a nervous man as a rule, and I never thought to have the fear of death put upon me as it was to-night.'

'My dear boy, you take the matter too seriously,' said his companion. 'Your nerves are out of order with your work, and you make too much of it. How could such a thing as this stride about the streets of Oxford, even at night, without being seen?'

'It has been seen. There is quite a scare in the town about an escaped ape, as they imagine the creature to be. It is the talk of the place.'

'Well, it's a striking chain of events. And yet, my dear fellow, you must allow that each incident in itself is capable of a more natural explanation.'

'What! even my adventure of to-night?'

'Certainly. You come out with your nerves all unstrung, and your head full of this theory of yours. Some gaunt, half-famished tramp steals after you, and seeing you run, is emboldened to pursue you. Your fears and imagination do the rest.'

'It won't do, Peterson; it won't do.'

'And again, in the instance of your finding the mummy case empty, and then a few moments later with an occupant, you know that it was lamp-light, that the lamp was half turned down, and that you had no special reason to look hard at the case. It is quite possible that you may have overlooked the creature in the first instance.'

'No, no; it is out of the question.'

'And then Lee may have fallen into the river, and Norton been garrotted. It is certainly a formidable indictment that you have against Bellingham; but if you were to place it before a police magistrate, he would simply laugh in your face.'

'I know he would. That is why I mean to take the matter into my own hands.'

'Eh?'

'Yes; I feel that a public duty rests upon me, and, besides, I must do it for my own safety, unless I choose to allow myself to be hunted by this beast out of the college, and that would be a little too feeble. I have quite made up my mind what I shall do. And first of all, may I use your paper and pens for an hour?'

'Most certainly. You will find all that you want upon that side-table.'

Abercrombie Smith sat down before a sheet of foolscap, and for an hour, and then for a second hour his pen travelled swiftly over it. Page after page was finished and tossed aside while his friend leaned back in his arm-chair, looking across at him with patient curiosity. At last, with an exclamation of satisfaction, Smith sprang to his feet, gathered his papers up into order, and laid the last one upon Peterson's desk.

'Kindly sign this as a witness,' he said.

'A witness? Of what?'

'Of my signature, and of the date. The date is the most important. Why, Peterson, my life might hang upon it.'

'My dear Smith, you are talking wildly. Let me beg you to go to bed.'

'On the contrary, I never spoke so deliberately in my life. And I will promise to go to bed the moment you have signed it.'

'But what is it?'

'It is a statement of all that I have been telling you to-night. I wish you to witness it.'

'Certainly,' said Peterson, signing his name under that of his companion. 'There you are! But what is the idea?'

'You will kindly retain it, and produce it in case I am arrested.'

'Arrested? For what?'

'For murder. It is quite on the cards. I wish to be ready for every event. There is only one course open to me, and I am determined to take it.'

'For Heaven's sake, don't do anything rash!'

'Believe me, it would be far more rash to adopt any other course. I hope that we won't need to bother you, but it will ease my mind to know that you have this statement of my motives. And now I am ready to take your advice and to go to roost, for I want be to at my best in the morning.'

Abercrombie Smith was not an entirely pleasant man to have as an enemy. Slow and easy-tempered, he was formidable when driven to action. He brought to every purpose in life the same deliberate resoluteness which had distinguished him as a scientific student. He had laid his studies aside for a day, but he intended that the day should not be wasted. Not a word did he say to his host as to his plans, but by nine o'clock he was well on his way to Oxford.

In the High Street he stopped at Clifford's, the gunmaker's, and bought a heavy revolver, with a box of central-fire cartridges. Six of them he slipped into the chambers, and half-cocking the weapon, placed it in the pocket of his coat. He then made his way to Hastie's rooms, where the big oarsman was lounging over his breakfast, with the *Sporting Times* propped up against the coffee-pot.

'Hullo! What's up?' he asked. 'Have some coffee?'

'No thank you. I want you to come with me, Hastie, and do what I ask you.'

'Certainly, my boy.'

'And bring a heavy stick with you.'

'Hullo!' Hastie stared. 'Here's a hunting crop that would fell an ox.'

'One other thing. You have a box of amputating knives. Give me the longest of them.'

'There you are. You seem to be fairly on the war trail. Anything else?'

'No; that will do.' Smith placed the knife inside his coat, and led the way to the quadrangle. 'We are neither of us chickens, Hastie,' said he. 'I think I can do this job alone, but I take you as a precaution. I am going to have a little talk with Bellingham. If I have only him to deal with, I won't, of course, need you. If I shout, however, up you come, and lam out with your whip as hard as you can lick. Do you understand?'

'All right. I'll come if I hear you bellow.'

'Stay here, then. I may be a little time, but don't budge until I come down.'

'I'm a fixture.'

Smith ascended the stairs, opened Bellingham's door and stepped in. Bellingham was seated behind his table, writing. Beside him, among his litter of strange possessions, towered the mummy case, with its sale number 249 still stuck upon its front, and its hideous occupant stiff and stark within it. Smith looked very deliberately round him, closed the door, and then, stepping across to the fireplace, struck a match and set the fire alight. Bellingham sat staring, with amazement and rage upon his bloated face.

'Well, really now, you make yourself at home,' he gasped.

Smith sat himself deliberately down, placing his watch upon the table, drew out his pistol, cocked it, and laid it in his lap. Then he took the long amputating knife from his bosom, and threw it down in front of Bellingham.

'Now, then,' said he, 'just get to work and cut up that mummy.'

'Oh, is that it?' said Bellingham with a sneer.

'Yes, that is it. They tell me that the law can't touch you. But I have a law that will set matters straight. If in five minutes you have not set to work, I swear by the God who made me that I will put a bullet through your brain!'

'You would murder me?'

Bellingham had half-risen, and his face was the colour of putty.

'Yes.'

'And for what?'

'To stop your mischief. One minute has gone.'

'But what have I done?'

'I know and you know.'

'This is mere bullying.'

'Two minutes are gone.'

'But you must give reasons. You are a madman – a dangerous madman. Why should I destroy my own property? It is a valuable mummy.'

'You must cut it up, and you must burn it.'

'I will do no such thing.'

'Four minutes are gone.'

Smith took up the pistol and he looked towards Bellingham with an inexorable face. As the secondhand stole round, he raised his hand, and the finger twitched upon the trigger.

'There! there! I'll do it!' screamed Bellingham.

In frantic haste he caught up the knife and hacked at the figure of the mummy, ever glancing round to see the eye and the weapon of his terrible visitor bent upon him. The creature crackled and snapped under every stab of the keen blade. A thick, yellow dust rose up from it. Spices and dried essences rained down upon the floor. Suddenly, with a rending crack, its backbone snapped asunder, and it fell, a brown heap of sprawling limbs, upon the floor.

'Now into the fire!' said Smith.

The flames leaped and roared as the dried and tinder-like debris was piled upon it. The little room was like the stoke-hole of a steamer and the sweat ran down the faces of the two men; but still the one stooped and worked, while the other sat watching him with a set face. A thick, fat smoke oozed out from the fire, and a heavy smell of burned resin and singed hair filled the air. In a quarter of an hour a few charred and brittle sticks were all that was left of Lot No. 249.

'Perhaps that will satisfy you,' snarled Bellingham, with hate and fear in his little grey eyes as he glanced back at his tormentor.

'No; I must make a clean sweep of all your materials. We must have no more devil's tricks. In with all these leaves! They may have something to do with it.'

'And what now?' asked Bellingham, when the leaves also had been added to the blaze.

'Now the roll of papyrus which you had on the table that night. It is in that drawer, I think.'

'No, no,' shouted Bellingham. 'Don't burn that! Why, man, you don't know what you do. It is unique; it contains wisdom which is nowhere else to be found.'

'Out with it!'

'But look here, Smith, you can't really mean it. I'll share the knowledge with you. I'll teach you all that is in it. Or, stay, let me only copy it before you burn it!'

Smith stepped forward and turned the key in the drawer. Taking out the yellow, curled roll of paper, he threw it into the fire, and pressed it down with his heel. Bellingham screamed, and grabbed at it; but Smith pushed him back and stood over it until it was reduced to a formless, grey ash.

'Now, Master B.,' said he, 'I think I have pretty well drawn your teeth. You'll hear from me again, if you return to your old tricks. And now good morning, for I must go back to my studies.'

And such is the narrative of Abercrombie Smith as to the singular events which occurred in Old College, Oxford, in the spring of '84. As Bellingham left the university immediately afterwards, and was last heard of in the Soudan, there is no one who can contradict his statement. But the wisdom of men is small, and the ways of Nature are strange, and who shall put a bound to the dark things which may be found by those who seek for them?

J. Kaden-Bandrowski

The Sentence

'Yakób . . . Yakób . . . Yakób!'

The old man was repeating his name to himself, or rather he was inwardly listening to the sound of it which he had been accustomed to hear for so many years. He had heard it in the stable, in the fields, and on the grazing-ground, on the steps of the manor-house and at the Jew's, but never like this. It seemed to issue from unknown depths, summoning sounds never heard before, sights never yet seen, producing a confusion which he had never experienced. He saw it, felt it everywhere; it was itself the cause of a hopeless despair.

This despair crept silently into Yakób's fatalistic and submissive soul. He felt it under his hand, as though he were holding another hand. He was as conscious of it as of his hairy chest, his cold and starved body. This despair, moreover, was blended with a kind of patient expectancy which was expressed by the whispering of his pale, trembling lips, the tepid sweat under his armpits, the saliva running into his throat and making his tongue feel rigid like a piece of wood.

This is what happened: he tried to remember how it had all happened.

They had come swarming in from everywhere; they had taken the men away; it was firearms everywhere . . . everywhere firearms, noise and hubbub. The whole world was pushing, running, sweating or freezing. They arrived from this side or from that; they asked questions, they hunted people down, they followed up a trail, they fought. Of course, one must not betray one's brothers, but then . . . who are one's brothers?

They placed watches in the mountains, in the forests, on the fields; they even drove people into the mountain-passes and told them to hold out at any cost.

THE SENTENCE

Yakób had been sitting in the chimney-corner in the straw and dust, covered with his frozen rags. The wind swept over the mountains and penetrated into the cottage, bringing with it a white covering of hoarfrost; it was sighing eerily in the fields; the fields themselves seemed to flee from it, and to be alive, running away into the distance. The earth in white convulsions besieged the sky, and and sky got entangled in the mountain-forests.

Yakób was looking at the snow which was falling thickly, and tried to penetrate the veil with his eyes. Stronger and faster raged the blizzard. Yakób's stare became vacant under the rumbling of the storm and the driving of the snow; one could not have told whether he was looking with eyes or with lumps of ice.

Shadows were flitting across the snowdrifts. They were the outlines of objects lit by the fire; they trembled on the window-frames; the fire flickered, and the shadows treacherously caressed the images of saints on the walls. The beam played on the window, threw a red light on the short posts of the railing, and disappeared in pursuit of the wind in the fields.

'Yakób . . . Yakób . . . Yakób!'

And he had really had nothing to do with it! It had all gone against him continuously, pertinaciously, and to no purpose. It had attached itself to him, clung to the dry flour that flew about in atoms in the tin where the bit of cheese also was kept. It had bewitched the creaking of the windows on their hinges; it had stared from the empty seats along the walls.

But he kept on beating his breast. His forehead was wrinkled in dried-up folds, his brows bristled fantastically into shaggy, dirty tufts. His heavy, blunt nose, powdered with hairs at the tip, stood out obstinately between two deep folds on either side. These folds overhung the corners of his mouth, and were joined below the chin by a network of pallid veins. A noise, light as a beetle's wing, came in puffs from the half-open lips; they were swollen and purple like an overgrown bean.

Yakób had been sitting in Turkish fashion, his hands crossed over his chest, breathing forth his misery so quietly that it covered him, together with the hoar-frost, stopped his ears and made the tufts of hair on his chest glitter. He was hugging his sorrow to himself, abandoning the last remnant of hope, and longing for deliverance. Behind the wrinkles of his forehead there swarmed a multitude not so much of pictures as of ghosts of the past, yet vividly present.

At last he got up and sat down on the bench in the chimney-corner, drew a pipe from his trouser-pocket and put it between his teeth, forgetting to light it. He laid his heavy hands round the stem. Beyond the blizzard and the shadow-play of the flame, there appeared to him the scene of his wife and daughters' flight. He had given up everything he possessed, had taken off his sheepskin, had himself loosened the cow from the post. For a short moment he had caught sight of his wife and daughters again in the distance, tramping through the snow as they passed the cross-roads, then they had been swallowed up in a mass of people, horses, guns, carts, shouts and curses. Since then he had constantly fancied that he was being called, yet he knew that there was no one to call him. His thoughts were entirely absorbed in what he had seen then. With his wife all his possessions had gone. Now there was nothing but silence, surrounding him with a sharp breath of pain and death.

By day and by night Yakób had listened to the shots that struck his cottage and his pear-trees. He chewed a bit of cheese from time to time, and gulped down with it the bitter fear that his cottage might be set on fire.

For here and there, like large red poppies on the snow, the glare of burning homesteads leapt up into the sky.

'Here I am . . . watching,' he said to himself, when he looked at these blood-red graves. He smiled at the sticks of firewood on his hearth, which was the dearest thing on earth to him. The walls of his cottage were one with his inmost being, and every moment when he saw them standing, seemed to him like precious savings which he was putting away. So he watched for several days; the vermin were over-running the place, and he was becoming desperate. Since mid-day the silence had deepened; the day declined, and there was nothing in the world but solitude and snow.

Yakób went over to the window. The snow was lying deep on the fields, like a shimmering coat of varnish; the world was bathed in the light of a pale, wan moon. The forest-trees stood out here and there in blue points, like teeth. Large and brilliant the stars looked down, and above the milky way, veiled in vapours, hung the sickle of the moon.

While in the immensity of the night cold and glittering worlds were bowing down before the eternal, Yakób looked, and noticed something approaching from the mountains. Along the heights and slopes there was a long chain of lights; it was opening out from the centre into two lines on either side, which looked as though they were lost in the forest. Below them there were confused gleams in the fields, and behind, in the distance, the glow of the burning homesteads.

'They have burned the vicarage,' thought Yakób, and his heart answered: 'and here am I . . . watching.'

He pressed against the window-frame, glued his grey face to the panes and, trembling with cold, sent out an obstinate and hostile glance into space, as though determined to obtain permission to keep his own heritage.

THE SENTENCE

Suddenly he pricked up his ears. Something was approaching from the distance across the forest very cautiously. The snow was creaking under the advancing steps. In the great silence it sounded like the forging of iron. Those were horses' hoofs stamping the snow.

This sound, suppressed as it was, produced in him a peculiar sensation which starts in the head and grips you in the nape of the neck, the consciousness that someone is hiding close to you.

Yakób stood quite still at the window, not even moving his pipe from one corner of his mouth to the other. Not he himself seemed to be trembling, only his rags.

The door was suddenly thrown open and a soldier appeared on the threshold. The light of a lantern which was suspended on his chest, filled the room.

Yakób's blood was freezing. Cossacks, hairy like bears, were standing in the opening of the door, the snow which covered them was shining like a white flame. In the courtyard there were steaming horses; lance-heads were glittering like reliquaries.

Yakób understood that they were calling him 'old man', and asking him questions. He extended his hands to express that he knew nothing. Some of the Cossacks entered, and made signs to him to make up the fire.

He noticed that they were bringing more horses into the yard, small, shaggy ponies like wolves.

He became calmer, and his fear disappeared; he only remained cautious and observant; everything that happened seemed to take hours, yet he saw it with precision.

'It is cold . . . it is cold!'

He made up the fire for these bandits who stretched themselves on the benches; he felt they were talking and laughing about him, and he turned to them and nodded; he thought it would please them if he showed that he approved of them.

They asked him about God knows what, where they were, and where they were not.

As though he knew!

Then they started all over again, while they swung their booted legs under the seats. One of them came up to the hearth, and clapped the crouching Yakób on his back for fun, but it hurt. It was a resounding smack. Yakób scratched himself and rumpled his hair, unable to understand.

They boiled water and made tea; a smell of sausages spread about the room. Yakób bit his jaws together and looked at the fire. He sat in his place as though he had been glued to it.

His ears were tingling when he heard the soldiers grinding their teeth on their food, tearing the skin off the sausages and smacking their lips.

A large and painful void was gaping in his inside.

They devoured their food fast and noisily, and an odour of brandy began to fill the room, and contracted Yakób's throat.

He understood that they were inviting him to share the meal, but he felt uneasy about that, and though his stomach seemed to have shrunk, and the sausage-skins and bones which they had thrown away lay quite close to him, he could not make up his mind to move and pick them up.

'Come on!'

The soldier beckoned to him. 'Come here!'

The old man felt that he was weakening, the savoury smell took possession of him.

But, 'I shan't go,' he thought. The soldier, gnawing a bone, repeated, 'Come on!'

'I shan't go,' thought Yakób, and spat into the fire, to assure himself that he was not going. All the same . . . the terribly tempting smell made him more and more feeble.

At last two of them got up, took him under the arms, and sat him down between them.

They made signs to him, they held the sausage under his nose; the tea was steaming, the brandy smelt delicious.

Yakób put his hands on the table, then put them behind him. Black shadows were gesticulating on the walls. He felt unhappy about sharing a meal with people without knowing what they were, never having seen or known them before. They were Russians, thus much he knew. He had a vision of something that happened long ago, he could not distinctly remember what it was, for it happened so very long ago; his grandfather had come home from the fair that was held in the town, shivering and groaning. There had been outcries and curses.

'They are going to poison me like a dog,' he thought.

The wind was changing and moaning under the roof. The fire flickered up and went down; the red flame and the darkness were dancing together on the walls. The wan moon was looking in at the window. Yakób was sitting on the bench among the soldiers like his own ghost.

'They are surely going to poison me,' he kept repeating to himself. He was still racking his memory as to what it was that had happened so long ago to his grandfather during the fair, at the inn. God knows what it was . . . who could know anything?

'They are going to poison me!'

His sides were heaving with his breath, he was trying to breathe carefully, so as not to smell the repast.

The shadows on the walls seemed to jeer at him. The soldiers were beginning to talk thickly; their mouths, their fingers were shining with grease. They took off their belts and laid their swords aside. The one next to Yakób put his arm round his neck and whispered in his ear; his red mouth was quite close; he passed his hand over Yakób's head, and brought his arm right round his throat. He was young and he was talking of his father.

'Daddy,' he said, and put the sausage between his teeth.

Yakób tried to clench his teeth; but he bit the sausage at the same time.

'Daddy,' said the young soldier again, holding out the sausage for another bite; he stroked his head, looked into his eyes, and laughed. Yakób was sorry for himself. Was he to be fed like a half-blind old man? Couldn't he eat by himself?

When the soldiers saw that Yokób was eating, they burst into shouts of laughter, and stamped their feet, rattling their spurs.

He knew they were laughing at him, and it made him easier in his mind to see that he was affording them pleasure. He purposely made himself ridiculous with the vague idea that he must do something for them in payment of what they were giving him; they struck him on the shoulder-blades to see him gasp with his beanlike mouth, and to see the frightened smile run over his face like a flash of lightning.

He ate as though from bravado, but he ate well. They started drinking again. Yakób looked at them with eagerness, his arms folded over his stomach, his head bent forward; the hairy hand of the captain put the bottle to his mouth.

Now he could laugh his own natural laugh again, and not only from bravado, for he felt quite happy. His frozen body was getting warmed through.

He felt as if a great danger had irrevocably passed.

Gradually he became garrulous, although they hardly understood what he was talking about: 'Yes, the sausage was good . . . to be sure!' He nodded his head and clicked his tongue; he also approved of the huge chunks of bread, and whenever the bottle was passed round, he put his head on one side and folded his hands, as if he were listening to a sermon. From his neighbour's encircling black sleeve the old face peeped out with equanimity, looking like a withering poppy.

'Daddy,' the loquacious Cossack would say from time to time, and point in the direction of the mountains; tears were standing in his eyes.

Yakób put his swollen hand on his, and waited for him to say more.

The soldier held his hand, pointed in the direction of the mountains again, and sniffled.

'He respects old age . . . they are human, there's no denying it,' thought Yakób, and got up to put more wood on the fire.

They seized hold of him, they would not allow him to do it. A young soldier jumped up: 'Sit down, you are old.'

Yakób held out his empty pipe, and the captain himself filled it.

So there he sat, among these armed bandits. They were dressed in sheepskins and warm materials, had sheepskin caps on their heads; there was he with his bare arms, in well-worn grey trousers, his shirt fastened together at the neck with a piece of wood. Sitting among them, defenceless as a centipede, without anyone belonging to him, puffing clouds of smoke, he inwardly blessed this adventure, in which everything had turned out so well. The Cossacks looked at the fire and they too said; 'This is very nice, very nice.'

To whom would not a blazing fire on a cold winter's night appeal?

They got more and more talkative and asked: 'Where are your wife and children?' They probably too had wives and children!

'My wife,' he said, 'has gone down to the village, she was afraid.' They laughed and tapped their chests: 'War is a bad thing, who would not be afraid?' Yakób assented all the more readily as he felt that for him the worst was over.

'Do you know the way to the village?' suddenly asked the captain. He was almost hidden in clouds of tobacco-smoke, but in his eyes there was a gleam, hard and sinister, like a bullet in a puff of smoke.

Yakób did not answer. How should he not know the way?

They started getting up, buckled on their belts and swords.

Yakób jumped up to give them the rest of the sausages and food which had been left on the plates. But they would only take the brandy, and left the tobacco and the broken meat.

'That will be for you . . . afterwards,' said the young Cossack, took a red muffler off his neck and put it round Yakób's shoulder.

'That will keep you warm.'

Yakób laughed back at him, and submitted to having the muffler knotted tightly round his throat. The young soldier drew a pair of trousers from his kitbag: 'Those will keep you warm, you are old.' He told him a long story about the trousers; they had belonged to his brother who had been killed.

'You know, it's lucky to wear things like that. Poor old fellow!'

Yakób stood and looked at the breeches. In the fire-light they seemed to be trembling like feeble and stricken legs. He laid his hand on them and smiled, a little defiant and a little touched.

'You may have them, you may have them,' grunted the captain, and insisted on his putting them on at once.

When he had put them on in the chimney-corner and showed himself, they were all doubled up with laughter. He looked appalling in the black trousers which were much too large for him, a grey hood and the red muffler. His head wobbled above the red line as if it had been fixed on a bleeding neck. The rags on his chest showed the thin, hairy body, the stiff folds of the breeches produced an effect as if he were not walking on the ground but floating above it.

The captain gave the command, the soldiers jumped up and looked once more round the cottage; the young Cossack put the sausage and meat in a heap and covered it with a piece of bread. 'For you,' he said once more, and they turned to leave.

Yakób went out with them to bid them God-speed. A vague presentiment seized him on the threshold, when he looked out at the frozen world, the stars, like nails fixed into the sky, and the light of the moon on everything. He was afraid.

The men went up to their horses, and he saw that there were others outside. The wind ruffled the shaggy little ponies' manes and threw snow upon them. The horses, restless, began to bite each other, and the Cossacks, scattered on the snow like juniper-bushes, reined them in.

The cottage-door remained open. The lucky horseshoe, nailed to the threshold, glittered in the light of the hearth, which threw blood-red streaks between the legs of the table, across the door and beyond it on to the snow.

'I wonder whether they will ever return to their families?' he thought, and: 'How queer it is that one should meet people like that.'

He was sorry for them.

The captain touched his arm and asked the way.

'Straight on.'

'Far?'

'No, not far, not at all far.'

'Where is it?'

The little group stood in front of him by the side of their wolf-like ponies. He drew back into the cottage.

The thought confusedly crossed his mind: 'After all, we did sit together and ate together, two and two, like friends.'

He began hurriedly, 'Turn to the left at the cross-roads, then across the fields as far as Gregor's cottage . . .'

The captain made a sign that he did not understand.

He thought: 'Perhaps they will lose their way and make a fuss; then they will come back to the cottage and eat the meat. I will go with them as far as the cross-roads.'

They crept down the road, passed the clump of pine-trees which came out in a point beside the brook, and went along the valley on the slippery stones. A large block of ice lay across the brook, shaped like a silver plough; the waves surrounded it as with golden crescents. The snow creaked under the soldiers' feet. Yakób walked beside them on his sandals, like a silent ghost.

'Now keep straight on as far as the cross,' he said, pointing to a dark object with a long shadow.

'I can't see anything,' said the captain.

He accompanied them as far as the cross, by the side of which stood a little shrine; the wan saint was wearing a crown of icicles.

From that point the village could be seen across the fields. Yakób discovered that the chain of lights which he had observed earlier in the evening, had come down from the mountains, for it now seemed to be close to the village.

Silence reigned in the sleeping world, every step could be heard.

This silence filled Yakób's heart with a wild fear; he turned round with a feeling of helplessness and looked back at his cottage. Probably the fire was now going out; a red glow appeared and disappeared on the windows.

Beyond the cross the road lay through low-lying ground, and was crossed by another road which led abruptly downwards into fields.

Yakób hesitated.

'Come on, old man, come on,' they called to him, and walked on without waiting for his answer.

The Cossacks dug their heels into the rugged ice of the road, and tumbled about in all directions. They had left their horses at the cross-roads. Each one kept a close hold on his gun, so that there should be no noise. They were whispering to each other; it sounded as if a congregation were murmuring their prayers. Yakób led them, and mentally he held fast to every bush, every lump of ice, saying to himself at every step that now he was going to leave them, they could not miss the road now. But he was afraid.

They no longer whispered, they had become taciturn as they pushed onwards, stumbling, breathing hard.

'As far as Gregor's cottage, and then no more!'

The effect of the drink was passing off. He rubbed his eyes, drew his rags across his chest. 'What was he doing, leading these people about on this night?'

He suddenly stopped where the field-road crossed theirs; the soldiers in front and behind threw themselves down. It was as if the ground had swallowed them.

A black horse was standing in the middle of the road, with extended nostrils. Its black mane, covered with hoar-frost, was tossed about its head; the saddle-bags, which were fur-lined, swung in the breeze; large dark drops were falling from its leg to the ground.

'Damn it!' cursed the captain.

The horse looked meekly at them, and stretched its head forward submissively. Yakób was sorry for the creature; perhaps one could do something for it. He stood still beside it, and again pointed out the road.

THE SENTENCE

'I have done enough, I shan't go any further!' He scratched his head and smiled, thinking that this was a good opportunity for escape.

'Come on,' hissed the captain so venomously in his ear that he marched forward without delay; they followed.

A dull fear mixed with resentment gripped him with terrible force. He now ran at the head like a sheep worried by watch-dogs.

They stopped in front of the cottage, silent, breathless, expectant.

Yakób looked at his companions with boundless astonishment. Their faces under their fur-caps had a tense, cruel look, their brows were wrinkled, their eyes glittered.

From all sides other Cossacks were advancing.

He noticed only now that there were some lying concealed behind the fence on the straw in a confused mass.

He shuddered; thick drops of perspiration stood on his forehead. The beating of his heart filled his head like the noise of a hammer, it seemed to fill everything. In spite of the feeling that he was being forced to do this thing, he again heard the voice calling: 'Yakób, Yakób!'

Up the hillock where Gregor's cottage stood, they advanced on all fours.

He clambered upwards, thinking of his wife, and of the cow he had loosed. Fear veiled his eyes, he saw black spots dancing.

Gregor's cottage was empty as a graveyard. It had been abandoned; the open doors creaked on their hinges. Under the window stood a cradle, covered with snow.

Silently the soldiers surrounded the cottage, and Yakób went with them, as though mesmerized by terror, mute and miserable.

They had hardly got round, when a red glow shot up from the other side of the village. The soldiers threw themselves down in the snow.

The thundering of guns began on all sides; blood-red lights came flying overhead. An appalling noise broke out, reinforced by the echo from the mountains, as though the whole world were going to perish. The Cossacks advanced, trembling.

Yakób advanced with them, for the captain had hit him across the head. He saw stars when he received the blow, gesticulated wildly, and staggered along the road.

He could distinguish the road running out from the forest like a silver thread. As they advanced, they came under a diabolically heavy rifle fire; bullets were raining upon them from all sides.

Here and there he heard moans already, when one of the soldiers fell bleeding on the snow. Close to him fell the young Cossack who had given him the muffler and breeches. He held out his hand, groaning. Yakób wanted to stop, but the captain would not let him, but rapped him over the head again with his knuckles.

The soldiers lay in heaps. The rest wavered, fell back, hid in the ditch or threw themselves down. The rifle-fire came nearer, the outlines and the faces of the advancing enemy could already be distinguished. Another blow on the head stretched Yakób to the ground, and he feigned death. The Cossacks retreated, the others advanced, and he understood that they belonged to his friends.

When he got up, he was immediately surrounded by them, taken by the scruff of the neck and so violently shaken, that he tumbled on his knees.

Gunfire was roaring from the mountains, shadows of soldiers flitted past him, the wounded Cossacks groaned in the snow. Young, well-nourished looking men were bending over him. Looking up into their faces, he crossed his hands over his chest and laughed joyfully.

'Ah, those Russians, those Russians . . . the villains!' he croaked, 'aho, aho, ho hurlai!' He rolled his tear-filled eyes.

Things were happening thick and fast. From where the chimney stood close to the water, near the manor-house, the village was burning. He could feel the heat and soot and hear the shouting of the crowd through the noise of the gunfire. Now he would see his wife and children again, the friendly soldiers surely had saved them. The young Cossack was still struggling on the ground; now he stretched himself out for his eternal sleep.

'Ah, the villains!' Yakób repeated; the great happiness which filled his heart rushed to his lips in incoherent babblings. 'The villains, they have served me nicely!'

He felt his bleeding head, crouched on his heels and got up. The fleshy red faces were still passing close to him, breathing harder and harder. Fear rose and fell in him like the flames of the burning village; again everything was swallowed up in indescribable noise.

Suddenly Yakób began to sob; he threw himself down at the soldiers' feet and wept bitterly, as though he would weep out his soul and the marrow of his bones.

They lifted him up, almost unconscious, and took him along the high road, under escort with fixed bayonets. His tears fell fast upon the snow, and thus he came into his own village, among his own people, pale as a corpse, with poison in his heart.

He looked dully at the blazing wooden church-spire where it stood enveloped in flames as though wrapped in an inflated glittering cloak. Dully he let his eyes wander over the hedges and fences; everything seemed unreal, as things seen across a distant wave or a downpour of rain, out of reach and strange.

He was standing where the field-path joined the high road. The soldiers sat down on a heap of stones and lighted their cigarettes.

Yakób, trembling all over, looked at his own black shadow; fugitives

THE SENTENCE

arrived from the burning village and swarmed past him; the rifle fire now sounded from the direction of the mountains.

Suddenly Gregor's cottage burst into flames. A blood-red glow inflated the clouds of smoke, trembled on the snow and ran over the pine-trees like gold.

Soldiers were arriving from that direction, streaming with blood, supported by their comrades.

Yakób stood motionless, looking at his shadow; fear was burning within him. He looked at the sky above the awful chaos on the earth, and became calmer. He tried to remember how it had all happened.

They had come, had given him food. His wife and children were probably safe in the manor-house. Blinking his swollen eyelids, he tried to deceive himself, crouched down near the guard who was smoking, and asked him for fire. His fear miraculously disappeared.

He began to talk rapidly to the soldier: 'I was sitting . . . the wind was moaning . . .' he told him circumstantially how he was sitting, what he had been thinking, how the shots had struck his cottage.

The soldier put his rifle between his knees, crossed his hands over his sleeves, spat out and sighed.

'But you have had underhand dealings with the Russians.'

'No . . . no.'

'Tell that to another.'

'I shall,' replied Yakób calmly.

'And who showed them the way?'

'Who?' said Yakób.

'Who showed them the way over here? Or did they find it on the map?'

'Yes, on the map,' assented Yakób, as though he were quite convinced.

'Well, who did?' said the soldier, wagging his head.

'Who?' repeated Yakób like an echo.

'I suppose it wasn't I?' said the soldier.

'I?' asked Yakób.

The other three soldiers approached inquisitively to where Yakób was crouching.

'A nice mess you've made,' one of them said, pointing to the wounded who were arriving across the fields. 'Do you understand?'

Yakób fixed his eyes on the soldiers' boots, and would not look in that direction. But he could not understand what it all meant . . . all this noise, and the firing that ran from hill to hill.

'Nice mess this you've made, old man.'

'Yes.'

'You!'

Yakób looked up at them, and had the sensation of being deep down at the bottom of a well instead of crouching at their feet.

'That is a lie, a lie, a lie!' he cried, beating his chest; his hair stood on end. The soldiers sat down in a row on the stones. They were young, cold, tired.

'But now they'll play the deuce with you.'

'Why?' said Yakób softly, glancing sideways at them.

'You're an old ass,' remarked one of them.

'But,' he began again, 'I was sitting, looking at the snow. . . .'

He had a great longing to talk to them, they looked as if they would understand, although they were so young.

'I was sitting . . . give me some fire . . . do you come from these parts yourselves?'

They did not answer.

He thought of his cottage, the bread and sausage, the black horse at the cross-roads.

'They beat me,' he sobbed, covering his face with his rags.

The soldiers shrugged their shoulders: 'Why did you let them?'

'O . . . o . . . o!' cried the old man. But tears would no longer wash away a conviction which was taking possession of him, searing his soul as the flames seared the pines.

'Why did you let them? Aren't you ashamed of yourself?'

No, he was not ashamed of himself for that. But that he had shown them the way . . . the way they had come by . . . what did it all mean? All his tears would not wash away this conviction: that he had shown them the way . . . the way they had come by.

Guns were thundering from the hills, the village was burning, the mill was burning . . . a black mass of people was surrounding him. More and more wounded came in from the fields, covered with grey mud. The flying sparks from the mill fell at his feet.

A detachment of soldiers was returning.

'Get up, old man,' cried his guard; 'we're off!'

Yakób jumped to his feet, hitched up his trousers, and went off perplexed, under cover of four bayonets that seemed to carry a piece of sky between them like a starred canopy.

His fear grew as he approached the village. He did not see the familiar cottages and hedges; he felt as though he were moving onwards without a goal. Moving onwards and yet not getting any farther. Moving onwards and yet hoping not to get to the end of the journey.

He sucked his pipe and paid no attention to anything; but the village was on his conscience.

The fear which filled his heart was not like that which he had felt when the Cossacks arrived, but a senseless fear, depriving him of sight and hearing . . . as though there were no place for him in the world.

THE SENTENCE

'Are we going too fast?' asked the guard hearing Yakób's heavy breathing.

'All right, all right,' he answered cheerfully. The friendly words had taken his fear away.

'Take it easy,' said the soldier. 'We will go more slowly. Here's a dry cigarette, smoke.'

Without turning round, he offered Yakób a cigarette, which he put behind his ear.

They entered the village. It smelt of burning, like a gipsy camp. The road seemed to waver in the flickering of the flames, the wind howled in the timber.

Yakób looked at the sky. Darkness and stars melted into one.

He would not look at the village. He knew there were only women and children in the cottages, the men had all gone. This thought was a relief to him, he hardly knew why.

Meanwhile the detachment of soldiers, instead of going to the manor-house, had turned down a narrow road which led to the mill. They stopped and formed fours. Every stone here was familiar to Yakób, and yet, standing in the snow up to his knees, he was puzzled as to where he was. If he could only sleep off this nightmare . . . he did not recognize the road . . . the night was far advanced, and the village not asleep as usual . . . if they would only let him go home!

He would return to-morrow.

The mill was burning out. Cinders were flying across from the granaries; the smoke bit into the eyes of the people who were standing about looking upwards, with their arms crossed.

Everything showed up brilliantly in the glare; the water was dripping from rung to rung of the silent wheel, and mixed its sound with that of the fire.

The adjoining buildings were fenced round with a small running fire; smoke whirled round the tumbling roof like a shock of hair shot through with flames. The faces of the bystanders assumed a metallic glow.

The wails of the miller and his family could be heard through the noise of battle, of water, and of fire.

It was as if the crumbling walls, the melting joints, the smoke, the cries were dripping down the wheel, transformed into blood, and were carried down by the black waves and swallowed up in the infinite abyss of the night.

'They beat me. . . .' Yakób justified himself to himself, when the tears rose to his eyes again. No tears could wash away the conviction that it was he who had shown them the way by which they had come.

The first detachment was waiting for the arrival of the second. It arrived, bringing in prisoners, Cossacks. A large number of them were being marched along; they did not walk in order but irregularly, like tired peasants. They were laughing, smoking cigarettes, and pushing against each other. Among them were those who had come to his cottage; he recognized the captain and others.

When they saw Yakób they waved their hands cordially and called out to him, 'Old man, old man!'

Yakób did not reply; he shrunk into himself. Shame filled his soul. He looked at them vacantly. His forehead was wrinkled as with a great effort to remember something, but he could think of nothing but a huge millwheel turning under red, smooth waves. Suddenly he remembered: it was the young Cossack who had given him his brother's clothes.

'The other one,' he shouted, pointing to his muffler, 'where did you leave him?'

Soldiers came between them and pushed the crowd away.

There was a terrific crash in the mill; a thick red cloud rushed upwards, dotted with sparks. Under this cloud an ever-increasing mass of people was flocking towards the spot where Yakób was; they were murmuring, pulling the soldiers by their cloaks. Women, children, and old men pressed in a circle round him, gesticulating, shouting: 'It was he . . . he . . . he!'

Words were lost in the chaos of sounds, faces became merely a dense mass, above which fists were flung upwards like stones.

Yakób tripped about among the soldiers like a fawn in a cage, raised and lowered his head, and clutched his rags; he could not shut his quivering mouth, and from his breast came a cry like the sob of a child.

The crowd turned upon him with fists and nails; he hid his face in his rags, stopped his ears with his fingers, and shook his head.

The prisoners had been dispatched, and it was Yakób's turn to be taken before the officer in command of the battalion.

'Say that I . . . that I . . .' Yakób entreated his guard.

'What are you in such a hurry for?'

'Say that I . . .'

The soldiers were sitting round a camp-fire, piling up the faggots. Soup was boiling in a cauldron.

'Say that I . . .' he begged again, standing in the thick smoke.

At last he was taken into the school-house.

The officer in command stood in the middle of the room with a cigarette between his fingers.

'I . . . I . . .' groaned Yakób, already in the door. His dishevelled hair made him look like a sea-urchin; his face was quite disfigured with black marks of violence; behind his bleeding left ear still stuck the cigarette. His swollen upper lip was drawn sideways and gave him the expression of a ghastly smile. His eyes looked out helpless, dispirited, from his swollen lids.

'What do you want to say?' asked the officer, without looking at him. Something suddenly came over him.

'It was I,' he said hoarsely.

The soldier made his report.

'They gave me food,' Yakób said, 'and this muffler and breeches, and they beat me.'

'It was you who showed them the way?'

'It was.'

'You did show them the way?'

He nodded.

'Did they beat you in the cottage?'

Yakób hesitated. 'In the cottage we were having supper.'

'They beat you afterwards, on the way?'

He again hesitated, and looked into the officer's eyes. They were clear, calm eyes. The guard came a step nearer.

The officer looked down, turned towards the window and asked more gently: 'You had supper together in the cottage. Then you went out with them. Did they beat you on the way?'

He turned suddenly and looked at Yakób. The peasant stood, looked at the grey snowflakes outside the window, and his face, partly black, partly pallid, wrinkled in deep folds.

'Well, what have you got to say?'

'It was I . . .' This interrogation made him alternately hot and cold.

'You who beat them, and not they who beat you?' laughed the officer.

'The meat is still there in the cottage, and here is what they gave me,' he said, holding up the muffler and tobacco.

The officer threw his cigarette away and turned on his heel. Yakób's eyes became dull, his arm with the muffler dropped.

The officer wrote an order. 'Take him away.'

They passed the schoolmaster and some women and soldiers in the passage.

'Well . . . well . . .' they whispered, leaning against the wall.

The guard made a sign with his hand. Yakób, behind him, looked dully into the startled faces of the bystanders.

'How frightened he looks . . . how they have beaten him . . . how frightened he looks!' they murmured.

He put the muffler round his neck again, for he felt cold.

'That's him, that's him,' growled the crowd outside.

The manor-house was reached. The light from the numerous windows fell upon horses and gun-carriages drawn up in the yard.

'What do you want?' cried the sentry to the crowd, pushing them back.

He nodded towards Yakób. 'Where is he to go?'

'That sort . . .' murmured the crowd. Yakób's guard delivered his order. They stopped in the porch. The pillars threw long shadows which lost themselves towards the fence and across the waves of the stream beyond, in the darkness of the night.

The heat in the waiting-room was overpowering. This was the room where the bailiff had so often given him his pay. The office no longer existed. Soldiers were lying asleep everywhere.

They passed on into a brilliantly lighted room. The staff was quartered there. The general took a few steps across the room, murmured something and stood still in front of Yakób.

'Ah, that is the man?' he turned and looked at Yakób with his blue eyes that shot glances quick as lightning from under bushy grey eyebrows.

'It was I,' ejaculated Yakób hoarsely.

'It was you who showed them the way?'

Yakób became calmer. He felt he would be able to make himself more quickly understood here. 'It was.'

'You brought them here?'

'Yes.'

He passed his hand over his hair and shrank into himself again. He looked at the brilliant lights.

'Do you know what is the punishment for that?'

The general came a step nearer; Yakób felt overawed by the feeling of strength and power that emanated from him. He was choking. Yes, he understood and yet did not understand.

'What have you got to say for yourself?'

'We had supper together . . .' he began, but stopped, for the general frowned and eyed him coldly. Yakób looked towards the window and listened to hear the sound of wind and waves. The general was still looking at him, and so they stood for a moment which seemed an eternity to Yakób, the man in the field-grey uniform who looked as if he had been sculptured in stone, and the quailing, shrunken, shivering form, covered with dirt and rags. Yakób felt as though a heavy weight were resting on him. Then both silently looked down.

'Take him back to the battalion.'

The steely sound of the command moved something in the souls of the soldiers, and took the enjoyment of their sleep from them.

They returned to the school-house. The crowd, as though following a thief caught in the act, ran by their side again.

They found room for the old man in a shed, some one threw him a blanket. Soldiers were sleeping in serried ranks. Their heavy breathing mixed with the sound of wind and waves, and the cold blue light of the moon embraced everything.

151

The Sentence

Yakób buried himself in the straw, looked out through a hole in the boarding and wept bitterly.

'What are you crying for?' asked the sentry outside, and tapped his shoulder with his gun.

Yakób did not answer.

'Thinking of your wife?' the soldier gossiped, walking up and down outside the shed. 'You're old, what good is your wife to you?' The soldier stopped and stretched his arms till the joints cracked.

'Or your children? Never mind, they'll get on in the world without a helpless old man like you.'

Yakób was silent, and the soldier crouched down near him.

'Old man, you ought . . .'

'No . . .' tremblingly came from the inside.

'You see,' the soldier paced up and down again, 'you are thinking of your cottage. I can understand that. But do you think the cottage will be any worse off for your death?'

The soldier's simple and dour words outside in the blue night, his talk of Yakób's death, of his own death which might come at any moment, slowly brought sleep to Yakób.

In the morning he woke with a start. The sun was shining on the snow, the mountains glittered like glass. The trees on the slopes were covered with millions of shining crystals; freshness floated between heaven and earth. Yakób stepped out of the shed, greeted the sentry and sat down on the boards, blinking his eyes.

The air was fresh and cold, tiny atoms of hoar-frost were flying about. Yakób felt the sun's warmth thawing his limbs, caressing him. He let himself be absorbed into the pure, rosy morning.

Doors creaked, and voices rang out clear and fresh. Opposite to him a squadron of Uhlans were waiting at the farrier's, who came out, black as a charcoal-burner, and chatted with them. They were laughing, their eyes shone. From inside the forge the hammer rang out like a bell. Yakób held his head in his hand and listened. At each stroke he shut his eyes. The soldiers brought him a cup of hot coffee; he drank it and lighted his pipe.

The murmuring of the brook, punctuated by the hammer-strokes, stimulated his thoughts till they became clearer, limpid as the stream.

'It was I . . . it was I . . .' he silently confided to all the fresh voices of the morning.

The guard again took him away with fixed bayonets. He knew where he was going. They would go through the village and stop at the wall of the cemetery.

The sky was becoming overcast, the beauty of the morning was waning. They called at the school-house for orders. Yakób remained outside the open window.

'I won't . . .' he heard a voice.

'Nor I . . .' another.

Yakób leant against the fence, supported his temples on his fists and watched the snow-clouds and mists.

A feeling of immense, heavy weariness came over him, and made him limp. He could see the ruins of the mill, the tumbled-down granaries, the broken doors. The water trickled down the wheel; smoke and soot were floating on the water, yet the water flowed on.

Guilty . . . not guilty. . . . What did it all matter?

'Do you hear?' he asked of the water. 'Do you hear?' he asked of his wife and children and his little property.

They took him here and they took him there. They made him wait outside houses, and he sat down on the steps as if he had never been used to anything else. He picked up a dry branch and gently tapped the snow with it and waited. He waited as in a dream, going round and round the wish that it might all be over soon.

While he was waiting, the crowd amused themselves with shaking their fists at him; he was thankful that his wife seemed to have gone away to the town and did not see him.

At last his guard went off in a bad temper. A soldier on horseback remained with him.

'Come on, old man,' he said, 'no one will have anything to do with it.'

Yakób glanced at him; the soldier and his horse seemed to be towering above the cottages, above the trees of the park with their flocks of circling crows. He looked into the far distance.

'It was I.'

'You're going begging, old man.'

Again they began their round, and behind them followed the miller's wife and other women. His legs were giving way, as though they were rushes. He took off his cap and gave a tired look in the direction of his cottage.

At last they joined a detachment which was starting off on the old road. They went as far as Gregor's cottage, then to the cross-roads, and in single file down the path. From time to time isolated gunshots rang out.

They sat down by the side of a ditch.

'We've got to finish this business,' said the sergeant, and scratched his head. 'No one would come forward voluntarily . . . I have been ordered. . . .'

The soldiers looked embarrassed and drew away, looking at Yakób.

He hid his head between his knees, and his thoughts dwelt on everything, sky, water, mountains, fire.

THE SENTENCE

His heart was breaking; a terrible sweat stood on his brows.
Shots rang out.
A deep groan escaped from Yakób's breast, a groan like a winter-wind.
He sprang up, stood on the edge of the ditch, sighed with all the strength
of his old breast and fell like a branch.
Puffs of smoke rose from the ditch and from the forests.

A. E. Coppard

Arabesque: the Mouse

In the main street amongst tall establishments of mart and worship was a high narrow house pressed between a coffee factory and a bootmaker's. It had four flights of long dim echoing stairs, and at the top, in a room that was full of the smell of dried apples and mice, a man in the middle age of life had sat reading Russian novels until he thought he was mad. Late was the hour, the night outside black and freezing, the pavements below empty and undistinguishable when he closed his book and sat motionless in front of the glowing but flameless fire. He felt he was very tired, yet he could not rest. He stared at a picture on the wall until he wanted to cry; it was a colour-print by Utamaro of a suckling child caressing its mother's breasts as she sits in front of a black-bound mirror. Very chaste and decorative it was, in spite of its curious anatomy. The man gazed, empty of sight though not of mind, until the sighing of the gas-jet maddened him. He got up, put out the light, and sat down again in the darkness trying to compose his mind before the comfort of the fire. And he was just about to begin a conversation with himself when a mouse crept from a hole in the skirting near the fireplace and scurried into the fender. The man had the crude dislike for such sly nocturnal things, but this mouse was so small and bright, its antics so pretty, that he drew his feet carefully from the fender and sat watching it almost with amusement. The mouse moved along the shadows of the fender, out upon the hearth, and sat before the glow, rubbing its head, ears and tiny belly with its paws, as if it were bathing itself with the warmth, until, sharp and sudden, the fire sank, an ember fell, and the mouse flashed into its hole.

The man reached forward to the mantelpiece and put his hand upon a pocket lamp. Turning on the beam, he opened the door of a cupboard beside the fireplace. Upon one of the shelves there was a small trap baited with cheese, a trap made with a wire spring, one of those that smashed down to break the back of ingenuous and unwary mice.

'Mean – so mean,' he mused, 'to appeal to the hunger of any living thing just in order to destroy it.'

He picked up the empty trap as if to throw it in the fire.

'I suppose I had better leave it, though – the place swarms with them.' He still hesitated. 'I hope that little beastie won't go and do anything foolish.' He put the trap back quite carefully, closed the door of the cupboard, sat down again and extinguished the lamp.

Was there anyone else in the world so squeamish and foolish about such things! Even his mother, mother so bright and beautiful, even she had laughed at his childish horrors. He recalled how once in his child-hood, not long after his sister Yosine was born, a friendly neighbour had sent him home with a bundle of dead larks tied by the feet 'for supper'. The pitiful inanimity of the birds had brought a gush of tears; he had run weeping home and into the kitchen, and there he had found the strange thing doing. It was dusk; mother was kneeling before the fire. He dropped the larks.

'Mother!' he exclaimed softly.

She looked at his tearful face.

'What's the matter, Filip?' she asked, smiling too, at his astonishment.

'Mother! What are you doing?'

Her bodice was open and she was squeezing her breasts; long thin streams of milk spurted into the fire with a plunging noise.

'Weaning your little sister,' laughed mother. She took his inquisitive face and pressed it against the delicate warmth of her bosom, and he forgot the dead birds behind him.

'Let me do it, Mother,' he cried, and doing so he discovered the throb of the heart in his mother's breast. Wonderful it was for him to experience it, although she could not explain it to him.

'Why does it do that?'

'If it did not beat, little son, I should die and the Holy Father would take me from you.'

'God?'

She nodded. He put his hand upon his own breast. 'Oh feel it, Mother!' he cried. Mother unbuttoned his little coat and felt the gentle *tick tick* with her warm palm.

'Beautiful!' she said.

'Is it a good one?'

She kissed his smiling lips. 'It is good if it beats truly. Let it always beat truly, Filip; let it always beat truly.'

There was the echo of a sigh in her voice, and he had divined some grief, for he was very wise. He kissed her bosom in his tiny ecstasy and whispered soothingly: 'Little Mother! Little Mother!' In such joys he forgot his horror of the dead larks; indeed he helped mother to pluck them and spit them for supper.

It was a black day that succeeded, and full of tragedy for the child. A great bay horse with a tawny mane had knocked down his mother in the lane, and a heavy cart had passed over her, crushing both her hands. She was borne away moaning with anguish to the surgeon who cut off the two hands. She died in the night. For years the child's dreams were filled with the horror of the stumps of arms bleeding unendingly. Yet he had never seen them, for he was sleeping when she died.

While this old woe was come vividly before him he again became aware of the mouse. His nerves stretched upon him in repulsion, but he soon relaxed to a tolerant interest, for it was really a most engaging little mouse. It moved with curious staccato scurries, stopping to rub its head or flicker with its ears; they seemed almost transparent ears. It spied a red cinder and skipped innocently up to it . . . sniffing . . . sniffing . . . until it jumped back scorched. It would crouch as a cat does, blinking in the warmth, or scamper madly as if dancing, and then roll upon its side rubbing its head with those pliant paws. The melancholy man watched it until it came at last to rest and squatted meditatively upon its haunches, hunched up, looking curiously wise, a pennyworth of philosophy; then once more the coals sank with a rattle and again the mouse was gone.

The man sat on before the fire and his mind filled again with unaccountable sadness. He had grown into manhood with a burning generosity of spirit and rifts of rebellion in him that proved too exacting for his fellows and seemed mere wantonness to men of casual rectitudes. 'Justice and Sin,' he would cry, 'Property and Virtue – incompatibilities! There can be no sin in a world of justice, no property in a world of virtue!' With an engaging extravagance and a certain clear-eyed honesty of mind he had put his two and two together and seemed then to rejoice, as in some topsy-turvy dream, in having rendered unto Caesar, as you might say, the things that were due to Napoleon! But this kind of thing could not pass unexpiated in a world of men having an infinite regard to Property and a pride in their traditions of Virtue and Justice. They could indeed forgive him his sins, but they could not forgive him his compassions. So he had to go seek for more melodious-minded men and fair unambiguous women. But rebuffs can deal more deadly blows than daggers; he became timid – a timidity not of fear but of pride – and grew with the years into misanthropy, susceptible to trivial griefs and despairs, a vessel of emotion that emptied as easily as it filled, until he came at last to know that his griefs were half deliberate, his despairs half unreal, and to live but for beauty – which is tranquillity – to put her wooing hand upon him.

Now, while the mouse hunts in the cupboard, one fair recollection stirs in the man's mind – of Cassia and the harmony of their only meeting, Cassia who had such rich red hair, and eyes, yes, her eyes were full of starry inquiry like the eyes of mice. It was so long ago that he had forgotten how he came to be in it, that unaccustomed orbit of vain vivid things – a village festival, all oranges and hoop-la. He could not remember how he came to be there, but at night, in the court hall, he had danced with Cassia – fair and unambiguous indeed – who had come like the wind from among the roses and swept into his heart.

'It is easy to guess,' he had said to her, 'what you like most in the world.'

She laughed. 'To dance? Yes, and you . . . ?'

'To find a friend.'

'I know, I know,' she cried, caressing him with recognitions. 'Ah, at times I quite love my friends – until I begin to wonder how much they hate me!'

He had loved at once that cool pale face, the abundance of her strange hair as light as the autumn's clustered bronze, her lilac dress and all the sweetness about her like a bush of lilies. How they had laughed at the two old peasants whom they had overheard gabbling of trifles like sickness and appetite!

'There's a lot of nature in a parsnip,' said one, a fat person of the kind that swells grossly when stung by a bee, 'a lot of nature when it's young, but when it's old it's like everything else.'

'True it is.'

'And I'm very fond of vegetables, yes, and I'm very fond of bread.'

'Come out with me,' whispered Cassia to Filip, and they walked out in the blackness of midnight into what must have been a garden.

'Cool it is here,' she said, 'and quiet, but too dark even to see your face – can you see mine?'

'The moon will not rise until after dawn,' said he, 'it will be white in the sky when the starlings whistle in your chimney.'

They walked silently and warily about until they felt the chill of the air. A dull echo of the music came to them through the walls, then stopped, and they heard the bark of a fox away in the woods.

'You are cold,' he whispered, touching her bare neck with timid fingers. 'Quite, quite cold,' drawing his hand tenderly over the curves of her chin and face. 'Let us go in,' he said, moving with discretion from the rapture he desired.

'We will come out again,' said Cassia.

But within the room the ball was just at an end, the musicians were packing up their instruments and the dancers were flocking out and homewards, or to the buffet which was on a platform at one end of the room. The two old peasants were there, munching hugely.

'I tell you,' said one of them, 'there's nothing in the world for it but the grease of an owl's liver. That's it, that's it! Take something on your stomach now, just to offset the chill of the dawn!'

Filip and Cassia were beside them, but there were so many people crowding the platform that Filip had to jump down. He stood then looking up adoringly at Cassia, who had pulled a purple cloak around her.

'For Filip, Filip, Filip,' she said, pushing the last bite of her sandwich into his mouth, and pressing upon him her glass of Loupiac. Quickly he drank it with a great gesture, and, flinging the glass to the wall, took Cassia into his arms, shouting, 'I'll carry you home, the whole way home, yes, I'll carry you!'

'Put me down!' she cried, beating his head and pulling his ear, as they passed among the departing dancers. 'Put me down, you wild thing!'

Dark, dark was the lane outside, and the night an obsidian net, into which he walked carrying the girl. But her arms were looped around him; she discovered paths for him, clinging more tightly as he staggered against a wall, stumbled upon a gulley, or when her sweet hair was caught in the boughs of a little lime tree.

'Do not loose me, Filip, will you? Do not loose me,' Cassia said, putting her lips against his temple.

His brain seemed bursting, his heart rocked within him, but he adored the rich grace of her limbs against his breast. 'Here it is,' she murmured, and he carried her into a path that led to her home in a little lawned garden where the smell of ripe apples upon the branches and the heavy lustre of roses stole upon the air. Roses and apples! Roses and apples! He carried her right into the porch before she slid down and stood close to him with her hands still upon his shoulders. He could breathe happily at the release, standing silent and looking round at the sky sprayed with wondrous stars but without a moon.

'You are stronger than I thought you, stronger than you look; you are really very strong,' she whispered, nodding her head to him. Opening the buttons of his coat, she put her palm against his breast.

'Oh, how your heart does beat! Does it beat truly – and for whom?'

He had seized her wrists in a little fury of love, crying, 'Little mother, little mother!'

'What are you saying?' asked the girl; but before he could continue there came a footstep sounding behind the door, and the clack of a bolt. . .

What was that? Was that really a bolt or was it . . . was it . . . the snap of the trap? The man sat up in his room intently listening, with nerves quivering again, waiting for the trap to kill the little philosopher. When he felt it was all over he reached guardedly in the darkness for the lantern, turned on the beam, and opened the door of the cupboard. Focusing the light upon the trap, he was amazed to see the mouse sitting on its haunches before it, uncaught. Its head was bowed, but its bead-like eyes were full of brightness, and it sat blinking, it did not flee.

'Shoosh!' said the man, but the mouse did not move.

'Why doesn't it go? Shoosh!' he said again, and suddenly the reason of the mouse's strange behaviour was made clear. The trap had not caught it completely, but it had broken off both its forefeet, and the thing crouched there holding out its two bleeding stumps humanely, too stricken to stir.

Horror flooded the man, and conquering his repugnance he plucked the mouse up quickly by the neck. Immediately the little thing fastened its teeth in his finger; the touch was no more than the slight prick of a pin. The man's impulse then exhausted itself. What should he do with it? He put his hand behind him, he dared not look, but there was nothing to be done except kill it at once, quickly, quickly. Oh, how should he do it? He bent towards the fire as if to drop the mouse into its quenching glow; but he paused and shuddered, he would hear its cries, he would have to listen. Should he crush it with finger and thumb? A glance towards the window decided him. He opened the sash with one hand and flung the wounded mouse far into the dark street. Closing the window with a crash, he sank into a chair, limp with pity too deep for tears.

So he sat for two minutes, five minutes, ten minutes. Anxiety and shame filled him with heat. He opened the window again, and the freezing air poured in and cooled him. Seizing his lantern, he ran down the echoing stairs, into the dark empty street, searching long and vainly for the little philosopher until he had to desist and return to his room, shivering, frozen to his very bones.

When he had recovered some warmth he took the trap from its shelf. The two feet dropped into his hand; he cast them into the fire. Then he once more set the trap and put it back carefully into the cupboard.

Luigi Pirandello

Cinci

The dog squatted there patiently on its hind legs, in front of the closed door, waiting for someone to open it and let him in. The nearest he came to protesting was to let out an occasional low whine, as he lifted a paw and scratched himself.

He was a dog, so he knew there was nothing more he could do.

When Cinci got back from afternoon school, with his textbooks and his exercise books all strapped together and tucked under his arm, he found the dog stuck there outside the door. It irritated him to see it waiting there, patiently like that, so he gave it a kick. Then he gave the door a good kicking, too, even though he knew it was locked and there was nobody at home. Finally, if only because he felt they were the worst of his burdens, he flung his bundle of books furiously against the door – just to get rid of them – as if he had some daft idea that they'd pass straight through the woodwork and land up in the house. Contrary to any such expectation, however, the door flung them straight back at his chest with the same force with which he'd hurled them originally. Cinci was quite surprised: it was as if this were some wonderful game that the door was suggesting they might play. So he threw the bundle back at the door. Then, since there were already three of them playing this game – Cinci, the bundle of books, and the door – the dog thought he'd join in as well. Every time Cinci slung the books at the door and every time they bounced back, he'd leap in the air, barking away. Several passers-by stopped to watch. A few of them smiled, almost ashamed of themselves, of course, because of the utter silliness of the game and because of the equal silliness of the dog, who was having such a riotous time. Others waxed highly indignant, because of the way those poor books were being treated. Books cost money, you know. People oughtn't to be allowed to treat them like that, with so little regard. Cinci brought the show to an end, dropped his bundle of books on the ground, and slumped to a sitting position by sliding his backbone down the wall. It had been his intention to sit on the books, but the bundle slid from under him and he landed on the ground with a sudden jolt. He gave a wry, comic grin and looked around, while the dog bounded back and eyed him speculatively.

All the devilment that passed through Cinci's mind was – well, you could almost see it written all over that untidy thatch of straw-coloured hair of his, and in those sharp green eyes, which seemed almost to be wriggling with life. He was at the awkward age, all gawky and sallow. He'd left his handkerchief at home when he'd gone back to school that afternoon. Now, as a consequence, he'd every so often give a snuffle, as he sat there on the ground. He drew his enormous knees up until they almost reached his chin. His huge legs were bare, because he was still wearing short trousers – and shouldn't have been. When he ran, his legs splayed out sideways. There wasn't a pair of shoes that could stand up to the treatment he meted out to them; the ones he had on then were right through already. He was bored stiff. He folded his arms round his knees, gave a huge, puffing sigh, and then dragged his spine up the wall again until he was standing upright once more. The dog got up too, and it was just as if he was asking, 'Well, where are we off to now?' Yes, where were we going? Out into the country, to have a snack? Knock off the odd fig or apple? It was an idea. He hadn't quite made up his mind, though.

The paved road ended at their house, and the cinder-path took over, and if you went on and on through their suburb you landed in the country. What a wonderful sensation it must be – if you were riding in a carriage, that is – when the horses' hooves and the carriage-wheels passed from the hard surface of the stridently noisy paving, to the soft, silent cinder-road. It's probably like what happens when the teacher who's been busy shouting your head off – oh, you've made him so angry! – starts talking to you gently, kindly, with a sort of resigned melancholy. You find it so much more agreeable, because it puts a safe distance between you and the punishment you were afraid you were in for. Yes, it would be a good idea to go into the country, to get away, out along the narrow stretch of road flanked by the last houses of this stinking suburb, down to where the road widened out into the little square that marked the end of the town. The new hospital was down there now, the walls of which were so freshly white-washed that when the sun was shining on them you had to shut your eyes, or you got blinded. In the last few days they'd been busy bringing down all the patients from the old hospital – ambulances and stretchers galore there'd been. It had been as good as a procession, as they all filed along. The ambulances in front, with all their curtains fluttering away at the windows, and then, for the more seriously ill patients, those lovely hammock-trolley things, bouncing along on their springs, like a lot of spiders' webs. It was pretty late now, though, and the sun was just about to set, so there wouldn't be the occasional convalescent patient up at one or other of the huge windows, wearing his grey nightshirt and his white nightcap, and sadly looking at the little old church opposite, as it stood there among a cluster of houses as old as itself and the odd tree or two. Once you'd left that little square, the road became a country-lane and went on up the side of the little hill.

Cinci stopped and gave another huge puffing sigh. Ought he to go? Really? He set off again in a resentful sort of way, because he was beginning to feel boiling away in his guts all the horrible feelings that kept welling up inside him because of so many things that he couldn't explain to himself. His mother, now: how did she live and what did she live on? Never at home, still stubbornly insisting on sending him to that damned school. Yes, that *damned* school – miles away from home it was! Every day he went there – and you had to run like hell for at least three-quarters of an hour to get there in time, from where they lived, out there on the outskirts, that is. Then another three-quarters of an hour sprint to get back home at midday; then another three-quarters of an hour to get back again, after he'd managed to bolt down a couple of mouthfuls – how the hell was he supposed to do it in the time? And his mother busy telling him that he wasted all his time playing with the dog, that he was an idle layabout. And, oh bloody hell! Always throwing the same old muck in his face: he didn't study, he always looked dirty, and if she sent him out to buy something at the shop, they always fobbed him off with any old rubbish.

Where was Fox?

There he was, trotting along behind him, poor little beast. Huh, at least he knew what he had to do: just follow his master. To do something. That's what all the frenzy of life's about – not knowing *what* to do. She could leave him the key, couldn't she – his mother, he meant – when she went off, as she did every day, to sew in gentlemen's houses? (That's what she told him she did.) Oh, no! She said he wasn't to be trusted, and that if she wasn't back by the time he got in from school, she couldn't possibly be long, and that he was to wait. Where? Outside the door, like a lemon? There'd been times when he'd waited for two whole hours, out in the cold – out in the rain, even. As a matter of fact, on *that* particular occasion, he'd deliberately not taken shelter, but had gone and stood under the overflow, so that when she came in she'd find him all sopping wet. Finally she'd appeared, all out of breath, her face flushed, and carrying a borrowed umbrella, her eyes bright, unable to meet his,

CINCI

and so nervy that she couldn't even find the key in her purse.

'Are you soaked? Shan't be a moment now. I had to stay late.'

Cinci frowned. There were certain things he preferred not to think about. He'd never known his father. They'd told him he was dead, that he'd died even before he was born. But they didn't tell him who he'd been. And now he no longer had any desire to know, or to ask any more questions. He might even have been that cripple, the one who was paralysed down one side, but who still managed to drag himself along to the pub, stout fellow. Fox used to rush up to him and bark at him. It was probably the crutch he didn't like. And look at those women standing around in a huddle – all that belly and not one of them pregnant. No, maybe one of them was. The one with her skirt hoicked up a good six inches at the front and sweeping the street behind. And that other one with the baby in her arms, fishing out a breast to—— *Ugh*! What a horrible blubbery mass of flesh! His mother was beautiful, and still very young, and when he'd been a baby, she'd given him milk from her breast, just like that. And perhaps it had been in a house in the country, or out in the sun, in the yard where they did the threshing. Cinci had a vague recollection of a house in the country. Perhaps it was there – always supposing he hadn't dreamt it – that he'd lived when he was a tiny child. Or perhaps he'd seen it somewhere when he was small. Heaven only knows where, though. Certainly now when, from a distance, he saw houses in the country, he felt that same sort of melancholy which you feel *must* come into those houses when it begins to get evening. When the lamps are lit – the sort you fill with paraffin and carry about in your hand from one room to another – and you see the light disappearing from one window and reappearing at another.

He'd reached the little square by this time. And now he could see the whole vast expanse of the sky. The last rays of the setting sun had disappeared and, over the now darkened hill, the sky was the tenderest of clear blues. The shadow of evening was already upon the earth, and the great white wall of the hospital was muted to a dull grey. The occasional old woman hurried along to the little church, late for Vespers. Cinci suddenly felt a desire to go in himself. Fox stood and looked at him. He knew perfectly well that he wasn't allowed into churches. In the church doorway the old woman who was late was panting and moaning away as she struggled with the leather curtain. It was far too heavy for her to cope with. Cinci helped her to hold it to one side but, instead of thanking him, she only gave him a nasty look. She'd realized only too clearly, of course, that he hadn't gone into that church for devotional reasons. The little church was freezing; cold as a cave. On the main altar two candles burned fitfully, while scattered here and there about the church there were a few dismayed-looking little oil-lamps. The dust of ages lay thick on everything in that little old church and, there in the crude dampness, the very dust itself had a smell of decay about it. And it was for all the world as if the shadow-filled silence were lying in ambush for the slightest noise, so that it could go crashing off into echo upon echo upon echo. Cinci felt a terrible temptation to let out a mighty yell, just to start all those echoes bounding about the place. The pious old dears had already filed into their pews. No, it wouldn't be a good idea to give a yell. But why not throw that bundle of books on to the ground? Well, they were awfully heavy, and they might quite well have dropped from his arm by sheer accident. . . . Why not? He hurled them to the ground, and instantly, the moment they hit the ground, the echoes came raining down upon him, thundering in his ears, crushing him beneath their weight – almost contemptuously. Cinci had often (and with very great relish) tried this experiment of raising echoes. He liked to feel the echo pouncing on a noise and crushing it to the ground, just like a dog that's been irked by something while he's asleep. There was no need for him to tempt the patience of those scandalized and pious old bodies any further, so he mooched out of the church, where he found Fox all ready to follow him, and off he set again along the road leading to the little hill. He felt the need to lay his hands on some fruit somewhere – something he could get his teeth into. Over the low wall he went, and hurled himself among the trees. He felt an enormous sense of tormented longing. But whether it was simply because of that frenzy which was biting into his guts, the frenzy to do something, he just couldn't say.

It was a country road, steep and lonely, strewn with pebbles that got caught by the hooves of passing donkeys, got sent rolling for a little way, and then – where they stopped, there they stayed. Look, there was one of them! He gave it a kick with the toe of his shoe. Go on, stone, enjoy yourself! Oh, it flies through the air with the greatest of ease . . . ! Grass was growing by the roadside and, at the foot of the low walls, long plumed stalks of oats which were very pleasant to chew on – when you'd stripped off the little plumes. They came off like a bouquet when you ran them through your fingers. Then you threw them at somebody, and the number of them that stuck on her (assuming she was a woman), was the number of husbands she was going to have – or, if it was a man, the number of wives. Cinci thought he'd try it out on Fox. Seven wives! No less than seven wives was his ration! It didn't really count, though, because they all stuck on Fox's black coat, the whole lot of them. And Fox, the silly old stupid, just stood there with his eyes shut! He didn't get the joke! There he was, with seven wives on his back.

Cinci didn't feel like going any farther. He was tired and he was bored. He swerved to the left and sat down on the low wall beside the road. And as he sat there he began to study the new moon, whose pale gold crescent was just beginning to gleam brightly through the green light that filled the sky in those last moments of sunset. He saw the moon and yet somehow he didn't see it – it was like so many things that were wandering through his mind, one thing merging into another, and every single one of them receding farther and farther away from that young body of his as it sat there, so motionless that he was no longer aware of it. If he'd caught sight then of his own hand on his knee, it would have seemed like a stranger's to him – just as his own leg would have done, as it dangled there, with his dirty, broken-down shoe at the end of it. He was no longer in his body. He was in all those things which he saw and didn't see: the sky that grew darker as the day died; the moon that was getting brighter and brighter; he was there in those gloomy clumps of trees, which stood so sharply in the empty air, and in the earth over there – the fresh, black, recently hoed earth, from which there still breathed that smell of damp, rotting vegetation, so characteristic of the sultry tedium of the end of October, when the days are still very warm and sunny.

While he was sitting there, completely absorbed, an extraordinary and unidentifiable *something* suddenly ran through his body, distracting him. Instinctively he raised his hand to his ear. A shrill little laugh came from behind the wall. A boy of about his own age, a well-built peasant lad, had been hiding behind it, on the field side. He too had plucked and stripped a long blade of oats for himself. He'd made a little noose at the top of it, and then, very, very quietly, he'd raised his arm and tried to hitch the noose over Cinci's ear. This annoyed Cinci, but the moment he turned round, the boy immediately gestured to him to shush, and held the blade of oats along the wall, towards where the head of a lizard was popping out from between a couple of stones. He'd been trying for the last hour to snare that lizard with his noose. Cinci leant backwards and down, anxiously trying to see what happened. Without realizing what it was doing, the little creature had popped its head into the noose which had been put there in the hope that it would be just so obliging. There was a long way to go yet, however. You had to wait till it stuck its head out a little farther. And it might well be that, instead of doing so, it would withdraw, especially if the hand which was holding the blade of oats trembled and so gave it warning of the ambush. At that very moment it might be on the point of darting out like an arrow, in order to escape from that refuge which had become a prison. Yes! Oh, yes! But you had to stand by, ready to give the jerk that would put the noose round its neck, just at the right moment. It was the work of an instant! There, he'd got it! The lizard was squirming like a fish at the end of that blade of oats. Cinci couldn't resist! He jumped down from the wall. But the other boy, afraid, perhaps, that he was planning to take over the little creature, whirled his arm round several times in the air, and smashed the lizard ferociously down again and again on a huge slab of stone that lay there among the weeds.

'No!' screamed Cinci, but it was too late. The lizard lay motionless on the slab of stone, with the white of its belly gleaming in the light of the moon. Cinci flew into a rage. Yes, he too had wanted that poor little creature to get caught, because he himself had for the moment been overpowered by that instinct to hunt which lurks insidiously in every single one of us. But to kill it like that, without even taking a close look at it; without looking into those eyes – those sharp, almost frantically sharp little eyes; without studying the steady rhythm of its sides as it breathed, and the whole trembling mass of its tiny green body. No, that had been stupid and utterly shameful! Cinci hurled himself at the boy, and punched him in the chest with all his might, sending him sprawling on the ground. He landed a little farther away than he might have done, because he'd been a bit off-balance when Cinci had hit him, and he'd tried and tried to prevent himself from falling. But, no sooner had he hit the ground, than he leapt up again, livid with fury, dug a clod of earth out of the ground and hurled it in Cinci's face. Cinci stood there for a moment, blinded by the dirt. The damp taste in his mouth only gave him a worse sense of outrage. He became like an animal in his fury. Now he grabbed a clod of earth, and hurled it back. The fight immediately became desperate. It was a duel now. The other boy was quicker on his feet, however, and a much more skilled fighter. He never missed. He moved in steadily, getting closer and closer, keeping up a bombardment with those clods of earth, which, even if they didn't actually injure Cinci still hit him pretty hard, as they rained down on him. It was like a hailstorm as they disintegrated with a thud on his chest or in his face. The dirt got in his hair, and in his eyes – even into his shoes. Choked with dirt, and completely at a loss to know how to defend himself or shield his body, Cinci, now quite beside himself with rage, leapt in the air, stretched out his arm, and snatched a stone from the top of the wall. He was vaguely aware that something scurried away – Fox, probably. He hurled the stone, and all of a sudden— How did it happen? Everything had been spinning round before. Sort of upside-down. Dancing in front of his eyes. Those clumps of trees. The moon, like a sliver of light in the sky. And now, nothing was moving any more. Almost as if Time itself, and everything else in the world too, were standing still in amazement and stupefaction at the sight of that boy stretched out there, face downwards on the ground.

Cinci, still panting, and with his heart in his mouth, gazed at it all in utter terror. His back against the wall, he gazed at the incredible, silent stillness of the countryside, with the moon high above. He gazed at that

CINCI

boy, lying there with his face half-hidden in the ground, and he felt growing within him, as a formidable reality, the sensation of an eternal solitude, from which he must immediately run away. It wasn't him! He hadn't wanted it to happen! He didn't know anything about it! And then, just as if he really hadn't done it, just as if he were simply going over to him out of curiosity, he took a step forward. Then another, and leant over him to have a look. The boy's head was bashed in, and his mouth was black where blood had dripped through it and on to the ground. You could see part of one of his legs, where his trousers had ridden up above the top of his cotton sock. He was dead, just as if he'd always been dead. Everything lay there, as if it were in a dream. He really must wake up, if he was to get away in time. Over there – just as if it were in a dream – that lizard, lying on its back on the stone, belly upwards to the moon, and with the blade of oats still hanging round its neck. Off he went, with his bundle of books under his arm once again, and Fox trotting along behind him. He didn't know anything about it either.

Gradually, as he went down the slope and moved farther and farther away from the spot, he got more and more the – yes, a strange feeling of being safe. So he didn't even bother to hurry. He reached the little square – it was quite deserted by this time. The moon was shining there too. It was another moon, though. One that didn't know anything at all about – things. It was busy lighting up the white façade of the hospital. He'd reached the road for their part of the suburb by this time, just like before. He reached home. His mother still hadn't got back. So he wouldn't even have to tell her where he'd been. He'd been there all the time, waiting for her. And this statement, which immediately became true as far as his mother was concerned, immediately became true as far as he himself was concerned. Yes, as a matter of fact, there he was, with his shoulders resting against the wall by the door.

It would be quite sufficient for all concerned, if he let her find him like that.

Dorothy L. Sayers

Suspicion

As the atmosphere of the railway carriage thickened with tobacco smoke, Mr Mummery became increasingly aware that his breakfast had not agreed with him.

There could have been nothing wrong with the breakfast itself. Brown bread, rich in vitamin content, as advised by the *Morning Star's* health expert; bacon fried to a delicious crispness; eggs just nicely set; coffee made as only Mrs Sutton knew how to make it. Mrs Sutton had been a real find, and that was something to be thankful for. For Ethel, since her nervous breakdown in the summer, had really not been fit to wrestle with the untrained girls who had come and gone in tempestuous succession. It took very little to upset Ethel nowadays, poor child. Mr Mummery, trying hard to ignore his growing internal discomfort, hoped he was not in for an illness. Apart from the trouble it would cause at the office, it would worry Ethel terribly, and Mr Mummery would cheerfully have laid down his rather uninteresting little life to spare Ethel a moment's uneasiness.

He slipped a digestive tablet into his mouth – he had taken lately to carrying a few tablets about with him – and opened his paper. There did not seem to be very much news. A question had been asked in the House about Government typewriters. The Prince of Wales had smilingly opened an all-British exhibition of footwear. A further split had occurred in the Liberal party. The police were still looking for the woman who was supposed to have poisoned a family in Lincoln. Two girls had been trapped in a burning factory. A film star had obtained her fourth decree nisi.

At Paragon Station, Mr Mummery descended and took a tram. The internal discomfort was taking the form of a definite nausea. Happily he contrived to reach his office before the worst occurred. He was seated at his desk, pale but in control of himself, when his partner came breezing in.

' 'Morning, Mummery,' said Mr Brookes in his loud tones, adding inevitably, 'cold enough for you?'

'Quite,' replied Mr Mummery. 'Unpleasantly raw, in fact.'

'Beastly, beastly,' said Mr Brookes. 'Your bulbs all in?'

'Not quite all,' confessed Mr Mummery. 'As a matter of fact I haven't been feeling—'

'Pity,' interrupted his partner. 'Great pity. Ought to get 'em in early. Mine were in last week. My little place will be a picture in the spring. For a town garden, that is. You're lucky, living in the country. Find it better than Hull, I expect, eh? Though we get plenty of fresh air up in the Avenues. How's the missus?'

'Thank you, she's very much better.'

'Glad to hear that, very glad. Hope we shall have her about again this winter as usual. Can't do without her in the Drama Society, you know. By Jove I shan't forget her acting last year in *Romance*. She and young Welbeck positively brought the house down, didn't they? The Welbecks were asking after her only yesterday.'

'Thank you, yes. I hope she will soon be able to take up her social activities again. But the doctor says she mustn't overdo it. No worry, he says – that's the important thing. She is to go easy and not rush about or undertake too much.'

'Quite right, quite right. Worry's the devil and all. I cut out worrying years ago and look at me! Fit as a fiddle, for all I shan't see fifty again. *You're* not looking altogether the thing, by the way.'

'A touch of dyspepsia,' said Mr Mummery. 'Nothing much. Chill on the liver, that's what I put it down to.'

'That's what it is,' said Mr Brookes, seizing his opportunity. 'Is life worth living? It depends upon the liver. Ha, ha! Well now, well now – we must do a spot of work, I suppose. Where's that lease of Ferraby's?'

Mr Mummery, who did not feel at his conversational best that morning, rather welcomed this suggestion, and for half an hour was allowed to proceed in peace with the duties of an estate agent. Presently, however, Mr Brookes burst into speech again.

'By the way,' he said abruptly, 'I suppose your wife doesn't know of a good cook, does she?'

'Well, no,' replied Mr Mummery. 'They aren't so easy to find nowadays. In fact, we've only just got suited ourselves. But why? Surely your old Cookie isn't leaving you?'

'Good lord, no!' Mr Brookes laughed heartily. 'It would take an earthquake to shake off old Cookie. No. It's for the Philipsons. Their girl's getting married. That's the worst of girls. I said to Philipson, "You mind what you're doing," I said. "Get somebody you know something about, or you may find yourself landed with this poisoning woman – what's her name – Andrews. Don't want to be sending wreaths to your funeral yet awhile," I said. He laughed, but it's no laughing matter and so I told him. What we pay the police for I simply don't know. Nearly a month now, and they can't seem to lay hands on the woman. All they say is, they think she's hanging about the neighbourhood and "may seek a situation as cook." As cook! Now I ask you!'

'You don't think she committed suicide, then?' suggested Mr Mummery.

'Suicide my foot!' retorted Mr Brookes coarsely. 'Don't you believe it, my boy. That coat found in the river was all eyewash. *They* don't commit suicide, that sort don't.'

'What sort?'

'Those arsenic maniacs. They're too damned careful of their own skins. Cunning as weasels, that's what they are. It's only to be hoped they'll manage to catch her before she tries her hand on anybody else. As I told Philipson—'

'You think Mrs Andrews did it, then?'

'Did it? Of course she did it. It's plain as the nose on your face. Looked after her old father, and he died suddenly – left her a bit of money, too. Then she keeps house for an elderly gentleman, and *he* dies suddenly. Now there's this husband and wife – man dies and woman taken very ill, of arsenic poisoning. Cook runs away, and you ask, did she do it? I don't mind betting that when they dig up the father and the other old bird they'll find *them* bung full of arsenic, too. Once that sort gets started, they don't stop. Grows on 'em, as you might say.'

'I suppose it does,' said Mr Mummery. He picked up his paper again and studied the photograph of the missing woman. 'She looks harmless enough,' he remarked. 'Rather a nice, motherly-looking kind of woman.'

'She's got a bad mouth,' pronounced Mr Brookes. He had a theory that character showed in the mouth. 'I wouldn't trust that woman an inch.'

As the day went on, Mr Mummery felt better. He was rather nervous about his lunch, choosing carefully a little boiled fish and custard pudding and being particular not to rush about immediately after the meal. To his great relief, the fish and custard remained where they were put, and he was not visited by that tiresome pain which had become almost habitual in the last fortnight. By the end of the day he became quite light-hearted. The bogey of illness and doctor's bills ceased to haunt him. He brought a bunch of bronze chrysanthemums to carry home to Ethel, and it was with a feeling of pleasant anticipation that he left the train and walked up the garden path of *Mon Abri*.

He was a little dashed by not finding his wife in the sitting-room. Still clutching the bunch of chrysanthemums he pattered down the passage and pushed open the kitchen door.

Nobody was there but the cook. She was sitting at the table with her back to him, and started up almost guiltily as he approached.

'Lor,' sir,' she said, 'you give me quite a start. I didn't hear the front door go.'

'Where is Mrs Mummery? Not feeling bad again, is she?'

'Well, sir, she's got a bit of a headache, poor lamb. I made her lay down and took her up a nice cup o' tea at half-past four. I think she's dozing nicely now.'

'Dear, dear,' said Mr Mummery.

'It was turning out the dining-room done it, if you ask me,' said Mrs Sutton. ' "Now, don't you overdo yourself, ma'am," I says to her, but you know how she is, sir. She gets that restless, she can't abear to be doing nothing.'

'I know,' said Mr Mummery. 'It's not your fault, Mrs Sutton. I'm sure you look after us both admirably. I'll just run up and have a peep at her. I won't disturb her if she's asleep. By the way, what are we having for dinner?'

'Well, I *had* made a nice steak-and-kidney pie,' said Mrs Sutton, in accents suggesting that she would readily turn it into a pumpkin or a coach and four if it was not approved of.

'Oh!' said Mr Mummery. 'Pastry? Well, I—'

'You'll find it beautiful and light,' protested the cook, whisking open the oven door for Mr Mummery to see. 'And it's made with butter, sir, you having said that you found lard indigestible.'

'Thank you, thank you,' said Mr Mummery. 'I'm sure it will be most excellent. I haven't been feeling altogether the thing just lately, and lard does not seem to suit me nowadays.'

'Well, it don't suit some people, and that's a fact,' agreed Mrs Sutton. 'I shouldn't wonder if you've got a bit of a chill on the liver. I'm sure this weather is enough to upset anybody.'

She bustled to the table and cleared away the picture paper which she had been reading.

'Perhaps the mistress would like her dinner sent up to her?' she suggested.

Mr Mummery said he would go and see, and tiptoed his way upstairs. Ethel was lying snuggled under the eiderdown and looked very small and fragile in the big double bed. She stirred as he came in and smiled up at him.

'Hullo, darling!' said Mr Mummery.

'Hullo! You back? I must have been asleep. I got tired and headachy, and Mrs Sutton packed me off upstairs.'

'You've been doing too much, sweetheart,' said her husband, taking her hand in his and sitting down on the edge of the bed.

'Yes – it was naughty of me. What lovely flowers, Harold. All for me?'

'All for you, Tiddleywinks,' said Mr Mummery tenderly. 'Don't I deserve something for that?'

Mrs Mummery smiled, and Mr Mummery took his reward several times over.

'That's quite enough, you sentimental old thing,' said Mrs Mummery. 'Run away, now, I'm going to get up.'

'Much better go to bed, my precious, and let Mrs Sutton send your dinner up,' said her husband.

Ethel protested, but he was firm with her. If she didn't take care of herself, she wouldn't be allowed to go to the Drama Society meetings. And everybody was so anxious to have her back. The Welbecks had been asking after her and saying that they really couldn't get on without her.

'Did they?' said Ethel with some animation. 'It's very sweet of them to want me. Well, perhaps I'll go to bed after all. And how has my old Hubby been all day?'

'Not too bad, not too bad.'

'No more tummyaches?'

'Well, just a *little* tummyache. But it's quite gone now. Nothing for Tiddleywinks to worry about.'

Mr Mummery experienced no more distressing symptoms the next day or the next. Following the advice of the newspaper expert, he took to drinking orange juice, and was delighted with the results of the treatment. On Thursday, however, he was taken so ill in the night that Ethel was alarmed and insisted on sending for the doctor. The doctor felt his pulse and looked at his tongue and appeared to take the matter lightly. An inquiry into what he had been eating elicited the fact that dinner had consisted of pig's trotters, followed by a milk pudding, and that, before retiring, Mr Mummery had consumed a large glass of orange juice, according to his new régime.

'There's your trouble,' said Dr Griffith cheerfully. 'Orange juice is an excellent thing, and so are trotters, but not in combination. Pig and oranges together are extraordinarily bad for the liver. I don't know why they should be, but there's no doubt that they are. Now I'll send you round a little prescription and you stick to slops for a day or two and keep off pork. And don't you worry about him, Mrs Mummery, he's as sound as a trout. *You're* the one we've got to look after. I don't want to see those black rings under the eyes, you know. Disturbed night, of course – yes. Taking your tonic regularly? That's right. Well, don't be alarmed about your hubby. We'll soon have him out and about again.'

The prophecy was fulfilled, but not immediately. Mr Mummery, though confining his diet to Benger's food, bread and milk, and beef tea skilfully prepared by Mrs Sutton and brought to his bedside by Ethel, remained very seedy all through Friday, and was only able to stagger rather shakily downstairs on Saturday afternoon. He had evidently suffered a 'thorough upset.' However, he was able to attend to a few papers which Brookes had sent down from the office for his signature, and to deal with the household books. Ethel was not a business woman, and Mr Mummery always ran over the accounts with her. Having settled up with the butcher, the baker, the dairy, and the coal merchant, Mr Mummery looked up inquiringly.

'Anything more, darling?'

'Well, there's Mrs Sutton. This is the end of her month, you know.'

'So it is. Well, you're quite satisfied with her, aren't you, darling?'

'Yes, rather – aren't you? She's a good cook, and a sweet, motherly old thing, too. Don't you think it was a real brain wave of mine, engaging her like that, on the spot?'

'I do, indeed,' said Mr Mummery.

'It was a perfect providence, her turning up like that, just after that wretched Jane had gone off without even giving notice. I was in absolute *despair*. It was a little bit of a gamble, of course, taking her without any references, but naturally, if she's been looking after a widowed mother, you couldn't expect her to give references.'

'N-no,' said Mr Mummery. At the time he had felt uneasy about the matter, though he had not liked to say much because, of course, they simply had to have somebody. And the experiment had justified itself so triumphantly in practice that one couldn't say much about it now. He had once rather tentatively suggested writing to the clergyman of Mrs Sutton's parish but, as Ethel had said, the clergyman wouldn't have been able to tell them anything about cooking, and cooking, after all, was the chief point.

Mr Mummery counted out the month's money.

'And by the way, my dear,' he said, 'you might just mention to Mrs Sutton that if she must *read* the morning paper before I come down, I should be obliged if she would fold it neatly afterwards.'

'What an old fuss-box you are, darling,' said his wife.

Mr Mummery sighed. He could not explain that it was somehow important that the morning paper should come to him fresh and prim, like a virgin. Women did not feel these things.

On Sunday, Mr Mummery felt very much better – quite his old self, in fact. He enjoyed the *News of the World* over breakfast in bed, reading the murders rather carefully. Mr Mummery got quite a lot of pleasure out of murders – they gave him an agreeable thrill of vicarious adventure, for, naturally, they were matters quite remote from daily life in the outskirts of Hull.

He noticed that Brookes had been perfectly right. Mrs Andrews' father and former employer had been 'dug up' and had, indeed, proved to be 'bung full' of arsenic.

He came downstairs for dinner – roast sirloin, with the potatoes done under the meat, and Yorkshire pudding of delicious lightness, and an apple tart to follow. After three days of invalid diet, it was delightful to savour the crisp fat and underdone lean. He ate moderately, but with a sensuous enjoyment. Ethel, on the other hand, seemed a little lacking in appetite, but then, she had never been a great meat eater. She was fastidious and, besides, she was (quite unnecessarily) afraid of getting fat.

It was a fine afternoon, and at three o'clock, when he was quite certain that the roast beef was 'settling' properly, it occurred to Mr Mummery that it would be a good thing to put the rest of those bulbs in. He slipped on his old gardening coat and wandered out to the potting-shed. Here he picked up a bag of tulips and a trowel, and then, remembering that he was wearing his good trousers, decided that it would be wise to take a mat to kneel on. When had he had the mat last? He could not recollect, but he rather fancied he had put it away in the corner under the potting-shelf. Stooping down, he felt about in the dark among the flower pots. Yes, there it was, but there was a tin of something in the way. He lifted the tin carefully out. Of course – yes – the remains of the weed-killer.

Mr Mummery glanced at the pink label, printed in staring letters with the legend: 'ARSENICAL WEED-KILLER. *Poison*,' and observed, with a mild feeling of excitement, that it was the same brand of stuff that had been associated with Mrs Andrews' latest victim. He was rather pleased about it. It gave him a sensation of being remotely but definitely in touch with important events. Then he noticed, with surprise and a little annoyance, that the stopper had been put in quite loosely.

'However'd I come to leave it like that?' he grunted. 'Shouldn't wonder if all the goodness has gone off.' He removed the stopper and squinted into the can, which appeared to be half-full. Then he rammed the thing home again, giving it a sharp thump with the handle of the trowel for better security. After that he washed his hands carefully at the scullery tap, for he did not believe in taking risks.

SUSPICION

He was a trifle disconcerted, when he came in after planting the tulips, to find visitors in the sitting-room. He was always pleased to see Mrs Welbeck and her son, but he would rather have had warning, so that he could have scrubbed the garden mould out of his nails more thoroughly. Not that Mrs Welbeck appeared to notice. She was a talkative woman and paid little attention to anything but her own conversation. Much to Mr Mummery's annoyance, she chose to prattle about the Lincoln Poisoning Case. A most unsuitable subject for the tea-table, thought Mr Mummery, at the best of times. His own 'upset' was vivid enough in his memory to make him queasy over the discussion of medical symptoms, and besides, this kind of talk was not good for Ethel. After all, the poisoner was still supposed to be in the neighbourhood. It was enough to make even a strong-nerved woman uneasy. A glance at Ethel showed him that she was looking quite white and tremulous. He must stop Mrs Welbeck somehow, or there would be a repetition of one of the old, dreadful, hysterical scenes.

He broke into the conversation with violent abruptness.

'Those forsythia cuttings, Mrs Welbeck,' he said. 'Now is just about the time to take them. If you care to come down the garden I will get them for you.'

He saw a relieved glance pass between Ethel and young Welbeck. Evidently the boy understood the situation and was chafing at his mother's tactlessness. Mrs Welbeck, brought up all standing, gasped slightly and then veered off with obliging readiness on the new tack. She accompanied her host down the garden and chattered cheerfully about horticulture while he selected and trimmed the cuttings. She complimented Mr Mummery on the immaculacy of his gravel paths. 'I simply *cannot* keep the weeds down,' she said.

Mr Mummery mentioned the weed-killer and praised its efficacy.

'That stuff!' Mrs Welbeck stared at him. Then she shuddered. 'I wouldn't have it in my place for a thousand pounds,' she said, with emphasis.

Mr Mummery smiled. 'Oh, we keep it well away from the house,' he said. 'Even if I were a careless sort of person—'

He broke off. The recollection of the loosened stopper had come to him suddenly, and it was as though, deep down in his mind, some obscure assembling of ideas had taken place. He left it at that, and went into the kitchen to fetch a newspaper to wrap up the cuttings.

Their approach to the house had evidently been seen from the sitting-room window, for when they entered, young Welbeck was already on his feet and holding Ethel's hand in the act of saying good-bye. He manoeuvred his mother out of the house with tactful promptness, and Mr Mummery returned to the kitchen to clear up the newspapers he had fished out of the drawer. To clear them up and to examine them more closely. Something had struck him about them, which he wanted to verify. He turned them over very carefully, sheet by sheet. Yes – he had been right. Every portrait of Mrs Andrews, every paragraph and line about the Lincoln Poisoning Case, had been carefully cut out.

Mr Mummery sat down by the kitchen fire. He felt as though he needed warmth. There seemed to be a curious cold lump of something at the pit of his stomach – something that he was chary of investigating.

He tried to recall the appearance of Mrs Andrews as shown in the newspaper photographs, but he had not a good visual memory. He remembered having remarked to Brookes that it was a 'motherly' face. then he tried counting up the time since the disappearance. Nearly a month, Brookes had said – and that was a week ago. Must be over a month now. A month. He has just paid Mrs Sutton her month's money.

'Ethel!' was the thought that hammered at the door of his brain. At all costs, he must cope with this monstrous suspicion on his own. He must spare her any shock or anxiety. And he must be sure of his ground. To dismiss the only decent cook they had ever had out of sheer, unfound-ed panic, would be wanton cruelty to both women. If he did it at all, it would have to be done arbitrarily, preposterously – he could not suggest horrors to Ethel. However it was done, there would be trouble. Ethel would not understand and he dared not tell her.

But if by any chance there was anything in this ghastly doubt – how could he expose Ethel to the appalling danger of having the woman in the house a moment longer? He thought of the family at Lincoln – the husband dead, the wife escaped by a miracle with her life. Was not any shock, any risk, better than that?

Mr Mummery felt suddenly very lonely and tired. His illness had taken it out of him.

Those illnesses – they had begun, when? Three weeks ago he had had the first attack. Yes, but then he had always been rather subject to gastric troubles. Bilious attacks. Not so violent, perhaps, as these last, but undoubted bilious attacks.

He pulled himself together and went, rather heavily, into the sitting-room. Ethel was tucked up in a corner of the chesterfield.

'Tired, darling?'

'Yes, a little.'

'That woman has worn you out with talking. She oughtn't to talk so much.'

'No.' Her head shifted wearily in the cushions. 'All about that horrible case. I don't like hearing about such things.'

'Of course not. Still, when a thing like that happens in the neighbour-hood, people will gossip and talk. It would be a relief if they caught the woman. One doesn't like to think—'

'I don't want to think of anything so hateful. She must be a horrible creature.'

'Horrible. Brookes was saying the other day—'

'I don't want to hear what he said. I don't want to hear about it at all. I want to be quiet. I want to be quiet!'

He recognized the note of rising hysteria.

'Tiddleywinks shall be quiet. Don't worry, darling. We won't talk about horrors.'

No. It would not do to talk about them.

Ethel went to bed early. It was understood that on Sundays Mr Mummery should sit up till Mrs Sutton came in. Ethel was a little anxious about this, but he assured her that he felt quite strong enough. In body, indeed, he did; it was his mind that felt weak and confused. He had decided to make a casual remark about the mutilated newspapers – just to see what Mrs Sutton would say.

He allowed himself the usual indulgence of a whisky and soda as he sat waiting. At a quarter to ten he heard the familiar click of the garden gate. Footsteps passed up the gravel – squeak, squeak, to the back door. Then the sound of the latch, the shutting of the door, the rattle of the bolts being shot home. Then a pause. Mrs Sutton would be taking off her hat. The moment was coming.

The step sounded in the passage. The door opened. Mrs Sutton in her neat black dress stood on the threshold. He was aware of a reluctance to face her. Then he looked up. A plump-faced woman, her eyes obscured by thick horn-rimmed spectacles. Was there, perhaps, something hard about the mouth? Or was it just that she had lost most of her front teeth?

'Would you be requiring anything to-night, sir, before I go up?'

'No, thank you, Mrs Sutton.'

'I hope you are feeling better, sir.' Her eager interest in his health seemed to him almost sinister, but the eyes, behind the thick glasses, were inscrutable.

'Quite better, thank you, Mrs Sutton.'

'Mrs Mummery is not indisposed, is she, sir? Should I take her up a glass of hot milk or anything?'

'No, thank you, no.' He spoke hurriedly, and fancied that she looked disappointed.

'Very well, sir. Good night, sir.'

'Good night. Oh! by the way, Mrs Sutton—'

'Yes, sir?'

'Oh, nothing,' said Mr Mummery, 'nothing.'

Next morning, Mr Mummery opened his paper eagerly. He would have been glad to learn that an arrest had been made over the week-end. But there was no news for him. The chairman of a trust company had blown out his brains, and the headlines were all occupied with tales about lost millions and ruined shareholders. Both in his own paper and in those he purchased on the way to the office, the Lincoln Poisoning Tragedy had been relegated to an obscure paragraph on a back page, which informed him that the police were still baffled.

The next few days were the most uncomfortable that Mr Mummery had ever spent. He developed a habit of coming down early in the morning and prowling about the kitchen. This made Ethel nervous, but Mrs Sutton offered no remark. She watched him tolerantly, even, he thought, with something like amusement. After all, it was ridiculous. What was the use of supervising the breakfast, when he had to be out of the house every day between half-past nine and six?

At the office, Brookes rallied him on the frequency with which he rang up Ethel. Mr Mummery paid no attention. It was reassuring to hear her voice and to know that she was safe and well.

Nothing happened, and by the following Thursday he began to think that he had been a fool. He came home late that night. Brookes had persuaded him to go with him to a little bachelor dinner for a friend who was about to get married. He left the others at eleven o'clock, however, refusing to make a night of it. The household was in bed when he got back but a note from Mrs Sutton lay on the table, informing him that there was cocoa for him in the kitchen, ready for hotting up. He hotted it up accordingly in the little saucepan where it stood. There was just one good cupful.

He sipped it thoughtfully, standing by the kitchen stove. After the first sip, he put the cup down. Was it his fancy, or was there something queer about the taste? He sipped it again, rolling it upon his tongue. It seemed to him to have a faint tang, metallic and unpleasant. In a sudden dread he ran out to the scullery and spat the mouthful into the sink.

After this, he stood quite still for a moment or two. Then, with a curious deliberation, as though his movements had been dictated to him, he fetched an empty medicine bottle from the pantry shelf, rinsed it under the tap and tipped the contents of the cup carefully into it. He slipped the bottle into his coat pocket and moved on tiptoe to the back door. The bolts were difficult to draw without noise, but he managed it at last. Still on tiptoe, he stole across the garden to the potting-shed. stooping down, he struck a match. He knew exactly where he had left the tin of weed-killer, under the shelf behind the pots at the back. Cautiously he lifted it out. The match flared up and burnt his fingers, but before he could light another his sense of touch had told him what he wanted to know. The stopper was loose again.

Panic seized Mr Mummery, standing there in the earthy-smelling shed, in his dress suit and overcoat, holding the tin in one hand and the match box in the other. He wanted very badly to run and tell somebody what he had discovered.

Instead, he replaced the tin exactly where he had found it and went back to the house. As he crossed the garden again, he noticed a light in Mrs Sutton's bedroom window. This terrified him more than anything which had gone before. Was she watching him? Ethel's window was dark. If she had drunk anything deadly there would be lights everywhere, movements, calls for the doctor, just as when he himself had been attacked. Attacked – that was the right word, he thought.

Still, with the same odd presence of mind and precision, he went in, washed out the utensils and made a second brew of cocoa, which he left standing in the saucepan. He crept quietly to his bedroom. Ethel's voice greeted him on the threshold.

'How late you are, Harold. Naughty old boy! Have a good time?'

'Not bad. You all right, darling?'

'Quite all right. Did Mrs Sutton leave something hot for you? She said she would.'

'Yes, but I wasn't thirsty.'

Ethel laughed. 'Oh! it was *that* sort of party, was it?'

Mr Mummery did not attempt any denials. He undressed and got into bed and clutched his wife to him as though defying death and hell to take her from him. Next morning he would act. He thanked God that he was not too late.

Mr Dimthorpe, the chemist, was a great friend of Mr Mummery's. They had often sat together in the untidy little shop on Spring Bank and exchanged views on green-fly and club-root. Mr Mummery told his story frankly to Mr Dimthorpe and handed over the bottle of cocoa. Mr Dimthorpe congratulated him on his prudence and intelligence.

'I will have it ready for you by this evening,' he said, 'and if it's what you think it is, then we shall have a clear case on which to take action.'

Mr Mummery thanked him, and was extremely vague and inattentive at business all day. But that hardly mattered, for Mr Brookes, who had seen the party through to a riotous end in the small hours, was in no very observant mood. At half-past four, Mr Mummery shut up his desk decisively and announced that he was off early, he had a call to make.

Mr Dimthorpe was ready for him.

'No doubt about it,' he said. 'I used Marsh's test. It's a heavy dose – no wonder you tasted it. There must be four or five grains of pure arsenic in that bottle. Look, here's the mirror. You can see it for yourself.'

Mr Mummery gazed at the little glass tube with its ominous purple-black stain.

'Will you ring up the police from here?' asked the chemist.

'No,' said Mr Mummery. 'No – I want to get home. God knows what's happening there. And I've only just time to catch my train.'

'All right,' said Mr Dimthorpe. 'Leave it to me. I'll ring them up for you.'

The local train did not go fast enough for Mr Mummery. Ethel – poisoned – dying – dead – Ethel – poisoned – dying – dead – the wheels drummed in his ears. He almost ran out of the station and along the road. A car was standing at his door. He saw it from the end of the street and broke into a gallop. It had happened already. The doctor was there. Fool, murderer that he was to have left things so late.

Then, while he was still a hundred and fifty yards off, he saw the front door open. A man came out followed by Ethel herself. The visitor got into his car and was driven away. Ethel went in again. She was safe – safe!

He could hardly control himself to hang up his hat and coat and go in looking reasonably calm. His wife had returned to the arm-chair by the fire and greeted him in some surprise. There were tea things on the table.

'Back early, aren't you?'

'Yes – business was slack. Somebody been to tea?'

'Yes, young Welbeck. About the arrangements for the Drama Society.' She spoke briefly but with an undertone of excitement.

A qualm came over Mr Mummery. Would a guest be any protection? His face must have shown his feelings, for Ethel stared at him in amazement.

'What's the matter, Harold, you look so queer?'

'Darling,' said Mr Mummery, 'there's something I want to tell you about.' He sat down and took her hand in his. 'Something a little unpleasant, I'm afraid—'

'Oh, ma'am!'

The cook was in the doorway.

'I beg your pardon, sir – I didn't know you was in. Will you be taking tea or can I clear away? And, oh, ma'am, there was a young man at the fishmonger's and he's just come from Grimsby and they've caught that dreadful woman – that Mrs Andrews. Isn't it a good thing? It's worritted me dreadful to think she was going about like that, but they've caught her. Taken a job as housekeeper she had to two elderly ladies and they found the wicked poison on her. Girl as spotted her will get a reward. I been keeping my eyes open for her, but it's at Grimsby she was all the time.'

SUSPICION

Mr Mummery clutched at the arm of his chair. It had all been a mad mistake then. He wanted to shout or cry. He wanted to apologize to this foolish, pleasant, excited woman. All a mistake.

But there had been the cocoa. Mr Dimthorpe. Marsh's test. Five grains of arsenic, Who, then—?

He glanced around at his wife, and in her eyes he saw something that he had never seen before. . . .

Cornell Woolrich

Dead on Her Feet

'And another thing I've got against these non-stop shindigs,' orated the chief to his slightly bored listeners, 'is they let minors get in 'em and dance for days until they wind up in a hospital with the D. T.'s, when the whole thing's been fixed ahead of time and they haven't a chance of copping the prize anyway. Here's a Missus Mollie McGuire been calling up every hour on the half-hour all day long, and bawling the eardrums off me because her daughter Toodles ain't been home in over a week and she wants this guy Pasternack arrested. So you go over there and tell Joe Pasternack I'll give him until tomorrow morning to fold up his contest and send his entries home. And tell him for me he can shove all his big and little silver loving-cups—'

For the first time his audience looked interested, even expectant, as they waited to hear what it was Mr P. could do with his loving-cups, hoping for the best.

'—back in their packing-cases,' concluded the chief chastely, if somewhat disappointingly. 'He ain't going to need 'em any more. He has promoted his last marathon in this neck of the woods.'

There was a pause while nobody stirred. 'Well, what are you all standing there looking at me for?' demanded the chief testily. 'You, Donnelly, you're nearest the door. Get going.'

Donnelly gave him an injured look. 'Me, Chief? Why, I've got a red-hot lead on that payroll thing you were so hipped about. If I don't keep after it it'll cool off on me.'

'All right, then you Stevens!'

'Why, I'm due in Yonkers right now,' protested Stevens virtuously. 'Machine-gun Rosie has been seen around again and I want to have a little talk with her—'

'That leaves you, Doyle,' snapped the merciless chief.

'Gee, Chief,' whined Doyle plaintively, 'gimme a break, can't you? My wife is expecting—' Very much under his breath he added: '—me home early tonight.'

'Congratulations,' scowled the chief, who had missed hearing the last part of it. He glowered at them. 'I get it!' he roared. 'It's below your dignity, ain't it! It's too petty-larceny for you! Anything less than the St Valentine's Day massacre ain't worth going out after, is that it? You figure it's a detail for a bluecoat, don't you?' His open palm hit the desktop with a sound like a firecracker going off. Purple became the dominant colour of his complexion. 'I'll put you all back where you started, watching pickpockets in the subway! I'll take some of the high-falutinness out of you! I'll – I'll—' The only surprising thing about it was that foam did not appear at his mouth.

It may have been that the chief's bark was worse than his bite. At any rate no great amount of apprehension was shown by the culprits before him. One of them cleared his throat inoffensively. 'By the way, Chief, I understand that rookie, Smith, has been swiping bananas from Tony on the corner again, and getting the squad a bad name after you told him to pay for them.'

The chief took pause and considered this point.

The others seemed to get the idea at once. 'They tell me he darned near wrecked a Chinese laundry because the Chinks tried to pass him somebody else's shirts. You could hear the screeching for miles.'

Doyle put the artistic finishing touch. 'I overheard him say he wouldn't be seen dead wearing the kind of socks you do. He was asking me did I think you had lost an election bet or just didn't know any better.'

The chief had become dangerously quiet all at once. A faint drumming sound from somewhere under the desk told what he was doing with his fingers. 'Oh he did, did he?' he remarked, very slowly and very ominously.

At this most unfortunate of all possible moments the door blew open and in breezed the maligned one in person. He looked very tired and at the same time enthusiastic, if the combination can be imagined. Red rimmed his eyes, blue shadowed his jaws, but he had a triumphant look on his face, the look of a man who has done his job well and expects a kind word. 'Well, Chief,' he burst out, 'it's over! I got both of 'em. Just brought 'em in. They're in the back room right now—'

An oppressive silence greeted him. Frost seemed to be in the air. He blinked and glanced at his three pals for enlightenment.

The silence didn't last long, however. The chief cleared his throat. 'Hrrrmph. Zat so?' he said with deceptive mildness. 'Well now, Smitty, as long as your engine's warm and you're hitting on all six, just run over to Joe Pasternack's marathon dance and put the skids under it. It's been going on in that old armoury on the west side—'

Smitty's face had become a picture of despair. He glanced mutely at the clock on the wall. The clock said four – A.M., not P.M. The chief, not being a naturally hard-hearted man, took time off to glance down at his own socks, as if to steel himself for this bit of cruelty. It seemed to work beautifully. 'An election bet!' he muttered cryptically to himself, and came up redder than ever.

'Gee, Chief,' pleaded the rookie, 'I haven't even had time to shave since yesterday morning.' In the background unseen nudgings and silent strangulation were rampant.

'You ain't taking part in it, you're putting the lid on it,' the chief reminded him morosely. 'First you buy your way in just like anyone else and size it up good and plenty, see if there's anything against it on moral grounds. Then you dig out one Toodles McGuire from under, and don't let her stall you she's of age either. Her old lady says she's sixteen and she ought to know. Smack her and send her home. You seal everything up tight and tell Pasternack and whoever else is backing this thing with him it's all off. And don't go 'way. You stay with him and make sure he refunds any money that's coming to anybody and shuts up shop good and proper. If he tries to squawk about there ain't no ordinance against marathons just lemme know. We can find an ordinance against anything if we go back far enough in the books—'

Smitty shifted his hat from northeast to southwest and started reluctantly towards the great outdoors once more. 'Anything screwy like this that comes up, I'm always It,' he was heard to mutter rebelliously. 'Nice job, shooing a dancing contest. I'll probably get bombarded with powder-puffs—'

The chief reached suddenly for the heavy brass inkwell on his desk, whether to sign some report or to let Smitty have it, Smitty didn't wait to find out. He ducked hurriedly out the door.

'Ah me,' sighed the chief profoundly, 'what a bunch of crumbs. Why didn't I listen to me old man and join the fire department instead!'

Young Mr Smith, muttering bad language all the way, had himself driven over to the unused armoury where the peculiar enterprise was taking place.

'Sixty cents,' said the taxi-driver.

Smitty took out a little pocket account-book and wrote down – *Taxifare – $1.20.* 'Send me out after nothing at four in the morning, will he!' he commented. After which he felt a lot better.

There was a box-office outside the entrance but now it was dark and untenanted. Smitty pushed through the unlocked doors and found a combination porter and doorman, a gentleman of colour, seated on the inside, who gave him a stub of pink pasteboard in exchange for fifty-five cents, then promptly took the stub back again and tore it in half. 'Boy,' he remarked affably, 'you is either up pow'ful early or up awful late.'

'I just is plain up,' remarked Smitty, and looked around him.

It was an hour before daylight and there were a dozen people left in the armoury, which was built to hold two thousand. Six of them were dancing, but you wouldn't have known it by looking at them. It had been going on nine days. There was no one watching them any more. The last of the paid admissions had gone home hours ago, even the drunks and the Park Avenue stay-outs. All the big snow-white arc lights hanging from the rafters had been put out, except one in the middle, to save expenses. Pasternack wasn't in this for his health. The one remaining light, spitting and sizzling way up overhead, and sending down violet and white rays that you could see with the naked eye, made everything look ghostly, unreal. A phonograph fitted with an amplifier was grinding away at one end of the big hall, tearing a dance-tune to pieces, giving it the beating of its life. Each time the needle got to the end of the record it was swept back to the beginning by a sort of stencil fitted over the turn-table.

Six scarecrows, three men and three girls, clung ludicrously together in pairs out in the middle of the floor. They were not dancing and they were not walking, they were tottering by now, barely moving enough to keep from standing still. Each of the men bore a number on his back. *3*, *8*, and *14* the numbers were. They were the 'lucky' couples who had outlasted all the others, the scores who had started with them at the bang of a gun a week and two days ago. There wasn't a coat or vest left among the three men – or a necktie. Two of them had replaced their shoes with carpet-slippers to ease their aching feet. The third had on a pair of canvas sneakers.

One of the girls had a wet handkerchief plastered across her forehead. Another had changed into a chorus-girl's practice outfit – shorts and a blouse. The third was a slip of a thing, a mere child, her head hanging limply down over her partner's shoulder, her eyes glazed with exhaustion.

Smitty watched her for a moment. There wasn't a curve in her whole body. If there was anyone here under age, it was she. She must be Toodles McGuire, killing herself for a plated loving-cup, a line in the newspapers, a contract to dance in some cheap honky-tonk, and a thousand dollars that she wasn't going to get anyway – according to the chief. He was probably right, reflected Smitty. There wasn't a thousand dollars in the whole set-up, much less three prizes on a sliding scale. Pasternack would probably pocket whatever profits there were and blow, letting the fame-struck suckers whistle. Corner-lizards and dance-hall belles like these couldn't even scrape together enough to bring suit. Now was as good a time as any to stop the lousy racket.

Smitty sauntered over to the bleachers where four of the remaining six the armoury housed just then were seated and sprawled in various attitudes. He looked them over. One was an aged crone who acted as matron to the female participants during the brief five-minute rest-periods that came every half-hour. She had come out of her retirement for the time being, a towel of dubious cleanliness slung over her arm, and was absorbed in the working-out of a crossword puzzle, mumbling to herself all the while. She had climbed halfway up the reviewing stand to secure privacy for her occupation.

Two or three rows below her lounged a greasy-looking counterman from some one-arm lunchroom, guarding a tray that held a covered tin pail of steaming coffee and a stack of wax-paper cups. One of the rest periods was evidently approaching and he was ready to cash in on it.

The third spectator was a girl in a dance dress, her face twisted with pain. Judging by her unkempt appearance and the scornful bitter look in her eyes as she watched the remaining dancers, she had only just recently disqualified herself. She had one stockingless foot up before her and was rubbing the swollen instep with alcohol and cursing softly under her breath.

The fourth and last of the onlookers (the fifth being the darky at the door) was too busy with his arithmetic even to look up when Smitty parked before him. He was in his shirt-sleeves and wore blue elastic armbands and a green celluloid eye-shade. A soggy-looking stogie protruded from his mouth. A watch, a megaphone, a whistle, and a blank-cartridge pistol lay beside him on the bench. He appeared to be computing the day's receipts in a pocket notebook, making them up out of his head as he went along. 'Get out of my light,' he remarked ungraciously as Smitty's shadow fell athwart him.

'You Pasternack?' Smitty wanted to know, not moving an inch.

'Naw, he's in his office taking a nap.'

'Well, get him out here, I've got news for him.'

'He don't wanna hear it,' said the pleasant party on the bench.

Smitty turned over his lapel, then let it curl back again. 'Oh, the lor,' commented the auditor, and two tens left the day's receipts and were left high and dry in Smitty's right hand. 'Buy yourself a drop of schnapps,' he said without even looking up. 'Stop in and ask for me tomorrow when there's more in the kitty—'

Smitty plucked the nearest armband, stretched it out until it would have gone around a piano, then let it snap back again. The business manager let out a yip. Smitty's palm with the two sawbucks came up

flat against his face, clamped itself there by the chin and bridge of the
nose, and executed a rotary motion, grinding them in. 'Wrong guy,' he
said and followed the financial wizard into the sanctum where Pasternack
lay in repose, mouth fixed to catch flies.

'Joe,' said the humbled side-kick, spitting out pieces of ten-dollar-bill,
'the lor.'

Pasternack got vertical as though he worked by a spring. 'Where's
your warrant?' he said before his eyes were even open. 'Quick, get me
my mouth on the phone, Moe!'

'You go out there and blow your whistle,' said Smitty, 'and call the
bally off – or do I have to throw this place out in the street?' He turned
suddenly, tripped over something unseen, and went staggering halfway
across the room. The telephone went flying out of Moe's hand at one
end and the sound-box came ripping off the baseboard of the wall at
the other. '*Tch, tch,* excuse it please,' apologized Smitty insincerely. 'Just
when you needed it most, too!'

He turned back to the one called Moe and sent him headlong out into
the auditorium with a hearty shove at the back of the neck. 'Now do like
I told you,' he said, 'while we're waiting for the telephone repairman to
get here. And when their dogs have cooled, send them all in here to me.
That goes for the cannibal and the washroom dame, too.' He motioned
towards the desk. 'Get out your little tin box, Pasternack. How much
you got on hand to pay these people?'

It wasn't in a tin box but in a briefcase. 'Close the door,' said Pasternack in an insinuating voice. 'There's plenty here, and plenty more will
be coming in. How big a cut will square you? Write your own ticket.'

Smitty sighed wearily. 'Do I have to knock your front teeth down the
back of your throat before I can convince you I'm one of these old-
fashioned guys that likes to work for my money?'

Outside a gun boomed hollowly and the squawking of the phonograph
stopped. Moe could be heard making an announcement through the
megaphone. 'You can't get away with this!' stormed Pasternack.
'Where's your warrant?'

'Where's your licence,' countered Smitty, 'if you're going to get tech-
nical? C'mon, don't waste any more time, you're keeping me up! Get
the dough ready for the pay-off.' He stepped to the door and called out
into the auditorium: 'Everybody in here. Get your things and line up.'
Two of the three couples separated slowly like sleepwalkers and began
to trudge painfully over towards him, walking zig-zag as though their
metabolism was all shot.

The third pair, Number 14, still clung together out on the floor, the
man facing towards Smitty. They didn't seem to realize it was over.
They seemed to be holding each other up. They were in the shape of a

human tent, their feet about three feet apart on the floor, their faces and shoulders pressed closely together. The girl was that clothes-pin, that stringbean of a kid he had already figured for Toodles McGuire. So she was going to be stubborn about it, was she? He went over to the pair bellicosely. 'C'mon, you heard me, break it up!'

The man gave him a frightened look over her shoulder. 'Will you take her off me please, Mac? She's passed out or something, and if I let her go she'll crack her conk on the floor.' He blew out his breath. 'I can't hold her up much longer!'

Smitty hooked an arm about her middle. She didn't weigh any more than a discarded topcoat. The poor devil who had been bearing her weight, more or less, for nine days and nights on end, let go and folded up into a squatting position at her feet like a shrivelled Buddha. 'Just lemme stay like this,' he moaned, 'it feels so good.' The girl, meanwhile, had begun to bend slowly double over Smitty's supporting arm, closing up like a jackknife. But she did it with a jerkiness, a deliberateness, that was almost grisly, slipping stiffly down a notch at a time, until her upside-down head had met her knees. She was like a walking doll whose spring has run down.

Smitty turned and barked over one shoulder at the washroom hag. 'Hey you! C'mere and gimme a hand with this girl! Can't you see she needs attention? Take her in there with you and see what you can do for her—'

The old crone edged fearfully nearer, but when Smitty tried to pass the inanimate form to her she drew hurriedly back. 'I – I ain't got the stren'th to lift her,' she mumbled stubbornly. 'You're strong, you carry her in and set her down—'

'I can't go in there,' he snarled disgustedly. 'That's no place for me! What're you here for if you can't—'

The girl who had been sitting on the sidelines suddenly got up and came limping over on one stockingless foot. 'Give her to me,' she said. 'I'll take her in for you.' She gave the old woman a long hard look before which the latter quailed and dropped her eyes. 'Take hold of her feet,' she ordered in a low voice. The hag hurriedly stooped to obey. They sidled off with her between them, and disappeared around the side of the orchestra-stand, towards the washroom. Their burden sagged low, until it almost touched the floor.

'Hang onto her,' Smitty thought he heard the younger woman say. 'She won't bite you!' The washroom door banged closed on the weird little procession. Smitty turned and hoisted the deflated Number 14 to his feet. 'C'mon,' he said. 'In you go, with the rest!'

They were all lined up against the wall in Pasternack's 'office', so played-out that if the wall had suddenly been taken away they would have all toppled flat like a pack of cards. Pasternack and his shill had gone into a huddle in the opposite corner, buzzing like a hive of bees.

'Would you two like to be alone?' Smitty wanted to know, parking Number 14 with the rest of the droops.

Pasternack evidently believed in the old adage, 'He who fights and runs away lives to fight, etc.' The game, he seemed to think, was no longer worth the candle. He unlatched the briefcase he had been guarding under his arm, walked back to the desk with it, and prepared to ease his conscience. 'Well folks,' he remarked genially, 'on the advice of this gentleman here' (big pally smile for Smitty) 'my partner and I are calling off the contest. While we are under no legal obligation to any of you' (business of clearing his throat and hitching up his necktie) 'we have decided to do the square thing, just so there won't be any trouble, and split the prize money among all the remaining entries. Deducting the rental for the armoury, the light bill, and the cost of printing tickets and handbills, that would leave—'

'No you don't!' said Smitty, 'That comes out of your first nine-days profits. What's on hand now gets divvied without any deductions. Do it your way and they'd all be owing you money!' He turned to the doorman. 'You been paid, sunburnt?'

'Nossuh! I'se got five dolluhs a night coming at me—'

'Forty-five for you,' said Smitty.

Pasternack suddenly blew up and advanced menacingly upon his partner. 'That's what I get for listening to you, know-it-all! So New York was a sucker town, was it! So there was easy pickings here, was there! Yah!'

'Boys, boys,' remonstrated Smitty, elbowing them apart.

'Throw them a piece of cheese, the rats,' remarked the girl in shorts. There was a scuffling sound in the doorway and Smitty turned in time to see the lamed girl and the washroom matron each trying to get in ahead of the other.

'You don't leave me in there!'

'Well I'm not staying in there alone with her. It ain't my job! I resign!'

The one with the limp got to him first. 'Listen, mister, you better go in there yourself,' she panted. 'We can't do anything with her. I think she's dead.'

'She's cold as ice and all stiff-like,' corroborated the old woman.

'Oh my God, I've killed her!' someone groaned. Number 14 sagged to his knees and went out like a light. Those on either side of him eased him down to the floor by his arms, too weak themselves to support him.

'Hold everything!' barked Smitty. He gripped the pop-eyed doorman by the shoulder. 'Scram out front and get a cop. Tell him to put in a call for an ambulance, and then have him report in here to me. And if you try lighting out, you lose your forty-five bucks and get the electric chair.'

'I'se pracktilly back inside again,' sobbed the terrified darky as he fled.

'The rest of you stay right where you are. I'll hold you responsible, Pasternack, if anybody ducks.'

'As though we could move an inch on these howling dogs,' muttered the girl in shorts.

Smitty pushed the girl with one shoe ahead of him. 'You come and show me,' he grunted. He was what might be termed a moral coward at the moment; he was going where he'd never gone before.

'Straight ahead of you,' she scowled, halting outside the door. 'Do you need a road-map?'

'C'mon, I'm not going in there alone,' he said and gave her a shove through the forbidden portal.

She was stretched out on the floor where they'd left her, a bottle of rubbing alcohol that hadn't worked uncorked beside her. His face was flaming as he squatted down and examined her. She was gone all right. She was as cold as they'd said and getting more rigid by the minute. 'Overtaxed her heart most likely,' he growled. 'That guy Pasternack ought to be hauled up for this. He's morally responsible.'

The cop, less well-brought-up than Smitty, stuck his head in the door without compunction.

'Stay by the entrance,' Smitty instructed him, 'Nobody leaves.' Then, 'This was the McGuire kid, wasn't it?' he asked his feminine companion.

'Can't prove it by me,' she said sulkily. 'Pasternack kept calling her Rose Lamont all through the contest. Why don't-cha ask the guy that was dancing with her? Maybe they got around to swapping names after nine days. Personally,' she said as she moved towards the door, 'I don't know who she was and I don't give a damn!'

'You'll make a swell mother for some guy's children,' commented Smitty following her out. 'In there,' he said to the ambulance doctor who had just arrived, 'but it's the morgue now, and not first-aid. Take a look.'

Number 14, when he got back to where they all were, was taking it hard and self-accusing. 'I didn't mean to do it, I didn't mean to!' he kept moaning.

'Shut up, you sap, you're making it tough for yourself,' someone hissed.

'Lemme see a list of your entries,' Smitty told Pasternack.

The impresario fished a ledger out of the desk drawer and held it out to him. 'All I got out of this enterprise was kicks in the pants! Why didn't I stick to the sticks where they don't drop dead from a little dancing? Ask me, why didn't I!'

'Fourteen,' read Smitty. 'Rose Lamont and Gene Monahan. That your real name, guy? Back it up.' 14 jerked off the coat that someone had slipped around his shoulders and turned the inner pocket inside out. The name was inked onto the label. The address checked too. 'What about her, was that her real tag?'

'McGuire was her real name,' admitted Monahan, 'Toodles McGuire She was going to change it anyway, pretty soon, if we'dda won that thousand' – he hung his head – 'so it didn't matter.'

'Why'd you say you did it? Why do you keep saying you didn't mean to?'

'Because I could feel there was something the matter with her in my arms. I knew she oughtta quit, and I wouldn't let her. I kept begging her to stick it out a little longer, even when she didn't answer me. I went crazy, I guess, thinking of that thousand dollars. We needed it to get married on. I kept expecting the others to drop out any minute, there were only two other couples left, and no one was watching us any more. When the rest-periods came, I carried her in my arms to the washroom door, so no one would notice she couldn't make it herself, and turned her over to the old lady in there. She couldn't do anything with her either, but I begged her not to let on, and each time the whistle blew I picked her up and started out from there with her—'

'Well, you've danced her into her grave,' said Smitty bitterly. 'If I was you I'd go out and stick both my feet under the first trolley-car that came along and hold them there until it went by. It might make a man of you!'

He went out and found the ambulance doctor in the act of leaving. 'What was it, her heart?'

The A.D. favoured him with a peculiar look, starting at the floor and ending at the top of his head. 'Why wouldn't it be? Nobody's heart keeps going with a seven- or eight-inch metal pencil jammed into it.'

He unfolded a handkerchief to reveal a slim coppery cylinder, tapering to needle-like sharpness at the writing end, where the case was pointed over the lead to protect it. It was aluminium – encrusted blood was what gave it its copper sheen. Smitty nearly dropped it in consternation – not because of what it had done but because he had missed seeing it.

'And another thing,' went on the A.D. 'You're new to this sort of thing, aren't you? Well, just a friendly tip. No offence, but you don't call an ambulance that long after they've gone, our time is too val—'

'I don't getcha,' said Smitty impatiently. 'She needed help; who am

I supposed to ring in, potter's field, and have her buried before she's quit breathing?'

This time the look he got was withering. 'She was past help hours ago.' The doctor scanned his wrist. 'It's five now. She's been dead since three, easily. I can't tell you when exactly, but your friend the medical examiner'll tell you whether I'm right or not. I've seen too many of 'em in my time. She's been gone two hours anyhow.'

Smitty had taken a step back, as though he were afraid of the guy. 'I came in here at four thirty,' he stammered excitedly, 'and she was dancing on that floor there – I saw her with my own eyes – fifteen, twenty minutes ago!' His face was slightly sallow.

'I don't care whether you saw her dancin' or saw her doin' double-hand-springs on her left ear, she was dead!' roared the ambulance man testily. 'She was celebrating her own wake then, if you insist!' He took a look at Smitty's horrified face, quieted down, spit emphatically out of one corner of his mouth, and remarked: 'Somebody was dancing with her dead body, that's all. Pleasant dreams, kid!'

Smitty started to burn slowly. 'Somebody was,' he agreed, gritting his teeth. 'I know who Somebody is, too. His number was Fourteen until a little while ago; well, it's Thirteen from now on!'

He went in to look at her again, the doctor whose time was so valuable trailing along. 'From the back, eh? That's how I missed it. She was lying on it the first time I came in and looked.'

'I nearly missed it myself,' the interne told him. 'I thought it was a boil at first. See this little pad of gauze? It had been soaked in alcohol and laid over it. There was absolutely no external flow of blood, and the pencil didn't protrude, it was in up to the hilt. In fact I had to use forceps to get it out. You can see for yourself, the clip that fastens to the wearer's pocket, which would have stopped it halfway, is missing. Probably broken off long before.'

'I can't figure it,' said Smitty. 'If it went in up to the hilt, what room was there left for the grip that sent it home?'

'Must have just gone in an inch or two at first and stayed there,' suggested the interne. 'She probably killed herself on it by keeling over backwards and hitting the floor or the wall, driving it the rest of the way in.' He got to his feet. 'Well, the pleasure's all yours.' He flipped a careless salute, and left.

'Send the old crow in that had charge in here,' Smitty told the cop.

The old woman came in fumbling with her hands, as though she had the seven-day itch.

'What's your name?'

'Josephine Falvey – Mrs Josephine Falvey.' She couldn't keep her eyes off what lay on the floor.

'It don't matter after you're forty,' Smitty assured her drily. 'What'd you bandage that wound up for? D'you know that makes you an accessory to a crime?'

'I didn't do no such a—' she started to deny whitely.

He suddenly thrust the postage-stamp of folded gauze, rusty on one side, under her nose. She cawed and jumped back. He followed her retreat. 'You didn't stick this on? C'mon, answer me!'

'Yeah, I did!' she cackled, almost jumping up and down, 'I did, I did – but I didn't mean no harm. Honest, mister, I—'

'When'd you do it?'

'The last time, when you made me and the girl bring her in here. Up to then I kept rubbing her face with alcohol each time he brought her back to the door, but it didn't seem to help her any. I knew I should of gone out and reported it to Pasternack, but he – that feller you know – begged me not to. He begged me to give them a break and not get them ruled out. He said it didn't matter if she acted all limp that way, that she was just dazed. And anyway, there wasn't so much difference between her and the rest any more, they were all acting dopy like that. Then after you told me to bring her in the last time, I stuck my hand down the back of her dress and I felt something hard and round, like a carbuncle or berl, so I put a little gauze application over it. And then me and her decided, as long as the contest was over anyway, we better go out and tell you—'

'Yeah,' he scoffed, 'and I s'pose if I hadn't shown up she'd still be dancing around out there, until the place needed disinfecting! When was the first time you noticed anything the matter with her?'

She babbled: 'About two thirty, three o'clock. They were all in here – the place was still crowded – and someone knocked on the door. He was standing out there with her in his arms and he passed her to me and whispered, "Look after her, will you?" That's when he begged me not to tell anyone. He said he'd—' She stopped.

'Go on!' snapped Smitty.

'He said he'd cut me in on the thousand if they won it. Then when the whistle blew and they all went out again, he was standing there waiting to take her back in his arms – and off he goes with her. They all had to be helped out by that time, anyway, so nobody noticed anything wrong. After that, the same thing happened each time – until you came. But I didn't dream she was dead.' She crossed herself. 'If I'da thought that, you couldn't have got me to touch her for love nor money—'

'I've got my doubts,' Smitty told her, 'about the money part of that, anyway. Outside – and consider yourself a material witness.'

If the old crone was to be believed, it had happened outside on the dance floor under the bright arc lights, and not in here. He was pretty sure it had, at that. Monahan wouldn't have dared try to force his way in here. The screaming of the other occupants would have blown the roof off. Secondly, the very fact that the floor had been more crowded at that time than later, had helped cover it up. They'd probably quarrelled when she tried to quit. He'd whipped out the pencil and struck her while she clung to him. She'd either fallen and killed herself on it, and he'd picked her up again immediately before anyone noticed, or else the Falvey woman had handled her carelessly in the washroom and the impaled pencil had reached her heart.

Smitty decided he wanted to know if any of the feminine entries had been seen to fall to the floor at any time during the evening. Pasternack had been in his office from ten on, first giving out publicity items and then taking a nap, so Smitty put him back on the shelf. Moe, however, came across beautifully.

'Did I see anyone fall?' he echoed shrilly. 'Who didn't! Such a commotion you never saw in your life. About half-past two. Right when we were on the air, too.'

'Go on, this is getting good. What'd he do, pick her right up again?'

'Pick her up! She wouldn't get up. You couldn't go near her! She just sat there swearing and screaming and throwing things. I thought we'd have to send for the police. Finally they sneaked up behind her and hauled her off on her fanny to the bleachers and disqualified her—'

'Wa-a-ait a minute,' gasped Smitty. 'Who you talking about?'

Moe looked surprised. 'That Standish dame, who else? You saw her, the one with the bum pin. That was when she sprained it and couldn't dance any more. She wouldn't go home. She hung around saying she was framed and gypped and we couldn't get rid of her—'

'Wrong number,' said Smitty disgustedly. 'Back where you came from.' And to the cop: 'Now we'll get down to brass tacks. Let's have a crack at Monahan—'

He was thumbing his notebook with studied absorption when the fellow was shoved in the door. 'Be right with you,' he said offhandedly, tapping his pockets, 'soon as I jot down – Lend me your pencil a minute, will you?'

'I – I had one, but I lost it,' said Monahan dully.

'How come?' asked Smitty quietly.

'Fell out of my pocket, I guess. The clip was broken.'

'This it?'

The fellow's eyes grew big, while it almost touched their lashes, twirling from left to right and right to left. 'Yeah, but what's the matter with it, what's it got on it?'

'You asking me that?' leered Smitty. 'Come on, show me how you did it!'

Monahan cowered back against the wall, looked from the body on the floor to the pencil, and back again. 'Oh no,' he moaned, 'no. Is that what happened to her? I didn't even know—'

'Guys as innocent as you rub me the wrong way,' said Smitty. He reached for him, hauled him out into the centre of the room, and then sent him flying back again. His head bonged the door and the cop looked in inquiringly. 'No, I didn't knock,' said Smitty, 'that was just his dome.' He sprayed a little of the alcohol into Monahan's stunned face and hauled him forward again. 'The first peep out of you was, "I killed her." Then you keeled over. Later on you kept saying "I'm to blame, I'm to blame." Why try to back out now?'

'But I didn't mean I did anything to her,' wailed Monahan, 'I thought I killed her by dancing too much. She was all right when I helped her in here about two. Then when I came back for her, the old dame whispered she couldn't wake her up. She said maybe the motion of dancing would bring her to. She said, "You want that thousand dollars, don't you? Here, hold her up, no one'll be any the wiser." And I listened to her like a fool and faked it from then on.'

Smitty sent him hurling again. 'Oh, so now it's supposed to have happened in here – with your pencil, no less! Quit trying to pass the buck!'

The cop, who didn't seem to be very bright, again opened the door, and Monahan came sprawling out at his feet. 'Geez, what a hard head he must have,' he remarked.

'Go over and start up that phonograph over there,' ordered Smitty. 'We're going to have a little demonstration – of how he did it. If banging his conk against the door won't bring back his memory, maybe dancing with her will do it.' He hoisted Monahan upright by the scruff of the neck. 'Which pocket was the pencil in?'

The man motioned towards his breast. Smitty dropped it in point-first. The cop fitted the needle into the groove and threw the switch. A blare came from the amplifier. 'Pick her up and hold her,' grated Smitty.

An animal-like moan was the only answer he got. The man tried to back away. The cop threw him forward again. 'So you won't dance, eh?'

'I won't dance,' gasped Monahan.

When they helped him up from the floor, he would dance.

'You held her like that dead, for two solid hours,' Smitty reminded him. 'Why mind an extra five minutes or so?'

The moving scarecrow crouched down beside the other inert scarecrow on the floor. Slowly his arms went around her. The two scarecrows rose to their feet, tottered drunkenly together, then moved out of the doorway into the open in time to the music. The cop began to perspire.

Smitty said: 'Any time you're willing to admit you done it, you can quit.'

'God forgive you for this!' said a tomb-like voice.

'Take out the pencil,' said Smitty, 'without letting go of her – like you did the first time .'

'This is the first time,' said that hollow voice. 'The time before – it dropped out.' His right hand slipped slowly away from the corpse's back, dipped into his pocket.

The others had come out of Pasternack's office, drawn by the sound of the macabre music, and stood huddled together, horror and unbelief written all over their weary faces. A corner of the bleachers hid both Smitty and the cop from them; all they could see was that grisly couple moving slowly out into the centre of the big floor, alone under the funeral heliotrope arc light. Monahan's hand suddenly went up, with something gleaming in it; stabbed down again and was hidden against his partner's back. There was an unearthly howl and the girl with the turned ankle fell flat on her face amidst the onlookers.

Smitty signalled the cop; the music suddenly broke off. Monahan and his partner had come to a halt again and stood there like they had when the contest first ended, upright, tent-shaped, feet far apart, heads locked together. One pair of eyes was as glazed as the other now.

'All right break, break!' said Smitty.

Monahan was clinging to her with a silent, terrible intensity as though he could no longer let go.

The Standish girl had sat up, but promptly covered her eyes with both hands and was shaking all over as if she had a chill.

'I want that girl in here,' said Smitty. 'And you, Moe. And the old lady.'

He closed the door on the three of them. 'Let's see that book of entries again.'

Moe handed it over jumpily.

'Sylvia Standish, eh?' The girl nodded, still sucking in her breath from the fright she'd had.

'Toodles McGuire was Rose Lamont – now what's your real name?' He thumbed at the old woman. 'What are you two to each other?'

The girl looked away. 'She's my mother, if you gotta know,' she said.

'Might as well admit it, it's easy enough to check up on,' he agreed. 'I had a hunch there was a tie-up like that in it somewhere. You were too ready to help her carry the body in here the first time.' He turned to the cringing Moe. 'I understood you to say she carried on like nobody's never-mind when she was ruled out, had to be hauled off the floor by main force and wouldn't go home. Was she just a bum loser, or what was her grievance?'

'She claimed it was done purposely,' said Moe. 'Me, I got my doubts. It was like this. That girl the feller killed, she had on a string of glass beads, see? So the string broke and they rolled all over the floor under everybody's feet. So this one, she slipped on 'em, fell and turned her ankle and couldn't dance no more. Then she starts hollering blue murder.' He shrugged. 'What should we do, call off the contest because she couldn't dance no more?'

'She did it purposely,' broke in the girl hotly, 'so she could hook the award herself! She knew I had a better chance than anyone else—'

'I suppose it was while you were sitting there on the floor you picked up the pencil Monahan had dropped,' Smitty said casually.

'I did like hell! It fell out in the bleachers when he came over to apolo—' She stopped abruptly. 'I don't know what pencil you're talking about.'

'Don't worry about a little slip-up like that,' Smitty told her. 'You're down for it anyway – and have been ever since you folded up out there just now. You're not telling me anything I don't know already.'

'Anyone woulda keeled over; I thought I was seeing her ghost—'

'That ain't what told me. It was seeing him pretend to do it that told me he never did it. It wasn't done outside at all, in spite of what your old lady tried to hand me. Know why? The pencil didn't go through her dress. There's no hole in the back of her dress. Therefore she had her dress off and was cooling off when it happened. Therefore it was done here in the restroom. For Monahan to do it outside he would have had to hitch her whole dress up almost over her head in front of everybody – and maybe that wouldn't have been noticed!

'He never came in here after her; your own mother would have been the first one to squawk for help. You did, though. She stayed a moment after the others. You came in the minute they cleared out and stuck her with it. She fell on it and killed herself. Then your old lady tried to cover you by putting a pad on the wound and giving Monahan the idea she was stupefied from fatigue. When he began to notice the coldness, if he did, he thought it was from the alcohol-rubs she was getting every rest-period. I guess he isn't very bright anyway – a guy like that, that dances for his coffee-and. He didn't have any motive. He wouldn't have done it even if she wanted to quit, he'd have let her. He was too penitent later on when he thought he'd tired her to death. But you had all the motive I need – those broken beads. Getting even for what you thought she did. Have I left anything out?'

'Yeah,' she said curtly, 'look up my sleeve and tell me if my hat's on straight!'

On the way out to the Black Maria that had backed up to the entrance, with the two Falvey women, Pasternack, Moe, and the other four dancers marching single file ahead of him, Smitty called to the cop: 'Where's Monahan? Bring him along!'

The cop came up mopping his brow. 'I finally pried him loose,' he said, 'when they came to take her away, but I can't get him to stop laughing. He's been laughing ever since. I think he's lost his mind. Makes your blood run cold. Look at that!'

Monahan was standing there, propped against the wall, a lone figure under the arclight, his arms still extended in the half-embrace in which he had held his partner for nine days and nights, while peal after peal of macabre mirth came from him, shaking him from head to foot.

Geoffrey Household

Taboo

I had this story from Lewis Banning, the American; but as I also know
Shiravieff pretty well and have heard some parts of it from him since, I
think I can honestly reconstruct his own words.

Shiravieff had asked Banning to meet Colonel Romero, and after
lunch took them, as his habit is, into his consulting-room; his study, I
should call it, for there are no instruments or white enamel to make a
man unpleasantly conscious of the workings of his own body, nor has
Shiravieff, among the obscure groups of letters that he is entitled to write
after his name, any one which implies a medical degree. It is a long,
restful room, its harmony only broken by sporting trophies. The muzzle
of an enormous wolf grins over the mantelpiece, and there are fine heads
of ibex and aurochs on the opposite wall. No doubt Shiravieff put them
there deliberately. His patients from the counties came in expecting a
quack doctor but at once gained confidence when they saw he had killed
wild animals in a gentlemanly manner.

The trophies suit him. With his peaked beard and broad smile, he
looks more the explorer than the psychologist. His unvarying calm is not
the priestlike quality of the doctor; it is the disillusionment of the
traveller and exile, of one who has studied the best and the worst in
human nature and discovered that there is no definable difference
between them.

Romero took a dislike to the room. He was very sensitive to atmosphere, though he would have denied it indignantly.

'A lot of silly women,' he grumbled obscurely, 'pouring out emotions.'

They had, of course, poured out plenty of emotions from the same
chair that he was occupying; but, since Shiravieff made his reputation
on cases of shell-shock, there must have been a lot of silly men too.

Romero naturally would not mention that. He preferred to think that hysteria was confined to the opposite sex. Being a Latin in love with England, he worshipped and cultivated our detachment.

'I assure you that emotions are quite harmless once they are out of the system,' answered Shiravieff, smiling. 'It's when they stay inside that they give trouble.'

'*Cá!* I like people who keep their emotions inside,' said Romero. 'It is why I live in London. The English are not cold – it is nonsense to say they are cold – but they are well bred. They never show a sign of what hurts them most. I like that.'

Shiravieff tapped his long forefinger on the table in a fast, nervous rhythm.

'And what if they *must* display emotion?' he asked irritably. 'Shock them – shock them, you understand, so that they must! They can't do it, and they are hurt for life.'

They had never before seen him impatient. Nobody had. It was an unimaginable activity, as if your family doctor were to come and visit you without his trousers. Romero had evidently stirred up the depths.

'I've shocked them, and they displayed plenty of emotion,' remarked Banning.

'Oh, I do not mean their little conventions,' said Shiravieff slowly and severely. 'Shock them with some horrid fact that they can't blink away, something that would outrage the souls of any of us. Do you remember de Maupassant's story of the man whose daughter was buried alive – how she returned from the grave and how all his life he kept the twitching gesture with which he tried to push her away? Well, if that man had shrieked or thrown a fit or wept all night he mightn't have suffered from the twitch.'

'Courage would have saved him,' announced the colonel superbly.

'No!' shouted Shiravieff. 'We're all cowards, and the healthiest thing we can do is to express fear when we feel it.'

'The fear of death—' began Romero.

'I am not talking about the fear of death. It is not that. It is our horror of breaking a taboo that causes shock. Listen to me. Do either of you remember the Zweibergen case in 1926?'

'The name's familiar,' said Banning. 'But I can't just recall . . . was it a haunted village?'

'I congratulate you on your healthy mind,' said Shiravieff ironically. 'You can forget what you don't want to remember.'

He offered them cigars and lit one himself. Since he hardly ever smoked it calmed him immediately. His grey eyes twinkled as if to assure them that he shared their surprise at his irritation. Banning had never before realized, so he said, that the anti-smoke societies were right, that tobacco was a drug.

'I was at Zweibergen that summer. I chose it because I wanted to be alone. I can only rest when I am alone,' began Shiravieff abruptly. 'The eastern Carpathians were remote ten years ago – cut off from the tourists by too many frontiers. The Hungarian magnates who used to shoot the forests before the war had vanished, and their estates were sparsely settled. I didn't expect any civilized company.

'I was disappointed to find that a married couple had rented the old shooting-box. They were obviously interesting, but I made no advances to them beyond passing the time of day whenever we met on the village street. He was English and she American – one of those delightful women who are wholly and typically American. No other country can fuse enough races to produce them. Her blood, I should guess, was mostly Slav. They thought me a surly fellow, but respected my evident desire for privacy – until the time when all of us in Zweibergen wanted listeners. Then the Vaughans asked me to dinner.

'We talked nothing but commonplaces during the meal, which was, by the way, excellent. There were a joint of venison and some wild strawberries, I remember. We took our coffee on the lawn in front of the house, and sat for a moment in silence – the mountain silence – staring out across the valley. The pine forest, rising tier upon tier, was very black in the late twilight. White, isolated rocks were scattered through it. They looked as if they might move on at any minute – like the ghosts of great beasts pasturing upon the tree-tops. Then a dog howled on the alp above us. We all began talking at once. About the mystery, of course.

'Two men had been missing in that forest for nearly a week. The first of them belonged to a little town about ten miles down the valley; he was returning after nightfall from a short climb in the mountains. He might have vanished into a snowdrift or ravine, for the paths were none too safe. There were no climbing clubs in that district to keep them up. But it seemed to be some less common accident that had overtaken him. He was out of the high peaks. A shepherd camping on one of the lower alps had exchanged a goodnight with him, and watched him disappear among the trees on his way downwards. That was the last that had been seen or heard of him.

'The other was one of the search party that had gone out on the following day. The man had been posted as a stop, while the rest beat the woods towards him. It was the last drive, and already dark. When the line came up to his stand he was not there.

'Everybody suspected wolves. Since 1914 there had been no shooting over the game preserves, and animal life of all sorts was plentiful. But the wolves were not in pack, and the search parties did not find a trace of blood. There were no tracks to help. There was no sign of a struggle.

Vaughan suggested that we were making a mystery out of nothing – probably the two men had become tired of domestic routine, and taken the opportunity to disappear. By now, he expected, they were on their way to the Argentine.

'His cool dismissal of tragedy was inhuman. He sat there, tall, distant, and casually strong. His face was stamped ready-made out of that pleasant upper-class mould. Only his firm mouth and thin sensitive nostrils showed that he had any personality of his own. Kyra Vaughan looked at him scornfully.

' "Is that what you really think?" she asked.

' "Why not?" he answered. "If those men had been killed it must have been by something prowling about and waiting for its chance. And there isn't such a thing."

' "If you want to believe the men aren't dead, believe it!" Kyra said.

'Vaughan's theory that the men had disappeared of their own free will was, of course, absurd; but his wife's sudden coldness to him seemed to me to be needlessly impatient. I understood when I knew them better. Vaughan – your reserved Englishman, Romero! – was covering up his thoughts and fears, and chose, quite unconsciously, to appear stupid rather than to show his anxiety. She recognized the insincerity without understanding its cause, and it made her angry.

'They were a queer pair, those two; intelligent, cultured, and so interested in themselves and each other that they needed more than one life to satisfy their curiosity. She was a highly strung creature, with swift brown eyes and a slender, eager body that seemed to grow like a flower from the ground under her feet. And natural! I don't mean she couldn't act. She could – but when she did, it was deliberate. She was defenceless before others' suffering and joy, and she didn't try to hide it.

'Lord! She used to live through enough emotions in one day to last her husband for a year!

'Not that he was unemotional. Those two were very much alike, though you'd never have guessed it. But he was shy of tears and laughter, and he had armed his whole soul against them. To a casual observer he seemed the calmer of the two, but at bottom he was an extremist. He might have been a poet, a Saint Francis, a revolutionary. But was he? No! He was an Englishman. He knew he was in danger of being swayed by emotional ideas, of giving his life to them. And so? And so he balanced every idea with another, and secured peace for himself between the scales. She, of course, would always jump into one scale or the other. And he loved her for it. But his non-committal attitudes got on her nerves.'

'She could do no wrong in your eyes,' said Romero indignantly. His sympathies had been aroused on behalf of the unknown Englishman. He admired him.

'I adored her,' said Shiravieff frankly. 'Everybody did. She made one live more intensely. Don't think I undervalued him, however. I couldn't help seeing how his wheels went round, but I liked him thoroughly. He was a man you could trust, and good company as well. A man of action. What he did had little relation to the opinions he expressed.

'Well, after that dinner with the Vaughans I had no more desire for a lonely holiday; so I did the next best thing, and took an active interest in everything that was going on. I heard all the gossip, for I was staying in the general clearing-house, the village inn. In the evenings I often joined the district magistrate as he sat in the garden with a stein of beer in front of him and looked over the notes of the depositions which he had taken that day.

'He was a very solid functionary – a good type of man for a case like that. A more imaginative person would have formed theories, found evidence to fit them, and only added to the mystery. He did not want to discuss the case. No, he had no fear of an indiscretion. It was simply that he had nothing to say, and was clear-headed enough to realize it. He admitted that he knew no more than the villagers whose depositions filled his portfolio. But he was ready to talk on any other subject – especially politics – and our long conversations gave me a reputation for profound wisdom among the villagers. Almost I had the standing of a public official.

'So, when a third man disappeared, this time from Zweibergen itself, the mayor and the village constable came to me for instructions. It was the local grocer who was missing. He had climbed up through the forest in the hope of bagging a blackcock at dusk. In the morning the shop did not open. Only then was it known that he had never returned. A solitary shot had been heard about 10.30 p.m., when the grocer was presumably trudging homewards.

'All I could do, pending the arrival of the magistrate, was to send out search parties. We quartered the forest, and examined every path. Vaughan and I, with one of the peasants, went up to my favourite place for blackcock. It was there, I thought, that the grocer would have gone. Then we inspected every foot of the route which he must have taken back to the village. Vaughan knew something about tracking. He was one of those surprising Englishmen whom you may know for years without realizing that once there were coloured men in Africa or Burma or Borneo who knew him still better, and drove game for him, and acknowledged him as someone juster than their gods, but no more comprehensible.

'We had covered some four miles when he surprised me by suddenly showing interest in the undergrowth. Up to then I had been fool enough to think that he was doing precisely nothing.

' "Someone has turned aside from the path here," he said. "He was in a hurry. I wonder why."

'A few yards from the path there was a white rock about thirty feet high. It was steep, but projecting ledges gave an easy way up. A hot spring at the foot of it bubbled out of a cavity hardly bigger than a fox's earth. When Vaughan showed me the signs, I could see that the scrub which grew between the rocks and the path had been roughly pushed aside. But I pointed out that no one was likely to dash off the path through that thicket.

' "When you know you're being followed, you like to have a clear space around you," Vaughan answered. "It would be comforting to be on top of that rock with a gun in your hands – if you got there in time. Let's go up."

'The top was bare stone, with clumps of creeper and ivy growing from the crannies. Set back some three yards from the edge was a little tree, growing in a pocket of soil. One side of its base was shattered into slivers. It had received a full charge of shot at close quarters. The peasant crossed himself. He murmured:

' "They say there's always a tree between you and it."

'I asked him what "it" was. He didn't answer immediately, but played with his stick casually, and as if ashamed, until the naked steel point was in his hand. Then he muttered:

' "The werewolf."

'Vaughan laughed and pointed to the shot marks six inches from the ground.

' "The werewolf must be a baby one, if it's only as tall as that," he said. "No, the man's gun went off as he fell. Perhaps he was followed too close as he scrambled up. About there is where his body would have fallen."

'He knelt down to examine the ground.

' "What's that?" he asked me. "If it's blood, it has something else with it."

'There was only a tiny spot on the bare rock. I looked at it. It was undoubtedly brain tissue. I was surprised that there was no more of it. It must, I suppose, have come from a deep wound in the skull. Might have been made by an arrow, or a bird's beak, or perhaps a tooth.

'Vaughan slid down the rock, and prodded his stick into the sulphurous mud of the stream bed. Then he hunted about in the bushes like a dog.

' "There was no body dragged away in that direction," he said.

'We examined the farther side of the rock. It fell sheer, and seemed an impossible climb for man or beast. The edge was matted with growing things. I was ready to believe that Vaughan's eyes could tell if anything had passed that way.

' "Not a sign!" he said. "Where the devil has his body gone to?"

'The three of us sat on the edge of the rock in silence. The spring bubbled and wept beneath, and the pines murmured above us. There was no need of a little particle of human substance, recognizable only to a physiologist's eye, to tell us that we were on the scene of a kill. Imagination? Imagination is so often only a forgotten instinct. The man who ran up that rock wondered in his panic why he gave way to his imagination.

'We found the magistrate in the village when we returned and reported our find to him.

' "Interesting! But what does it tell us?" he said.

'I pointed out that at least we knew the man was dead or dying.

' "There's no certain proof. Show me his body. Show me any motive for killing him." '

'Vaughan insisted that it was the work of an animal. The magistrate disagreed. If it were wolf, he said, we might have some difficulty in collecting the body, but none in finding it. And as for bear – well, they were so harmless that the idea was ridiculous.

'Nobody believed in any material beast, for the whole countryside had been beaten. But tales were told in the village – the old tales. I should never have dreamed that those peasants accepted so many horrors as fact if I hadn't heard those tales in the village inn. The odd thing is that I couldn't say then, and I can't say now, that they were altogether wrong. You should have seen the look in those men's eyes as old Weiss, the game warden, told how time after time his grandfather had fired point-blank at a grey wolf whom he met in the woods at twilight. He had never killed it until he loaded his gun with silver. Then the wolf vanished after the shot, but Heinrich the cobbler was found dying in his house with a beaten silver dollar in his belly.

'Josef Weiss, his son, who did most of the work on the preserves and was seldom seen in the village unless he came down to sell a joint or two of venison, was indignant with his father. He was a heavily built, sullen fellow, who had read a little. There's nobody so intolerant of superstition as your half-educated man. Vaughan, of course, agreed with him – but then capped the villagers' stories with such ghastly tales from native folklore and mediæval literature that I couldn't help seeing he had been brooding on the subject. The peasants took him seriously. They came and went in pairs. No one would step out into the night without a companion. Only the shepherd was unaffected. He didn't disbelieve, but he was a mystic. He was used to passing to and fro under the trees at night.

' "You've got to be a part of those things, sir," he said to me, "then you'll not be afraid of them. I don't say a man can turn himself into a wolf – the Blessed Virgin protect us! – but I know why he'd want to."

'That was most interesting.

' "I think I know too," I answered. "But what does it feel like?"

' "It feels as if the woods had got under your skin, and you want to walk wild and crouch at the knees."

' "He's perfectly right," said Vaughan convincingly.

'That was the last straw for those peasants. They drew away from Vaughan, and two of them spat into the fire to avert his evil eye. He seemed to them much too familiar with the black arts.

' "How do you explain it?" asked Vaughan, turning to me.

'I told him it might have a dozen different causes, just as fear of the dark has. And physical hunger might also have something to do with it.

'I think our modern psychology is inclined to give too much importance to sex. We forget that man is, or was, a fleet-footed hunting animal equipped with all the necessary instincts.

'As soon as I mentioned hunger, there was a chorus of assent – though they really didn't know what I or the shepherd or Vaughan was talking about. Most of those men had experienced extreme hunger. The innkeeper was reminded of a temporary famine during the war. The shepherd told us how he had once spent a week stuck on the face of a cliff before he was found. Josef Weiss, eager to get away from the supernatural, told his experiences as a prisoner of war in Russia. With his companions he had been forgotten behind the blank walls of a fortress while their guards engaged in revolution. Those poor devils had been reduced to very desperate straits indeed.

'For a whole week Vaughan and I were out with the search parties day and night. Meanwhile Kyra wore herself out trying to comfort the womenfolk. They couldn't help loving her – yet half suspected that she herself was at the bottom of the mystery. I don't blame them. They couldn't be expected to understand her intense spirituality. To them she was like a creature from another planet, fascinating and terrifying. Without claiming any supernatural powers for her, I've no doubt that Kyra could have told the past, present, and future of any of those villagers much more accurately than the travelling gipsies.

'On our first day of rest I spent the afternoon with the Vaughans. He and I were refreshed by twelve hours' sleep, and certain that we could hit on some new solution to the mystery that might be the right one. Kyra joined in the discussion. We went over the old theories again and again, but could make no progress.

' "We shall be forced to believe the tales they tell in the village," I said at last.

' "Why don't you?" asked Kyra Vaughan.

'We both protested. Did she believe them, we asked.

' "I'm not sure," she answered. "What does it matter? But I know that evil has come to those men. Evil . . ." she repeated

'We were startled You smile, Romero, but you don't realize how that atmosphere of the uncanny affected us.

'Looking back on it, I see how right she was. Women – good Lord, they get hold of the spiritual significance of something, and we take them literally!

'When she left us I asked Vaughan whether she really believed in the werewolf.

' "Not exactly," he explained. "What she means is that our logic isn't getting us anywhere – that we ought to begin looking for something which, if it isn't a werewolf, has the spirit of the werewolf. You see, even if she saw one, she would be no more worried than she is. The outward form of things impresses her so little."

'Vaughan appreciated his wife. He didn't know what in the world she meant, but he knew that there was always sense in her parables, even if it took one a long time to make the connection between what she actually said and the way in which one would have expressed the same thing oneself. That, after all, is what understanding means.

'I asked what he supposed she meant by evil.

' "Evil?" he replied. "Evil forces – something that behaves as it has no right to behave. She means almost – possession. Look here! Let's find out in our own way what she means. Assuming it's visible, let's see this thing."

'It was, he still thought, an animal. Its hunting had been successful, and now that the woods were quiet it would start again. He didn't think it had been driven away for good.

' "It wasn't driven away by the first search parties," he pointed out. "They frightened all the game for miles around, but this thing simply took one of them. It will come back, just as surely as a man-eating lion comes back. And there's only one way to catch it – bait!"

' "Who's going to be the bait?" I asked.

' "You and I."

'I suppose I looked startled. Vaughan laughed. He said that I was getting fat, that I would make most tempting bait. Whenever he made jokes in poor taste, I knew that he was perfectly serious.

' "What are you going to do?" I asked. "Tie me to a tree and watch out with a gun?"

' "That's about right, except that you needn't be tied up – and as the idea is mine you can have first turn with the gun. Are you a good shot?"

'I am and so was he. To prove it, we practised on a target after dinner, and found that we could trust each other up to fifty yards in clear moonlight. Kyra disliked shooting. She had a horror of death. Vaughan's excuse didn't improve matters. He said that we were going deer-stalking the next night and needed some practice.

' "Are you going to shoot them while they are asleep?" she asked disgustedly.

' "While they are having their supper, dear."

' "Before, if possible," I added.

'I disliked hurting her by jokes that to her were pointless, but we chose that method deliberately. She couldn't be told the truth, and now she would be too proud to ask questions.

'Vaughan came down to the inn the following afternoon, and we worked out a plan of campaign. The rock was the starting-point of all our theories, and on it we decided to place the watcher. From the top there was a clear view of the path for fifty yards on either side. The watcher was to take up his stand, while covered by the ivy, before sunset, and at a little before ten the bait was to be on the path and within shot. He should walk up and down, taking care never to step out of sight of the rock, until midnight, when the party would break up. We reckoned that our quarry, if it reasoned, would take the bait to be a picket posted in that part of the forest.

'The difficulty was getting home. We had to go separately in case we were observed, and hope for the best. Eventually we decided that the man on the path, who might be followed, should go straight down to the road as fast as he could. There was a timber slide quite close, by which he could cut down in ten minutes. The man on the rock should wait awhile and then go home by the path.

' "Well, I shall not see you again until to-morrow morning," said Vaughan as he got up to go. "You'll see me but I shan't see you. Just whistle once, very softly, as I come up the path, so that I know you're there."

'He remarked that he had left a letter for Kyra with the notary in case of accidents, and added, with an embarrassed laugh, that he supposed it was silly.

'I thought it was anything but silly, and said so.

'I was on the rock by sunset. I wormed my legs and body back into the ivy, leaving head and shoulders free to pivot with the rifle. It was a little .300 with a longish barrel. I felt certain that Vaughan was as safe as human science and a steady hand could make him.

'The moon came up, and the path was a ribbon of silver in front of me. There's something silent about moonlight. It's not light. It's a state of things. When there was sound it was unexpected, like the sudden shiver on the flank of a sleeping beast. A twig cracked now and then. An owl hooted. A fox slunk across the pathway, looking back over his shoulder. I wished that Vaughan would come. Then the ivy rustled

TABOO

behind me. I couldn't turn round. My spine became very sensitive, and a point at the back of my skull tingled as if expecting a blow. It was no good my telling myself that nothing but a bird could possibly be behind me – but of course it was a bird. A nightjar whooshed out of the ivy, and my body became suddenly cold with sweat. That infernal fright cleared all vague fears right out of me. I continued to be uneasy, but I was calm.

'After a while I heard Vaughan striding up the path. Then he stepped within range, a bold, clear figure in the moonlight. I whistled softly, and he waved his hand from the wrist in acknowledgment. He walked up and down, smoking a cigar. The point of light marked his head in the shadows. Wherever he went, my sights were lined a yard or two behind him. At midnight he nodded his head towards my hiding-place and trotted rapidly away to the timber slide. A little later I took the path home.

'The next night our rôles were reversed. It was my turn to walk the path. I found that I preferred to be the bait. On the rock I had longed for another pair of eyes, but after an hour on the ground I did not even want to turn my head. I was quite content to trust Vaughan to take care of anything going on behind me. Only once was I uneasy. I heard, as I thought, a bird calling far down in the woods. It was a strange call, almost a whimper. It was like the little frightened exclamation of a woman. Birds weren't popular with me just then. I had a crazy memory of some Brazilian bird which drives a hole in the back of your head and lives on brains. I peered down through the trees, and caught a flicker of white in a moonlight clearing below. It showed only for a split second, and I came to the conclusion that it must have been a ripple of wind in the silver grass. When the time was up I went down the timber slide and took the road home to the inn. I fell asleep wondering whether we hadn't let our nerves run away with us.

'I went up to see the Vaughans in the morning. Kyra looked pale and worried. I told her at once that she must take more rest.

' "She won't," said Vaughan. "She can't resist other people's troubles."

' "You see, I can't put them out of my mind as easily as you," she answered provocatively.

' "Oh Lord!" Vaughan exclaimed. "I'm not going to start an argument."

' "No – because you know you're in the wrong. Have you quite forgotten this horrible affair?"

'I gathered up the reins of the conversation, and gentled it into easier topics. As I did so, I was conscious of resistance from Kyra; she evidently wanted to go on scrapping. I wondered why. Her nerves, no doubt, were overstrained, but she was too tired to wish to relieve them by a quarrel.

I decided that she was deliberately worrying her husband to make him admit how he was spending his evenings.

'That was it. Before I left, she took me apart on the pretext of showing me the garden and pinned the conversation to our shooting expeditions. Please God I'm never in the dock if the prosecuting counsel is a woman! As it was, I had the right to ask questions in my turn, and managed to slip from under her cross-examination without allowing her to feel it. It hurt. I couldn't let her know the truth, but I hated to leave her in that torment of uncertainty. She hesitated an instant before she said goodbye to me. Then she caught my arm, and cried:

' "Take care of him!"

'I smiled and told her that she was overwrought, that we were doing nothing dangerous. What else could I say?

'That night, the third of the watching, the woods were alive. The world which lives just below the fallen leaves – mice and moles and big beetles – was making its surprising stir. The night birds were crying. A deer coughed far up in the forest. There was a slight breeze blowing, and from my lair on top of the rock I watched Vaughan trying to catch the scents it bore. He crouched down in the shadows. A bear ambled across the path up wind, and began to grub for some succulent morsel at the roots of a tree. It looked as woolly and harmless as a big dog. Clearly neither it nor its kind were the cause of our vigil. I saw Vaughan smile, and knew that he was thinking the same thought.

'A little after eleven the bear looked up, sniffed the air, and disappeared into the black bulk of the undergrowth as effortlessly and completely as if a spotlight had been switched off him. One by one the sounds of the night ceased. Vaughan eased the revolver in his pocket. The silence told its own tale. The forest had laid aside its business, and was watching like ourselves.

'Vaughan walked up the path to the far end of his beat. I looked away from him an instant, and down the path through the trees my eyes caught that same flicker of white. He turned to come back, and by the time that he was abreast of the rock I had seen it again. A bulky object it seemed to be, soft white, moving fast. He passed me, going towards it, and I lined my sights on the path ahead of him. Bounding up through the woods it came, then into the moonlight, and on to him. I was saved only by the extreme difficulty of the shot. I took just a fraction of a second longer than I needed, to make very sure of not hitting Vaughan. In that fraction of a second, thank God, she called to him! It was Kyra. A white ermine coat and her terrified running up the path had made of her a strange figure.

'She clung to him while she got her breath back. I heard her say:

' "I was frightened. There was something after me. I know it."

'Vaughan did not answer, but held her very close and stroked her hair. His upper lip curled back a little from his teeth. For once his whole being was surrendered to a single emotion: the desire to kill whatever had frightened her.

' "How did you know I was here?" he asked.

' "I didn't. I was looking for you. I looked for you last night, too."

' "You mad, brave girl!" he said.

' "But you mustn't, mustn't be alone. Where's Shiravieff?"

' "Right there." He pointed to the rock.

' "Why don't you hide yourself, too?"

' "One of us must show himself," he answered.

'She understood instantly the full meaning of his reply.

' "Come back with me!" she cried. "Promise me to stop it!"

' "I'm very safe, dear," he answered. "Look!"

'I can hear his tense voice right now, and remember their exact words. Those things eat into the memory. He led her just below the rock. His left arm was round her. At the full stretch of his right arm he held out his handkerchief by two corners. He did not look at me, nor alter his tone.

' "Shiravieff," he said, "make a hole in that!"

'It was just a theatrical bit of nonsense, for the handkerchief was the easiest of easy marks. At any other time I would have been as sure as he of the result of the shot. But what he didn't know was that I had so nearly fired at another white and much larger mark – I was trembling so that I could hardly hold the rifle. I pressed the trigger. The hole in the handkerchief was dangerously near his hand. He put it down to bravado rather than bad shooting.

'Vaughan's trick had its effect. Kyra was surprised. She did not realize how easy it was, any more than she knew how much harder to hit is a moving mark seen in a moment of excitement.

' "But let me stay with you," she appealed.

' "Sweetheart, we're going back right now. Do you think I'm going to allow my most precious possession to run wild in the woods?"

' "What about mine?" she said, and kissed him.

'They went away down the short cut. He made her walk a yard in front of him, and I caught the glint of moonlight on the barrel of his revolver. He was taking no risks.

'I myself went back by the path – carelessly, for I was sure that every living thing had been scared away by the voices and the shot. I was nearly down when I knew I was being followed. You've both lived in strange places – do you want me to explain the sensation? No? Well then, I knew I was being followed. I stopped and faced back up the path. Instantly something moved past me in the bushes, as if to cut off my retreat. I'm not superstitious. Once I heard it, I felt safe, for I knew where it was. I was sure I could move faster down that path than anything in the undergrowth – and if it came out into the open, it would have to absorb five steel explosive bullets. I ran. So far as I could hear, it didn't follow.

'I told Vaughan the next morning what had happened.

' "I'm sorry," he said, "I had to take her back. You understand, don't you?"

' "Of course," I answered in surprise. "What else could you do?"

' "Well, I didn't like leaving you alone. We had advertised our presence pretty widely. True, we should have frightened away any animal – but all we know about this animal is that it doesn't behave like one. There was a chance of our attracting instead of frightening it. We're going to get it to-night," he added savagely.

'I asked if Kyra would promise to stay at home.

' "Yes. She says we're doing our duty, and that she won't interfere. Do you think this is our duty?"

' "No!" I said.

' "Nor do I. I never feel that anything which I enjoy can possibly be my duty. And, by God, I enjoy this now!"

'I think he did enjoy it as he waited on the rock that night. He wanted revenge. There was no reason to believe that Kyra had been frightened by anything more than night and loneliness, but he was out against the whole set of circumstances that had dared to affect her. He wanted to be the bait instead of the watcher – I believe, with some mad hope of getting his hands on his enemy. But I wouldn't let him. After all, it was my turn.

'Bait! As I walked up and down the path, the word kept running through my mind. There wasn't a sound. The only moving thing was the moon which passed from tree-top to tree-top as the night wore on. I pictured Vaughan on the rock, the foresight of his rifle creeping backwards and forwards in a quarter-circle as it followed my movements. I visualized the line of his aim as a thread of light passing down and across in front of my eyes. Once I heard Vaughan cough. I knew that he had seen my nervousness and was reassuring me. I stood by a clump of bushes some twenty yards away, watching a silver leaf that shook as some tiny beast crawled up it.

'Hot breath on the back of my neck – crushing weight on my shoulders – hardness against the back of my skull – the crack of Vaughan's rifle – they were instantaneous, but not too swift for me to know all the terror of death. Something leapt away from me, and squirmed into the spring-head beneath the rock.

' "Are you all right?" shouted Vaughan, crashing down through the ivy.

TABOO

' "What was it?"

' "A man. I've winged him. Come on! I'm going in after him!"

'Vaughan was berserk mad. I've never seen such flaming disregard of danger. He drew a deep breath, and tackled the hole as if it were a man's ankles. Head and shoulders, he sloshed into the mud of the cavity, emptying his Winchester in front of him. If he couldn't wriggle forward swiftly without drawing breath he would be choked by the sulphur fumes or drowned. If his enemy were waiting for him, he was a dead man. He disappeared and I followed. No, I didn't need any courage. I was covered by the whole length of Vaughan's body. But it was a vile moment. We'd never dreamed that anything could get in and out through that spring. Imagine holding your breath, and trying to squirm through hot water, using your hips and shoulders like a snake, not knowing how you would return if the way forward was barred. At last I was able to raise myself on my hands and draw a breath. Vaughan had dragged himself clear and was on his feet, holding a flashlight in front of him.

' "Got him!" he said.

'We were in a low cave under the rock. There was air from the cracks above us. The floor was of dry sand, for the hot stream flowed into the cave close to the hole by which it left. A man lay crumpled up at the far end of the hollow. We crossed over to him. He held a sort of long pistol in his hand. It was a spring humane-killer. The touch of that wide muzzle against my skull is not a pleasant memory. The muzzle is jagged, you see, so that it grips the scalp while the spike is released.

'We turned the body over – it was Josef Weiss. Werewolf? Possession? I don't know. I would call it an atavistic neurosis. But that's a name, not an explanation.

'Beyond the body there was a hole some six feet in diameter, as round as if it had been bored by a rotary drill. The springs which had forced that passage had dried up, but the mottled-yellow walls were smooth as marble with the deposit left by the water. Evidently Weiss had been trying to reach that opening when Vaughan dropped him. We climbed that natural sewer pipe. For half an hour the flashlight revealed nothing but the sweating walls of the hole. Then we were stopped by a roughly hewn ladder which sprawled across the passage. The rungs were covered with mud, and here and there were dark stains on the wood. We went up. It led to a hollow evidently dug out with spade and chisel. The roof was of planks, with a trap-door at one end. We lifted it with our shoulders, and stood up within the four walls of a cottage. A fire was smouldering on the open hearth, and as we let in the draught of air, a log burst into flame. A gun stood in the ingle. On a rack were some iron traps and a belt of cartridges. There was a table in the centre of the room with a long knife on it. That was all we saw with our first glance. With our second we saw a lot more. Weiss had certainly carried his homicidal mania to extremes. I imagine his beastly experiences as a prisoner of war had left a kink in the poor devil's mind. Then, digging out a cellar or repairing the floor, he had accidentally discovered the dry channel beneath the cottage, and followed it to its hidden outlet. That turned his secret desires into action. He could kill and remove his victim without any trace. And so he let himself go.

'At dawn we were back at the cottage with the magistrate. When he came out, he was violently, terribly sick. I have never seen a man be so sick. It cleared him. No, I'm not being humorous. It cleared him mentally. He needed none of those emotional upheavals which we have to employ to drive shock out of our system. Didn't I tell you he was unimaginative? He handled the subsequent inquiry in a masterly fashion. He accepted as an unavoidable fact the horror of the thing, but he wouldn't listen to tales which could not be proved. There was never any definite proof of the extra horror in which the villagers believed.'

There was an exclamation from Lewis Banning.

'Ah – you remember now. I thought you would. The press reported that rumour as a fact, but there was no definite proof, I tell you.

'Vaughan begged me to keep it from his wife. I was to persuade her to go away at once before a breath of it could reach her. I was to tell her that he might have received internal injuries, and should be examined without delay. He himself believed the tale that was going round, but he was very conscious of his poise. I suspect that he was feeling a little proud of himself – proud that he was unaffected. But he dreaded the effect of the shock on his wife.

'We were too late. The cook had caught the prevailing fever, and told that unpleasant rumour to Kyra. She ran to her husband, deadly pale, desperate, instinctively seeking protection against the blow. He could protect himself, and would have given his life to be able to protect her. He tried, but only gave her words and more words. He explained that, looking at the affair calmly, it didn't matter; that no one could have known; that the best thing was to forget it; and so on. It was absurd. As if anyone who believed what was being said could look at the affair calmly!

'Sentiments of that kind were no comfort to his wife. She expected him to show his horror, not to isolate himself as if he had shut down a lid, not to leave her spiritually alone. She cried out at him that he had no feeling and rushed to her room. Perhaps I should have given her a sedative, but I didn't. I knew that the sooner she had it out with herself, the better, and that her mind was healthy enough to stand it.

'I said so to Vaughan, but he did not understand. Emotion, he thought, was dangerous. It mustn't be let loose. He wanted to tell her again not to "worry". He didn't see that he was the only person within ten miles who wasn't "worried".

'She came down later. She spoke to Vaughan scornfully, coldly, as if she had found him unfaithful to her. She said to him:

' "I can't see the woman again. Tell her to go, will you?"

'She meant the cook. Vaughan challenged her. He was just obstinately logical and fair.

' "It's not her fault," he said. "She's an ignorant woman, not an anatomist. We'll call her in, and you'll see how unjust you are."

' "Oh no!" she cried – and then checked herself.

' "Send for her then!" she said.

'The cook came in. How could she know, she sobbed – she had noticed nothing – she was sure that what she had bought from Josef Weiss was really venison – she didn't think for a moment. . . . Well, blessed are the simple!

' "My God! Be quiet!" Kyra burst out. "You all of you think what you want to think. You all lie to yourselves and pretend and have no feelings!"

'I couldn't stand any more. I begged her not to torture herself and not to torture me. It was the right note. She took my hands and asked me to forgive her. Then the tears came. She cried, I think, till morning. At breakfast she had a wan smile for both of us, and I knew that she was out of danger – clear of the shock for good. They left for England the same day.

'I met them in Vienna two years ago, and they dined with me. We never mentioned Zweibergen. They still adored one another, and still quarrelled. It was good to hear them talk and watch them feeling for each other's sympathy.

'Vaughan refused his meat at dinner, and said that he had become a vegetarian.

' "Why?" I asked deliberately.

'He answered that he had recently had a nervous breakdown – could eat nothing, and had nearly died. He was all right now, he said; no trace of the illness remained but his distaste for meat . . . it had come over him quite suddenly . . . he could not think why.

'I tell you the man was absolutely serious. He could *not* think why. Shock had lain hidden in him for ten years, and then had claimed its penalty.'

'And you?' asked Banning. 'How did you get clear of shock? You had to control your emotions at the time.'

'A fair question,' said Shiravieff. 'I've been living under a suspended sentence. There have been days when I thought I should visit one of my colleagues and ask him to clean up the mess. If I could only have got the story out of my system, it would have helped a lot – but I couldn't bring myself to tell it.'

'You have just told it,' said Colonel Romero solemnly.

Graham Greene

A Little Place off the
Edgware Road

Craven came up past the Achilles statue in the thin summer rain. It was only just after lighting-up time, but already the cars were lined up all the way to the Marble Arch, and the sharp acquisitive faces peered out ready for a good time with anything possible which came along. Craven went bitterly by with the collar of his mackintosh tight round his throat: it was one of his bad days.

All the way up the Park he was reminded of passion, but you needed money for love. All that a poor man could get was lust. Love needed a good suit, a car, a flat somewhere, or a good hotel. It needed to be wrapped in cellophane. He was aware all the time of the stringy tie beneath the mackintosh, and the frayed sleeves: he carried his body about with him like something he hated. (There were moments of happiness in the British Museum reading-room, but the body called him back.) He bore, as his only sentiment, the memory of ugly deeds committed on park chairs. People talked as if the body died too soon – that wasn't the trouble, to Craven, at all. The body kept alive – and through the glittering tinselly rain, on his way to a rostrum, he passed a little man in a black suit carrying a banner, 'The Body shall rise again'. He remembered a dream from which three times he had woken trembling: he had been alone in the huge dark cavernous burying ground of all the world. Every grave was connected to another under the ground: the globe was honeycombed for the sake of the dead, and on each occasion of dreaming he had discovered anew the horrifying fact that the body doesn't decay. There are no worms and dissolution. Under the ground the world was littered with masses of dead flesh ready to rise again with their warts and boils and eruptions. He had lain in bed and remembered – as 'tidings of great joy' – that the body after all was corrupt.

He came up into the Edgware Road walking fast – the Guardsmen were out in couples, great languid elongated beasts – the bodies like worms in their tight trousers. He hated them, and hated his hatred because he knew what it was, envy. He was aware that every one of them had a better body than himself: indigestion creased his stomach: he felt sure that his breath was foul – but who could he ask? Sometimes he secretly touched himself here and there with scent: it was one of his ugliest secrets. Why should he be asked to believe in the resurrection of this body he wanted to forget? Sometimes he prayed at night (a hint of religious belief was lodged in his breast like a worm in a nut) that *his* body at any rate should never rise again.

He knew all the side streets round the Edgware Road only too well: when a mood was on, he simply walked until he tired, squinting at his own image in the windows of Salmon & Gluckstein and the A.B.C.s. So he noticed at once the posters outside the disused theatre in Culpar Road. They were not unusual, for sometimes Barclays Bank Dramatic Society would hire the place for an evening – or an obscure film would be trade-shown there. The theatre had been built in 1920 by an optimist who thought the cheapness of the site would more than counter-balance its disadvantage of lying a mile outside the conventional theatre zone. But no play had ever succeeded, and it was soon left to gather rat-holes and spider-webs. The covering of the seats was never renewed, and all that ever happened to the place was the temporary false life of an amateur play or a trade show.

Craven stopped and read – there were still optimists it appeared, even in 1939, for nobody but the blindest optimist could hope to make money out of the place as 'The Home of the Silent Film'. The first season of 'primitives' was announced (a high-brow phrase): there would never be a second. Well, the seats were cheap, and it was perhaps worth a shilling to him, now that he was tired, to get in somewhere out of the rain. Craven bought a ticket and went in to the darkness of the stalls.

In the dead darkness a piano tinkled something monotonous recalling Mendelssohn: he sat down in a gangway seat, and could immediately feel the emptiness all round him. No, there would never be another season. On the screen a large woman in a kind of toga wrung her hands, then wobbled with curious jerky movements towards a couch. There she sat and stared out like a sheep-dog distractedly through her loose and black and stringy hair. Sometimes she seemed to dissolve altogether into dots and flashes and wiggly lines. A sub-title said, 'Pompilia betrayed by her beloved Augustus seeks an end to her troubles.'

Craven began at last to see – a dim waste of stalls. There were not twenty people in the place – a few couples whispering with their heads touching, and a number of lonely men like himself, wearing the same uniform of the cheap mackintosh. They lay about at intervals like corpses – and again Craven's obsession returned: the tooth-ache of horror. He thought miserably – I am going mad: other people don't feel like this. Even a disused theatre reminded him of those interminable caverns where the bodies were waiting for resurrection.

'A slave to his passion Augustus calls for yet more wine.'

A gross middle-aged Teutonic actor lay on an elbow with his arm round a large woman in a shift. The Spring Song tinkled ineptly on, and the screen flickered like indigestion. Somebody felt his way through the darkness, scrabbling past Craven's knees – a small man: Craven experienced the unpleasant feeling of a large beard brushing his mouth. Then there was a long sigh as the newcomer found the next chair, and on the screen events had moved with such rapidity that Pompilia had already stabbed herself – or so Craven supposed – and lay still and buxom among her weeping slaves.

A low breathless voice sighed out close to Craven's ear, 'What's happened? Is she asleep?'

'No. Dead.'

'Murdered?' the voice asked with a keen interest.

'I don't think so. Stabbed herself.'

Nobody said 'Hush': nobody was enough interested to object to a voice. They drooped among the empty chairs in attitudes of weary inattention.

The film wasn't nearly over yet: there were children somehow to be considered: was it all going on to a second generation? But the small bearded man in the next seat seemed to be interested only in Pompilia's death. The fact that he had come in at that moment apparently fascinated him. Craven heard the word 'coincidence' twice, and he went on talking to himself about it in low out-of-breath tones. 'Absurd when you come to think of it,' and then 'no blood at all'. Craven didn't listen: he sat with his hands clasped between his knees, facing the fact as he had faced it so often before, that he was in danger of going mad. He had to pull himself up, take a holiday, see a doctor (God knew what infection moved in his veins). He became aware that his bearded neighbour had addressed him directly. 'What?' he asked impatiently, 'what did you say?'

'There would be more blood than you can imagine.'

'What are you talking about?'

When the man spoke to him, he sprayed him with damp breath. There was a little bubble in his speech like an impediment. He said, 'When you murder a man . . .'

'This was a woman,' Craven said impatiently.

'That wouldn't make any difference.'

'And it's got nothing to do with murder anyway.'

'That doesn't signify.' They seemed to have got into an absurd and meaningless wrangle in the dark.

'I know, you see,' the little bearded man said in a tone of enormous conceit.

'Know what?'

'About such things,' he said with guarded ambiguity.

Craven turned and tried to see him clearly. Was he mad? Was this a warning of what he might become – babbling incomprehensibly to strangers in cinemas? He thought, By God, no, trying to see: I'll be sane yet. I *will* be sane. He could make out nothing but a small black hump of body. The man was talking to himself again. He said, 'Talk. Such talk. They'll say it was all for fifty pounds. But that's a lie. Reasons and reasons. They always take the first reason. Never look behind. Thirty years of reasons. Such simpletons,' he added again in that tone of breathless and unbounded conceit. So this was madness. So long as he could realize that, he must be sane himself – relatively speaking. Not so sane perhaps as the seekers in the park or the Guardsmen in the Edgware Road, but saner than this. It was like a message of encouragement as the piano tinkled on.

Then again the little man turned and sprayed him. 'Killed herself, you say? But who's to know that? It's not a mere question of what hand holds the knife.' He laid a hand suddenly and confidingly on Craven's: it was damp and sticky: Craven said with horror as a possible meaning came to him, 'What are you talking about?'

'I know,' the little man said. 'A man in my position gets to know almost everything.'

'What is your position?' Craven asked, feeling the sticky hand on his, trying to make up his mind whether he was being hysterical or not – after all, there were a dozen explanations – it might be treacle.

'A pretty desperate one *you'd* say.' Sometimes the voice almost died in the throat altogether. Something incomprehensible had happened on the screen – take your eyes from these early pictures for a moment and the plot had proceeded on at such a pace. . . . Only the actors moved slowly and jerkily. A young woman in a nightdress seemed to be weeping in the arms of a Roman centurion: Craven hadn't seen either of them before. '*I am not afraid of death, Lucius – in your arms.*'

The little man began to titter – knowingly. He was talking to himself again. It would have been easy to ignore him altogether if it had not been for those sticky hands which he now removed: he seemed to be fumbling at the seat in front of him. His head had a habit of lolling sideways – like an idiot child's. He said distinctly and irrelevantly: 'Bayswater Tragedy.'

'What was that?' Craven said. He had seen those words on a poster before he entered the park.

'What?'

'About the tragedy.'

'To think they call Cullen Mews Bayswater.' Suddenly the little man began to cough – turning his face towards Craven and coughing right at him: it was like vindictiveness. The voice said, 'Let me see. My umbrella.' He was getting up.

'You didn't have an umbrella.'

'My umbrella,' he repeated. 'My —' and seemed to lose the word altogether. He went scrabbling out past Craven's knees.

Craven let him go, but before he had reached the billowy dusty curtains of the Exit the screen went blank and bright – the film had broken, and somebody immediately turned up one dirt-choked chandelier above the circle. It shone down just enough for Craven to see the smear on his hands. This wasn't hysteria: this was a fact. He wasn't mad: he had sat next a madman who in some mews – what was the name, Colon, Collin. . . . Craven jumped up and made his own way out: the black curtain flapped in his mouth. But he was too late: the man had gone and there were three turnings to choose from. He chose instead a telephone-box and dialled with a sense odd for him of sanity and decision 999.

It didn't take two minutes to get the right department. They were interested and very kind. Yes, there had been a murder in a mews – Cullen Mews. A man's neck had been cut from ear to ear with a bread knife – a horrid crime. He began to tell them how he had sat next the murderer in a cinema: it couldn't be anyone else: there was blood on his hands – and he remembered with repulsion as he spoke the damp beard. There must have been a terrible lot of blood. But the voice from the Yard interrupted him. 'Oh no,' it was saying, 'we have the murderer – no doubt of it at all. It's the body that's disappeared.'

Craven put down the receiver. He said to himself aloud, 'Why should this happen to *me*? Why to *me*?' He was back in the horror of his dream – the squalid darkening street outside was only one of the innumerable tunnels connecting grave to grave where the imperishable bodies lay. He said, 'It was a dream, a dream,' and leaning forward he saw in the mirror above the telephone his own face sprinkled by tiny drops of blood like dew from a scent-spray. He began to scream, 'I won't go mad. I won't go mad. I'm sane. I won't go mad.' Presently a little crowd began to collect, and soon a policeman came.

C. M. Kornbluth

The Words of Guru

Yesterday, when I was going to meet Guru in the woods a man stopped me and said: 'Child, what are you doing out at one in the morning? Does your mother know where you are? How old are you, walking around this late?'

I looked at him, and saw that he was white-haired, so I laughed. Old men never see; in fact men hardly see at all. Sometimes young women see part, but men rarely ever see at all. 'I'm twelve on my next birthday,' I said. And then, because I would not let him live to tell people, I said, 'And I'm out this late to see Guru.'

'Guru?' he asked. 'Who is Guru? Some foreigner, I suppose? Bad business mixing with foreigners, young fellow. Who is Guru?'

So I told him who Guru was, and just as he began talking about cheap magazines and fairy tales I said one of the words that Guru taught me and he stopped talking. Because he was an old man and his joints were stiff he didn't crumple up but fell in one piece, hitting his head on the stone. Then I went on.

Even though I'm going to be only twelve on my next birthday I know many things that old people don't. And I remember things that other boys can't. I remember being born out of darkness, and I remember the noises that people made about me. Then when I was two months old I began to understand that the noises meant things like the things that were going on inside my head. I found out that I could make the noises too, and everybody was very much surprised. 'Talking!' they said, again and again. 'And so very young! Clara, what do you make of it?' Clara was my mother.

And Clara would say: 'I'm sure I don't know. There never was any genius in my family, and I'm sure there was none in Joe's.' Joe was my father.

THE WORDS OF GURU

Once Clara showed me a man I had never seen before, and told me that he was a reporter – that he wrote things in newspapers. The reporter tried to talk to me as if I were an ordinary baby. I didn't even answer him, but just kept looking at him until his eyes fell and he went away. Later Clara scolded me and read me a little piece in the reporter's newspaper that was supposed to be funny – about the reporter asking me very complicated questions and me answering with baby noises. It was not true, of course. I didn't say a word to the reporter, and he didn't ask me even one of the questions.

I heard her read the little piece, but while I listened I was watching the slug crawling on the wall. When Clara was finished I asked her: 'What is that grey thing?'

She looked where I pointed, but couldn't see it. 'What grey thing, Peter?' she asked. I had her call me by my whole name, Peter, instead of anything silly like Petey. 'What grey thing?'

'It's as big as your hand, Clara, but soft. I don't think it has any bones at all. It's crawling up, but I don't see any face on the topward side. And there aren't any legs.'

I think she was worried, but she tried to baby me by putting her hand on the wall and trying to find out where it was. I called out whether she was right or left of the thing. Finally she put her hand right through the slug. And then I realized that she really couldn't see it, and didn't believe it was there. I stopped talking about it then and only asked her a few days later: 'Clara, what do you call a thing which one person can see and another person can't?'

'An illusion, Peter,' she said. 'If that's what you mean.' I said nothing, but let her put me to bed as usual, but when she turned out the light and went away I waited a little while and then called out softly, 'Illusion! Illusion!'

At once Guru came for the first time. He bowed, the way he always has since, and said: 'I have been waiting.'

'I didn't know that was the way to call you,' I said.

'Whenever you want me I will be ready. I will teach you, Peter – if you want to learn. Do you know what I will teach you?'

'If you will teach me about the grey thing on the wall,' I said, 'I will listen. And if you will teach me about real things and unreal things I will listen.'

'These things,' he said thoughtfully, 'very few wish to learn. And there are some things that nobody ever wished to learn. And there are some things that I will not teach.'

Then I said: 'The things nobody has ever wished to learn I will learn. And I will even learn the things you do not wish to teach.'

He smiled mockingly. 'A master has come,' he said, half-laughing. 'A master of Guru.'

That was how I learned his name. And that night he taught me a word which would do little things, like spoiling food.

From that day, to the time I saw him last night he has not changed at all, though now I am as tall as he is. His skin is still as dry and shiny as ever it was, and his face is still bony, crowned by a head of very coarse, black hair.

When I was ten years old I went to bed one night only long enough to make Joe and Clara suppose I was fast asleep. I left in my place something which appears when you say one of the words of Guru and went down the drainpipe outside my window. It always was easy to climb down and up, ever since I was eight years old.

I met Guru in Inwood Hill Park. 'You're late,' he said.

'Not too late,' I answered. 'I know it's never too late for one of these things.'

'How do you know?' he asked sharply. 'This is your first.'

'And maybe my last,' I replied. 'I don't like the idea of it. If I have nothing more to learn from my second than my first I shan't go to another.'

'You don't know,' he said. 'You don't know what it's like – the voices, and the bodies slick with unguent, leaping flames, mind-filling ritual! You can have no idea at all until you've taken part.'

'We'll see,' I said. 'Can we leave from here?'

'Yes,' he said. Then he taught me the word I would need to know, and we both said it together.

The place we were in next was lit with red lights, and I think that the walls were of rock. Though of course there was no real seeing there, and so the lights only seemed to be red, and it was not real rock.

As we were going to the fire one of them stopped us. 'Who's with you?' she asked, calling Guru by another name. I did not know that he was also the person bearing that name, for it was a very powerful one.

He cast a hasty, sidewise glance at me and then said: 'This is Peter of whom I have often told you.'

She looked at me then and smiled, stretching out her oily arms. 'Ah,' she said, softly, like the cats when they talk at night to me. 'Ah, this is Peter. Will you come to me when I call you, Peter? And sometimes call for me – in the dark – when you are alone?'

'Don't do that!' said Guru, angrily pushing past her. 'He's very young – you might spoil him for his work.'

She screeched at our backs: 'Guru and his pupil – fine pair! Boy, he's no more real than I am – you're the only real thing here!'

'Don't listen to her,' said Guru. 'She's wild and raving. They're

THE WORDS OF GURU

always tight-strung when this time comes around.'

We came near the fires then, and sat down on rocks. They were killing animals and birds and doing things with their bodies. The blood was being collected in a basin of stone, which passed through the crowd. The one to my left handed it to me. 'Drink,' she said, grinning to show me her fine, white teeth. I swallowed twice from it and passed it to Guru.

When the bowl had passed all around we took off our clothes. Some, like Guru, did not wear them, but many did. The one to my left sat closer to me, breathing heavily at my face. I moved away. 'Tell her to stop, Guru,' I said. 'This isn't part of it, I know.'

Guru spoke to her sharply in their own language, and she changed her seat, snarling.

Then we all began to chant, clapping our hands and beating our thighs. One of them rose slowly and circled about the fires in a slow pace, her eyes rolling wildly. She worked her jaws and flung her arms about so sharply that I could hear the elbows crack. Still shuffling her feet against the rock floor she bent her body backwards down to her feet. Her belly muscles were bands standing out from her skin, nearly, and the oil rolled down her body and legs. As the palms of her hands touched the ground she collapsed in a twitching heap and began to set up a thin wailing noise against the steady chant and hand-beat that the rest of us were keeping up.

Another of them did the same as the first, and we chanted louder for her and still louder for the third. Then, while we still beat our hands and thighs, one of them took up the third, laid her across the altar and made her ready with a stone knife. The fire's light gleamed off the chipped edge of obsidian. As her blood drained down the groove cut as a gutter into the rock of the altar, we stopped our chant and the fires were snuffed out.

But still we could see what was going on, for these things were, of course, not happening at all – only seeming to happen, really, just as all the people and things there only seemed to be what they were. Only I was real. That must be why they desired me so.

As the last of the fires died Guru excitedly whispered: 'The Presence!' He was very deeply moved.

From the pool of blood from the third dancer's body there issued the Presence. It was the tallest one there, and when it spoke its voice was deeper, and when it commanded its commands were obeyed.

'Let blood!' it commanded, and we gashed ourselves with flints. It smiled and showed teeth bigger and sharper and whiter than any of the others.

'Make water!' it commanded, and we all spat on each other. It flapped its wings and rolled its eyes, that were bigger and redder than any of the others.

'Pass flame!' it commanded, and we breathed smoke and fire on our limbs. It stamped its feet, let blue flames roar from its mouth, and they were bigger and wilder than any of the others.

Then it returned to the pool of blood and we lit the fires again. Guru was staring straight before him; I tugged his arm. He bowed as though we were meeting for the first time that night.

'What are you thinking of?' I asked. 'We shall go now.'

'Yes,' he said heavily. 'Now we shall go.' Then we said the word that had brought us there.

The first man I killed was Brother Paul, at the school where I went to learn the things that Guru did not teach me.

It was less than a year ago, but it seems like a very long time. I have killed so many times since then.

'You're a very bright boy, Peter,' said the brother.

'Thank you, brother.'

'But there are things about you that I don't understand. Normally I'd ask your parents but – I feel that they don't understand either. You were an infant prodigy, weren't you?'

'Yes, brother.'

'There's nothing very unusual about that – glands, I'm told. You know what glands are?'

Then I was alarmed. I had heard of them, but I was not certain whether they were the short, thick green men who wear only metal or the things with many legs with whom I talked in the woods.

'How did you find out?' I asked him.

'But Peter! You look positively frightened, lad! I don't know a thing about them myself, but Father Frederick does. He has whole books about them, though I sometimes doubt whether he believes them himself.'

'They aren't good books, brother,' I said. 'They ought to be burned.'

'That's a savage thought, my son. But to return to your own problem—'

I could not let him go any further knowing what he did about me. I said one of the words Guru taught me and he looked at first very surprised and then seemed to be in great pain. He dropped across his desk and I felt his wrist to make sure, for I had not used that word before. But he was dead.

There was a heavy step outside and I made myself invisible. Stout Father Frederick entered, and I nearly killed him too with the word, but I knew that that would be very curious. I decided to wait, and went through the door as Father Frederick bent over the dead monk. He thought he was asleep.

I went down the corridor to the book-lined office of the stout priest and, working quickly, piled all his books in the centre of the room and lit them with my breath. Then I went down to the schoolyard and made myself visible again when there was nobody looking. It was very easy. I killed a man I passed on the street the next day.

There was a girl named Mary who lived near us. She was fourteen then, and I desired her as those in the Cavern out of Time and Space had desired me.

So when I saw Guru and he had bowed, I told him of it, and he looked at me in great surprise. 'You are growing older, Peter,' he said.

'I am, Guru. And there will come a time when your words will not be strong enough for me.'

He laughed. 'Come, Peter,' he said. 'Follow me if you wish. There is something that is going to be done—' He licked his thin, purple lips and said: 'I have told you what it will be like.'

'I shall come,' I said. 'Teach me the word.' So he taught me the word and we said it together.

The place we were in next was not like any of the other places I had been to before with Guru. It was No-place. Always before there had been the seeming passage of time and matter, but here there was not even that. Here Guru and the others cast off their forms and were what they were, and No-place was the only place where they could do this.

It was not like the Cavern, for the Cavern had been out of time and space, and this place was not enough of a place even for that. It was No-place.

What happened there does not bear telling, but I was made known to certain ones who never departed from there. All came to them as they existed. They had not colour or the seeming of colour, or any seeming of shape.

There I learned that eventually I would join with them; that I had been selected as the one of my planet who was to dwell without being forever in that No-place.

Guru and I left, having said the word.

'Well?' demanded Guru, staring me in the eye.

'I am willing,' I said. 'But teach me one word now—'

'Ah,' he said grinning. 'The girl?'

'Yes,' I said. 'The word that will mean much to her.'

Still grinning, he taught me the word.

Mary, who had been fourteen, is now fifteen and what they call incurably mad.

Last night I saw Guru again and for the last time. He bowed as I approached him. 'Peter,' he said warmly.

'Teach me the word,' said I.

'It is not too late.'

'Teach me the word.'

'You can withdraw – with what you master you can master also this world. Gold without reckoning; sardonyx and gems, Peter! Rich crushed velvet – stiff, scraping, embroidered tapestries!'

'Teach me the word.'

'Think, Peter, of the house you could build. It could be of white marble, and every slab centred by a winking ruby. Its gate could be of beaten gold within and without and it could be built about one slender tower of carven ivory, rising mile after mile into the turquoise sky. You could see the clouds float underneath your eyes.'

'Teach me the word.'

'Your tongue could crush the grapes that taste like melted silver. You could hear always the song of the bulbul and the lark that sounds like the dawnstar made musical. Spikenard that will bloom a thousand thousand years could be ever in your nostrils. Your hands could feel the down of purple Himalayan swans that is softer than a sunset cloud.'

'Teach me the word.'

'You could have women whose skin would be from the black of ebony to the white of snow. You could have women who would be as hard as flints or as soft as a sunset cloud.'

'Teach me the word.'

Guru grinned and said the word.

Now, I do not know whether I will say that word, which was the last that Guru taught me, today or tomorrow or until a year has passed.

It is a word that will explode this planet like a stick of dynamite in a rotten apple.

Robert Bloch

Yours truly, Jack the Ripper

I looked at the stage Englishman. He looked at me.

'Sir Guy Hollis?' I asked.

'Indeed. Have I the pleasure of addressing John Carmody, the psychiatrist?'

I nodded. My eyes swept over the figure of my distinguished visitor. Tall, lean, sandy-haired – with the traditional tufted moustache. And the tweeds. I suspected a monocle concealed in a vest pocket, and wondered if he'd left his umbrella in the outer office.

But more than that, I wondered what the devil had impelled Sir Guy Hollis of the British Embassy to seek out a total stranger here in Chicago.

Sir Guy didn't help matters any as he sat down. He cleared his throat, glanced around nervously, tapped his pipe against the side of the desk. Then he opened his mouth.

'What do you think of London?' he said.

'Why—'

'I'd like to discuss London with you, Mr Carmody.'

I meet all kinds. So I merely smiled, sat back, and gave him his head.

'Have you ever noticed anything strange about that city?' he asked.

'Well, the fog is famous.'

'Yes, the fog. That's important. It usually provides the perfect setting.'

'Setting for what?'

Sir Guy Hollis gave me an enigmatic grin.

'Murder,' he murmured.

'Murder?'

'Yes. Hasn't it struck you that London, of all cities, has a peculiar affinity for those who contemplate homicide?'

They don't talk that way, except in books. Still, it was an interesting thought. London as an ideal spot for a murder!

'As you mentioned,' said Sir Guy, 'there is a natural reason for this. The fog is an ideal background. And then too the British have a peculiar attitude in such matters. You might call it their sporting instinct. They regard murder as sort of a game.'

I sat up straight. Here was a theory.

'Yes, I needn't bore you with homicide statistics. The record is there. Aesthetically, temperamentally, the Englishman is interested in crimes of violence.

'A man commits murder. Then the excitement begins. The game starts. Will the criminal outwit the police? You can read between the lines in their newspaper stories. Everybody is waiting to see who will score.

'British law regards a prisoner as guilty until proven innocent. That's *their* advantage. But first they must catch their prisoner. And London bobbies are not allowed to carry fire-arms. That's a point for the fugitive. You see? All part of the rules of the game.'

I wondered what Sir Guy was driving at. Either a point or a strait jacket. But I kept my mouth shut and let him continue.

'The logical result of this British attitude towards murder is – Sherlock Holmes,' he said.

'Have you ever noticed how popular the theme of murder is in British fiction and drama?'

I smiled. I was back on familiar ground.

'*Angel Street*,' I suggested.

'*Ladies in Retirement*,' he continued. '*Night Must Fall*.'

'*Payment Deferred*,' I added. '*Laburnum Grove. Kind Lady. Love from a Stranger. Portrait of a Man with Red Hair. Black Limelight.*'

He nodded. 'Think of the motion pictures of Alfred Hitchcock and Emlyn Williams. The actors – Wilfred Lawson and Leslie Banks.'

'Charles Laughton,' I continued for him. 'Edmund Gwenn. Basil Rathbone. Raymond Massey. Sir Cedric Hardwicke.'

'You're quite an expert on this sort of thing yourself,' he told me.

'Not at all.' I smiled. 'I'm a psychiatrist.'

Then I leaned forward. I didn't change my tone of voice. 'All I want to know,' I said sweetly, 'is why you come up to my office and discuss murder melodramas with me.'

It stung him. He sat back and blinked a little.

'That isn't my intention,' he murmured. 'No. Not at all. I was just advancing a theory—'

'Stalling,' I said. 'Stalling. Come on, Sir Guy – spit it out.'

Talking like a gangster is all part of the applied psychiatric technique.

At least, it worked for me.

It worked this time.

Sir Guy stopped bleating. His eyes narrowed. When he leaned forward again he meant business.

'Mr Carmody,' he said, 'have you ever heard of – Jack the Ripper?'

'The murderer?' I asked.

'Exactly. The greatest monster of them all. Worse than Spring-heel Jack or Crippen. Jack the Ripper. Red Jack.'

'I've heard of him,' I said.

'Do you know his history?'

I got tough again. 'Listen, Sir Guy,' I muttered. 'I don't think we'll get any place swapping old wives' tales about famous crimes of history.'

Another bull's-eye. He took a deep breath.

'This is no old wives' tale. It's a matter of life or death.'

He was so wrapped up in his obsession he even talked that way. Well – I was willing to listen. We psychiatrists get paid for listening.

'Go ahead,' I told him. 'Let's have the story.'

Sir Guy lit a cigarette and began to talk.

'London, 1888,' he began. 'Late summer and early fall. That was the time. Out of nowhere came the shadowy figure of Jack the Ripper – a stalking shadow with a knife, prowling through London's East End. Haunting the squalid dives of Whitechapel, Spitalfields. Where he came from no one knew. But he brought death. Death in a knife.

'Six times that knife descended to slash the throats and bodies of London's women. Drabs and alley sluts. August 7th was the date of the first butchery. They found her body lying there with thirty-nine stab wounds. A ghastly murder. On August 31st, another victim. The press became interested. The slum inhabitants were more deeply interested still.

'Who was this unknown killer who prowled in their midst and struck at will in the deserted alleyways of night-town? And what was more important – when would he strike again?

'September 8th was the date. Scotland Yard assigned special deputies. Rumours ran rampant. The atrocious nature of the slayings was the subject for shocking speculation.

'The killer used a knife -- expertly. He cut throats. He chose victims and settings with a fiendish deliberation. No one saw him or heard him. But watchmen making their grey rounds in the dawn would stumble across the hacked and horrid thing that was the Ripper's handiwork.

'Who was he? What was he? A mad surgeon? A butcher? An insane scientist? A pathological degenerate escaped from an asylum? A deranged nobleman? A member of the London police?

'Then the poem appeared in the newspapers. The anonymous poem, designed to put a stop to speculations – but which only aroused public interest to a further frenzy. A mocking little stanza:

> *I'm not a butcher, I'm not a kid*
> *Nor yet a foreign skipper,*
> *But I'm your own true loving friend,*
> *Yours truly – Jack the Ripper.*

'And on September 30th, two more throats were slashed open.'

I interrupted Sir Guy for a moment.

'Very interesting,' I commented. I'm afraid a faint hint of sarcasm crept into my voice.

He winced, but didn't falter in his narrative.

'There was silence, then, in London for a time. Silence, and a nameless fear. When would Red Jack strike again? They waited through October. Every figment of fog concealed his phantom presence. Concealed it well – for nothing was learned of the Ripper's identity, or his purpose. The drabs of London shivered in the raw wind of early November. Shivered, and were thankful for the coming of each morning's sun.

'November 9th. They found her in her room. She lay there very quietly, limbs neatly arranged. And beside her, with equal neatness, were laid her head and heart. The Ripper had outdone himself in execution.

'Then, panic. But needless panic. For though press, police and populace alike awaited in sick dread, Jack the Ripper did not strike again.

'Months passed. A year. The immediate interest died, but not the memory. They said Jack had skipped to America. That he had committed suicide. They said – and they wrote. They've written ever since. Theories, hypotheses, arguments, treatises. But to this day no one knows who Jack the Ripper was. Or why he killed. Or why he stopped killing.'

Sir Guy was silent. Obviously he expected some comment from me.

'You tell the story well,' I remarked. 'Though with a slight emotional bias.'

'I've got all the documents,' said Sir Guy Hollis. 'I've made a collection of existing data and studied it.'

I stood up. 'Well,' I yawned, in mock fatigue, 'I've enjoyed your little bedtime story a great deal, Sir Guy. It was kind of you to abandon your duties at the British Embassy to drop in on a poor psychiatrist and regale him with your anecdotes.'

Goading him always did the trick.

'I suppose you want to know why I'm interested?' he snapped.

'Yes. That's exactly what I'd like to know. Why are you interested?'

'Because,' said Sir Guy Hollis, 'I am on the trail of Jack the Ripper now. I think he's here – in Chicago!'

I sat down again. This time I did the blinking act.

'Say that again,' I stuttered.

'Jack the Ripper is alive, in Chicago, and I'm out to find him.'

'Wait a minute,' I said. 'Wait – a – minute!'

He wasn't smiling. It wasn't a joke.

'See here,' I said. 'What was the date of these murders?'

'August to November 1888.'

'1888? But if Jack the Ripper was an able-bodied man in 1888, he'd surely be dead today! Why look, man – if he were merely *born* in that year, he'd be fifty-five years old today!'

'Would he?' smiled Sir Guy Hollis. 'Or should I say, "Would she?"' Because Jack the Ripper may have been a woman. Or any number of things.'

'Sir Guy,' I said. 'You came to the right person when you looked me up. You definitely need the services of a psychiatrist.'

'Perhaps. Tell me, Mr Carmody, do you think I'm crazy?'

I looked at him and shrugged. But I had to give him a truthful answer.

'Frankly – no.'

'Then you might listen to the reasons I believe Jack the Ripper is alive today.'

'I might.'

'I've studied these cases for thirty years. Been over the actual ground. Talked to officials. Talked to friends and acquaintances of the poor drabs who were killed. Visited with men and women in the neighbourhood. Collected an entire library of material touching on Jack the Ripper. Studied all the wild theories or crazy notions.

'I learned a little. Not much, but a little. I won't bore you with my conclusions. But there was another branch of inquiry that yielded more fruitful returns. I have studied unsolved crimes. Murders.

'I could show you clippings from the papers of half the world's great cities. San Francisco. Shanghai. Calcutta. Omsk. Paris. Berlin. Pretoria. Cairo. Milan. Adelaide.

'The trail is there, the pattern. Unsolved crimes. Slashed throats of women. With the peculiar disfigurations and removals. Yes, I've followed a trail of blood. From New York westward across the continent. Then to the Pacific. From there to Africa. During the World War of 1914–18 it was Europe. After that, South America. And since 1930, the United States again. Eighty-seven such murders – and to the trained criminologist, all bear the stigma of the Ripper's handiwork.

'Recently there were the so-called Cleveland torso slayings. Remember? A shocking series. And finally, two recent deaths in Chicago. Within the past six months. One out on South Dearborn. The other somewhere up on Halsted. Same type of crime, same technique. I tell you, there are unmistakable indications in all these affairs – indications of the work of Jack the Ripper!'

I smiled.

'A very tight theory,' I said. 'I'll not question your evidence at all, or the deductions you draw. You're the criminologist, and I'll take your word for it. Just one thing remains to be explained. A minor point, perhaps, but worth mentioning.'

'And what is that?' asked Sir Guy.

'Just how could a man of, let us say, eighty-five years commit these crimes? For if Jack the Ripper was around thirty in 1888 and lived, he'd be eighty-five today.'

Sir Guy Hollis was silent. I had him there. But—

'*Suppose he didn't get any older?*' whispered Sir Guy.

'What's that?'

'Suppose Jack the Ripper didn't grow old? Suppose he is still a young man today?'

'All right,' I said. 'I'll suppose for a moment. Then I'll stop supposing and call for my nurse to restrain you.'

'I'm serious,' said Sir Guy.

'They all are,' I told him. 'That's the pity of it all, isn't it? They *know* they hear voices and see demons. But we lock them up just the same.'

It was cruel, but it got results. He rose and faced me.

'It's a crazy theory, I grant you,' he said. 'All the theories about the Ripper are crazy. The idea that he was a doctor. Or a maniac. Or a woman. The reasons advanced for such beliefs are flimsy enough. There's nothing to go by. So why should my notion be any worse?'

'Because people grow older,' I reasoned with him. 'Doctors, maniacs and women alike.'

'What about – *sorcerers*?'

'Sorcerers?'

'Necromancers. Wizards. Practisers of Black Magic?'

'What's the point?'

'I studied,' said Sir Guy. 'I studied everything. After a while I began to study the dates of the murders. The pattern those dates formed. The rhythm. The solar, lunar, stellar rhythm. The sidereal aspect. The astrological significance.'

He *was* crazy. But I still listened.

'Suppose Jack the Ripper didn't murder for murder's sake alone? Suppose he wanted to make – a sacrifice?'

'What kind of a sacrifice?'

Sir Guy shrugged. 'It is said that if you offer blood to the dark gods they grant boons. Yes, if a blood offering is made at the proper time – when the moon and the stars are right – and with the proper ceremonies – they grant boons. Boons of youth. Eternal youth.'

'But that's nonsense!'

'No. That's – Jack the Ripper.'

I stood up. 'A most interesting theory,' I told him. 'But Sir Guy – there's just one thing I'm interested in. Why do you come here and tell it to me? I'm not an authority on witchcraft. I'm not a police official or criminologist. I'm a practising psychiatrist. What's the connection?'

Sir Guy smiled.

'You are interested, then?'

'Well, yes. There must be some point.'

'There is. But I wished to be assured of your interest first. Now I can tell you my plan.'

'And just what is that plan?'

Sir Guy gave me a long look. Then he spoke.

'John Carmody,' he said, 'you and I are going to capture Jack the Ripper.'

That's the way it happened. I've given the gist of that first interview in all its intricate and somewhat boring detail, because I think it's important. It helps to throw some light on Sir Guy's character and attitude. And in view of what happened after that—

But I'm coming to those matters.

Sir Guy's thought was simple. It wasn't even a thought. Just a hunch.

'You know the people here,' he told me. 'I've inquired. That's why I came to you as the ideal man for my purpose. You number among your acquaintances many writers, painters, poets. The so-called intelligentsia. The Bohemians. The lunatic fringe from the near north side.

'For certain reasons – never mind what they are – my clues lead me to infer that Jack the Ripper is a member of that element. He chooses to pose as an eccentric. I've a feeling that with you to take me around and introduce me to your set, I might hit upon the right person.'

'It's all right with me,' I said. 'But just how are you going to look for him? As you say, he might be anybody, anywhere. And you have no idea what he looks like. He might be young or old. Jack the Ripper – a Jack of all trades? Rich man, poor man, beggar man, thief, doctor, lawyer – how will you know?'

'We shall see.' Sir Guy sighed heavily. 'But I must find him. At once.'

'Why the hurry?'

Sir Guy sighed again. 'Because in two days he will kill again.'

'Are you sure?'

'Sure as the stars. I've plotted his chart, you see. All eighty-seven of the murders correspond to certain astrological rhythm patterns. If, as I suspect, he makes a blood sacrifice to renew his youth, he must murder within two days. Notice the pattern of his first crimes in London. August 7th. Then August 31st. September 8th. September 30th. November 9th. Intervals of 24 days, 9 days, 22 days – he killed two this time – and then 40 days. Of course there were crimes in between. There had to be. But they weren't discovered and pinned on him.

'At any rate, I've worked out a pattern for him, based on all my data. And I say that within the next two days he kills. So I must seek him out, somehow, before then.'

'And I'm still asking you what you want me to do.'

'Take me out,' said Sir Guy. 'Introduce me to your friends. Take me to parties.'

'But where do I begin? As far as I know, my artistic friends, despite their eccentricities, are all normal people.'

'So is the Ripper. Perfectly normal. Except on certain nights.' Again that faraway look in Sir Guy's eyes. 'Then he becomes an ageless pathological monster, crouching to kill, on evenings when the stars blaze down in the blazing patterns of death.'

'All right,' I said. 'All right. I'll take you to parties, Sir Guy. I want to go myself, anyway. I need the drinks they'll serve there, after listening to your kind of talk.'

We made our plans. And that evening I took him over to Lester Baston's studio.

As we ascended to the penthouse roof in the elevator I took the opportunity to warn Sir Guy.

'Baston's a real screwball,' I cautioned him. 'So are his guests. Be prepared for anything and everything.'

'I am.' Sir Guy Hollis was perfectly serious. He put his hand in his trousers pocket and pulled out a gun.

'What the—' I began.

'If I see him I'll be ready,' Sir Guy said. He didn't smile, either.

'But you can't go running around at a party with a loaded revolver in your pocket, man!'

'Don't worry, I won't behave foolishly.'

I wondered. Sir Guy Hollis was not, to my way of thinking, a normal man.

We stepped out of the elevator, went towards Baston's apartment door.

'By the way,' I murmured, 'just how do you wish to be introduced? Shall I tell them who you are and what you are looking for?'

'I don't care. Perhaps it would be best to be frank.'

'But don't you think that the Ripper – if by some miracle he or she is present – will immediately get the wind up and take cover?'

'I think the shock of the announcement that I am hunting the Ripper would provoke some kind of betraying gesture on his part,' said Sir Guy.

'You'd make a pretty good psychiatrist yourself,' I conceded. 'It's a fine theory. But I warn you, you're going to be in for a lot of ribbing. This is a wild bunch.'

Sir Guy smiled.

'I'm ready,' he announced. 'I have a little plan of my own. Don't be shocked by anything I do,' he warned me.

I nodded and knocked on the door.

Baston opened it and poured out into the hall. He teetered back and forth regarding us very gravely. He squinted at my square-cut homburg hat and Sir Guy's moustache.

'Aha,' he intoned. 'The Walrus and the Carpenter.'

I introduced Sir Guy.

'Welcome,' said Baston, gesturing us inside with over-elaborate courtesy. He stumbled after us into the garish parlour.

I stared at the crowd that moved restlessly through the fog of cigarette smoke.

It was the shank of the evening for this mob. Every hand held a drink. Every face held a slightly hectic flush. Over in one corner the piano was going full blast.

Sir Guy got a monocle-full right away. He saw LaVerne Gonnister, the poetess, hit Hymie Kralik in the eye. He saw Hymie sit down on the floor and cry until Dick Pool accidentally stepped on his stomach as he walked through to the dining-room for a drink.

He heard Nadia Vilinoff the commercial artist tell Johnny Odcutt that she thought his tattooing was in dreadful taste.

His zoological observations might have continued indefinitely if Lester Baston hadn't stepped to the centre of the room and called for silence by dropping a vase on the floor.

'We have distinguished visitors in our midst,' bawled Lester, waving his empty glass in our direction. 'None other than the Walrus and the Carpenter. The Walrus is Sir Guy Hollis, a something-or-other from the British Embassy. The Carpenter, as you all know, is our own John Carmody, the prominent dispenser of libido-liniment.'

He turned and grabbed Sir Guy by the arm, dragging him to the middle of the carpet. For a moment I thought Hollis might object, but a quick wink reassured me. He was prepared for this.

'It is our custom, Sir Guy,' said Baston, loudly, 'to subject our new friends to a little cross-examination. Just a little formality at these very formal gatherings, you understand. Are you prepared to answer questions?'

Sir Guy nodded and grinned.

'Very well,' Baston muttered. 'Friends – I give you this bundle from Britain. Your witness.'

Then the ribbing started. I meant to listen, but at that moment Lydia Dare saw me and dragged me off into the vestibule for one of those Darling-I-waited-for-your-call-all-day routines.

By the time I got rid of her and went back, the impromptu quiz session was in full swing. From the attitude of the crowd, I gathered that Sir Guy was doing all right for himself.

Then Baston himself interjected a question that upset the applecart.

'And what, may I ask, brings you to our midst tonight? What is your mission, oh Walrus?'

'I'm looking for Jack the Ripper.'

Nobody laughed.

Perhaps it struck them all the way it did me. I glanced at my neighbours and began to *wonder*.

LaVerne Gonnister. Hymie Kralik. Harmless. Dick Pool. Nadia Vilinoff. Johnny Odcutt and his wife. Barclay Melton. Lydia Dare. All harmless.

But what a forced smile on Dick Pool's face! And that sly, self-conscious smirk that Barclay Melton wore!

Oh, it was absurd, I grant you. But for the first time I saw these people in a new light. I wondered about their lives – their secret lives beyond the scenes of parties.

How many of them were playing a part, concealing something?

Who here would worship Hecate and grant that horrid goddess the dark boon of blood?

Even Lester Baston might be masquerading.

The mood was upon us all, for a moment. I saw questions flicker in the circle of eyes around the room.

Sir Guy stood there, and I could swear he was fully conscious of the situation he'd created, and enjoyed it.

I wondered idly just what was *really* wrong with him. Why he had this odd fixation concerning Jack the Ripper. Maybe he was hiding secrets, too . . .

Baston, as usual, broke the mood. He burlesqued it.

'The Walrus isn't kidding, friends,' he said. He slapped Sir Guy on the back and put his arm around him as he orated. 'Our English cousin is really on the trail of the fabulous Jack the Ripper. You all remember Jack the Ripper, I presume? Quite a cutup in the old days, as I recall.

Really had some ripping good times when he went out on a tear.

'The Walrus has some idea that the Ripper is still alive, probably prowling around Chicago with a Boy Scout knife. In fact' – Baston paused impressively and shot it out in a rasping stage-whisper – 'in fact, he has reason to believe that Jack the Ripper might even be right here in our midst tonight.'

There was the expected reaction of giggles and grins. Baston eyed Lydia Dare reprovingly. 'You girls needn't laugh,' he smirked. 'Jack the Ripper might be a woman, too, you know. Sort of a Jill the Ripper.'

'You mean you actually suspect one of us?' shrieked LaVerne Gonnister, simpering up to Sir Guy. 'But that Jack the Ripper person disappeared ages ago, didn't he? In 1888?'

'Aha!' interrupted Baston. 'How do you know so much about it, young lady? Sounds suspicious! Watch her, Sir Guy – she may not be as young as she appears. These lady poets have dark pasts.'

The tension was gone, the mood was shattered, and the whole thing was beginning to degenerate into a trivial party joke.

Then Baston caught it.

'Guess what?' he yelled. 'The Walrus has a gun.'

His embracing arm had slipped and encountered the hard outline of the gun in Sir Guy's pocket. He snatched it out before Hollis had the opportunity to protest.

I stared hard at Sir Guy, wondering if this thing had carried far enough. But he flicked a wink my way and I remembered he had told me not to be alarmed.

So I waited as Baston broached a drunken inspiration.

'Let's play fair with our friend the Walrus,' he cried. 'He came all the way from England to our party on this mission. If none of you is willing to confess, I suggest we give him a chance to find out – the hard way.'

'What's up?' asked Johnny Odcutt.

'I'll turn out the lights for one minute. Sir Guy can stand here with his gun. If anyone in this room is the Ripper he can either run for it or take the opportunity to – well, eradicate his pursuer. Fair enough?'

It was even sillier than it sounds, but it caught the popular fancy. Sir Guy's protests went unheard in the ensuing babble. And before I could stride over and put in my two cents' worth, Lester Baston had reached the light switch.

'Don't anybody move,' he announced, with fake solemnity. 'For one minute we will remain in darkness – perhaps at the mercy of a killer. At the end of that time, I'll turn up the lights again and look for bodies. Choose your partners, ladies and gentlemen.'

The lights went out.

Somebody giggled.

I heard footsteps in the darkness. Mutterings.

A hand brushed my face.

The watch on my wrist ticked violently. But even louder, rising above it, I heard another thumping. The beating of my heart.

Absurd. Standing in the dark with a group of tipsy fools. And yet there was real terror lurking here, rustling through the velvet blackness.

Jack the Ripper prowled in darkness like this. And Jack the Ripper had a knife. Jack the Ripper had a madman's brain and a madman's purpose.

But Jack the Ripper was dead, dead and dust these many years – by every human law.

Only there are no human laws when you feel yourself in the darkness, when the darkness hides and protects and the outer mask slips off your face and you feel something welling up within you, a brooding shapeless purpose that is brother to the blackness.

Sir Guy Hollis shrieked.

There was a grisly thud.

Baston had the lights on.

Everybody screamed.

Sir Guy Hollis lay sprawled on the floor in the centre of the room. The gun was still clutched in his hand.

I glanced at the faces, marvelling at the variety of expressions human beings can assume when confronting horror.

All the faces were present in the circle. Nobody had fled. And yet Sir Guy Hollis lay there . . .

LaVerne Gonnister was wailing and hiding her face.

'All right.'

Sir Guy rolled over and jumped to his feet. He was smiling.

'Just an experiment, eh? If Jack the Ripper *were* among those present, and thought I had been murdered, he would have betrayed himself in some way when the lights went on and he saw me lying there.

'I am convinced of your individual and collective innocence. Just a gentle spoof, my friends.'

Hollis stared at the goggling Baston and the rest of them crowding in behind him.

'Shall we leave, John?' he called to me. 'It's getting late, I think.'

Turning, he headed for the closet. I followed him. Nobody said a word.

It was a pretty dull party after that.

I met Sir Guy the following evening as we agreed, on the corner of 29th and South Halsted.

After what had happened the night before, I was prepared for almost anything. But Sir Guy seemed matter-of-fact enough as he stood huddled against a grimy doorway and waited for me to appear.

'Boo!' I said, jumping out suddenly. He smiled. Only the betraying gesture of his left hand indicated that he'd instinctively reached for his gun when I startled him.

'All ready for our wild goose chase?' I asked.

'Yes.' He nodded. 'I'm glad that you agreed to meet me without asking questions,' he told me. 'It shows you trust my judgment.' He took my arm and edged me along the street slowly.

'It's foggy tonight, John,' said Sir Guy Hollis. 'Like London.'

I nodded.

'Cold, too, for November.'

I nodded again and half-shivered my agreement.

'Curious,' mused Sir Guy. 'London fog and November. The place and the time of the Ripper murders.'

I grinned through darkness. 'Let me remind you, Sir Guy, that this isn't London, but Chicago. And it isn't November 1888. It's over fifty years later.'

Sir Guy returned my grin, but without mirth. 'I'm not so sure, at that,' he murmured. 'Look about you. These tangled alleys and twisted streets. They're like the East End. Mitre Square. And surely they are as ancient as fifty years, at least.'

'You're in the poor neighbourhood off South Clark Street,' I said, shortly. 'And why you dragged me down here I still don't know.'

'It's a hunch,' Sir Guy admitted. 'Just a hunch on my part, John. I want to wander around down here. There's the same geographical conformation in these streets as in those courts where the Ripper roamed and slew. That's where we'll find him, John. Not in the bright lights of the Bohemian neighbourhood, but down here in the darkness. The darkness where he waits and crouches.'

'Is that why you brought a gun?' I asked. I was unable to keep a trace of sarcastic nervousness from my voice. All of this talk, this incessant obsession with Jack the Ripper, got on my nerves more than I cared to admit.

'We may need the gun,' said Sir Guy, gravely. 'After all, tonight is the appointed night.'

I sighed. We wandered on through the foggy, deserted streets. Here and there a dim light burned above a doorway. Otherwise, all was darkness and shadow. Deep, gaping alley-ways loomed as we proceeded down a slanting side street.

We crawled through that fog, alone and silent, like two tiny maggots floundering within a shroud.

When that thought hit me, I winced. The atmosphere was beginning to get *me*, too. If I didn't watch my step I'd go as loony as Sir Guy.

'Can't you see there's not a soul around these streets?' I said, tugging at his coat impatiently.

'He's bound to come,' said Sir Guy. 'He'll be drawn here. This is what I've been looking for. A *genius loci*. An evil spot that attracts evil. Always, when he slays, it's in the slums.

'You see, that must be one of his weaknesses. He has a fascination for squalor. Besides, the women he needs for sacrifice are more easily found in the dives and stewpots of a great city.'

I smiled. 'Well, let's go into one of the dives or stewpots,' I suggested. 'I'm cold. Need a drink. This fog gets into your bones. You Britishers can stand it, but I like warmth and dry heat.'

We emerged from our side street and stood upon the threshold of an alley.

Through the white clouds of mist ahead, I discerned a dim blue light, a naked bulb dangling from a beer sign above an alley tavern.

'Let's take a chance,' I said. 'I'm beginning to shiver.'

'Lead the way,' said Sir Guy. I led him down the alley passage. We halted before the door of the dive.

'What are you waiting for?' he asked.

'Just looking in,' I told him. 'This is a tough neighbourhood, Sir Guy. Never know what you're liable to run into. And I'd prefer we didn't get into the wrong company.'

'Good idea, John.'

I finished my inspection through the doorway. 'Looks deserted,' I murmured. 'Let's try it.'

We entered a dingy bar. A feeble light flickered above the counter and railing, but failed to penetrate the farther gloom of the back booths.

A gigantic Negro lolled across the bar. He scarcely stirred as we came in, but his eyes flickered open quite suddenly and I knew he noted our presence and was judging us.

'Evening,' I said.

He took his time before replying. Still sizing us up. Then he grinned.

'Evening, gents. What's your pleasure?'

'Gin,' I said. 'Two gins. It's a cold night.'

'That's right, gents.'

He poured, I paid, and took the glasses over to one of the booths. We wasted no time in emptying them. The fiery liquor warmed.

I went over to the bar and got the bottle. Sir Guy and I poured ourselves another drink. The big Negro went back into his doze, with one wary eye half-open against any sudden activity.

The clock over the bar ticked on. The wind was rising outside, tearing the shroud of fog to ragged shreds. Sir Guy and I sat in the warm booth and drank our gin.

He began to talk, and the shadows crept up about us to listen.

He rambled a great deal. He went over everything he'd said in the office when I met him, just as though I hadn't heard it before. The poor devils with obsessions are like that.

I listened very patiently. I poured Sir Guy another drink. And another.

But the liquor only made him more talkative. How he did run on! About ritual killings and prolonging life unnaturally – the whole fantastic tale came out again. And, of course, he maintained his unyielding conviction that the Ripper was abroad tonight.

I suppose I was guilty of goading him.

'Very well,' I said, unable to keep the impatience from my voice. 'Let us say that your theory is correct – even though we must overlook every natural law and swallow a lot of superstition to give it any credence.

'But let us say, for the sake of argument, that you are right. Jack the Ripper was a man who discovered how to prolong his own life through making human sacrifices. He did travel around the world as you believe. He is in Chicago now and he is planning to kill. In other words, let us suppose that everything you claim is gospel truth. So what?'

'What do you mean, "so what"?' said Sir Guy.

'I mean – so what?' I answered. 'If all this is true, it still doesn't prove that by sitting down in a dingy gin-mill on the South Side, Jack the Ripper is going to walk in here and let you kill him, or turn him over to the police. And come to think of it, I don't even know now just what you intend to *do* with him if you ever did find him.'

Sir Guy gulped his gin. 'I'd capture the bloody swine,' he said. 'Capture him and turn him over to the government, together with all the papers and documentary evidence I've collected against him over a period of many years. I've spent a fortune investigating this affair, I tell you, a fortune! His capture will mean the solution of hundreds of unsolved crimes, of that I am convinced.

'I tell you, a mad beast is loose on this world! An ageless, eternal beast, sacrificing to Hecate and the dark gods!'

In vino veritas. Or was all this babbling the result of too much gin? It didn't matter. Sir Guy Hollis had another. I sat there and wondered what to do with him. The man was rapidly working up to a climax of hysterical drunkenness.

'One other point,' I said, more for the sake of conversation than in any hopes of obtaining information. 'You still don't explain how it is that you hope to just blunder into the Ripper.'

'He'll be around,' said Sir Guy. 'I'm psychic. I know.'

Sir Guy wasn't psychic. He was maudlin.

The whole business was beginning to infuriate me. We'd been sitting here an hour, and during all this time I'd been forced to play nursemaid and audience to a babbling idiot. After all, he wasn't a regular patient of mine.

'That's enough,' I said, putting out my hand as Sir Guy reached for the half-emptied bottle again. 'You've had plenty. Now I've got a suggestion to make. Let's call a cab and get out of here. It's getting late and it doesn't look as though your elusive friend is going to put in his appearance. Tomorrow, if I were you, I'd plan to turn all those papers and documents over to the F.B.I. If you're so convinced of the truth of your wild theory, they are competent to make a very thorough investigation and find your man.'

'No.' Sir Guy was drunkenly obstinate. 'No cab.'

'But let's get out of here anyway,' I said, glancing at my watch. 'It's past midnight.'

He sighed, shrugged, and rose unsteadily. As he started for the door, he tugged the gun free from his pocket.

'Here, give me that!' I whispered. 'You can't walk around the street brandishing that thing.'

I took the gun and slipped it inside my coat. Then I got hold of his right arm and steered him out of the door. The Negro didn't look up as we departed.

We stood shivering in the alleyway. The fog had increased. I couldn't see either end of the alley from where we stood. It was cold. Damp. Dark. Fog or no fog, a little wind was whispering secrets to the shadows at our cacks.

The fresh air hit Sir Guy just as I had expected it would. Fog and gin fumes don't mingle very well. He lurched as I guided him slowly through the mist.

Sir Guy, despite his incapacity, still stared apprehensively at the alley, as though he expected to see a figure approaching.

Disgust got the better of me.

'Childish foolishness,' I snorted. 'Jack the Ripper, indeed! I call this carrying a hobby too far.'

'Hobby?' He faced me. Through the fog I could see his distorted face. 'You call this a hobby?'

'Well, what is it?' I grumbled. 'Just why else are you so interested in tracking down this mythical killer?'

My arm held him. But his stare held me.

'In London,' he whispered. 'In 1888 . . . one of those women the

Ripper slew . . . was my mother.'

'What?'

'My father and I swore to give our lives to find the Ripper. My father was the first to search. He died in Hollywood in 1926 – on the trail of the Ripper. They said he was stabbed by an unknown assailant in a brawl. But I know who that assailant was.

'So I've taken up his work, do you see, John? I've carried on. And I will carry on until I do find him and kill him with my own hands.

'He took my mother's life and the lives of hundreds to keep his own hellish being alive. Like a vampire, he battens on blood. Like a ghoul, he is nourished by death. Like a fiend, he stalks the world to kill. He is cunning, devilishly cunning. But I'll never rest until I find him, never!'

I believed him then. He wouldn't give up. He wasn't just a drunken babbler any more. He was as fanatical, as determined, as relentless as the Ripper himself.

Tomorrow he'd be sober. He'd continue the search. Perhaps he'd turn those papers over to the F.B.I. Sooner or later, with such persistence – and with his motive – he'd be successful. I'd always known he had a motive.

'Let's go,' I said, steering him down the alley.

'Wait a minute,' said Sir Guy. 'Give me back my gun.' He lurched a little. 'I'd feel better with the gun on me.'

He pressed me into the dark shadows of a little recess.

I tried to shrug him off, but he was insistent.

'Let me carry the gun now, John,' he mumbled.

'All right,' I said.

I reached into my coat, brought my hand out.

'But that's not a gun,' he protested. 'That's a knife.'

'I know.'

I bore down on him swiftly.

'John!' he screamed.

'Never mind the "John",' I whispered, raising the knife. 'Just call me . . . Jack.'

Ray Bradbury

The Veld

'George, I wish you'd look at the nursery.'

'What's wrong with it?'

'I don't know.'

'Well, then.'

'I just want you to look at it, is all, or call a psychologist in to look at it.'

'What would a psychologist want with a nursery?'

'You know very well what he'd want.' His wife paused in the middle of the kitchen and watched the stove busy humming to itself, making supper for four.

'It's just that the nursery is different now than it was.'

'All right, let's have a look.'

They walked down the hall of their sound-proofed, Happy-life Home, which had cost them thirty thousand dollars installed, this house which clothed and fed and rocked them to sleep and played and sang and was good to them. Their approach sensitised a switch somewhere and the nursery light flicked on when they came within ten feet of it. Similarly, behind them, in the halls, lights went on and off as they left them behind, with a soft automaticity.

'Well,' said George Hadley.

They stood on the thatched floor of the nursery. It was forty feet across by forty feet long and thirty feet high, it had cost half again as much as the rest of the house. 'But nothing's too good for our children,' George had said.

The nursery was silent. It was empty as a jungle glade at hot high noon. The walls were blank and two-dimensional. Now, as George and Lydia Hadley stood in the centre of the room, the walls began to purr and recede into crystalline distance, it seemed, and presently an African veld appeared, in three dimensions, on all sides, in colour, reproduced to the final pebble and bit of straw. The ceiling above them became a deep sky with a hot yellow sun.

George Hadley felt the perspiration start on his brow.

'Let's get out of this sun,' he said. 'This is a little too real. But I don't see anything wrong.'

'Wait a moment, you'll see,' said his wife.

Now the hidden odorophonics were beginning to blow a wind o odour at the two people in the middle of the baked veldland. The hot straw smell of lion grass, the cool green smell of the hidden water hole, the great rusty smell of animals, the smell of dust like a red paprika in the hot air. And now the sounds: the thump of distant antelope feet on grassy sod, the papery rustling of vultures. A shadow passed through the sky. The shadow flickered on George Hadley's upturned, sweating face.

'Filthy creatures,' he heard his wife say.

'The vultures.'

'You see, there are the lions, far over, that way. Now they're on their way to the water hole. They've just been eating,' said Lydia. 'I don't know what.'

'Some animal.' George Hadley put his hand up to shield off the burning light from his squinted eyes. 'A zebra or a baby giraffe, maybe.'

'Are you *sure*?' His wife sounded peculiarly tense.

'No, it's a little late to be *sure*,' he said, amused. 'Nothing over there I can see but cleaned bone, and the vultures dropping for what's left.'

'Did you hear that scream?' she asked.

'No.'

'About a minute ago?'

'Sorry, no.'

The lions were coming. And again George Hadley was filled with admiration for the mechanical genius who had conceived this room. A miracle of efficiency selling for an absurdly low price. Every home should have one. Oh, occasionally they frightened you with their clinical accuracy, they startled you, gave you a twinge, but most of the time what fun for everyone, not only your own son and daughter, but for yourself when you felt like a quick jaunt to a foreign land, a quick change of scenery. Well, here it was!

And here were the lions now, fifteen feet away, so real, so feverishly and startlingly real that you could feel the prickling fur on your hand, and your mouth was stuffed with the dusty upholstery smell of their heated pelts, and the yellow of them was in your eyes like the yellow of an exquisite French tapestry, the yellows of lions and summer grass, and the sound of the matted lion lungs exhaling on the silent noontide, and the smell of meat from the panting, dripping mouths.

The lions stood looking at George and Lydia Hadley with terrible green-yellow eyes.

'Watch out!' screamed Lydia.

The lions came running at them.

Lydia bolted and ran. Instinctively, George sprang after her. Outside, in the hall, with the door slammed, he was laughing and she was crying, and they both stood appalled at the other's reaction.

'George!'

'Lydia! Oh, my dear poor sweet Lydia!'

'They almost got us!'

'Walls, Lydia, remember; crystal walls, that's all they are. Oh, they look real, I must admit – Africa in your parlour – but it's all dimensional super-reactionary, super-sensitive colour film and mental tape film behind glass screens. It's all odorophonics and sonics, Lydia. Here's my handkerchief.'

'I'm afraid.' She came to him and put her body against him and cried steadily. 'Did you see? Did you feel? It's too real.'

'Now, Lydia . . .'

'You've got to tell Wendy and Peter not to read any more on Africa.'

'Of course – of course.' He patted her.

'Promise?'

'Sure.'

'And lock the nursery for a few days until I get my nerves settled.'

'You know how difficult Peter is about that. When I punished him a month ago by locking the nursery for even a few hours – the tantrum he threw! And Wendy too. They live for the nursery.'

'It's got to be locked, that's all there is to it.'

'All right.' Reluctantly he locked the huge door. 'You've been working too hard. You need a rest.'

'I don't know – I don't know,' she said, blowing her nose, sitting down in a chair that immediately began to rock and comfort her. 'Maybe I don't have enough to do. Maybe I have time to think too much. Why don't we shut the whole house off for a few days and take a vacation?'

'You mean you want to fry my eggs for me?'

'Yes.' She nodded.

'And darn my socks?'

'Yes.' A frantic, watery-eyed nodding.

'And sweep the house?'

'Yes, yes – oh, yes!'

'But I thought that's why we bought this house, so we wouldn't have to do anything?'

'That's just it. I feel like I don't belong here. The house is wife and mother now and nursemaid. Can I compete with an African veld? Can I have a bath and scrub the children as efficiently or quickly as the automatic scrub bath can? I cannot. And it isn't just me. It's you. You've been awfully nervous lately.'

'I suppose I have been smoking too much.'

'You look as if you didn't know what to do with yourself in this house, either. You smoke a little more every morning and drink a little more every afternoon and need a little more sedative every night. You're beginning to feel unnecessary too.'

'Am I?' He paused and tried to feel into himself to see what was really there.

'Oh, George!' She looked beyond him, at the nursery door. 'Those lions can't get out of there, can they?'

He looked at the door and saw it tremble as if something had jumped against it from the other side.

'Of course not,' he said.

At dinner they ate alone, for Wendy and Peter were at a special plastic carnival across town and had televised home to say they'd be late, to go ahead eating. So George Hadley, bemused, sat watching the dining-room table produce warm dishes of food from its mechanical interior.

'We forgot the ketchup,' he said.

'Sorry,' said a small voice within the table, and ketchup appeared.

As for the nursery, thought George Hadley, it won't hurt for the children to be locked out of it awhile. Too much of anything isn't good for anyone. And it was clearly indicated that the children had been spending a little too much time on Africa. That *sun*. He could feel it on his neck, still, like a hot paw. And the *lions*. And the smell of blood. Remarkable how the nursery caught the telepathic emanations of the children's minds and created life to fill their every desire. The children thought lions, and there were lions. The children thought zebras, and there were zebras. Sun – sun. Giraffes – giraffes. Death and death.

That *last*. He chewed tastelessly on the meat that the table had cut for him. Death thoughts. They were awfully young, Wendy and Peter, for death thoughts. Or, no, you were never too young, really. Long before you knew what death was you were wishing it on someone else. When you were two years old you were shooting people with cap pistols.

But this – the long, hot African veld – the awful death in the jaws of a lion. And repeated again and again.

'Where are you going?'

He didn't answer Lydia. Preoccupied, he let the lights glow softly on ahead of him, extinguish behind him as he padded to the nursery door. He listened against it. Far away, a lion roared.

He unlocked the door and opened it. Just before he stepped inside, he heard a far-away scream. And then another roar from the lions, which subsided quickly.

He stepped into Africa. How many times in the last year had he opened this door and found Wonderland, Alice, the Mock Turtle, or Aladdin and his Magical Lamp, or Jack Pumpkinhead of Oz, or Dr Doolittle, or the cow jumping over a very real-appearing moon – all the delightful contraptions of a make-believe world. How often had be seen Pegasus flying in the sky ceiling, or seen fountains of red fireworks, or heard angel voices singing. But now, this yellow hot Africa, this bake oven with murder in the heat. Perhaps Lydia was right. Perhaps they needed a little vacation from the fantasy which was growing a bit too real for ten-year-old children. It was all right to exercise one's mind with gymnastic fantasies, but when the lively child mind settled on one pattern . . ?

It seemed that, at a distance, for the past month, he had heard lions roaring, and smelled their strong odour seeping as far away as his study door. But, being busy, he had paid it no attention.

George Hadley stood on the African grassland alone. The lions looked up from their feeding, watching him. The only flaw to the illusion was the open door through which he could see his wife, far down the dark hall, like a framed picture, eating her dinner abstractedly.

'Go away,' he said to the lions.

They did not go.

He knew the principle of the room exactly. You sent out your thoughts. Whatever you thought would appear.

'Let's have Aladdin and his lamp,' he snapped.

The veldland remained, the lions remained.

'Come on, room! I demand Aladdin!' he said.

Nothing happened. The lions mumbled in their baked pelts.

'Aladdin!'

He went back to dinner. 'The fool room's out of order,' he said. 'It won't respond.'

'Or—'

'Or what?'

'Or it *can't* respond,' said Lydia, 'because the children have thought about Africa and lions and killing so many days that the room's in a rut.'

'Could be.'

'Or Peter's set it to remain that way.'

'*Set* it?'

'He may have got into the machinery and fixed something.'

'Peter doesn't know machinery.'

'He's a wise one for ten. That I.Q. of his—'

'Nevertheless—'

'Hello, Mom. Hello, Dad.'

The Hadleys turned. Wendy and Peter were coming in the front door, cheeks like peppermint candy, eyes like bright blue agate marbles, a smell of ozone on their jumpers from their trip in the helicopter.

'You're just in time for supper,' said both parents.

'We're full of strawberry ice cream and hot dogs,' said the children, holding hands. 'But we'll sit and watch.'

'Yes, come tell us about the nursery,' said George Hadley.

The brother and sister blinked at him and then at each other. 'Nursery?'

'All about Africa and everything,' said the father with false joviality.

'I don't understand,' said Peter.

'Your mother and I were just travelling through Africa with rod and reel; Tom Swift and his Electric Lion,' said George Hadley.

'There's no Africa in the nursery,' said Peter simply.

'Oh, come now, Peter. We know better.'

'I don't remember any Africa,' said Peter to Wendy. 'Do you?'

'No.'

'Run see and come tell.'

She obeyed.

'Wendy, come back here!' said George Hadley, but she was gone. The house lights followed her like a flock of fireflies. Too late, he realised he had forgotten to lock the nursery door after his last inspection.

'Wendy'll look and come tell us,' said Peter.

'She doesn't have to tell *me*. I've seen it.'

'I'm sure you're mistaken, Father.'

'I'm not, Peter. Come along now.'

But Wendy was back. 'It's not Africa,' she said breathlessly.

'We'll see about this,' said George Hadley, and they all walked down the hall together and opened the nursery door.

There was a green, lovely forest, a lovely river, a purple mountain, high voices singing, and Rima, lovely and mysterious, lurking in the trees with colourful flights of butterflies, like animated bouquets, lingering in her long hair. The African veldland was gone. The lions were gone. Only Rima was here now, singing a song so beautiful that it brought tears to your eyes.

George Hadley looked in at the changed scene. 'Go to bed,' he said to the children.

They opened their mouths.

'You heard me,' he said.

They went off to the air closet, where a wind sucked them like brown leaves up the flue to their slumber rooms.

George Hadley walked through the singing glade and picked up something that lay in the corner near where the lions had been. He walked slowly back to his wife.

'What is that?' she asked.

'An old wallet of mine,' he said.

He showed it to her. The smell of hot grass was on it and the smell of a lion. There were drops of saliva on it, it had been chewed, and there blood smears on both sides.

He closed the nursery door and locked it, tight.

In the middle of the night he was still awake and he knew his wife was awake. 'Do you think Wendy changed it?' she said at last, in the dark room.

'Of course.'

'Made it from a veld into a forest and put Rima there instead of lions?'

'Yes.'

'Why?'

'I don't know. But it's staying locked until I find out.'

'How did your wallet get there?'

'I don't know anything,' he said, 'except that I'm beginning to be sorry we bought that room for the children. If children are neurotic at all, a room like that—'

'It's supposed to help them work off their neuroses in a healthful way.'

'I'm starting to wonder.' He stared at the ceiling.

'We've given the children everything they ever wanted. Is this our reward – secrecy, disobedience?'

'Who was it said, "Children are carpets, they should be stepped on occasionally"? We've never lifted a hand. They're insufferable – let's admit it. They come and go when they like; they treat us as if *we* were offspring. They're spoiled and we're spoiled.'

'They've been acting funny ever since you forbade them to take the rocket to New York a few months ago.'

'They're not old enough to do that alone, I explained.'

'Nevertheless, I've noticed they've been decidedly cool toward us since.'

'I think I'll have David McClean come tomorrow morning to have a look at Africa.'

'But it's not Africa now, it's Green Mansions country and Rima.'

'I have a feeling it'll be Africa again before then.'

A moment later they heard the screams.

Two screams. Two people screaming from downstairs. And then a roar of lions.

'Wendy and Peter aren't in their rooms,' said his wife.

He lay in his bed with his beating heart. 'No,' he said. 'They've broken into the nursery.'

'Those screams – they sound familiar.'

'Do they?'

'Yes, awfully.'

And although their beds tried very hard, the two adults couldn't be rocked to sleep for another hour. A smell of cats was in the night air.

'Father?' said Peter.

'Yes.'

Peter looked at his shoes. He never looked at his father any more, nor at his mother. 'You aren't going to lock up the nursery for good, are you?'

'That all depends.'

'On what?' snapped Peter.

'On you and your sister. If you intersperse this Africa with a little variety – oh, Sweden perhaps, or Denmark or China—'

'I thought we were free to play as we wished.'

'You are, within reasonable bounds.'

'What's wrong with Africa, Father?'

'Oh, so now you admit you have been conjuring up Africa, do you?'

'I wouldn't want the nursery locked up,' said Peter coldly. 'Ever.'

'Matter of fact, we're thinking of turning the whole house off for about a month. Live sort of a carefree one-for-all existence.'

'That sounds dreadful! Would I have to tie my own shoes instead of letting the shoe tier do it? And brush my own teeth and comb my hair and give myself a bath?'

'It would be fun for a change, don't you think?'

'No, it would be horrid. I didn't like it when you took out the picture painter last month.'

'That's because I wanted you to learn to paint all by yourself, son.'

'I don't want to do anything but look and listen and smell; what else is there to do?'

'All right, go play in Africa.'

'Will you shut off the house sometime soon?'

'We're considering it.'

'I don't think you'd better consider it any more, Father.'

'I won't have any threats from my son!'

'Very well.' And Peter strolled off to the nursery.

'Am I on time?' said David McClean.

'Breakfast?' asked George Hadley.

'Thanks, had some. What's the trouble?'

'David, you're a psychologist.'

'I should hope so.'

'Well, then, have a look at our nursery. You saw it a year ago when you dropped by; did you notice anything peculiar about it then?'

'Can't say I did; the usual violences, a tendency toward a slight paranoia here or there, usual in children because they feel persecuted by parents constantly, but, oh, really nothing.'

They walked down the hall. 'I locked the nursery up,' explained the father, 'and the children broke back into it during the night. I let them stay so they could form the patterns for you to see.'

There was a terrible screaming from the nursery.

'There it is,' said George Hadley. 'See what you make of it.'

They walked in on the children without rapping.

The screams had faded. The lions were feeding.

'Run outside a moment, children,' said George Hadley. 'No, don't change the mental combination. Leave the walls as they are. Get!'

With the children gone, the two men stood studying the lions clustered at a distance, eating with great relish whatever it was they had caught.

'I wish I knew what it was,' said George Hadley. 'Sometimes I can almost see. Do you think if I brought highpowered binoculars here and—'

David McClean laughed dryly. 'Hardly.' He turned to study all four walls. 'How long has this been going on?'

'A little over a month.'

'It certainly doesn't feel good.'

'I want facts, not feelings.'

'My dear George, a psychologist never saw a fact in his life. He only hears about feelings; vague things. This doesn't feel good, I tell you. Trust my hunches and my instincts, I have a nose for something bad. This is very bad. My advice to you is to have the whole damn room torn down and your children brought to me every day during the next year for treatment.'

'Is it that bad?'

'I'm afraid so. One of the original uses of these nurseries was so that we could study the patterns left on the walls by the child's mind, study at our leisure, and help the child. In this case, however, the room has become a channel toward – destructive thoughts, instead of a release away from them.'

'Didn't you sense this before?'

'I sensed only that you had spoiled your children more than most. And now you're letting them down in some way. What way?'

'I wouldn't let them go to New York.'

'What else?'

'I've taken a few machines from the house and threatened them, a month ago, with closing up the nursery unless they did their homework. I did close it for a few days to show I meant business.'

'Ah, ha!'

'Does that mean anything?'

'Everything. Where before they had a Santa Claus now they have a Scrooge. Children prefer Santas. You've let this room and this house replace you and your wife in your children's affections. This room is their mother and father, far more important in their lives than their real parents. And now you come along and want to shut it off. No wonder there's hatred here. You can feel it coming out of the sky. Feel that sun. George, you'll have to change your life. Like too many others, you've built it around creature comforts. Why, you'd starve tomorrow if something went wrong in your kitchen. You wouldn't know how to tap an egg. Nevertheless, turn everything off. Start new. It'll take time. But we'll make good children out of bad in a year, wait and see.'

'But won't the shock be too much for the children, shutting the room up abruptly, for good?'

'I don't want them going any deeper into this, that's all.'

The lions were finished with their red feast.

The lions were standing on the edge of the clearing watching the two men.

'Now *I'm* feeling persecuted,' said McClean. 'Let's get out of here. I never have cared for these damned rooms. Make me nervous.'

'The lions look real, don't they?' said George Hadley. 'I don't suppose there's any way—'

'What?'

'– that they could *become* real?'

'Not that I know.'

'Some flaw in the machinery, a tampering or something?'

'No.'

They went to the door.

'I don't imagine the room will like being turned off,' said the father.

'Nothing ever likes to die – even a room.'

'I wonder if it hates me for wanting to switch it off?'

'Paranoia is thick around here today,' said David McClean. 'You can follow it like a spoor. Hello.' He bent and picked up a bloody scarf. 'This yours?'

'No.' George Hadley's face was rigid. 'It belongs to Lydia.'

They went to the fuse box together and threw the switch that killed the nursery.

The two children were in hysterics. They screamed and pranced and threw things. They yelled and sobbed and swore and jumped at the furniture.

'You can't do that to the nursery, you can't?'

'Now, children.'

The children flung themselves on to a couch, weeping.

'George,' said Lydia Hadley, 'turn on the nursery, just for a few moments. You can't be so abrupt.'

'No.'

'You can't be so cruel.'

'Lydia, it's off, and it stays off. And the whole damn house dies as of here and now. The more I see of the mess we've put ourselves in, the more it sickens me. We've been contemplating our mechanical, electronic navels for too long. My God, how we need a breath of honest air!'

And he marched about the house turning off the voice clocks, the stoves, the heaters, the shoe shiners, the shoe lacers, the body scrubbers and swabbers and massagers, and every other machine he could put his hand to.

The house was full of dead bodies, it seemed. It felt like a mechanical cemetery. So silent. None of the humming hidden energy of machines waiting to funtion at the tap of a button.

'Don't let them do it!' wailed Peter at the ceiling, as if he was talking to the house, the nursery. 'Don't let Father kill everything.' He turned to his father. 'Oh, I hate you!'

'Insults won't get you anywhere.'

'I wish you were dead!'

'We were, for a long while. Now we're going to really start living. Instead of being handled and massaged, we're going to live.'

Wendy was still crying and Peter joined her again. 'Just a moment, just one moment, just another moment of nursery,' they wailed.

'Oh George,' said the wife, 'it can't hurt.'

'All right – all right, if they'll only just shut up. One minute, mind you, and then off forever.'

'Daddy, Daddy, Daddy!' sang the children, smiling with wet faces.

'And then we're going on a vacation. David McClean is coming back in half an hour to help us move out and get to the airport. I'm going to dress. You turn the nursery on for a minute, Lydia, just a minute, mind you.'

And the three of them went babbling off while he let himself be vacuumed upstairs through the air flue and set about dressing himself. A minutes later Lydia appeared.

'I'll be glad when we get away,' she sighed.

'Did you leave them in the nursery?'

'I wanted to dress too. Oh, that horrid Africa. What can they see in it?'

'Well, in five minutes we'll be on our way to Iowa. Lord, how did we ever get in this house? What prompted us to buy a nightmare?'

'Pride, money, foolishness.'

'I think we'd better get downstairs before those kids get engrossed with those damned beasts again.'

Just then they heard the children calling, 'Daddy, Mommy, come quick – quick!'

They went downstairs in the air flue and ran down the hall. The children were nowhere in sight. 'Wendy? Peter!'

They ran into the nursery. The veldland was empty save for the lions waiting, looking at them. 'Peter, Wendy?'

The door slammed.

'Wendy, Peter!'

George Hadley and his wife whirled and ran back to the door.

'Open the door!' cried George Hadley, trying the knob. 'Why, they've locked it from the outside! Peter!' He beat at the door. 'Open up!'

He heard Peter's voice outside, against the door.

'Don't let them switch off the nursery and the house,' he was saying.

Mr and Mrs George Hadley beat at the door. 'Now, don't be ridiculous, children. It's time to go. Mr McClean'll be here in a minute and ...'

And then they heard the sounds.

The lions on three sides of them, in the yellow veld grass, padding through the dry straw, rumbling and roaring in their throats.

The lions.

Mr Hadley looked at his wife and they turned and looked back at the beasts edging slowly forward, crouching, tails stiff.

Mr and Mrs Hadley screamed.

And suddenly they realised why those other screams had sounded familiar.

'Well, here I am,' said David McClean in the nursery doorway. 'Oh, hello,' He stared at the two children seated in the centre of the open glade eating a little picnic lunch. Beyond them was the water hole and the yellow veldland; above was the hot sun. He began to perspire. 'Where are your father and mother?'

The children looked up and smiled. 'Oh, they'll be here directly.'

'Good, we must get going.' At a distance Mr McClean saw the lions fighting and clawing and then quieting down to feed in silence under the shady trees.

He squinted at the lions with his hand up to his eyes.

Now the lions were done feeding. They moved to the water hole to drink.

A shadow flickered over Mr McClean's hot face. Many shadows flickered. The vultures were dropping down the blazing sky.

'A cup of tea?' asked Wendy in the silence.

John Collier

Evening Primrose

March 21
In a pad of Highlife Bond, bought by Miss Sadie Broadribb at Bracey's for 25c

Today I made my decision. I would turn my back for good and all upon the *bourgeois* world that hates a poet. I would leave, get out, break away—

And I have done it. I am free! Free as the mote that dances in the sunbeam! Free as a house-fly crossing first-class in the largest of luxury liners! Free as my verse! Free as the food I shall eat, the paper I shall write upon, the lamb's-wool-lined, softly slithering slippers I shall wear.

This morning I had not so much as a car-fare. Now I am here, on velvet. You are itching to learn of this haven; you would like to organise trips here, spoil it, send your relations-in-law, perhaps even come yourself. After all, this journal will hardly fall into your hands till I am dead. I'll tell you.

I am at Bracey's Giant Emporium, as happy as a mouse in the middle of an immense cheese, and the world shall know me no more.

Merrily, merrily shall I live now, secure behind a towering pile of carpets, in a corner-nook which I propose to line with eiderdowns, angora vestments, and the Cleopatraean tops in pillows. I shall be cosy.

I nipped into this sanctuary late this afternoon, and soon heard the dying footfalls of closing time. From now on, my only effort will be to dodge the night-watchman. Poets can dodge.

I have already made my first mouse-like exploration. I tiptoed as far as the stationery department, and, timid, darted back with only these writing materials, the poet's first need. Now I shall lay them aside and seek other necessities: food, wine, the soft furniture of my couch, and a natty smoking-jacket. This place stimulates me. I shall write here.

Dawn, Next Day

I suppose no one in the world was ever more astonished and over-whelmed than I have been tonight. It is unbelievable. Yet I believe it. How interesting life is when things get like that!

I crept out, as I said I would, and found the great shop in mingled light and gloom. The central well was half illuminated; the circling galleries towered in a pansy Piranesi of toppling light and shade. The spidery stairways and flying bridges had passed from purpose into fantasy. Silks and velvets glimmered like ghosts, a hundred pantie-clad models offered simpers and embraces to the desert air. Ring, clips, and bracelets glittered frostily in a desolate absence of Honey and Daddy.

Creeping along the transverse aisles, which were in deeper darkness, I felt like a wandering thought in the dreaming brain of a chorus girl down on her luck. Only, of course, their brains are not so big as Bracey's Giant Emporium. And there was no man there.

None, that is, except the night-watchman. I had forgotten him. As I crossed an open space on the mezzanine floor, hugging the lee of a display of sultry shawls, I became aware of a regular thudding, which might almost have been that of my own heart. Suddenly it burst upon me that it came from outside. It was the sound of footsteps, and they were only a few paces away. Quick as a flash I seized a flamboyant mantilla, whirled it about me and stood with one arm outflung, like a Carmen petrified in a gesture of disdain.

I was successful. He passed me, jingling his little machine on its chain; humming his little tine; he eyes scaled with refractions of the blaring day. 'Go, worldling!' I whispered, and permitted myself a soundless laugh.

It froze on my lips. My heart faltered. A new fear seized me.

I was afraid to move. I was afraid to look round. I felt I was being watched, by something that could see right through me. This was a very different feeling from the ordinary emergency caused by the very ordinary night-watchman. My conscious impulse was the obvious one; to glance behind me. But my eyes knew better. I remained absolutely petrified, staring straight ahead.

My eyes were trying to tell me something that my brain refused to believe. They made their point. I was looking straight into another pair of eyes, human eyes, but large, flat, luminous. I have seen such eyes among the nocturnal creatures, which creep out under the artificial blue moonlight in the zoo.

The owner was only a dozen feet away from me. The watchman had passed between us, nearer him than me. Yet he had not seen him. I must have been looking straight at him for several minutes at a stretch. I had not seen him either.

He was half reclining against a low dais where, on a floor of russet leaves, and flanked by billows of glowing home-spun, the fresh-faced waxen girls modelled spectator sports suits in herringbones, checks, and plaids. He leaned against the skirt of one of these Dianas; its folds concealed perhaps his ear, his shoulder, and a little of his right-hand side. He, himself, was clad in dim but large-patterned Shetland tweeds of the latest cut, suede shoes, a shirt in a rather broad *motif* in olive, pink, and grey. He was as pale as a creature found under a stone. His long, thin arms ended in hands that hung floatingly, more like trailing, transparent fins, or wisps of chiffon, than ordinary hands.

He spoke. His voice was not a voice; it was a mere whistling under the tongue. 'Not bad, for a beginner!'

I grasped that he was complimenting me, rather satirically, on my own, more amateurish, feat of camouflage. I stuttered. I said, 'I'm sorry. I didn't know anyone else lived here.' I noticed, even as I spoke, that I was imitating his own whistling sibilant utterance.

'Oh, yes,' he said. '*We* live here. It's delightful.'

'We?'

'Yes, all of us. Look!'

We were near the edge of the first gallery. He swept his long hand round, indicating the whole well of the shop. I looked. I saw nothing. I could hear nothing, except the watchman's thudding step receding infinitely far along some basement aisle.

'Don't you see?'

You know the sensation one has, peering into the half-light of a vivarium? One sees bark, pebbles, a few leaves, nothing more. And then suddenly, a stone breathes – it is a toad; there is a chameleon, another, a coiled adder, a mantis among the leaves. The whole case seems crepitant with life. Perhaps the whole world is. One glances at one's sleeve, one's feet.

So it was with thet ad,n. I loo iked shopwas empty. I looked, and there was an old lady, clambering out from behind the monstrous clock. There were three girls, elderly *ingénues*, incredibly emaciated, simpering at the entrance of the perfumery. Their hair was a fine floss, pale as gossamer. Equally brittle and colourless was a man with the appearance of a colonel of southern extraction, who stood regarding me while he caressed moustachios that would have done credit to a crystal shrimp. A chintzy woman, possibly of literary tastes, swam forward from the curtains and drapes.

They came thick about me, fluttering, whistling, like a waving of gauze in the wind. Their eyes were wide and flatly bright. I saw there was no colour to the iris.

'How raw he looks!'

'A detective! Send for the Dark Men!'

'I'm not a detective. I am a poet. I have renounced the world.'

'He is a poet. He has come over to us. Mr Roscoe found him.'

'He admires us.'

'He must meet Mrs Vanderpant.'

I was taken to meet Mrs Vanderpant. She proved to be the Grand Old Lady of the store, almost entirely transparent.

'So you are a poet, Mr Snell? You will find inspiration here. I am quite the oldest inhabitant. Three mergers and a complete rebuilding, but they didn't get rid of me!'

'Tell how you went out by daylight, dear Mrs Vanderpant, and nearly got bought for Whistler's *Mother*.'

'That was in pre-war days. I was more robust then. But at the cash desk they suddenly remembered there was no frame. And when they came back to look at me—'

'—She was gone.'

Their laughter was like the stridulation of the ghosts of grasshoppers.

'Where is Ella? Where is my broth?'

'She is bringing it, Mrs Vanderpant. It will come.'

'Tiresome little creature! She is our foundling, Mr Snell. She is not quite our sort.'

'Is that so, Mrs Vanderpant? Dear, dear!'

'I lived alone here, Mr Snell, for many years. I took refuge here in the terrible times in the 'eighties. I was a young girl then, a beauty, people were kind enough to say, but poor Papa lost his money. Bracey's meant a lot to a young girl, in the New York of those days, Mr Snell. It seemed to me terrible that I should not be able to come here in the ordinary way. So I came here for good. I was quite alarmed when others began to come in, after the crash of 1907. But it was the dear Judge, the Colonel, Mrs Bilbee—'

I bowed. I was being introduced.

'Mrs Bilbee writes plays. *And* of a very old Philadelphia family. You will find us quite *nice* here, Mr Snell.'

'I feel it a great privilege, Mrs Vanderpant.'

'And of course, all our dear *young* people came in '29. *Their* poor papas jumped from skyscrapers.'

I did a great deal of bowing and whistling. The introductions took a long time. Who would have thought so many people lived in Bracey's?

'And here at last is Ella with my broth.'

It was then that I noticed the young people were not so young after all, in spite of their smiles, their little ways, the *ingénue* dress. Ella was in her teens. Clad only in something from the shop-soiled counter, she nevertheless had the appearance of a living flower in a French cemetery, or a mermaid among polyps.

'Come, you stupid thing!'

'Mrs Vanderpant is waiting.'

Her pallor was not like theirs; not like the pallor of something that glistens or scuttles when you turn over a stone. Hers was that of a pearl.

Ella! Pearl of this remotest, most fantastic cave! Little mermaid, brushed over, pressed down by objects of a deadlier white – tentacles – ! I can write no more.

March 28

Well, I am rapidly becoming used to my new and half-lit world, to my strange company. I am learning the intricate laws of silence and camouflage which dominate the apparently casual strollings and gatherings of the mid-night clan. How they detest the night-watchman, whose existence imposes these laws on their idle festivals!

'Odious, vulgar creature! He reeks of the coarse sun!'

Actually, he is quite a personable young man, very young for a night-watchman, so young that I think he must have been wounded in the war. But they would like to tear him to pieces.

They are very pleasant to me, though. They are pleased that a poet should have come among them. Yet I cannot like them entirely. My blood is a little chilled by the uncanny ease with which even the old ladies can clamber spider-like from balcony to balcony. Or is it because they are so unkind to Ella?

Yesterday we had a bridge party. Tonight, Mrs Bilbee's little play, *Love in Shadowland*, is going to be presented. Would you believe it? – another colony, from Wanamaker's, is coming over *en masse* to attend. Apparently people live in all the great stores. This visit is considered a great honour, for there is an intense snobbery in these creatures. They speak with horror of a social outcast who left a high-class Madison Avenue establishment, and now leads a wallowing, beachcomberish life in a delicatessen. And they relate with tragic emotions the story of the man in Altman's, who conceived such a passion for a model plaid dressing jacket that he emerged and wrested it from the hands of a purchaser. It seems that all the Altman colony, dreading an investigation, were forced to remove beyond the social pale, into a five-and-dime. Well, I must get ready to attend the play.

April 14

I have found an opportunity to speak to Ella. I dared not before;

here one has a sense always of pale eyes secretly watching. But last night, at the play, I developed a fit of hiccups. I was somewhat sternly told to go and secrete myself in the basement, among the garbage cans, where the watchman never comes.

There, in the rat-haunted darkness. I heard a stifled sob. 'What's that? Is it you? Is it Ella? What ails you, child? Why do you cry?'

'They wouldn't even let me see the play.'

'Is that all? Let me console you.'

'I am so unhappy.'

She told me her tragic little story. What do you think? When she was a child, a little tiny child of only six, she strayed away and fell asleep behind a counter, while her mother tried on a new hat. When she woke, the store was in darkness.

'And I cried, and they all came around, and took hold of me. "She will tell, if we let her go," they said. Some said, "Call in the Dark Men." "Let her stay here," said Mrs Vanderpant. "She will make me a nice little maid." '

'Who are these Dark Men, Ella? They spoke of them when I came here.'

'Don't you know? Oh, it's horrible! It's horrible!'

'Tell me, Ella. Let us share it.'

She trembled. 'You know the morticians, "Journey's End", who go to houses when people die?'

'Yes, Ella.'

'Well, in that shop, just like here, and at Gimbel's, and at Blooming-dale's, there are people living, people like these.'

'How disgusting! But what can they live upon, Ella, in a funeral home?'

'Don't ask me! Dead people are sent there, to be embalmed. Oh, they are terrible creatures! Even the people here are terrified of them. But if anyone dies, or if some poor burglar breaks in, and sees these people, and might tell—'

'Yes? Go on.'

'Then they send for the others, the Dark Men.'

'Good heavens!'

'Yes, and they put the body in Surgical Supplies – or the burglar, all tied up, if it's a burglar – and they send for these others, and then they all hide, and in they come, the others – Oh! They're like pieces of blackness. I saw them once. It was terrible.'

'And then?'

'They go in, to where the dead person is, or the poor burglar. And they have wax there – and all sorts of things. And when they're gone there's just one of these wax models left on the table. And then our people put a dress on it, or a bathing suit, and they mix it up with all the others, and nobody ever knows.'

'But aren't they heavier than the others, these wax models? You would think they'd be heavier.'

'No, they're not heavier. I think there's a lot of them – gone.'

'Oh, dear! So they were going to do that to you, when you were a little child?'

'Yes, only Mrs Vanderpant said I was to be her maid.'

'I don't like these people, Ella.'

'Nor do I. I wish I could see a bird.'

'Why don't you go into the pet shop?'

'It wouldn't be the same. I want to see it on a twig, with leaves.'

'Ella, let us meet often. Let us creep away down here and meet. I will tell you about birds, and twigs and leaves.'

May 1

For the last few nights the store has been feverish with the shivering whisper of a huge crush at Bloomingdale's. Tonight was the night.

'Not changed yet? We leave on the stroke of two.' Roscoe has appointed himself, or been appointed, my guide or my guard.

'Roscoe, I am still a greenhorn. I dread the streets.'

'Nonsense! There's nothing to it. We slip out by twos and threes, stand on the sidewalk, pick up a taxi. Were you never out late in the old days? If so, you must have seen us, many a time.'

'Good heavens, I believe I have! And often wondered where you came from. And it was from here! But, Roscoe, my brow is burning. I find it hard to breathe. I fear a cold.'

'In that case you must certainly remain behind. Our whole party would be disgraced in the unfortunate event of a sneeze.'

I had relied on their rigid etiquette, so largely based on fear of discovery, and I was right. Soon they were gone, drifting out like leaves aslant on the wind. At once I dressed in flannel slacks, canvas shoes and a tasteful sport shirt, all new in stock today. I found a quiet spot, safely off the track beaten by the night-watchman. There, in a model's lifted hand, I set a wide fern frond culled from the florist's shop, and at once had a young spring tree. The carpet was sandy, sandy as a lake-side beach. A snowy napkin; two cakes, each with a cherry on it; I had only to imagine the lake and to find Ella.

'Why, Charles, what's this?'

'I'm a poet, Ella, and when a poet meets a girl like you he thinks of a day in the country. Do you see this tree? Let's call it *our* tree. There's the lake – the prettiest lake imaginable. Here is grass, and there are flowers. There are birds too, Ella. You told me you like birds.'

'Oh, Charles, you're so sweet. I feel I hear them singing.'

'And here's our lunch. But before we eat, go behind the rock there, and see what you find.'

I heard her cry out in delight when she saw the summer dress I had put there for her. When she came back the spring day smiled to see her, and the lake shone brighter than before. 'Ella, let us have lunch. Let us have fun. Let us have a swim. I can just imagine you in one of those new bathing suits.'

'Let's just sit here, Charles, and talk.'

So we sat and talked, and the time was gone like a dream. We might have stayed there, forgetful of everything, had it not been for the spider.

'Charles, what are you doing?'

'Nothing, my dear. Just a naughty little spider, crawling over your knee. Purely imaginary, of course, but that sort are sometimes the worst. I had to try to catch him.'

'Don't Charles! It's late. It's terribly late. They'll be back any minute. I'd better go home.'

I took her home to the kitchenware on the sub-ground floor, and kissed here good-day. She offered me her cheek. This troubles me.

May 10

'Ella, I love you.'

I said it to her just like that. We have met many times. I have dreamt of her by day. I have not even kept up my journal. Verse has been out of the question.

'Ella, I love you. Let us move into the trousseau department. Don't look so dismayed, darling. If you like, we will go right away from here. We will live in that little restaurant in Central Park. There are thousands of birds there.'

'Please – please don't talk like that!'

'But I love you with all my heart.'

'You mustn't.'

'But I find I must. I can't help it. Ella, you don't love another?'

She wept a little. 'Oh, Charles, I do.'

'Love another, Ella? One of these? I thought you dreaded them all. It must be Roscoe. He is the only one that's any way human. We talk of art, life, and such things. And he has stolen your heart!'

'No, Charles, no. He's just like the rest, really. I hate them all. They make me shudder.'

'Who is it, then?'

'It's him.'

'Who?'

'The night-watchman.'

'Impossible!'

'No. He smells of the sun.'

'Oh, Ella, you have broken my heart.'

'Be my friend, though.'

'I will. I'll be your brother. How did you fall in love with him?'

'Oh, Charles, it was wonderful. I was thinking of birds, and I was careless. Don't tell on me, Charles. They'll punish me.'

'No. No. Go on.'

'I was careless, and there he was, coming round the corner. And there was no place for me; I had this blue dress on. There were some wax models in their underthings.'

'Please go on.'

'I couldn't help it. I slipped off my dress, and stood still.'

'I see.'

'And he stopped just by me, Charles. And he looked at me. And he touched my cheek.'

'Did he notice nothing?'

'No. It was cold. But Charles, he said – he said – "Say, honey, I wish they made 'em like you on Eighth Avenue." Charles, wasn't that a lovely thing to say?'

'Personally, I should have said Park Avenue.'

'Oh, Charles, don't get like these people here. Sometimes I think you're getting like them. It doesn't matter what street, Charles; it was a lovely thing to say.'

'Yes, but my heart's broken. And what can you do about him? Ella, he belongs to another world.'

'Yes, Charles, Eighth Avenue. I want to go there. Charles, are you truly my friend?'

'I'm your brother, only my heart's broken.'

'I'll tell you. I will. I'm going to stand there again. So he'll see me.'

'And then?'

'Perhaps he'll speak to me again.'

'My dearest Ella, you are torturing yourself. You are making it worse.'

'No, Charles. Because I shall answer him. He will take me away.'

'Ella, I can't bear it.'

'Ssh! There is someone coming. I shall see birds – real birds, Charles – and flowers growing. They're coming. You must go.'

May 13

The last three days have been torture. This evening I broke. Roscoe had joined me. He sat eyeing me for a long time. He put his hand on my shoulder.

He said, 'You're looking seedy, old fellow. Why don't you go over to Wanamaker's for some ski-ing?'

His kindness compelled a frank response. 'It's deeper than that, Roscoe. I'm done for. I can't eat, I can't sleep. I can't write, man. I can't even write.'

'What is it? Day starvation?'

'Roscoe – it's love.'

'Not one of the staff, Charles, or the customers? That's absolutely forbidden.'

'No, it's not that, Roscoe. But just as hopeless.'

'My dear fellow, I can't bear to see you like this. Let me help you. Let me share your trouble.'

Then it all came out. It burst out. I trusted him. I think I trusted him. I really think I had no intention of betraying Ella, of spoiling her escape, of keeping her here till her heart turned towards me. If I had, it was subconscious, I swear it.

But I told him all. He was sympathetic, but I detected a sly reserve in his sympathy. 'You will respect my confidence, Roscoe? This is to be a secret between us.'

'As secret as the grave, old chap.'

And he must have gone straight to Mrs Vanderpant. This evening the atmosphere has changed. People flicker to and fro, smiling nervously, horribly, with a sort of frightened sadistic exaltation. When I speak to them they answer evasively, fidget, and disappear. An informal dance has been called off. I cannot find Ella. I will creep out. I will look for her again.

Later

Heaven! It has happened. I went in desperation to the manager's office, whose glass front overlooks the whole shop. I watched till midnight. Then I saw a little group of them, like ants bearing a victim. They were carrying Ella. They took her to the surgical department. They took other things.

And, coming back here, I was passed by a flittering, whispering horde of them, glancing over their shoulders in a thrilled ecstasy of panic, making for their hiding places. I, too, hid myself. How can I describe the dark inhuman creatures that passed me, silent as shadows? They went there – where Ella is.

What can I do? There is only one thing. I will find the watchman. I will tell him. He and I will save her. And if we are overpowered— Well, I will leave this on a counter. Tomorrow, if we live, I can recover it.

If not, look in the windows. Look for three new figures; two men,

one rather sensitive-looking, and a girl. She has blue eyes, like peri-
winkle flowers, and her upper lip is lifted a little.

Look for us.

Smoke them out! Obliterate them! Avenge us!

Robert Silverberg

Back from the Grave

Massey woke slowly, as if the return to awareness were almost painful to him. He had the ghastly sensation of being closed in. The air around him was warm and moist and faintly foul-tasting as it passed into his lungs, and everything was dark.

He yawned, tried to stretch. Probably the windows were closed in the bedroom, that was all. That was why everything seemed so muggy in here. All he had to do was call his wife, have her get the maid or someone else to draw back the curtains and let some fresh air into the room. . . .

'Louise! Louise!'

His voice sounded oddly muffled, flat, and indistinct in his own ears. It seemed to bounce back at him from the walls and ceiling of his bedroom.

'Louise? I'm calling you!'

There was no answer.

Massey suddenly became conscious of the noxious humidity all about him. *Very well*, he thought, *if there's no one else here I'll have to open the windows myself!* He levered himself up on his elbows, tried to swing himself out of bed.

He realised that he was not in a bed at all.

A pallid quiver of fear lanced through him as he discovered he did not have room to rise to a sitting position. Above him, only inches above his head, he felt the smooth sheen of satin. There was satin all about. He reached to his left in the darkness and felt satin again, barely an inch from his shoulder. It was the same to his right.

Moment after moment, the air was growing murkier and harder to breathe. And he did not have room to move. He seemed to be in a container just about the length and width of his own body.

There is only one purpose for a container of such dimensions.

Massey felt the clammy hand of panic brush his cheeks. My *God*, he thought. *They've made a mistake! They thought I was dead and they buried me! I'm not dead! I'm – I'm – buried alive!*

Massey lay quite still for several moments after the terrible truth had become apparent. He did not want to panic. He was a reasonable man; he knew that to panic now would mean certain death. He had to be calm. Think this thing out. Don't panic.

The first fact to consider was that he was in a coffin. Coffins are not built with much air-space. Massey was a heavy-set man, and that meant not only that he needed a lot of air but that there could be little air in the coffin to begin with. And that air was rapidly being exhausted. He began taking shallower, and less frequent breaths.

Perhaps they had not buried him yet. Maybe he was still lying in state in a funeral parlour somewhere. They had lowered the coffin lid already, but there was still the chance they had not yet placed him in the grave. In that case –

He summoned up his energy and released it in one mighty cry for help. He waited.

Nothing happened.

Massey realised that such shouting was wasteful of oxygen. Probably they could not hear him through the heavy lid of the coffin. Or – he quivered at the possibility – perhaps they had lowered him into the ground already, said the proper words over him, shovelled the soil back into the cavity.

That would mean that five feet of packed-down earth lay above his head. Not even superman could raise a coffin lid with that kind of weight pressing down. Lying there in the darkness, Massey tried to force himself not to think of that possibility. Despite himself, the vision came – of himself, two yards beneath the ground, wasting his last strength in a desperate and ultimately futile attempt to raise a coffin lid held down by hundreds of pounds of soil Pushing and pushing, while the moist air around him gradually gave up its life-saving oxygen and became unfit to breathe, until finally he clutched at his purpling throat in agony, unable even to double up because of the dimensions of the coffin.

No, he thought. *I won't think of it!*

The only situation he would allow his numbed mind to consider was a hopeful one, that he was still above the surface of the ground. Otherwise there would be no hope, and he might as well lie back and die.

But. . . .

How could such a thing happen to me?

BACK FROM THE GRAVE

He had heard of cases of premature burial before. Most of them were apocryphal, of course – tales out of Poe, placed in real life by glib-tongued liars. But this was no lie, nor was it a story by Poe. Here he was: James Ronald Massey, forty-four years old, assets better than five hundred thousand dollars, holding responsible positions in no less than seven important corporations – here he was, lying in a coffin hardly bigger than his own body, while his life flickered like a dying candle.

It was like a dream – a nightmare. But it was real.

Massey allowed himself the luxury of a deep breath and raised his arms until his hands pressed against the satin-lined lid of the coffin. Tensing his body, he pushed upward until his wrists ached. Nothing happened; not even the smallest upward motion of the coffin lid was apparent.

He let his hands drop.

Droplets of sweat broke out all over his body. His clothes itched; he was wearing, not one of his own costly suits, but some cheap outfit supplied by the undertaker, and the coarse fabric felt rough and un-familiar against his skin.

He wondered how much more time he had, before the air would be totally vitiated. Ten minutes? An hour? A day, perhaps?

He wondered how he could possibly have been buried alive at all.

As he lay there, gathering his strength for another attempt to raise the lid, his thoughts drifted back – back over an entire lifetime, really, but centring on only the last three years, the years of his marriage to Louise. Massey had been past forty when he married her: she had been only twenty-three.

He had never had time to marry when he was young. He was always too busy, involved in complex corporate schemes, pyramiding his investments, building up his money to provide himself with a luxurious middle age. Despite himself he smiled ironically, lying in the coffin, as he recalled his frantic planning, the long hours of pacing the floor at night to devise yet another investment plan.

For what? Here at the age of forty-four he lay trapped alive in his coffin – with his life ticking away with every beat of his heart. Unless he freed himself through a miracle, there would be no old age for him.

And he would not have Louise any more.

The thoughts of Louise made the fear return. He had met her at a summer resort, one of his rare vacations; she was with her parents, and they had danced a few times, and before the two weeks were over Massey had astonished himself by proposing marriage to her. She had astonished him even more by accepting.

They had been married a month later. It was a small ceremony, though he did send announcements to all of his business associates, and they honeymooned for a month in South America. Massey could not spare more than a month away from his desk. Louise didn't seem to object to his devotion to his work, especially when he explained his financial status to her and their children after he was gone.

Those early married months had been the happiest of his life. Massey thought. To watch Louise moving around the big mansion was a delight; she seemed to bring a glowing radiance wherever she went.

I have to get out of here! The thought took on new urgency as he pictured Louise in his mind, tall, slim, so graceful she seemed to float instead of to walk, with her hair a golden halo round her head. So lovely, so warm, so loving.

Massey's breath came in panicky harsh gasps now even though he fought for control over his rebellious lungs. There still was plenty of time, he told himself. Just get in the right position and lift. How much can a coffin-lid weigh anyway?

Plenty, came the answer, *if there's a ton of dirt holding it down.*

'No! It isn't so!' Massey shouted, and the booming sound ricocheted mockingly from the walls of his coffin. 'I'm not underground yet! I can still get out!'

He squirmed around on one hip after a good deal of wriggling, and put his shoulder to the coffin lid. He took a deep breath.

Now – lift!

He pushed upward, anchoring himself with his left hand and pressing up with his right shoulder, until it seemed that his left arm would buckle under the strain. Bands of pain coursed through his body, across his chest, down his back.

The lid would not budge.

Massey's calmness began to desert him. The air was so close it stank, now, stank with musty graveyard odours and with his own perspiration and with the killing dankness of the carbon dioxide that was rapidly replacing its oxygen. He began to laugh hysterically, suddenly, without warning. He threw his head back and laughed, not seeming to care that by so laughing he was consuming more of his precious remnant of breathable air.

It was all so funny! He remembered his last day of consciousness. Remembered Louise – in Henry Marshall's arms!

Henry Marshall had arrived on the scene in the first year of Massey's marriage to Louise. She had told Massey, one night, in that casual way of hers, 'I'm having a guest for dinner.'

'Oh? Anyone I know?'

'A boy named Henry Marshall. An old playmate of mine; I haven't seen him for years.'

BACK FROM THE GRAVE

Massey had smiled indulgently. Above all else, he wanted Louise to be happy, and never to fear that because she had married a husband nearly twice her age she was condemned to a life of solemn loneliness.

Henry Marshall arrived at the dot of six that night. He was a boy of about twenty-five, tall and handsome, with wavy blond hair and an easy, likable manner about him. Something in his very charm made Massey dislike him almost on sight. He was too casual, took things too much for granted. Massey noticed that Henry Marshall was dressed rather shabbily, too.

It was not a pleasant evening. Louise and Henry Marshall reminisced together, chuckled over old times that meant nothing to Massey, told stories of friends long since unseen. Henry Marshall stayed late, past eleven, and when he finally left and Massey held Louise tightly in the quiet of her bedroom he sensed a certain remoteness about her that he had never felt before. It was as if she were making love mechanically, not really caring.

Massey brooded about that in the days that followed, though he never spoke a word to Louise. And Henry Marshall became a frequent visitor at the Massey's, coming sometimes for dinner, occasionally remaining as a house guest for two and three days. Massey resented the younger man's presence, but, as always, he remained silent out of deference to his wife's happiness.

He had almost come to accept Marshall's regular visits, even though they were occurring more frequently now, twice a month where once they had been only once a month. But, thought Massey as he lay in the clammy darkness of the coffin where he had been interred alive, this final visit – only a few days ago, was it, or had years gone by? – this final visit had been too much.

Young Marshall had arrived on Friday night in time for dinner, as usual. By now he was well known among the servants, and they gave him his usual room in the north wing of the building. He was gay and amusing at dinner and afterwards.

Massey retired early that night, pleading a headache. But he lay awake, tossing restlessly in his bed, perturbed half by the problems involved in a large steel manoeuvre coming up on Monday, half by the presence of this flippant youngster under his own roof.

Half the sleepless night went by, and visions danced before him: Louise, lovely, tempting, belonging to him. A current of excitement rose in Massey. He left his bed, donned a housecoat, and made his way down the hallway to his wife's bedroom. The great clock in the corridor told him that the time was past three in the morning, and the big house was quiet.

Louise had left the 'do not disturb' sign on her bedroom door. Massey opened the door gently, silently, thinking that if she were asleep he would not waken her, but hoping that perhaps she, too, had tossed and turned this evening, and would welcome him into her bed, into her arms.

He tiptoed towards the canopied bed.

Louise was not asleep. She was looking up at him, eyes bright with fear (or was it defiance?).

Louise was not alone.

Henry Marshall lay beside her, an arm thrown negligently over her bare shoulders.

In one stunned instant of understanding. Massey saw confirmed what he had barely dared to suspect, these past years when Henry Marshall had visited them so many times. Louise was deceiving him!

A hot ribbon of pain coursed across the front of his body, centring like a cauterising knife just behind his ribs. He gasped in agony and confusion.

'Louise – I didn't know –'

They were sitting up in bed, both of them, smiling at him. They were unafraid.

'Well, now you *do* know,' Henry Marshall said. 'And it's been going on for years. What are you going to do about it, old boy?'

Massey's heart thundered agonisingly. He staggered, nearly fell, grabbed a bedpost to support himself. His arms and legs felt cold with a deadly chill.

Louise said quietly, 'You were bound to find out about us sooner or later. Henry and I have been in love for years – ever since we were nineteen. But we couldn't afford to marry – and he agreed to wait a few years, when I met you. Only a few years; that's what your doctor told me, privately. He didn't want you to know.'

Massey put his hands to the fiery ball of palpitating hell that his heart had abruptly become. He could almost feel the blood circulating through his body, pounding at his brain.

Louise said, 'Dr Robinson said you had a serious heart defect – any shock was likely to carry you off. But he didn't want you to know about it; he said your days were numbered anyway, so you might just as well live them out in peace. But *I* knew – and Henry knew! And now we'll inherit your money, James. We're both still young, and we'll have each other for years to come!'

Massey took two uncertain steps towards the couple in the bed. Red flashes of light were interfering with his vision now, and his legs were numb.

'Louise – it isn't so, Louise – this is all a dream, isn't it?'

'You're wide awake! It's actually happening! Why don't you die, you old fool? Die! Die!'

BACK FROM THE GRAVE

And then he had started to fall, toppling into the thick wine-red carpet of Louise's bedroom, lying there with his hands dug deep into the high pile rug, while eddies of pain rippled through him, and above him sounded their mocking laughter and Louise's repeated cry of 'Die, you old fool! Die! Die!'

So that was the way it had been. Massey recalled everything, now, and he understood. The shock of finding Louise and Henry Marshall that way had touched off the heart attack that had been inevitable for so long. He had lain on the floor in Louise's bedroom, unconscious, in a coma, perhaps, and somehow – somehow – the doctors had decided he was dead.

It was incredible. Had life indeed been flickering so feebly in him that the high-price medicos had failed to realise he still lived? Or – the thought chilled Massey there in the darkness – had Louise and her lover found some complacent doctor who, for a fee, would certify death when death had not really come? What if Louise had known he was still alive, though unconscious, and had knowingly placed him in this coffin and sent him to the darkness of the grave?

A terrible passion came to life in Massey. He *would* get out! He had won before, in corporation matters, in proxy fights, in struggles of every kind. He was a mild-mannered man on the surface, but this will was all-consuming once it was aroused.

He would free himself.

Somehow.

Massey vowed to escape from this grave, whether he lay under a ton of soil or not. He would return to life, come back from the grave. Punish Louise for her crime, make her atone for her mocking infidelity.

I'll get out, he swore to himself. *I won't die here like a trapped rat.*

The word 'rat' brought a new and even more ghastly thought to mind. He had heard legends of the graveyard rats, great slug-shaped creatures with blazing red eyes and tails like scaled serpents, who tunnelled under the graveyards and gnawed their way into the new graves to devour the flesh of recent corpses.

Suppose they came for him? Suppose, even now as he lay here, the graveyard beasts squatted in their unmentionable tunnels below his coffin, nibbling at the wood with yellowed teeth, gnawing, biting, scratching, boring ominously inward.

How the rats would rejoice when they found a living man within the coffin!

Massey had always had a vivid imagination. Now with darkness settled like a cloak about him, he found himself unable to make that imagination cease functioning. Sharply in the eye of his mind he saw the gleeful cascade of rats pouring through the breach in the coffin wall, saw dozens of the foul beasts launching themselves on him with more burrowing greedily in from all sides. He pictured the rats madly joyous at the discovery of a live being, of fresh meat.

He saw their bristly snouts nuzzling at the soft pink flesh of his throat. He could picture their razor-keen teeth meeting beneath his chin, while his outraged blood spurted out over them. He could feel the animals quarrelling with each other for the right to devour the tender morsels that were his eyes.

What was that? That sound?

A fitful champing and chewing sound, was it? As of hundreds of rats patiently gnawing at the sleek fresh wood of his coffin?

No, he thought. More imagination. There was no sound. Everything was utterly silent. It was, he thought, the silence of – of the grave.

Then he wondered how he could still retain a sense of humour. How, for that matter, he could still retain any shred of his sanity, trapped like this.

He could no longer preserve the fiction that he was still lying in state in some undertaker's parlour. Coffins do not normally have locks; the only reason why he had been unable to lift the lid was that he was already in the ground. No doubt Louise and her lover had rushed him into the ground as fast as they could.

They would be in for a surprise, Massey thought with calmness that surprised himself. Calmness was what he needed now. In the same way as he had piloted so many complicated financial manoeuvres, James Ronald Massey now set to work to think of a way to escape from the living grave to which he had been condemned.

Pushing at the lid was futile. He had already tried that a dozen unsuccessful times. But perhaps he could break the lid, claw his way upward through the dirt till he reached the surface.

He felt in the darkness for the satin lining of the coffin. The air hung like a moist cloth around him now. He realised he had no more than a few minutes' air left, and then the hideous slow death of stragulation would start.

Better that than the rats, he told himself. I don't want to be alive if the rats break into the coffin. I'd rather choke to death than be eaten alive. Yes. Much better to choke.

His hands clawed at the satin and ripped it away, shredding the expensive cloth. Now he could feel the smooth, cool pine boards from which his coffin had been made. The wood had been planed and sanded to a perfect finish. He laughed, a little wildly. Probably Louise had bought him the most expensive coffin that could be found. 'Nothing but the best for my poor dead darling husband,' she must have told the undertaker.

He began to pound at the wood, hoping he would hear it splinter. But the wood held. He gasped for breath, knowing just a bit of fresh air remained, that now the torture would begin. He could barely fill his lungs. He drew in a deep breath and nearly retched at the nauseous taste of the stale air.

Weirdly he wondered if perhaps they had laid him in his grave upside-down. Perhaps he did not face the sky, and perhaps he was really digging at the bottom of his coffin instead of the top. In that case, even if he did succeed in breaking through the solid wood he would be far from free.

Impossible, he thought. *A joke of my tired mind.* He had to keep trying. Couldn't give up now. Not now, when the air would be gone in minutes, and the rats lay waiting, waiting for him.

His hands, which had never done any kind of manual labour, now clawed and scraped desperately at the unyielding wood of the coffin lid. His nails raked the mocking pine boards again and again, as if he thought to dig his way through the wood splinter by splinter. His nails ripped away one by one and blood streamed down his fingers, and he felt the bright hotness of the terrible pain, but still he clawed.

And screamed.

'Help me! Can't you hear me? I'm buried alive in here! Alive! I'll give ten thousand dollars to any man who gets me out! Twenty thousand! Fifty thousand! Do you hear me, fifty thousand dollars!'

He might just as well have offered the moon and the stars. No one heard his call; no one answered him. The funeral was probably long since over, the mourners dispersed. At this moment perhaps Louise and Henry Marshall were making love and laughing to each other about the fortune that now was theirs.

'Help me! Help me!'

His broken fingers clawed futilely at the wooden barrier above him, clawed until his nerves were numbed by constant agony and he could feel no more pain. The air was all but gone, now.

Part of his mind was still clear. Part was still engaged in formulating plans. Break a hole in the coffin lid, he thought. Widen it. Claw through the dirt to the surface. The soil will still be loose and soft. You can push it to one side if you can only get out of this coffin. Get your head above air, breathe the fresh air again, call for help.

Then settle with Louise and Henry.

It was all so simple – all but the first step. He could not get a purchase on the wood. The air was a vile moist thing now, and he could feel the cold hand of asphyxiation tightening steadily round his throat. The staleness of the air was making thought more difficult; he could barely think clearly any more. And he seemed to hear the rats again, chewing tirelessly at the wood, as if they knew that a living being lay in the wooden box, as if they yearned to get to Massey while the warm blood still pulsed in his veins.

And his heart – the heart whose sudden failure had been mistaken for death – his heart now pounded wildly from his exertions, and the pain that shot through him was ten times the torment he had experienced that night in Louise's bedroom. He wondered how long he could stand the combined assault.

The rats . . . the rats coming to get me . . . and the air almost gone . . . the darkness . . . my heart, my heart! . . . I'll need a miracle to get out of here now . . . my heart! The pain!

The pain!

Suddenly tranquillity stole over Massey. He smiled, and realised that the pain had diminished. He felt calm and assured now.

How foolish he had been to work so hard to get out of his coffin! There was such an easier way to do it!

All he had to do was drift. He drifted upward, passed lightly through the sturdy wood he had failed to break, drifted up through five feet of dark earth, and stood once more on the surface of the green land.

Free!

It was mid-afternoon. The sun glinted brightly, the sun Massey had thought never to see again. Fifty feet away, a group of people were gathered round a marble headstone, placing a wreath. Massey shouted to them.

'I'm free! They buried me, but I escaped from the grave! Get the sexton! Tell him there's been a mistake, please!'

Curiously, they ignored him. They did not even turn around to see who called. Massey repeated his words, to no avail.

He took a deep breath – and discovered for the first time that he could not taste the spring-like freshness of the air. He felt no cool fragrance in his nostrils.

Massey looked down. Then, suddenly, it was as if the ground parted beneath him, and he could see clearly the coffin lying deep in the earth, and he could see into the coffin, where the dead body of a middle-aged man lay – his fingers torn and bloodied, his face mottled with the discoloration of asphyxiation and the redness of a sudden and fatal heart attack.

William Faulkner

A Rose for Emily

I

When Miss Emily Grierson died, our whole town went to her funeral: the men through a sort of respectful affection for a fallen monument, the women mostly out of curiosity to see the inside of her house, which no one save an old man-servant – a combined gardener and cook – had seen in at least ten years.

It was a big, squarish frame house that had once been white, decorated with cupolas and spires and scrolled balconies in the heavily lightsome style of the 'seventies, set on what had once been our most select street. But garages and cotton gins had encroached and obliterated even the august names of that neighbourhood; only Miss Emily's house was left, lifting its stubborn and coquettish decay above the cotton wagons and the petrol pumps – an eyesore among eyesores. And now Miss Emily had gone to join the representatives of those august names where they lay in the cedar-bemused cemetery among the ranked and anonymous graves of Union and Confederate soldiers who fell at the battle of Jefferson.

Alive, Miss Emily had been a tradition, a duty, and a care; a sort of hereditary obligation upon the town, dating from that day in 1894 when Colonel Sartoris, the mayor – he who fathered the edict that no Negro woman should appear on the streets without an apron – remitted her taxes, the dispensation dating from the death of her father on into perpetuity. Not that Miss Emily would have accepted charity. Colonel Sartoris invented an involved tale to the effect that Miss Emily's father had loaned money to the town, which the town, as a matter of business, preferred this way of repaying. Only a man of Colonel Sartoris's generation and thought could have invented it, and only a woman could have believed it.

When the next generation, with its more modern ideas, became mayors and aldermen, this arrangement created some little dissatisfaction. On the first of the year they mailed her a tax notice. February came, and there was no reply. They wrote her a formal letter asking her to call at the sheriff's office at her convenience. A week later the mayor wrote her himself, offering to call or to send his car for her, and received in reply a note on paper of an archaic shape, in a thin, flowing calligraphy in faded ink, to the effect that she no longer went out at all. The tax notice was also enclosed, without comment.

They called a special meeting of the Board of Aldermen. A deputation waited upon her, knocked at the door through which no visitor had passed since she ceased giving china-painting lessons eight or ten years earlier. They were admitted by the old Negro into a dim hall from which a stairway mounted into still more shadow. It smelled of dust and disuse – a close, dank smell. The Negro led them into the parlour. It was furnished in heavy, leather-covered furniture. When the Negro opened the blinds of one window, they could see that the leather was cracked; and when they sat down, a faint dust rose sluggishly about their thighs, spinning with slow motes in the single sun-ray. On a tarnished gilt easel before the fireplace stood a crayon portrait of Miss Emily's father.

They rose when she entered – a small, fat woman in black, with a thin gold chain descending to her waist and vanishing into her belt, leaning on an ebony cane with a tarnished gold head. Her skeleton was small and spare; perhaps that was why what would have been merely plumpness in another was obesity in her. She looked bloated, like a body long submerged in motionless water, and of that pallid hue. Her eyes, lost in the fatty ridges of her face, looked like two small pieces of coal pressed into a lump of dough as they moved from one face to another while the visitors stated their errand.

She did not ask them to sit. She just stood in the doorway and listened quietly until the spokesman came to a stumbling halt. Then they could hear the invisible watch ticking at the end of the gold chain.

Her voice was dry and cold. 'I have no taxes in Jefferson. Colonel Sartoris explained it to me. Perhaps one of you can gain access to the city records and satisfy yourselves.'

'But we have. We are the city authorities, Miss Emily. Didn't you get a notice from the sheriff, signed by him?'

'I received a paper, yes,' Miss Emily said. 'Perhaps he considers himself the sheriff. . . . I have no taxes in Jefferson.'

'But there is nothing on the books to show that, you see. We must go by the—'

'See Colonel Sartoris. I have no taxes in Jefferson.'

'But, Miss Emily—'

'See Colonel Sartoris.' (Colonel Sartoris had been dead almost ten years.) 'I have no taxes in Jefferson. Tobe!' The Negro appeared. 'Show these gentlemen out.'

II

So she vanquished them, horse and foot, just as she had vanquished their fathers thirty years before about the smell. That was two years after her father's death and a short time after her sweetheart – the one we believed would marry her – had deserted her. After her father's death she went out very little; after her sweetheart went away, people hardly saw her at all. A few of the ladies had the temerity to call, but were not received, and the only sign of life about the place was the Negro man – a young man then – going in and out with a market basket.

'Just as if a man – any man – could keep a kitchen properly,' the ladies said; so they were not surprised when the smell developed. It was another link between the gross, teeming world and the high and mighty Griersons.

A neighbour, a woman, complained to the mayor, Judge Stevens, eighty years old.

'But what will you have me do about it, madam?' he said.

'Why, send her word to stop it,' the woman said. 'Isn't there a law?'

'I'm sure that won't be necessary,' Judge Stevens said. 'It's probably just a snake or a rat that nigger of hers killed in the yard. I'll speak to him about it.'

The next day he received two more complaints, one from a man who came in diffident deprecation. 'We really must do something about it, Judge. I'd be the last one in the world to bother Miss Emily, but we've got to do something.' That night the Board of Aldermen met – three greybeards and one younger man, a member of the rising generation.

'It's simple enough,' he said. 'Send her word to have her place cleaned up. Give her a certain time to do it in, and if she don't . . .'

'Dammit, sir,' Judge Stevens said, 'will you accuse a lady to her face of smelling bad?'

So the next night, after midnight, four men crossed Miss Emily's lawn and slunk about the house like burglars, sniffing along the base of the brickwork and at the cellar openings, while one of them performed a regular sowing motion with his hand out of a sack slung from his shoulder. They broke open the cellar door and sprinkled lime there, and in all the outbuildings. As they recrossed the lawn, a window that had been dark was lighted and Miss Emily sat in it, the light behind her, and her upright torso motionless as that of an idol. They crept quietly across the lawn and into the shadow of the locusts that lined the street. After a week or two the smell went away.

That was when people had begun to feel really sorry for her. People in our town, remembering how Old Lady Wyatt, her great-aunt, had gone completely crazy at last, believed that the Griersons held themselves a little too high for what they really were. None of the young men was quite good enough to Miss Emily and such. We had long thought of them as a tableau: Miss Emily a slender figure in white in the background, her father a spraddled silhouette in the foreground, his back to her and clutching a horsewhip, the two of them framed by the backflung front door. So when she got to be thirty and was still single, we were not pleased exactly, but vindicated; even with insanity in the family she wouldn't have turned down all of her chances if they had really materialised.

When her father died, it got about that the house was all that was left to her; and in a way, people were glad. At last they could pity Miss Emily. Being left alone, and a pauper, she had become humanised. Now she too would know the old thrill and the old despair of a penny more or less.

The day after his death all the ladies prepared to call at the house and offer condolence and aid, as is our custom. Miss Emily met them at the door, dressed as usual and with no trace of grief on her face. She told them that her father was not dead. She did that for three days, with the ministers calling on her, and the doctors, trying to persuade her to let them dispose of the body. Just as they were about to resort to law and force, she broke down, and they buried her father quickly.

We did not say she was crazy then. We believed she had to do that. We remembered all the young men her father had driven away, and we knew that, with nothing left, she would have to cling to that which had robbed her, as people will.

III

She was sick for a long time. When we saw her again, her hair was cut short, making her look like a girl, with a vague resemblance to those angels in coloured church windows – sort of tragic and serene.

The town had just let the contracts for paving the sidewalks, and in the summer after her father's death they began the work. The construction company came with niggers and mules and machinery, and a foreman named Homer Barron, a Yankee – a big, dark, ready man, with a big voice and eyes lighter than his face. The little boys would follow in groups to hear him cuss the niggers, and the niggers singing in time to the rise and fall of picks. Pretty soon he knew everybody in town.

A ROSE FOR EMILY

Whenever you heard a lot of laughing anywhere about the square, Homer Barron would be in the centre of the group. Presently we began to see him and Miss Emily on Sunday afternoons driving in the yellow-wheeled buggy and the matched team of bays from the livery stable.

At first we were glad that Miss Emily would have an interest, because the ladies all said, 'Of course a Grierson would not think seriously of a Northerner, a day labourer.' But there were still others, older people, who said that even grief could not cause a real lady to forget *noblesse oblige* – without calling it *noblesse oblige*. They just said, 'Poor Emily. Her kinsfolk should come to her.' She had some kin in Alabama; but years ago her father had fallen out with them over the estate of Old Lady Wyatt, the crazy woman, and there was no communication between the two families. They had not even been represented at the funeral.

And as soon as the old people said, 'Poor Emily,' the whispering began. 'Do you suppose it's really so?' they said to one another. 'Of course it is. What else could . . .' This behind their hands; rustling of craned silk and satin behind jalousies closed upon the sun of Sunday afternoon as the thin, swift clop-clop-clop of the matched team passed: 'Poor Emily.'

She carried her head high enough – even when we believed that she was fallen. It was as if she demanded more than ever the recognition of her dignity as the last Grierson; as if it had wanted that touch of earthiness to reaffirm her imperviousness. Like when she bought the rat poison, the arsenic. That was over a year after they had begun to say 'Poor Emily,' and while the two female cousins were visiting her.

'I want some poison,' she said to the druggist. She was over thirty then, still a slight woman, though thinner than usual, with cold, haughty black eyes in a face the flesh of which was strained across the temples and about the eye-sockets as you imagine a lighthouse-keeper's face ought to look. 'I want some poison,' she said.

'Yes, Miss Emily. What kind? For rats and such? I'd recom—'

'I want the best you have. I don't care what kind.'

The druggist named several. 'They'll kill anything up to an elephant. But what you want is—'

'Arsenic,' Miss Emily said. 'Is that a good one?'

'Is . . . arsenic? Yes, ma'am. But what you want—'

'I want arsenic.'

The druggist looked down at her. She looked back at him, erect, her face like a strained flag. 'Why, of course,' the druggist said. 'If that's what you want. But the law requires you to tell what you are going to use it for.'

Miss Emily just stared at him, her head tilted back in order to look him eye for eye, until he looked away and went and got the arsenic and wrapped it up. The Negro delivery boy brought her the package; the druggist didn't come back. When she opened the package at home there was written on the box, under the skull and bones: 'For rats.'

IV

So the next day we all said, 'She will kill herself'; and we said it would be the best thing. When she had first begun to be seen with Homer Barron, we had said, 'She will marry him.' Then we said, 'She will persuade him yet,' because Homer himself had remarked – he liked men, and it was known that he drank with the younger men in the Elks' Club – that he was not a marrying man. Later we said, 'Poor Emily' behind the jalousies as they passed on Sunday afternoon in the glittering buggy, Miss Emily with her head high and Homer Barron with his hat cocked and a cigar in his teeth, reins and whip in a yellow glove.

Then some of the ladies began to say that it was a disgrace to the town and a bad example to the young people. The men did not want to interfere, but at last the ladies forced the Baptist minister – Miss Emily's people were Episcopal – to call upon her. He would never divulge what happened during that interview, but he refused to go back again. The next Sunday they again drove about the streets, and the following day the minister's wife wrote to Miss Emily's relations in Alabama.

So she had blood-kin under her roof again and we sat back to watch developments. At first nothing happened. Then we were sure that they were to be married. We learned that Miss Emily had been to the jeweller's and ordered a man's toilet set in silver, with the letters H. B. on each piece. Two days later we learned that she had bought a complete outfit of men's clothing, including a night-shirt, and we said, 'They are married.' We were really glad. We were glad because the two female cousins were even more Grierson than Miss Emily had ever been.

So we were not surprised when Homer Barron – the streets had been finished some time since – was gone. We were a little disappointed that there was not a public blowing-off, but we believed that he had gone on to prepare for Miss Emily's coming, or to give her a chance to get rid of the cousins. (By that time it was a cabal, and we were all Miss Emily's allies to help circumvent the cousins.) Sure enough, after another week they departed. And, as we had expected all along, within three days Homer Barron was back in town. A neighbour saw the Negro man admit him at the kitchen door at dusk one evening.

And that was the last we saw of Homer Barron. And of Miss Emily for some time. The Negro man went in and out with the market basket, but the front door remained closed. Now and then we would see her at a window for a moment, as the men did that night when they sprinkled the lime, but for almost six months she did not appear on the streets. Then we knew that this was to be expected too; as if that quality of her father which had thwarted her woman's life so many times had been too virulent and too furious to die.

When we next saw Miss Emily, she had grown fat and her hair was turning grey. During the next few years it grew greyer and greyer until it attained an even pepper-and-salt iron-grey, when it ceased turning. Up to the day of her death at seventy-four it was still that vigorous iron-grey, like the hair of an active man.

From that time on her front door remained closed, save for a period of six or seven years, when she was about forty, during which she gave lessons in china-painting. She fitted up a studio in one of the downstairs rooms, where the daughters and granddaughters of Colonel Sartoris's contemporaries were sent to her with the same regularity and in the same spirit that they were sent to church on Sundays with a twenty-five cent piece for the collection plate. Meanwhile her taxes has been remitted.

Then the newer generation became the backbone and the spirit of the town, and the painting pupils grew up and fell away and did not send their children to her with boxes of colour and tedious brushes and pictures cut from the ladies' magazines. The front door closed upon the last one and remained closed for good. When the town got free postal delivery, Miss Emily alone refused to let them fasten the metal numbers above her door and attach a mail-box to it. She would not listen to them.

Daily, monthly, yearly we watched the Negro grow greyer and more stooped, going in and out with the market basket. Each December we sent her a tax notice, which would be returned by the post office a week later, unclaimed. Now and then we would see her in one of the downstairs windows – she had evidently shut up the top floor of the house – like the carven torso of an idol in a niche, looking or not looking at us, we could never tell which. Thus she passed from generation to generation – dear, inescapable, impervious, tranquil, and perverse.

And so she died. Fell ill in the house filled with dust and shadows, with only a doddering Negro man to wait on her. We did not even know she was sick; we had long since given up trying to get any information from the Negro. He talked to no one, probably not even to her, for his voice had grown harsh and rusty, as if from disuse.

She died in one of the downstairs rooms, in a heavy walnut bed with a curtain, her grey head propped on a pillow yellow and mouldy with age and lack of sunlight.

V

The Negro met the first of the ladies at the front door and let them in, with their hushed, sibilant voices, and their quick, curious glances, and then he disappeared. He walked right through the house and out the back and was not seen again.

The two female cousins came at once. They held the funeral on the second day, with the town coming to look at Miss Emily beneath a mass of bought flowers, with the crayon face of her father musing profoundly above the bier and the ladies sibilant and macabre; and the very old men – some in their brushed Confederate uniforms – on the porch and the lawn, talking of Miss Emily as if she had been a contemporary of theirs, believing that they had danced with her and courted her perhaps, confusing time with its mathematical progression, as the old do, to whom all the past is not a diminishing road but, instead, a huge meadow which no winter ever quite touches, divided from them now by the narrow bottle-neck of the most recent decade of years.

Already we knew that there was one room in that region above stairs which no one had seen in forty years, and which would have to be forced. They waited until Miss Emily was decently in the ground before they opened it.

The violence of breaking down the door seemed to fill this room with pervading dust. A thin, acrid pall as of the tomb seemed to lie everywhere upon this room decked and furnished as for a bridal: upon the valance curtains of faded rose colour, upon the rose-shaded lights, upon the dressing table, upon the delicate array of crystal and the man's toilet things backed with tarnished silver, silver so tarnished that the monogram was obscured. Among them lay a collar and tie, as if they had just been removed, which, lifted, left upon the surface a pale crescent in the dust. Upon a chair hung the suit, carefully folded; beneath it the two mute shoes and the discarded socks.

The man himself lay in the bed.

For a long while we just stood there, looking down at the profound and fleshless grin. The body had apparently once lain in the attitude of an embrace, but now the long sleep that outlasts love, that conquers even the grimace of love, had cuckolded him. What was left of him, rotted beneath what was left of the night-shirt, had become inextricable from the bed in which he lay; and upon him and upon the pillow beside him lay that even coating of the patient and biding dust.

Then we noticed that in the second pillow was the indentation of a head. One of us lifted something from it, and leaning forward, that faint and invisible dust, dry and acrid in the nostrils, we saw a long strand of iron-grey hair.

Flannery O'Connor

The Comforts of Home

Thomas withdrew to the side of the window and with his head between the wall and the curtain he looked down on the driveway where the car had stopped. His mother and the little slut were getting out of it. His mother emerged slowly, stolid and awkward, and then the little slut's long slightly bowed legs slid out, the dress pulled above the knees. With a shriek of laughter she ran to meet the dog, who bounded, overjoyed, shaking with pleasure, to welcome her. Rage gathered throughout Thomas's large frame with a silent ominous intensity, like a mob assembling.

It was now up to him to pack a suitcase, go to the hotel, and stay there until the house should be cleared.

He did not know where a suitcase was, he disliked to pack, he needed his books, his typewriter was not portable, he was used to an electric blanket, he could not bear to eat in restaurants. His mother, with her daredevil charity, was about to wreck the peace of the house.

The back door slammed and the girl's laugh shot up from the kitchen, through the back hall, up the stairwell and into his room, making for him like a bolt of electricity. He jumped to the side and stood glaring about him. His words of the morning had been unequivocal: 'If you bring that girl back into this house, I leave. You can choose – her or me.'

She had made her choice. An intense pain gripped his throat. It was the first time in his thirty-five years . . . He felt a sudden burning moisture behind his eyes. Then he steadied himself, overcome by rage. On the contrary: she had not made any choice. She was counting on his attachment to his electric blanket. She would have to be shown.

The girl's laughter rang upward a second time and Thomas winced. He saw again her look of the night before. She had invaded his room.

He had waked to find his door open and her in it. There was enough light from the hall to make her visible as she turned toward him. The face was like a comedienne's in a musical comedy – a pointed chin, wide apple cheeks and feline empty eyes. He had sprung out of his bed and snatched a straight chair and then he had backed her out the door, holding the chair in front of him like an animal trainer driving out a dangerous cat. He had driven her silently down the hall, pausing when he reached it to beat on his mother's door. The girl, with a gasp, turned and fled into the guest room.

In a moment his mother had opened her door and peered out apprehensively. Her face, greasy with whatever she put on it at night, was framed in pink rubber curlers. She looked down the hall where the girl had disappeared. Thomas stood before her, the chair still lifted in front of him as if he were about to quell another beast. 'She tried to get in my room,' he hissed, pushing in. 'I woke up and she was trying to get in my room.' He closed the door behind him and his voice rose in outrage. 'I won't put up with this! I won't put up with it another day!'

His mother, backed by him to her bed, sat down on the edge of it. She had a heavy body on which sat a thin, mysteriously gaunt and incongruous head.

'I'm telling you for the last time,' Thomas said, 'I won't put up with this another day.' There was an observable tendency in all of her actions. This was, with the best intentions in the world, to make a mockery of virtue, to pursue it with such a mindless intensity that everyone involved was made a fool of and virtue itself became ridiculous. 'Not another day,' he repeated.

His mother shook her head emphatically, her eyes still on the door.

Thomas put the chair on the floor in front of her and sat down on it. He leaned forward as if he were about to explain something to a defective child.

'That's just another way she's unfortunate,' his mother said. 'So awful, so awful. She told me the name of it but I forget what it is but it's something she can't help. Something she was born with. Thomas,' she said and put her hand to her jaw, 'suppose it were you?'

Exasperation blocked his windpipe. 'Can't I make you see,' he croaked, 'that if she can't help herself you can't help her?'

His mother's eyes, intimate but untouchable, were the blue of great distances after sunset. 'Nimpermaniac,' she murmured.

'Nymphomaniac,' he said fiercely. 'She doesn't need to supply you with any fancy names. She's a moral moron. That's all you need to know. Born without the moral faculty – like somebody else would be born without a kidney or a leg. Do you understand?'

'I keep thinking it might be you,' she said, her hand still on her jaw.

'If it were you, how do you think I'd feel if nobody took you in? What if you were a nimpermaniac and not a brilliant smart person and you did what you couldn't help and . . .'

Thomas felt a deep unbearable loathing for himself as if he were turning slowly into the girl.

'What did she have on?' she asked abruptly, her eyes narrowing.

'Nothing!' he roared. 'Now will you get her out of here!'

'How can I turn her out in the cold?' she said. 'This morning she was threatening to kill herself again.'

'Send her back to jail,' Thomas said.

'I would not send *you* back to jail, Thomas,' she said.

He got up and snatched the chair and fled the room while he was still able to control himself.

Thomas loved his mother. He loved her because it was his nature to do so, but there were times when he could not endure her love for him. There were times when it became nothing but pure idiot mystery and he sensed about him forces, invisible currents entirely out of his control. She proceeded always from the tritest of considerations – it was the *nice thing to do* – into the most foolhardly engagements with the devil, whom, of course, she never recognised.

The devil for Thomas was only a manner of speaking, but it was a manner appropriate to the situations his mother got into. Had she been in any degree intellectual, he could have proved to her from early Christian history that no excess of virtue is justified, that a moderation of good produces likewise a moderation in evil, that if Antony of Egypt had stayed at home and attended to his sister, no devils would have plagued him.

Thomas was not cynical and so far from being opposed to virtue, he saw it as the principle of order and the only thing that makes life bearable. His own life was made bearable by the fruits of his mother's saner virtues – by the well-regulated house she kept and the excellent meals she served. But when virtue got out of hand with her, as now, a sense of devils grew upon him, and these were not mental quirks in himself or the old lady, they were denizens with personalities, present though not visible, who might any moment be expected to shriek or rattle a pot.

The girl had landed in the county jail a month ago on a bad cheque charge and his mother had seen her picture in the paper. At the breakfast table she had gazed at it for a long time and then had passed it over the coffee pot to him. 'Imagine,' she said, 'only nineteen years old and in that filthy jail. And she doesn't look like a bad girl.'

Thomas glanced at the picture. It showed the face of a shrewd ragamuffin. He observed that the average age for ciminality was steadily lowering.

'She looks like a wholesome girl,' his mother said.

'Wholesome people don't pass bad cheques,' Thomas said.

'You don't know what you'd do in a pinch.'

'I wouldn't pass a bad cheque,' Thomas said.

'I think,' his mother said, 'I'll take her a little box of candy.'

If then and there he had put his foot down, nothing else would have happened. His father, had he been living, would have put his foot down at that point. Taking a box of candy was her favourite nice thing to do. When anyone within her social station moved to town, she called and took a box of candy; when any of her friend's children had babies or won a scholarship, she called and took a box of candy; when an old person broke his hip, she was at his bedside with a box of candy. He had been amused at the idea of her taking a box of candy to the jail.

He stood now in his room with the girl's laugh rocketing away in his head and cursed his amusement.

When his mother returned from the visit to the jail, she had burst into his study without knocking and had collapsed full-length on his couch, lifting her small swollen feet up on the arm of it. After a moment, she recovered herself enough to sit up and put a newspaper under them. Then she fell back again. 'We don't know how the other half lives,' she said.

Thomas knew that though her conversation moved from cliché to cliché there were real experiences behind them. He was less sorry for the girl's being in jail than for his mother having to see her there. He would have spared her all unpleasant sights. 'Well,' he said and put away his journal, 'you had better forget it now. The girl has ample reason to be in jail.'

'You can't imagine what all she's been through,' she said, sitting up again, 'listen.' The poor girl, Star, had been brought up by a stepmother with three children of her own, one an almost grown boy who had taken advantage of her in such dreadful ways that she had been forced to run away and find her real mother. Once found, her real mother had sent her to various boarding schools to get rid of her. At each of these she had been forced to run away by the presence of perverts and sadists so monstrous that their acts defied description. Thomas could tell that his mother had not been spared the details that she was sparing him. Now and again when she spoke vaguely, her voice shook and he could tell that she was remembering some horror that had been put to her graphically. He had hoped that in a few days the memory of all this would wear off, but it did not. The next day she returned to the jail with Kleenex and cold-cream and a few days later, she announced that she had consulted a lawyer.

It was at these times that Thomas truly mourned the death of his father though he had not been able to endure him in life. The old man would have had none of this foolishness. Untouched by useless compassion, he would (behind her back) have pulled the necessary strings with his crony, the sheriff, and the girl would have been packed off to the state penitentiary to serve her time. He had always been engaged in some enraged action until one morning when (with an angry glance at his wife as if she alone were responsible) he had dropped dead at the breakfast table. Thomas had inherited his father's reason without his ruthlessness and his mother's love of good without her tendency to pursue it. His plan for all practical action was to wait and see what developed.

The lawyer found that the story of the repeated atrocities was for the most part untrue, but when he explained to her that the girl was a psychopathic personality, not insane enough for the asylum, not criminal enough for the jail, not stable enough for society, Thomas's mother was more deeply affected than ever. The girl readily admitted that her story was untrue on account of her being a congenital liar; she lied, she said, because she was insecure. She had passed through the hands of several psychiatrists who had put the finishing touches to her education. She knew there was no hope for her. In the presence of such an affliction as this, his mother seemed bowed down by some painful mystery that nothing would make endurable but a redoubling of effort. To his annoyance, she appeared to look on *him* with compassion, as if her hazy charity no longer made distinctions.

A few days later she burst in and said that the lawyer had got the girl paroled – to her.

Thomas rose from his Morris chair, dropping the review he had been reading. His large bland face contracted in anticipated pain. 'You are not,' he said, 'going to bring that girl here!'

'No, no,' she said, 'calm yourself. Thomas.' She had managed with difficulty to get the girl a job in a pet shop in town and a place to board with a crotchety old lady of her acquaintance. People were not kind. They did not put themselves in the place of someone like Star who had everything against her.

Thomas sat down again and retrieved his review. He seemed just to have escaped some danger which he did not care to make clear to himself. 'Nobody can tell you anything,' he said, 'but in a few days that girl will have left town, having got what she could out of you. You'll never hear from her again.'

Two nights later he came home and opened the parlour door and was speared by a shrill depthless laugh. His mother and the girl sat close to the fireplace where the gas logs were lit. The girl gave the immediate impression of being physically crooked. Her hair was cut like a dog's or an elf's and she was dressed in the latest fashion. She was training on him a long familiar sparkling stare that turned after a second into an intimate grin.

'Thomas!' his mother said, her voice firm with the injunction not to bolt, 'this is Star you've heard so much about. Star is going to have supper with us.'

The girl called herself Star Drake. The lawyer had found that her real name was Sarah Ham.

Thomas neither moved nor spoke but hung in the door in what seemed a savage perplexity. Finally he said, 'How do you do, Sarah,' in a tone of such loathing that he was shocked at the sound of it. He reddened, feeling it beneath him to show contempt for any creature so pathetic. He advanced into the room, determined at least on a decent politeness and sat down heavily in a straight chair.

'Thomas writes history,' his mother said with a threatening look at him. 'He's president of the local Historical Society this year.'

The girl leaned forward and gave Thomas an even more pointed attention. 'Fabulous!' she said in a throaty voice.

'Right now Thomas is writing about the first settlers in this county,' his mother said.

'Fabulous!' the girl repeated.

Thomas by an effort of will managed to look as if he were alone in the room.

'Say, you know who he looks like?' Star asked, her head on one side, taking him in at an angle.

'Oh, someone very distinguished!' his mother said archly.

'This cop I saw in the movie I went to last night,' Star said.

'Star,' his mother said, 'I think you ought to be careful about the kind of movies you go to. I think you ought to see only the best ones. I don't think crime stories would be good for you.'

'Oh this was a crime-does-not-pay,' Star said, 'and I swear this cop looked exactly like him. They were always putting something over on the guy. He would look like he couldn't stand it a minute longer or he would blow up. He was a riot. And not bad looking,' she added with an appreciative leer at Thomas.

'Star,' his mother said, 'I think it would be grand if you developed a taste for music.'

Thomas sighed. His mother rattled on and the girl, paying no attention to her, let her eyes play over him. The quality of her look was such that it might have been her hands, resting now on his knees, now on his neck. Her eyes had a mocking glitter and he knew that she was well aware he could not stand the sight of her. He needed nothing to tell him he was in the presence of the very stuff of corruption, but blameless corruption because there was no responsible faculty behind it. He was looking at the most unendurable form of innocence. Absently he asked himself what the attitude of God was to this, meaning if possible to adopt it.

His mother's behaviour throughout the meal was so idiotic that he could barely stand to look at her and since he could less stand to look at Sarah Ham, he fixed on the sideboard across the room a continuous gaze of disapproval and disgust. Every remark of the girl's his mother met as if it deserved serious attention. She advanced several plans for the wholesome use of Star's spare time. Sarah Ham paid no more attention to this advice than if it came from a parrot. Once when Thomas inadvertently looked in her direction, she winked. As soon as he had swallowed the last spoonful of dessert, he rose and muttered, 'I have to go, I have a meeting.'

'Thomas,' his mother said. 'I want you to take Star home on your way. I don't want her riding in taxis by herself at night.'

For a moment Thomas remained furiously silent. Then he turned and left the room. Presently he came back with a look of obscure determination on his face. The girl was ready, meekly waiting at the parlour door. She cast up at him a great look of admiration and confidence. Thomas did not offer his arm but she took it anyway and moved out of the house and down the steps, attached to what might have been a miraculously moving monument.

'Be good!' his mother called.

Sarah Ham snickered and poked him in the ribs.

While getting his coat he had decided that this would be his opportunity to tell the girl that unless she ceased to be a parasite on his mother, he would see to it, personally, that she was returned to jail. He would let her know that he understood what she was up to, that he was not an innocent and that there were certain things he would not put up with. At his desk, pen in hand, none was more articulate than Thomas. As soon as he found himself shut into the car with Sarah Ham, terror seized his tongue.

She curled her feet up under her and said, 'Alone at last,' and giggled.

Thomas swerved the car away from the house and drove fast toward the gate. Once on the highway, he shot forward as if he were being pursued.

'Jesus!' Sarah Ham said, swinging her feet off the seat, 'where's the fire?'

Thomas did not answer. In a few seconds he could feel her edging closer. She stretched, eased nearer, and finally hung her hand limply over his shoulder. 'Tomsee doesn't like me,' she said, 'but I think he's fabulously cute.'

Thomas covered the three and a half miles into town in a little over four minutes. The light at the first intersection was red but he ignored it. The old woman lived three blocks beyond. When the car screeched to a halt at the place, he jumped out and ran around to the girl's door and opened it. She did not move from the car and Thomas was obliged to wait. After a moment one leg emerged, then her small white crooked face appeared and stared up at him. There was something about the look of it that suggested blindness but it was the blindness of those who don't know that they cannot see. Thomas was curiously sickened. The empty eyes moved over him. 'Nobody likes me,' she said in a sullen tone. 'What if you were me and I couldn't stand to ride you three miles?'

'My mother likes you,' he muttered.

'Her!' the girl said. 'She's just about seventy-five years behind the times!'

Breathlessly Thomas said, 'If I find you bothering her again, I'll have you put back in jail.' There was a dull force behind his voice though it came out barely above a whisper.

'You and who else?' she said and drew back in the car as if now she did not intend to get out at all. Thomas reached into it, blindly grasped the front of her coat, pulled her out by it and released her. Then he lunged back to the car and sped off. The other door was still hanging open and her laugh, bodiless but real, bounded up the street as if it were about to jump in the open side of the car and ride away with him. He reached over and slammed the door and then drove toward home, too angry to attend his meeting. He intended to make his mother well-aware of his displeasure. He intended to leave no doubt in her mind. The voice of his father rasped in his head.

Numbskull, the old man said, put your foot down now. Show her who's boss before she shows you.

But when Thomas reached home, his mother, wisely, had gone to bed.

The next morning he appeared at the breakfast table, his brow lowered and the thrust of his jaw indicating that he was in a dangerous humour. When he intended to be determined, Thomas began like a bull that, before charging, backs with his head lowered and paws the ground. 'All right now listen,' he began, yanking out his chair and sitting down, 'I have something to say to you about that girl and I don't intend to say it but once.' He drew breath. 'She's nothing but a little slut. She makes fun of you behind your back. She means to get everything she can out of you and you are nothing to her.'

His mother looked as if she too had spent a restless night. She did not dress in the morning but wore her bathrobe and a gray turban around her head, which gave her face a disconcerting omniscient look. He might have been breakfasting with a sibyl.

'You'll have to use canned cream this morning,' she said, pouring his coffee. 'I forgot the other.'

'All right, did you hear me?' Thomas growled.

'I'm not deaf,' his mother said and put the pot back on the trivet. 'I know I'm nothing but an old bag of wind to her.'

'Then why do you persist in this foolhardy . . .'

'Thomas,' she said, and put her hand to the side of her face, 'it might be . . .'

'It is not me!' Thomas said, grasping the table leg at his knee.

She continued to hold her face, shaking her head slightly. 'Think of all you have,' she began. 'All the comforts of home. And morals, Thomas. No bad inclinations, nothing bad you were born with.'

Thomas began to breathe like someone who feels the onset of asthma. 'You are not logical,' he said in a limp voice. '*He* would have put his foot down.'

The old lady stiffened. 'You,' she said, 'are not like him.'

Thomas opened his mouth silently.

'However,' his mother said, in a tone of such subtle accusation that she might have been taking back the compliment, 'I won't invite her back again since you're so dead set against her.'

'I am not set against her,' Thomas said. 'I am set against your making a fool of yourself.'

As soon as he left the table and closed the door of his study on himself, his father took up a squatting position in his mind. The old man had had the countryman's ability to converse squatting, though he was no countryman but had been born and brought up in the city and only moved to a smaller place later to exploit his talents. With steady skill he had made them think him one of them. In the midst of a conversation on the courthouse lawn, he would squat and his two or three companions would squat with him with no break in the surface of the talk. By gesture he had lived his lie; he had never deigned to tell one.

Let her run over you, he said. You ain't like me. Not enough to be a man.

Thomas began vigorously to read and presently the image faded. The girl had caused a disturbance in the depths of his being, somewhere out of the reach of his power of analysis. He felt as if he had seen a tornado pass a hundred yards away and had an intimation that it would turn again and head directly for him. He did not get his mind firmly on his work until mid-morning.

Two nights later, his mother and he were sitting in the den after their supper, each reading a section of the evening paper, when the telephone began to ring with the brassy intensity of a fire alarm. Thomas reached for it. As soon as the receiver was in his hand, a shrill female voice screamed into the room, 'Come get this girl! Come get her! Drunk!

Drunk in my parlour and I won't have it! Lost her job and come back here drunk! I won't have it!'

His mother leapt up and snatched the receiver.

The ghost of Thomas's father rose before him. Call the sheriff, the old man prompted. 'Call the sheriff,' Thomas said in a loud voice. 'Call the sheriff to go there and pick her up.'

'We'll be right there,' his mother was saying. 'We'll come and get her right away. Tell her to get her things together.'

'She ain't in no condition to get nothing together,' the voice screamed. 'You shouldn't have put something like her off on me! My house is respectable!'

'Tell her to call the sheriff,' Thomas shouted.

His mother put the receiver down and looked at him. 'I wouldn't turn a dog over to that man,' she said.

Thomas sat in the chair with his arms folded and looked fixedly at the wall.

'Think of the poor girl, Thomas,' his mother said, 'with nothing. Nothing. And we have everything.'

When they arrived, Sarah Ham was slumped spraddle-legged against the banister on the boarding house front-steps. Her tam was down on her forehead where the old woman had slammed it and her clothes were bulging out of her suitcase where the old woman had thrown them in. She was carrying on a drunken conversation with herself in a low personal tone. A streak of lipstick ran up one side of her face. She allowed herself to be guided by his mother to the car and put in the back seat without seeming to know who the rescuer was. 'Nothing to talk to all day but a pack of goddamned parakeets,' she said in a furious whisper.

Thomas, who had not got out of the car at all, or looked at her after the first revolted glance, said, 'I'm telling you, once and for all, the place to take her is the jail.'

His mother, sitting on the back seat, holding girl's hand, did not answer.

'All right, take her to the hotel,' he said.

'I cannot take a drunk girl to a hotel, Thomas,' she said. 'You know that.'

'Then take her to a hospital.'

'She doesn't need a jail or a hotel or a hospital,' his mother said, 'she needs a home.'

'She does not need mine,' Thomas said.

'Only for tonight, Thomas,' the old lady sighed. 'Only for tonight.'

Since then eight days had passed. The little slut was established in the guest room. Every day his mother set out to find her a job and a place to board, and failed, for the old woman had broadcast a warning.

Thomas kept to his room or the den. His home was to him home, workshop, church, as personal as the shell of a turtle and as necessary. He could not believe that it could be violated in this way. His flushed face had a constant look of stunned outrage.

As soon as the girl was up in the morning, her voice throbbed out in a blues song that would rise and waver, then plunge low with insinuations of passion about to be satisfied and Thomas, at his desk, would lunge up and begin frantically stuffing his ears with Kleenex. Each time he started from one room to another, one floor to another, she would be certain to appear. Each time he was halfway up or down the stairs, she would either meet him and pass, cringing coyly, or go up or down behind him, breathing small tragic spearmint-flavoured sighs. She appeared to adore Thomas's repugnance to her and to draw it out of him every chance she got as if it added delectably to her martyrdom.

The old man – small, wasp-like, in his yellowed panama hat, his seersucker suit, his pink carefully-soiled shirt, his small string tie – appeared to have taken up his station in Thomas's mind and from there, usually squatting, he shot out the same rasping suggestion every time the boy paused from his forced studies. Put your foot down. Go to see the sheriff.

The sheriff was another edition of Thomas's father except that he wore a checkered shirt and a Texas type hat and was ten years younger. He was as easily dishonest, and he had genuinely admired the old man. Thomas, like his mother, would have gone far out of his way to avoid his glassy pale blue gaze. He kept hoping for another solution, for a miracle.

With Sarah Ham in the house, meals were unbearable.

'Tomsee doesn't like me,' she said the third or fourth night at the supper table and cast her pouting gaze across at the large rigid figure of Thomas, whose face was set with the look of a man trapped by insufferable odours. 'He doesn't want me here. Nobody wants me anywhere.'

'Thomas's name is Thomas,' his mother interrupted. 'Not Tomsee.'

'I made Tomsee up,' she said. 'I think it's cute. He hates me.'

'Thomas does not hate you,' his mother said. 'We are not the kind of people who hate,' she added, as if this were an inperfection that had been bred out of them generations ago.

'Oh, I know when I'm not wanted,' Sarah Ham continued. 'They didn't even want me in jail. If I killed myself I wonder would God want me?'

'Try it and see,' Thomas muttered.

The girl screamed with laughter. Then she stopped abruptly, her face puckered and she began to shake. 'The best thing to do,' she said, her teeth clattering, 'is to kill myself. Then I'll be out of everybody's way. I'll go to hell and be out of God's way. And even the devil won't want me. He'll kick me out of hell, not even in hell . . .' she wailed.

Thomas rose, picked up his plate and knife and fork and carried them to the den to finish his supper. After that, he had not eaten another meal at the table but had had his mother serve him at his desk. At these meals, the old man was intensely present to him. He appeared to be tipping backwards in his chair, his thumbs beneath his galluses, while he said such things as, She never ran me away from my own table.

A few nights later, Sarah Ham slashed her wrists with a paring knife and had hysterics. From the den where he was closeted after supper, Thomas heard a shriek, then a series of screams, then his mother's scurrying footsteps through the house. He did not move. His first instant of hope that the girl had cut her throat faded as he realised she could not have done it and continue to scream the way she was doing. He returned to his journal and presently the screams subsided. In a moment his mother burst in with his coat and hat. 'We have to take her to the hospital,' she said. 'She tried to do away with herself. I have a tourniquet on her arm. Oh Lord, Thomas,' she said, 'imagine being so low you'd do a thing like that!'

Thomas rose woodenly and put on his hat and coat. 'We will take her to the hospital,' he said, 'and we will leave her there.'

'And drive her to despair again?' the old lady cried. 'Thomas!'

Standing in the centre of his room now, realising that he had reached the point where action was inevitable, that he must pack, that he must leave, that he must go, Thomas remained immovable.

His fury was directed not at the little slut but at his mother. Even though the doctor had found that she had barely damaged herself and had raised the girl's wrath by laughing at the tourniquet and putting only a streak of iodine on the cut, his mother could not get over the incident. Some new weight of sorrow seemed to have been thrown across her shoulders, and not only Thomas, but Sarah Ham was infuriated by this, for it appeared to be a general sorrow that would have found another object no matter what good fortune came to either of them. The experience of Sarah Ham had plunged the old lady into mourning for the world.

The morning after the attempted suicide, she had gone through the house and collected all the knives and scissors and locked them in a drawer. She emptied a bottle of rat poison down the toilet and took up the roach tablets from the kitchen floor. Then she came to Thomas's study and said in a whisper, 'Where is that gun of his? I want you to lock it up.'

'The gun is in my drawer,' Thomas roared, 'and I will not lock it up.

If she shoots herself, so much the better!'

'Thomas,' his mother said, 'she'll hear you!'

'Let her hear me!' Thomas yelled. 'Don't you know she has no intention of killing herself? Don't you know her kind never kill themselves? Don't you . . .'

His mother slipped out the door and closed it to silence him and Sarah Ham's laugh, quite close in the hall, came rattling into his room. 'Tomsee'll find out. I'll kill myself and then he'll be sorry he wasn't nice to me. I'll use his own lil gun, his own lil ol' pearl-handled revol-lervuh!' she shouted and let out a loud tormented-sounding laugh in imitation of a movie monster.

Thomas ground his teeth. He pulled out his desk drawer and felt for the pistol. It was an inheritance from the old man, whose opinion it had been that every house should contain a loaded gun. He had discharged two bullets one night into the side of a prowler, but Thomas had never shot anything. He had no fear that the girl would use the gun on herself and he closed the drawer. Her kind clung tenaciously to life and were able to wrest some histrionic advantage from every moment.

Several ideas for getting rid of her had entered his head but each of these had been suggestions whose moral tone indicated that they had come from a mind akin to his father's, and Thomas had rejected them. He could not get the girl locked up again until she did something illegal. The old man would have been able with no qualms at all to get her drunk and send her out on the highway in his car, meanwhile notifying the highway patrol of her presence on the road, but Thomas considered this below his moral stature. Suggestions continued to come to him, each more outrageous than the last.

He had not the vaguest hope that the girl would get the gun and shoot herself, but that afternoon when he looked in the drawer, the gun was gone. His study locked from the inside, not the out. He cared nothing about the gun, but the thought of Sarah Ham's hands sliding among his papers infuriated him. Now even his study was contaminated. The only place left untouched by her was his bedroom.

That night she entered it.

In the morning at breakfast, he did not eat and did not sit down. He stood beside his chair and delivered his ultimatum while his mother sipped her coffee as if she were both alone in the room and in great pain. 'I have stood this,' he said, 'for as long as I am able. Since I see plainly that you care nothing about me, about my peace or comfort or working conditions, I am about to take the only step open to me. I will give you one more day. If you bring the girl back into this house this afternoon, I leave. You can choose – her or me.' He had more to say but at that point his voice cracked and he left.

At ten o'clock his mother and Sarah Ham left the house.

At four he heard the car wheels on the gravel and rushed to the window. As the car stopped, the dog stood up, alert, shaking.

He seemed unable to take the first step that would set him walking to the closet in the hall to look for the suitcase. He was like a man handed a knife and told to operate on himself if he wished to live. His huge hands clenched helplessly. His expression was a turmoil of indecision and outrage. His pale blue eyes seemed to sweat in his broiling face. He closed them for a moment and on the back of his lids, his father's image leered at him. Idiot! the old man hissed, idiot! The criminal slut stole your gun! See the sheriff! See the sheriff!

It was a moment before Thomas opened his eyes. He seemed newly stunned. He stood where he was for at least three minutes, then he turned slowly like a large vessel reversing its direction and faced the door. He stood there a moment longer, then he left, his face set to see the ordeal through.

He did not know where he would find the sheriff. The man made his own rules and kept his own hours. Thomas stopped first at the jail where his office was, but he was not in it. He went to the courthouse and was told by a clerk that the sheriff had gone to the barber shop across the street. 'Yonder's the deppity,' the clerk said and pointed out the window to the large figure of a man in a checkered shirt, who was leaning against the side of a police car, looking into space.

'It has to be the sheriff,' Thomas said and left for the barber shop. As little as he wanted anything to do with the sheriff, he realised that the man was at least intelligent and not simply a mound of sweating flesh.

The barber said the sheriff had just left. Thomas started back to the courthouse and as he stepped onto the sidewalk from the street, he saw a lean, slightly stooped figure gesticulating angrily at the deputy.

Thomas approached with an aggressiveness brought on by nervous agitation. He stopped abruptly three feet away and said in an over-loud voice, 'Can I have a word with you?' without adding the sheriff's name, which was Farebrother.

Farebrother turned his sharp creased face just enough to take Thomas in, and the deputy did likewise, but neither spoke. The sheriff removed a very small piece of cigarette from his lip and dropped it at his feet. 'I told you what to do,' he said to the deputy. Then he moved off with a slight nod that indicated Thomas could follow him if he wanted to see him. The deputy slunk around the front of the police car and got inside.

Farebrother, with Thomas following, headed across the courthouse square and stopped beneath a tree that shaded a quarter of the front lawn. He waited, leaning slightly forward, and lit another cigarette.

Thomas began to blurt out his business. As he had not had time to prepare his words, he was barely coherent. By repeating the same thing over several times, he managed at length to get out what he wanted to say. When he finished, the sheriff was still leaning slightly forward, at an angle to him, his eyes on nothing in particular. He remained that way without speaking.

Thomas began again, slower and in a lamer voice, and Farebrother let him continue for some time before he said, 'We had her once.' He then allowed himself a slow, creased, all-knowing, quarter smile.

'I had nothing to do with that,' Thomas said. 'That was my mother.' Farebrother squatted.

'She was trying to help the girl,' Thomas said. 'She didn't know she couldn't be helped.'

'Bit off more than she could chew, I reckon,' the voice below him mused.

'She has nothing to do with this,' Thomas said. 'She doesn't know I'm here. The girl is dangerous with that gun.'

'*He*,' the sheriff said, 'never let anything grow under his feet. Particularly nothing a woman planted.'

'She might kill somebody with that gun,' Thomas said weakly, looking down at the round top of the Texas type hat.

There was a long time of silence.

'Where's she got it?' Farebrother asked.

'I don't know. She sleeps in the guest room. It must be in there, in her suitcase probably,' Thomas said.

Farebrother lapsed into silence again.

'You could come search the guest room,' Thomas said in a strained voice. 'I can go home and leave the latch off the front door and you can come in quietly and go upstairs and search her room.'

Farebrother turned his head so that his eyes looked boldly at Thomas's knees. 'You seem to know how it ought to be done,' he said. 'Want to swap jobs?'

Thomas said nothing because he could not think of anything to say, but he waited doggedly. Farebrother removed the cigarette butt from his lips and dropped it on the grass. Beyond him on the courthouse porch a group of loiterers who had been leaning at the left of the door moved over to the right where a patch of sunlight had settled. From one of the upper windows a crumpled piece of paper blew out and drifted down.

'I'll come along about six,' Farebrother said. 'Leave the latch off the door and keep out of my way – yourself and them two women too.'

Thomas let out a rasping sound of relief meant to be 'Thanks,' and struck off across the grass like someone released. The phrase, 'them two women,' stuck like a burr in his brain – the subtlety of the insult to his mother hurting him more than any of Farebrother's references to his own incompetence. As he got into his car, his face suddenly flushed. Had he delivered his mother over to the sheriff – to be a butt for the man's tongue? Was he betraying her to get rid of the little slut? He saw at once that this was not the case. He was doing what he was doing for her own good, to rid her of a parasite that would ruin their peace. He started his car and drove quickly home but once he had turned in the driveway, he decided it would be better to park some distance from the house and go quietly in by the back door. He parked on the grass and on the grass walked in a circle toward the rear of the house. The sky was lined with mustard-coloured streaks. The dog was asleep on the back doormat. At the approach of his master's step, he opened one yellow eye, took him in, and closed it again.

Thomas let himself into the kitchen. It was empty and the house was quiet enough for him to be aware of the loud ticking of the kitchen clock. It was a quarter to six. He tiptoed hurriedly through the hall to the front door and took the latch off it. Then he stood for a moment listening. From behind the closed parlour door, he heard his mother snoring softly and presumed that she had gone to sleep while reading. On the other side of the hall, not three feet from his study, the little slut's black coat and red pocketbook were slung on a chair. He heard water running upstairs and decided she was taking a bath.

He went into his study and sat down at his desk to wait, noting with distaste that every few moments a tremor ran through him. He sat for a minute or two doing nothing. Then he picked up a pen and began to draw squares on the back of an envelope that lay before him. He looked at his watch. It was eleven minutes to six. After a moment he idly drew the centre drawer of the desk out over his lap. For a moment he stared at the gun without recognition. Then he gave a yelp and leaped up. She had put it back!

Idiot! his father hissed, idiot! Go plant it in her pocketbook. Don't just stand there. Go plant it in her pocketbook!

Thomas stood staring at the drawer.

Moron! the old man fumed. Quick while there's time! Go plant it in her pocketbook.

Thomas did not move.

Imbecile! his father cried.

Thomas picked up the gun.

Make haste, the old man ordered.

Thomas started forward, holding the gun away from him. He opened the door and looked at the chair. The black coat and red pocketbook were lying on it almost within reach.

Hurry up, you fool, his father said.

From behind the parlour door the almost inaudible snores of his mother rose and fell. They seemed to mark an order of time that had nothing to do with the instants left to Thomas. There was no other sound.

Quick, you imbecile, before she wakes up, the old man said.

The snores stopped and Thomas heard the sofa springs groan. He grabbed the red pocketbook. It had a skin-like feel to his touch and as it opened, he caught an unmistakable odour of the girl. Wincing, he thrust in the gun and then drew back. His face burned an ugly dull red.

'What is Tomsee putting in my purse?' she called and her pleased laugh bounced down the staircase. Thomas whirled.

She was at the top of the stair, coming down in the manner of a fashion model, one bare leg and then the other thrusting out the front of her kimona in a definite rhythm. 'Tomsee is being naughty,' she said in a throaty voice. She reached the bottom and cast a possessive leer at Thomas whose face was now more gray than red. She reached out, pulled the bag open with her finger and peered at the gun.

His mother opened the parlour door and looked out.

'Tomsee put his pistol in my bag!' the girl shrieked.

'Ridiculous,' his mother said, yawning. 'What would Thomas want to put his pistol in your bag for?'

Thomas stood slightly hunched, his hands hanging helplessly at the wrists as if he had just pulled them up out of a pool of blood.

'I don't know what for,' the girl said, 'but he sure did it,' and she proceeded to walk around Thomas, her hands on her hips, her neck thrust forward and her intimate grin fixed on him fiercely. All at once her expression seemed to open as the purse had opened when Thomas touched it. She stood with her head cocked on one side in an attitude of disbelief. 'Oh boy,' she said slowly, 'is he a case.'

At that instant Thomas damned not only the girl but the entire order of the universe that made her possible.

'Thomas wouldn't put a gun in your bag,' his mother said. 'Thomas is a gentleman.'

The girl made a chortling noise. 'You can see it in there,' she said and pointed to the open purse.

You *found* it in her bag, you dimwit! the old man hissed.

'I found it in her bag!' Thomas shouted. 'The dirty criminal slut stole my gun!'

His mother gasped at the sound of the other presence in his voice. The old lady's sybil-like face turned pale.

'Found it my eye!' Sarah Ham shrieked and started for the pocket-book, but Thomas, as if his arm were guided by his father, caught it first and snatched the gun. The girl in a frenzy lunged at Thomas's throat and would actually have caught him around the neck had not his mother thrown herself forward to protect her.

Fire! the old man yelled.

Thomas fired. The blast was like a sound meant to bring an end to evil in the world. Thomas heard it as a sound that would shatter the laughter of sluts until all shrieks were stilled and nothing was left to disturb the peace of perfect order.

The echo died away in waves. Before the last one had faded, Farebrother opened the door and put his head inside the hall. His nose wrinkled. His expression for some few seconds was that of a man unwilling to admit surprise. His eyes were clear as glass, reflecting the scene. The old lady lay on the floor between the girl and Thomas.

The sheriff's brain worked instantly like a calculating machine. He saw the facts as if they were already in print: the fellow had intended all along to kill his mother and pin it on the girl. But Farebrother had been too quick for him. They were not yet aware of his head in the door. As he scrutinised the scene, further insights were flashed to him. Over her body, the killer and the slut were about to collapse into each other's arms. The sheriff knew a nasty bit when he saw it. He was accustomed to enter upon scenes that were not as bad as he had hoped to find them, but this one met his expectations.

Roald Dahl

Pig

I

Once upon a time, in the City of New York, a beautiful baby boy was born into this world, and the joyful parents named him Lexington.

No sooner had the mother returned home from the hospital carrying Lexington in her arms than she said to her husband, 'Darling, now you must take me out to a most marvellous restaurant for dinner so that we can celebrate the arrival of our son and heir.'

Her husband embraced her tenderly and told her that any woman who could produce such a beautiful child as Lexington deserved to go absolutely anywhere she wanted. But was she strong enough yet, he enquired, to start running around the city late at night?

'No,' she said, she wasn't. But what the hell.

So that evening they both dressed themselves up in fancy clothes, and leaving little Lexington in care of a trained infant's nurse who was costing them twenty dollars a day and was Scottish into the bargain, they went out to the finest and most expensive restaurant in town. There they each ate a giant lobster and drank a bottle of champagne between them, and after that, they went on to a nightclub, where they drank another bottle of champagne and then sat holding hands for several hours while they recalled and discussed and admired each individual physical feature of their lovely newborn son.

They arrived back at their house on the East Side of Manhattan at around two o'clock in the morning and the husband paid off the taxi driver and then began feeling in his pockets for the key to the front door. After a while, he announced that he must have left it in the pocket of his other suit, and he suggested they ring the bell and get the nurse to come down and let them in. An infant's nurse at twenty dollars a day must expect to be hauled out of bed occasionally in the night, the husband said.

So he rang the bell. They waited. Nothing happened. He rang it again, long and loud. They waited another minute. Then they both stepped back on to the street and shouted the nurse's name (McPottle) up at the nursery windows on the third floor, but there was still no response. The house was dark and silent. The wife began to grow apprehensive. Her baby was imprisoned in this place, she told herself. Alone with McPottle. And who was McPottle? They had known her for two days, that was all, and she had a thin mouth, a small disapproving eye, and a starchy bosom, and quite clearly she was in the habit of sleeping too soundly for safety. If she couldn't hear the front-door bell, then how on earth did she expect to hear a baby crying? Why, this very second the poor thing might be swallowing its tongue or suffocating on its pillow.

'He doesn't use a pillow,' the husband said. 'You are not to worry. But I'll get you in if that's what you want.' He was feeling rather superb after all the champagne, and now he bent down and undid the laces of one of his black patent-leather shoes, and took it off. Then, holding it by the toe, he flung it hard and straight through the dining-room window on the ground floor.

'There you are,' he said, grinning. 'We'll deduct it from McPottle's wages.'

He stepped forward and very carefully put a hand through the hole in the glass and released the catch. Then he raised the window.

'I shall lift you in first, little mother,' he said, and he took his wife around the waist and lifted her off the ground. This brought her big red mouth up level with his own, and very close, so he started kissing her. He knew from experience that women like very much to be kissed in this position, with their bodies held tight and their legs dangling in the air, so he went on doing it for quite a long time, and she wiggled her feet, and made loud gulping noises down in her throat. Finally, the husband turned her round and began easing her gently through the open window into the dining-room. At this point, a police patrol car came nosing silently along the street towards them. It stopped about thirty yards away, and three cops of Irish extraction leaped out of the car and started running in the direction of the husband and wife, brandishing revolvers.

'Stick 'em up!' the cops shouted. 'Stick 'em up!' But it was impossible for the husband to obey this order without letting go of his wife, and had he done this she would either have fallen to the ground or would have been left dangling half in and half out of the house, which is a terribly uncomfortable position for a woman; so he continued gallantly to push her upwards and inwards through the window. The cops, all of whom had received medals before for killing robbers, opened fire immediately, and although they were still running, and although the wife in particular was presenting them with a very small target indeed, they succeeded in scoring several direct hits on each body – sufficient anyway to prove fatal in both cases.

Thus, when he was no more than twelve days old, little Lexington became an orphan.

II

The news of this killing, for which the three policemen subsequently received citations, was eagerly conveyed to all relatives of the deceased couple by newspaper reporters, and the next morning, the closest of these relatives, as well as a couple of undertakers, three lawyers, and a priest, climbed into taxis and set out for the house with the broken window. They assembled in the living-room, men and women both, and they sat around in a circle on the sofas and armchairs, smoking cigarettes and sipping sherry and debating what on earth should be done now with the baby upstairs, the orphan Lexington.

It soon became apparent that none of the relatives was particularly keen to assume responsibility for the child, and the discussions and arguments continued all through the day. Everybody declared an enormous, almost an irresistible desire to look after him, and would have done so with the greatest of pleasure were it not for the fact that their apartment was too small, or that they already had one baby and couldn't possibly afford another, or that they wouldn't know what to do with the poor little thing when they went abroad in the summer, or that they were getting on in years, which surely would be most unfair to the boy when he grew up, and so on and so forth. They all knew, of course, that the father had been heavily in debt for a long time and that the house was mortgaged and that consequently there would be no money at all to go with the child.

They were still arguing like mad at six in the evening when suddenly, in the middle of it all an old aunt of the deceased father (her name was Glosspan) swept in from Virginia, and without even removing her hat and coat, not even pausing to sit down, ignoring all offers of a martini, a whisky, a sherry, she announced firmly to the assembled relatives that she herself intended to take sole charge of the infant boy from then on. What was more, she said, she would assume full financial responsibility on all counts, including education, and everyone else could go back home where they belonged and give their consciences a rest. So saying, she trotted upstairs to the nursery and snatched Lexington from his cradle and swept out of the house with the baby clutched tightly in her arms, while the relatives simply sat and stared and smiled and looked relieved, and McPottle the nurse stood stiff with disapproval at the head of the stairs, her lips compressed, her arms folded across her starched bosom.

And thus it was that the infant Lexington, when he was thirteen days old, left the City of New York and travelled southward to live with his Great Aunt Glosspan in the State of Virginia.

III

Aunt Glosspan was nearly seventy when she became guardian to Lexington, but to look at her you would never have guessed it for one minute. She was as sprightly as a woman half her age, with a small, wrinkled, but still quite beautiful face and two lovely brown eyes that sparkled at you in the nicest way. She was also a spinster, though you would never have guessed that either, for there was nothing spinsterish about Aunt Glosspan. She was never bitter or gloomy or irritable; she didn't have a moustache; and she wasn't in the least bit jealous of other people, which in itself is something you can seldom say about either a spinster or a virgin lady, although of course it is not known for certain whether Aunt Glosspan qualified on both counts.

But she was an eccentric old woman, there was no doubt about that. For the past thirty years she had lived a strange isolated life all by herself in a tiny cottage high up on the slopes of the Blue Ridge Mountains, several miles from the nearest village. She had five acres of pasture, a plot for growing vegetables, a flower garden, three cows, a dozen hens, and a fine cockerel.

And now she had little Lexington as well.

She was a strict vegetarian and regarded the consumption of animal flesh as not only unhealthy and disgusting, but horribly cruel. She lived upon lovely clean foods like milk, butter, eggs, cheese, vegetables, nuts, herbs, and fruit, and she rejoiced in the conviction that no living creature would be slaughtered on her account, not even a shrimp. Once, when a brown hen of hers passed away in the prime of life from being egg-bound, Aunt Glosspan was so distressed that she nearly gave up egg-eating altogether.

She knew not the first thing about babies, but that didn't worry her in the least. At the railway station in New York, while waiting for the train that would take her and Lexington back to Virginia, she bought six feeding-bottles, two dozen diapers, a box of safety pins, a carton of milk for the journey, and a small paper-covered book called *The Care of Infants*. What more could anyone want? And when the train got going, she fed the baby some milk, changed its nappies after a fashion, and laid it down on the seat to sleep. Then she read *The Care of Infants* from cover to cover.

'There is no problem here,' she said, throwing the book out of the window. 'No problem at all.'

And curiously enough there wasn't. Back home in the cottage everything went just as smoothly as could be. Little Lexington drank his milk and belched and yelled and slept exactly as a good baby should, and Aunt Glosspan glowed with joy whenever she looked at him, and showered him with kisses all day long.

IV

By the time he was six years old, young Lexington had grown into a most beautiful boy with long golden hair and deep blue eyes the colour of cornflowers. He was bright and cheerful, and already he was learning to help his old aunt in all sorts of different ways around the property, collecting the eggs from the chicken house, turning the handle of the butter churn, digging up potatoes in the vegetable garden, and searching for wild herbs on the side of the mountain. Soon Aunt Glosspan told herself, she would have to start thinking about his education.

But she couldn't bear the thought of sending him away to school. She loved him so much now that it would kill her to be parted from him for any length of time. There was, of course, that village school down in the valley, but it was a dreadful-looking place, and if she sent him there she just knew they would start forcing him to eat meat the very first day he arrived.

'You know what, my darling?' she said to him one day when he was sitting on a stool in the kitchen watching her make cheese. 'I don't really see why I shouldn't give you your lessons myself.'

The boy looked up at her with his large blue eyes, and gave her a lovely trusting smile. 'That would be nice,' he said.

'And the very first thing I should do would be to teach you how to cook.'

'I think I would like that, Aunt Glosspan.'

'Whether you like it or not, you're going to have to learn some time,' she said. 'Vegetarians like us don't have nearly so many foods to choose from as ordinary people, and therefore they must learn to be doubly expert with what they have.'

'Aunt Glosspan,' the boy said, 'what *do* ordinary people eat that we don't?'

'Animals,' she answered, tossing her head in disgust.

'You mean *live* animals?'

'No,' she said. 'Dead ones.'

The boy considered this for a moment.

'You mean when they die they *eat* them instead of *burying* them?'

'They don't wait for them to die, my pet. They kill them.'

'How do they kill them, Aunt Glosspan?'

'They usually slit their throats with a knife.'

'But what *kind* of animals?'

'Cows and pigs mostly, and sheep.'

'Cows!' the boy cried. 'You mean like Daisy and Snowdrop and Lily?'

'Exactly, my dear.'

'But *how* do they eat them, Aunt Glosspan?'

'They cut them up into bits and they cook the bits. They like it best when it's all red and bloody and sticking to the bones. They love to eat lumps of cow's flesh with the blood oozing out of it.'

'Pigs too?'

'They adore pigs.'

'Lumps of bloody pig's meat,' the boy said. 'Imagine that. What else do they eat, Aunt Glosspan?'

'Chickens.'

'Chickens!'

'Millions of them.'

'Feathers and all?'

'No, dear, not the feathers. Now run along outside and get Aunt Glosspan a bunch of chives, will you, my darling?'

Shortly after that, the lessons began. They covered five subjects, reading, writing, geography, arithmetic, and cooking, but the latter was by far the most popular with both teacher and pupil. In fact, it very soon became apparent that young Lexington possessed a truly remarkable talent in this direction. He was a born cook. He was dexterous and quick. He could handle his pans like a juggler. He could slice a single potato into twenty paper-thin slivers in less time than it took his aunt to peel it. His palate was exquisitely sensitive, and he could taste a pot of strong onion soup and immediately detect the presence of a single tiny leaf of sage. In so young a boy, all this was a bit bewildering to Aunt Glosspan, and to tell the truth she didn't quite know what to make of it. But she was proud as proud could be, all the same, and predicted a brilliant future for the child.

'What a mercy it is,' she said, 'that I have such a wonderful little fellow to look after me in my dotage.' And a couple of years later, she retired from the kitchen for good, leaving Lexington in sole charge of all household cooking. The boy was now ten years old, and Aunt Glosspan was nearly eighty.

V

With the kitchen to himself, Lexington straight away began experimenting with dishes of his own invention. The old favourites no longer interested him. He had a violent urge to create. There were hundreds of fresh ideas in his head. 'I will begin,' he said, 'by devising a chestnut soufflé.' He made it and served it up for supper that very night. It was terrific. 'You are a genius!' Aunt Glosspan cried, leaping up from her chair and kissing him on both cheeks. 'You will make history.'

From then on, hardly a day went by without some new delectable creation being set upon the table. There was Brazilnut soup, hominy cutlets, vegetable ragout, dandelion omelette, cream-cheese fritters, stuffed-cabbage surprise, stewed foggage, shallots à la bonne femme, beet-root mousse piquant, prunes Stroganoff, Dutch rarebit, turnips on horseback, flaming spruce-needle tarts, and many many other beautiful compositions. Never before in her life, Aunt Glosspan declared, had she tasted such food as this; and in the mornings, long before lunch was due, she would go out on to the porch and sit there in her rocking-chair, speculating about the coming meal, licking her chops, sniffing the aromas that came wafting out through the kitchen window.

'What's that you're making in there today, boy?' she would call out.

'Try to guess, Aunt Glosspan.'

'Smells like a bit of salsify fritters to me,' she would say, sniffing vigorously.

Then out he would come, this ten-year-old child, a little grin of triumph on his face, and in his hands a big steaming pot of the most heavenly stew made entirely of parsnips and lovage.

'You know what you ought to do,' his aunt said to him, gobbling the stew. 'You ought to set yourself down this very minute with paper and pencil and write a cooking-book.'

He looked at her across the table, chewing his parsnips slowly.

'Why not?' she cried. 'I've taught you how to write and I've taught you how to cook and now all you've got to do is put the two things together. You write a cooking-book, my darling, and it'll make you famous the whole world over.'

'All right,' he said. 'I will.'

And that very day, Lexington began writing the first page of that monumental work which was to occupy him for the rest of his life. He called it *Eat Good and Healthy*.

VI

Seven years later, by the time he was seventeen, he had recorded over nine thousand different recipes, all of them original, all of them delicious.

But now, suddenly, his labours were interrupted by the tragic death of Aunt Glosspan. She was afflicted in the night by a violent seizure, and Lexington, who had rushed into her bedroom to see what all the noise was about, found her lying on her bed yelling and cussing and twisting herself up into all manner of complicated knots. Indeed, she was a terrible sight to behold, and the agitated youth danced around her in his pyjamas, wringing his hands, and wondering what on earth he should do. Finally, in an effort to cool her down, he fetched a bucket of water from the pond in the cow field and tipped it over her head, but this only intensified the paroxysms, and the old lady expired within the hour.

'This is really too bad,' the poor boy said, pinching her several times to make sure that she was dead. 'And how sudden! How quick and sudden! Why only a few hours ago she seemed in the very best of spirits. She even took three large helpings of my most recent creation, devilled mushroom-burgers, and told me how succulent it was.'

After weeping bitterly for several minutes, for he had loved his aunt very much, he pulled himself together and carried her outside and buried her behind the cowshed.

The next day, while tidying up her belongings, he came across an envelope that was addressed to him in Aunt Glosspan's handwriting. He opened it and drew out two fifty-dollar bills and a letter. *Darling boy*, the letter said, *I know that you have never yet been down the mountain since you were thirteen days old, but as soon as I die you must put on a pair of shoes and a clean shirt and walk down to the village and find the doctor. Ask the doctor to give you a death certificate to prove that I am dead. Then take this certificate to my lawyer, a man called Mr Samuel Zuckermann, who lives in New York City and who has a copy of my will. Mr Zuckermann will arrange everything. The cash in this envelope is to pay the doctor for the certificate and to cover the cost of your journey to New York. Mr Zuckermann will give you more money when you get there, and it is my earnest wish that you use it to further your researches into culinary and vegetarian matters, and that you continue to work upon the great book of yours until you are satisfied that it is complete in every way. Your loving aunt – Glosspan.*

Lexington, who had always done everything his aunt told him, pocketed the money, put on a pair of shoes and a clean shirt, and went down the mountain to the village where the doctor lived.

'Old Glosspan?' the doctor said. 'My God, is *she* dead?'

'Certainly she's dead,' the youth answered. 'If you will come back home with me now I'll dig her up and you can see for yourself.'

'How deep did you bury her?' the doctor asked.

'Six or seven feet down, I should think.'

'And how long ago?'

'Oh, about eight hours.'

'Then she's dead,' the doctor announced. 'Here's the certificate.'

VII

Our hero now set out for the City of New York to find Mr Samuel Zuckermann. He travelled on foot, and he slept under hedges, and he lived on berries and wild herbs, and it took him sixteen days to reach the metropolis.

'What a fabulous place this is!' he cried as he stood at the corner of Fifty-seventh Street and Fifth Avenue, staring around him. 'There are no cows or chickens anywhere, and none of the women looks in the least like Aunt Glosspan.'

As for Mr Samuel Zuckermann, he looked like nothing that Lexington had ever seen before.

He was a small spongy man with livid jowls and a huge magenta nose, and when he smiled, bits of gold flashed at you marvellously from lots of different places inside his mouth. In his luxurious office, he shook Lexington warmly by the hand and congratulated him upon his aunt's death.

'I suppose you knew that your dearly beloved guardian was a woman of considerable wealth?' he said.

'You mean the cows and the chickens?'

'I mean half a million bucks,' Mr Zuckermann said.

'How much?'

'Half a million dollars, my boy. And she's left it all to you.' Mr Zuckermann leaned back in his chair and clasped his hands over his spongy paunch. At the same time, be began secretly working his right forefinger in through his waistcoat and under his shirt so as to scratch the skin around the circumference of his navel – a favourite exercise of his, and one that gave him a peculiar pleasure. 'Of course, I shall have to deduct fifty per cent for my services,' he said, 'but that still leaves you with two hundred and fifty grand.'

'I am rich!' Lexington cried. 'This is wonderful! How soon can I have the money?'

'Well,' Mr Zuckermann said, 'luckily for you, I happen to be on rather cordial terms with the tax authorities around here, and I am confident that I shall be able to persuade them to waive all death duties and back taxes.'

'How kind you are,' murmured Lexington.

'I should naturally have to give somebody a small honorarium.'

'Whatever you say, Mr Zuckermann.'

'I think a hundred thousand would be sufficient.'

'Good gracious, isn't that rather excessive?'

'Never undertip a tax inspector or a policeman,' Mr Zuckermann said. 'Remember that.'

'But how much does it leave for me?' the youth asked meekly.

'One hundred and fifty thousand. But then you've got the funeral expenses to pay out of that.'

'*Funeral* expenses?'

'You've got to pay the funeral parlour. Surely you know that?'

'But I buried her myself, Mr Zuckermann, behind the cowshed.'

'I don't doubt it,' the lawyer said. 'So what?'

'I never used a funeral parlour.'

'Listen,' Mr Zuckermann said patiently. 'You may not know it, but there is a law in this State which says that no beneficiary under a will may receive a single penny of his inheritance until the funeral parlour has been paid in full.'

'You mean that's a *law*?'

'Certainly it's a law, and a very good one it is, too. The funeral parlour is one of our great national institutions. It must be protected at all cost.'

Mr Zuckermann himself, together with a group of public-spirited doctors, controlled a corporation that owned a chain of nine lavish funeral parlours in the city, not to mention a casket factory in Brooklyn and a postgraduate school for embalmers in Washington Heights. The celebration of death was therefore a deeply religious affair in Mr Zuckermann's eyes. In fact, the whole business affected him profoundly, almost as profoundly, one might say, as the birth of Christ affected the shopkeeper.

'You had no right to go out and bury your aunt like that,' he said. 'None at all.'

'I'm very sorry, Mr Zuckermann.'

'Why, it's downright subversive.'

'I'll do whatever you say, Mr Zuckermann. All I want to know is how much I'm going to get in the end, when everything's paid.'

There was a pause. Mr Zuckermann sighed and frowned and continued secretly to run the tip of his finger around the rim of his navel.

'Shall we say fifteen thousand?' he suggested, flashing a big gold smile. 'That's a nice round figure.'

'Can I take it with me this afternoon?'

'I don't see why not.'

So Mr Zuckermann summoned his chief cashier and told him to give Lexington fifteen thousand dollars out of the petty cash, and to obtain a receipt. The youth, who by this time was delighted to be getting anything at all, accepted the money gratefully and stowed it away in his knapsack. Then he shook Mr Zuckermann warmly by the hand, thanked him for all his help, and went out of the office.

'The whole world is before me!' our hero cried as he emerged into the street. 'I now have fifteen thousand dollars to see me through until my book is published. And after that, of course, I shall have a great deal more.' He stood on the pavement, wondering which way to go. He turned left and began strolling slowly down the street, staring at the sights of the city.

'What a revolting smell,' he said, sniffing the air. 'I can't stand this.' His delicate olfactory nerves, tuned to receive only the most delicious kitchen aromas, were being tortured by the stench of the diesel-oil fumes pouring out of the backs of the buses.

'I must get out of this place before my nose is ruined altogether,' he said. 'But first, I've simply got to have something to eat. I'm starving.' The poor boy had had nothing but berries and wild herbs for the past two weeks, and now his stomach was yearning for solid food. I'd like a nice hominy cutlet, he told himself. Or maybe a few juicy salsify fritters.

He crossed the street and entered a small restaurant. The place was hot inside, and dark and silent. There was a strong smell of cooking-fat and cabbage water. The only other customer was a man with a brown hat on his head, crouching intently over his food, who did not look up as Lexington came in.

Our hero seated himself at a corner table and hung his knapsack on the back of his chair. This, he told himself, is going to be most interesting. In all my seventeen years I have tasted only the cooking of two people, Aunt Glosspan and myself – unless one counts Nurse McPottle, who must have heated my bottle a few times when I was an infant. But I am now about to sample the art of a new chef altogether, and perhaps, if I am lucky, I may pick up a couple of useful ideas for my book.

A waiter approached out of the shadows at the back, and stood beside the table.

'How do you do,' Lexington said. 'I should like a large hominy cutlet please. Do it twenty-five seconds each side, in a very hot skillet with sour cream, and sprinkle a pinch of lovage on it before serving – unless of course your chef knows of a more original method, in which case I should be delighted to try it.'

The waiter laid his head over to one side and looked carefully at his customer. 'You want the roast pork and cabbage?' he asked. 'That's all we got left.'

'Roast what and cabbage?'

The waiter took a soiled handkerchief from his trouser pocket and shook it open with a violent flourish, as though he were cracking a whip. Then he blew his nose loud and wet.

'You want it or don't you?' he said, wiping his nostrils.

'I haven't the foggiest idea what it is,' Lexington replied, 'but I should love to try it. You see, I am writing a cooking-book and . . .'

'One pork and cabbage!' the waiter shouted, and somewhere in the back of the restaurant, far away in the darkness, a voice answered him.

The waiter disappeared. Lexington reached into his knapsack for his personal knife and fork. These were a present from Aunt Glosspan, given him when he was six years old, made of solid silver, and he had never eaten with any other instruments since. While waiting for the food to arrive, he polished them lovingly with a piece of soft muslin.

Soon the waiter returned carrying a plate on which there lay a thick greyish-white slab of something hot. Lexington leaned forward anxiously to smell it as it was put down before him. His nostrils were wide open now to receive the scent, quivering and sniffing.

'But this is absolute heaven!' he exclaimed. 'What an aroma! It's tremendous!'

The waiter stepped back a pace, watching his customer carefully.

'Never in my life have I smelled anything as rich and wonderful as this!' our hero cried, seizing his knife and fork. 'What on earth is it made of?'

The man in the brown hat looked around and stared, then returned to his eating. The waiter was backing away towards the kitchen.

Lexington cut off a small piece of the meat, impaled it on his silver fork, and carried it up to his nose so as to smell it again. Then he popped it into his mouth and began to chew it slowly, his eyes half closed, his body tense.

'This is fantastic!' he cried. 'It is a brand-new flavour! Oh, Glosspan, my beloved Aunt, how I wish you were with me now so you could taste this remarkable dish! Waiter! Come here at once! I want you!'

The astonished waiter was now watching from the other end of the room, and he seemed reluctant to move any closer.

'If you will come and talk to me I will give you a present,' Lexington said, waving a hundred-dollar bill. 'Please come over here and talk to me.'

The waiter sidled cautiously back to the table, snatched away the money, and held it up close to his face, peering at it from all angles. Then he slipped it quickly into his pocket.

'What can I do for you, my friend?' he asked.

'Look,' Lexington said. 'If you will tell me what this delicious dish is made of, and exactly how it is prepared, I will give you another hundred.'

'I already told you,' the man said. 'It's pork.'

'And what exactly is pork?'

'You never had roast pork before?' the waiter asked, staring.

'For heaven's sake, man, tell me what it is and stop keeping me in suspense like this.'

'It's pig,' the waiter said. 'You just bung it in the oven.'

'*Pig!*'

'All pork is pig. Didn't you know that?'

'You mean *this* is *pig's meat*?'

'I guarantee it.'

'But . . . but . . . that's impossible,' the youth stammered. 'Aunt

PIG

Glosspan, who knew more about food than anyone else in the world, said that meat of any kind was disgusting, revolting, horrible, foul, nauseating, and beastly. And yet this piece that I have here on my plate is without doubt the most delicious thing that I have ever tasted. Now how on earth do you explain that? Aunt Glosspan certainly wouldn't have told me it was revolting if it wasn't.'

'Maybe your aunt didn't know how to cook it,' the waiter said.

'Is that possible?'

'You're damned right it is. Especially with pork. Pork has to be very well done or you can't eat it.'

'Eureka!' Lexington cried. 'I'll bet that's exactly what happened! She did it wrong!' He handed the man another hundred-dollar bill. 'Lead me to the kitchen,' he said. 'Introduce me to the genius who prepared this meat.'

Lexington was at once taken into the kitchen, and there he met the cook who was an elderly man with a rash on one side of his neck.

'This will cost you another hundred,' the waiter said.

Lexington was only too glad to oblige, but this time he gave the money to the cook. 'Now listen to me,' he said. 'I have to admit that I am really rather confused by what the waiter has just been telling me. Are you quite positive that the delectable dish which I have just been eating was prepared from pig's flesh?'

The cook raised his right hand and began scratching the rash on his neck.

'Well,' he said, looking at the waiter and giving him a sly wink, 'all I can tell you is that I *think* it was pig's meat.'

'You mean you're not sure?'

'One can't ever be sure.'

'Then what else could it have been?'

'Well,' the cook said, speaking very slowly and still staring at the waiter. 'There's just a chance, you see, that it might have been a piece of human stuff.'

'You mean a man?'

'Yes.'

'Good heavens.'

'Or a woman. It could have been either. They both taste the same.'

'Well – now you really do surprise me,' the youth declared.

'One lives and learns.'

'Indeed one does.'

'As a matter of fact, we've been getting an awful lot of it just lately from the butcher's in place of pork,' the cook declared.

'Have you really?'

'The trouble is, it's almost impossible to tell which is which. They're both very good.'

'The piece I had just now was simply superb.'

'I'm glad you liked it,' the cook said. 'But to be quite honest, I think that was a bit of pig. In fact, I'm almost sure it was.'

'You are?'

'Yes, I am.'

'In that case, we shall have to assume that you are right,' Lexington said. 'So now will you please tell me – and here is another hundred dollars for your trouble – will you please tell me precisely how you prepared it?'

The cook, after pocketing the money, launched out upon a colourful description of how to roast a loin of pork, while the youth, not wanting to miss a single word of so great a recipe, sat down at the kitchen table and recorded every detail in his notebook.

'Is that all?' he asked when the cook had finished.

'That's all.'

'But there must be more to it than that, surely?'

'You got to get a good piece of meat to start off with,' the cook said. 'That's half the battle. It's got to be a good hog and it's got to be butchered right, otherwise it'll turn out lousy which ever way you cook it.'

'Show me how,' Lexington said. 'Butcher me one now so I can learn.'

'We don't butcher pigs in the kitchen,' the cook said. 'That lot you just ate came from a packing-house over in the Bronx.'

'Then give me the address!'

The cook gave him the address, and our hero, after thanking them both many times for all their kindnesses, rushed outside and leapt into a taxi and headed for the Bronx.

VIII

The packing-house was a big four-storey brick building, and the air around it smelled sweet and heavy, like musk. At the main entrance gates, there was a large notice which said VISITORS WELCOME AT ANY TIME, and thus encouraged, Lexington walked through the gates and entered a cobbled yard which surrounded the building itself. He then followed a series of signposts (THIS WAY FOR THE GUIDED TOURS), and came eventually to a small corrugated-iron shed set well apart from the main building (VISITORS' WAITING-ROOM). After knocking politely on the door, he went in.

There were six other people ahead of him in the waiting-room. There was a fat mother with her two little boys aged about nine and eleven. There was a bright-eyed young couple who looked as though they might be on their honeymoon. And there was a pale woman with long white gloves, who sat very upright, looking straight ahead, with her hands folded on her lap. Nobody spoke. Lexington wondered whether they were all writing cooking-books, like himself, but when he put this question to them aloud, he got no answer. The grown-ups merely smiled mysteriously to themselves and shook their heads, and the two children stared at him as though they were seeing a lunatic.

Soon, the door opened and a man with a merry pink face popped his head into the room and said, 'Next, please.' The mother and the two boys got up and went out.

About ten minutes later, the same man returned. 'Next, please,' he said again, and the honeymoon couple jumped up and followed him outside.

Two new visitors came in and sat down – a middle-aged husband and a middle-aged wife, the wife carrying a wicker shopping-basket containing groceries.

'Next, please,' said the guide, and the woman with the long white gloves got up and left.

Several more people came in and took their places on the stiff-backed wooden chairs.

Soon the guide returned for the third time, and now it was Lexington's turn to go outside.

'Follow me, please,' the guide said, leading the youth across the yard towards the main building.

'How exciting this is!' Lexington cried, hopping from one foot to the other. 'I only wish that my dear Aunt Glosspan could be with me now to see what I am going to see.'

'I myself only do the preliminaries,' the guide said. 'Then I shall hand you over to someone else.'

'Anything you say,' cried the ecstatic youth.

First they visited a large penned-in area at the back of the building where several hundred pigs were wandering around. 'Here's where they start,' the guide said. 'And over there's where they go in.'

'Where?'

'Right there.' The guide pointed to a long wooden shed that stood against the outside wall of the factory. 'We call it the shackling-pen. This way, please.'

Three men wearing long rubber boots were driving a dozen pigs into the shackling-pen just as Lexington and the guide approached, so they all went in together.

'Now,' the guide said, 'watch how they shackle them.'

Inside, the shed was simply a bare wooden room with no roof, but there was a steel cable with hooks on it that kept moving slowly along the length of one wall, parallel with the ground, about three feet up. When it reached the end of the shed, this cable suddenly changed direction and climbed vertically upward through the open roof towards the top floor of the main building.

The twelve pigs were huddled together at the far end of the pen, standing quietly, looking apprehensive. One of the men in rubber boots pulled a length of metal chain down from the wall and advanced upon the nearest animal, approaching it from the rear. Then he bent down and quickly looped one end of the chain around one of the animal's hind legs. The other end he attached to a hook on the moving cable as it went by. The cable kept moving. The chain tightened. The pig's leg was pulled up and back, and then the pig itself began to be dragged backwards. But it didn't fall down. It was rather a nimble pig, and somehow it managed to keep its balance on three legs, hopping from foot to foot and struggling against the pull of the chain, but going back and back all the time until at the end of the pen where the cable changed direction and went vertically upward, the creature was suddenly jerked off its feet and borne aloft. Shrill protests filled the air.

'Truly a fascinating process,' Lexington said. 'But what was that funny cracking noise it made as it went up?'

'Probably the leg,' the guide answered. 'Either that or the pelvis.'

'But doesn't that matter?'

'Why should it matter?' the guide asked. 'You don't eat the bones.'

The rubber-booted men were busy shackling the rest of the pigs, and one after another they were hooked to the moving cable and hoisted up through the roof, protesting loudly as they went.

'There's a good deal more to this recipe than just picking herbs,' Lexington said. 'Aunt Glosspan would never have made it.'

At this point, while Lexington was gazing skyward at the last pig to go up, a man in rubber boots approached him quietly from behind and looped one end of a chain around the youth's own ankle, hooking the other end to the moving belt. The next moment, before he had time to realise what was happening, our hero was jerked off his feet and dragged backwards along the concrete floor of the shackling-pen.

'Stop!' he cried. 'Hold everything! My leg is caught!'

But nobody seemed to hear him, and five seconds later, the unhappy young man was jerked off the floor and hoisted vertically upward through the open roof of the pen, dangling upside down by one ankle, and wriggling like a fish.

'Help!' he shouted. 'Help! There's been a frightful mistake! Stop the engines! Let me down!'

The guide removed a cigar from his mouth and looked up serenely at the rapidly ascending youth, but he said nothing. The men in rubber boots were already on their way out to collect the next batch of pigs.

'Oh, save me!' our hero cried. 'Let me down! Please let me down!'

But he was now approaching the top floor of the building where the moving belt curled over like a snake and entered a large hole in the wall, a kind of doorway without a door; and there, on the threshold, waiting to greet him, clothed in a dark-stained yellow rubber apron, and looking for all the world like Saint Peter at the Gates of Heaven, the sticker stood.

Lexington saw him only from upside down, and very briefly at that, but even so he noticed at once the expression of absolute peace and benevolence on the man's face, the cheerful twinkle in the eyes, the little wistful smile, the dimples in his cheeks – and all this gave him hope.

'Hi there,' the sticker said, smiling.

'Quick! Save me!' our hero cried.

'With pleasure,' the sticker said, and taking Lexington gently by one ear with his left hand, he raised his right hand and deftly slit open the boy's jugular vein with a knife.

The belt moved on. Lexington went with it. Everything was still upside down and the blood was pouring out of his throat and getting into his eyes, but he could still see after a fashion, and he had a blurred impression of being in an enormously long room, and at the far end of the room there was a great smoking cauldron of water, and there were dark figures, half hidden in the steam, dancing around the edge of it, brandishing long poles. The conveyor-belt seemed to be travelling right over the top of the cauldron, and the pigs seemed to be dropping down one by one into the boiling water, and one of the pigs seemed to be wearing long white gloves on its front feet.

Suddenly our hero started to feel very sleepy, but it wasn't until his good strong heart had pumped the last drop of blood from his body that he passed on out of this, the best of all possible worlds, into the next.

Stanley Ellin

Robert

The windows of the Sixth Grade classroom were wide open to the June afternoon, and through them came all the sounds of the departing school: the thunder of bus motors warming up, the hiss of gravel under running feet, the voices raised in cynical fervour.

'So we sing all hail to thee,
District Schoo-wull Number Three . . .'

Miss Gildea flinched a little at the last high, shrill note, and pressed her fingers to her aching forehead. She was tired, more tired than she could ever recall being in her thirty-eight years of teaching, and, as she told herself, she had reason to be. It had not been a good term, not good at all, what with the size of the class, and the Principal's insistence on new methods, and then her mother's shocking death coming right in the middle of everything.

Perhaps she had been too close to her mother, Miss Gildea thought; perhaps she had been wrong, never taking into account that some day the old lady would have to pass on and leave her alone in the world. Well, thinking about it all the time didn't make it any easier. She should try to forget.

And, of course, to add to her troubles, there had been during the past few weeks this maddening business of Robert. He had been a perfectly nice boy, and then, out of a clear sky, had become impossible. Not bothersome or noisy really, but sunk into an endless daydream from which Miss Gildea had to sharply jar him a dozen times a day.

She turned her attention to Robert who sat alone in the room at the desk immediately before hers, a thin boy with neatly combed, colourless hair bracketed between large ears; mild blue eyes in a pale face fixed solemnly on hers.

'Robert.'

'Yes, Miss Gildea.'

'Do you know why I told you to remain after school, Robert?'

He frowned thoughtfully at this, as if it were some lesson he was being called on for, but had failed to memorise properly.

'I suppose for being bad,' he said, at last.

Miss Gildea sighed.

'No, Robert, that's not it at all. I know a bad boy when I see one, Robert, and you aren't one like that. But I do know there's something troubling you, something on your mind, and I think I can help you.'

'There's nothing bothering me, Miss Gildea. Honest, there isn't.'

Miss Gildea found the silver pencil thrust into her hair and tapped it in a nervous rhythm on her desk.

'Oh, come, Robert. During the last month every time I looked at you your mind was a million miles away. Now, what is it? Just making plans for vacation, or, perhaps, some trouble with the boys?'

'I'm not having trouble with anybody, Miss Gildea.'

'You don't seem to understand, Robert, that I'm not trying to punish you for anything. Your homework is good. You've managed to keep up with the class, but I do think your inattentiveness should be explained. What, for example, were you thinking this afternoon when I spoke to you directly for five minutes, and you didn't hear a word I said?'

'Nothing, Miss Gildea.'

She brought the pencil down sharply on the desk. 'There must have been *something*, Robert. Now, I insist that you think back, and try to explain yourself.'

Looking at his impassive face she knew that somehow she herself had been put on the defensive, that if any means of graceful retreat were offered now she would gladly take it. Thirty-eight years, she thought grimly, and I'm still trying to play mother-hen to ducklings. Not that there wasn't a bright side to the picture. Thirty-eight years passed meant only two more to go before retirement, the half-salary pension the chance to putter around the house, tend to the garden properly. The pension wouldn't buy you furs and diamonds, sure enough, but it could buy the right to enjoy your own home for the rest of your days instead of a dismal room in the County Home for Old Ladies. Miss Gildea had visited the County Home once, on an instructional visit, and preferred not to think about it.

'Well, Robert,' she said wearily, 'have you remembered what you were thinking?'

'Yes, Miss Gildea.'

'What was it?'

'I'd rather not tell, Miss Gildea.'

'I insist!'

'Well,' Robert said gently, 'I was thinking I wished you were dead, Miss Gildea. I was thinking I wished I could kill you.'

Her first reaction was simply blank incomprehension. She had been standing not ten feet away when that car had skidded up on the sidewalk and crushed her mother's life from her, and Miss Gildea had neither screamed nor fainted. She had stood there dumbly, because of the very unreality of the thing. Just the way she stood in court where they explained that the man got a year in jail, but didn't have a dime to pay for the tragedy he had brought about. And now the orderly ranks of desks before her, the expanse of blackboard around her, and Robert's face in the midst of it all were no more real. She found herself rising from her chair, walking toward Robert who shrank back, his eyes wide and panicky, his elbow half lifted as if to ward off a blow.

'Do you understand what you've just said?' Miss Gildea demanded hoarsely.

'No, Miss Gildea! Honest, I didn't mean anything.'

She shook her head unbelievingly. 'Whatever made you say it? Whatever in the world could make a boy say a thing like that, such a wicked, terrible thing!'

'You wanted to know! You kept asking me!'

The sight of that protective elbow raised against her cut as deep as the incredible words had.

'Put that arm down!' Miss Gildea said shrilly, and then struggled to get her voice under control. 'In all my years I've never struck a child, and I don't intend to start now!'

Robert dropped his arm and clasped his hands together on his desk, and Miss Gildea looking at the pinched white knuckles realised with surprise that her own hands were shaking uncontrollably. 'But if you think this little matter ends here, young-feller-me-lad,' she said, 'you've got another thought coming. You get your things together, and we're marching right up to Mr Harkness. He'll be very much interested in all this.'

Mr Harkness was the Principal. He had arrived only the term before, and but for his taste in eyeglasses (the large, black-rimmed kind which, Miss Gildea privately though, looked actorish) and his predilection for the phrase 'modern pedagogical methods' was, in her opinion, a rather engaging young man.

He looked at Robert's frightened face and then at Miss Gildea's pursed lips. 'Well,' he said pleasantly, 'what seems to be the trouble here?'

'That,' said Miss Gildea, 'is something I think Robert should tell you about.'

She placed a hand on Robert's shoulder, but he pulled away and backed slowly toward Mr Harkness, his breath coming in loud, shuddering sobs, his eyes riveted on Miss Gildea as if she were the only thing in the room beside himself. Mr Harkness put an arm around Robert and frowned at Miss Gildea.

'Now, what's behind all this, Miss Gildea? The boy seems frightened to death.'

Miss Gildea found herself sick of it all, anxious to get out of the room, away from Robert. 'That's enough, Robert,' she commanded. 'Just tell Mr Harkness exactly what happened.'

'I said the boy was frightened to death, Miss Gildea,' Mr Harkness said brusquely. 'We'll talk about it as soon as he understands we're his friends. Won't we, Robert?'

Robert shook his head vehemently. 'I didn't do anything bad! Miss Gildea said I didn't do anything bad!'

'Well, then!' said Mr Harkness triumphantly. 'There's nothing to be afraid of, is there?'

Robert shook his head again. 'She said I had to stay in after school.'

Mr Harkness glanced sharply at Miss Gildea. 'I suppose he missed the morning bus, is that it? And after I said in a directive that the staff was to make allowances—'

'Robert doesn't use a bus,' Miss Gildea protested. 'Perhaps I'd better explain all this, Mr Harkness. You see—'

'I think Robert's doing very well,' Mr Harkness said, and tightened his arm around Robert who nodded shakily.

'She kept me in,' he said, 'and then when we were alone she came up close to me and she said, "I know what you're thinking. You're thinking you'd like to see me dead! You're thinking you'd like to kill me, aren't you?"'

Robert's voice had dropped to an eerie whisper that bound Miss Gildea like a spell. It was broken only when she saw the expression on Mr Harkness's face.

'Why, that's a lie!' she cried. 'That's the most dreadful lie I ever heard any boy dare—'

Mr Harkness cut in abruptly. 'Miss Gildea! I *insist* you let the boy finish what he has to say.'

Miss Gildea's voice fluttered. 'It seems to me, Mr Harkness, that he has been allowed to say quite enough already!'

'Has he?' Mr Harkness asked.

'Robert has been inattentive lately, especially so this afternoon. After class I asked him what he had been thinking about, and he dared to say he was thinking how he wished I were dead! How he wanted to kill me!'

'Robert said that?'

'In almost those exact words. And I can tell you, Mr Harkness, that I was shocked, terribly shocked, especially since Robert always seemed like such a nice boy.'

'His record—?'

'His record is quite good. It's just—'

'And his social conduct?' asked Mr Harkness in the same level voice.

'As far as I know, he gets along with the other children well enough.'

'But for some reason,' persisted Mr Harkness, 'you found him annoying you.'

Robert raised his voice. 'I didn't! Miss Gildea said I didn't do anything bad. And I always liked her. I like her better than *any* teacher!'

Miss Gildea fumbled blindly in her hair for the silver pencil, and failed to find it. She looked around the floor distractedly.

'Yes?' said Mr Harkness.

'My pencil,' said Miss Gildea on the verge of tears. 'It's gone.'

'Surely, Miss Gildea,' said Mr Harkness in a tone of mild exasperation. 'This is not quite the moment—'

'It was very valuable,' Miss Gildea tried to explain hopelessly. 'It was my mother's.' In the face of Mr Harkness's stony surveillance she knew she must look a complete mess. Hems crooked, nose red, hair all dishevelled. 'I'm all upset, Mr Harkness. It's been a long term and now all this right at the end of it. I don't know what to say.'

Mr Harkness's face fell into sympathetic lines.

'That's quite all right, Miss Gildea. I know how you feel. Now, if you want to leave, I think Robert and I should have a long, friendly talk.'

'If you don't mind—'

'No, no,' Mr Harkness said heartily. 'As a matter of fact, I think that would be the best thing all around.'

After he had seen her out he closed the door abruptly behind her, and Miss Gildea walked heavily up the stairway and down the corridor to the Sixth Grade room. The silver pencil was there on the floor at Robert's desk, and she picked it up and carefully polished it with her handkerchief. Then she sat down at her desk with the handkerchief to her nose and wept soundlessly for ten minutes.

That night when the bitter taste of humiliation had grown faint enought to permit it, Miss Gildea reviewed the episode with all the honesty at her command. Honesty with oneself had always been a major point in her credo, had, in fact, been passed on through succeeding classes during the required lesson on The Duties of An American Citizen, when Miss Gildea, to sum up the lesson, would recite: 'This above all, To thine ownself be true . . .' while thumping her fist on her desk as an accompaniment to each syllable.

Hamlet, of course, was not in the syllabus of the Sixth Grade, whose reactions over the years never deviated from a mixed bewilderment and indifference. But Miss Gildea, after some prodding of the better minds into a discussion of the lines, would rest content with the knowledge that she had sown good seed on what, she prayed, was fertile ground.

Reviewing the case of Robert now, with her emotions under control, she came to the unhappy conclusion that it was she who had committed the injustice. The child had been ordered to stay after school, something that to him could mean only a punishment. He had been ordered to disclose some shadowy, childlike thoughts that had drifted through his mind hours before, and, unable to do so, either had to make up something out of the whole cloth, or blurt out the immediate thought in his immature mind.

It was hardly unusual, reflected Miss Gildea sadly, for a child badgered by a teacher to think what Robert had; she could well remember her own feelings toward a certain pompadoured harridan who still haunted her dreams. And the only conclusion to be drawn, unpleasant though it was, was that Robert, and not she, had truly put into practice those beautiful words from Shakespeare.

It was this, as well as the sight of his pale accusing face before her while she led the class through the morning session next day, which prompted her to put Robert in charge of refilling the water pitcher during recess. The duties of the water pitcher monitor were to leave the playground a little before the rest of the class and clean and refill the pitcher on her desk, but since the task was regarded as an honour by the class, her gesture, Miss Gildea felt with some self-approval, carried exactly the right note of conciliation.

She was erasing the blackboard at the front of the room near the end of the recess when she heard Robert approaching her desk, but much as she wanted to she could not summon up courage enough to turn and face him. As if, she thought, he were the teacher, and I were afraid of him. And she could feel her cheeks grow warm at the thought.

He re-entered the room on the sound of the bell that marked the end of recess, and this time Miss Gildea plopped the eraser firmly into its place beneath the blackboard and turned to look at him. 'Thank you very much, Robert,' she said as he set the pitcher down and neatly capped it with her drinking glass.

'You're welcome, Miss Gildea,' Robert said politely. He drew a handkerchief from his pocket, wiped his hands with it, then smiled gently at Miss Gildea. 'I bet you think I put poison or something into that water,' he said gravely, 'but I wouldn't do anything like that, Miss Gildea. Honest, I wouldn't.'

Miss Gildea gasped, then reached out a hand toward Robert's shoulder. She withdrew it hastily when he shrank away with the familiar panicky look in his eyes.

'Why did you say that, Robert?' Miss Gildea demanded in a terrible voice. 'That was plain impudence, wasn't it? You thought you were being smart, didn't you?'

At that moment the rest of the class surged noisily into the room, but Miss Gildea froze them into silence with a commanding wave of the hand. Out of the corner of her eye she noted the cluster of shocked and righteous faces allied with her in condemnation, and she felt a quick little sense of triumph in her position.

'I was talking to you, Robert,' she said. 'What do you have to say for yourself?'

Robert took another step backward and almost tumbled over a schoolbag left carelessly in the aisle. He caught himself, then stood there helplessly, his eyes never leaving Miss Gildea's.

'Well, Robert!'

He shook his head wildly. 'I didn't do it!' he cried. 'I didn't put anything in your water, Miss Gildea! I told you I didn't!'

Without looking Miss Gildea knew that the cluster of accusing faces had swung toward her now, felt her triumph turn to a sick bewilderment inside her. It was as if Robert, with his teary eyes and pale, frightened face and too large ears, had turned into a strange jelly-like creature that could not be pinned down and put in its place. As if he were retreating further and further down some dark, twisting path, and leading her on with him. And, she thought desperately, she had to pull herself free before she did something dreadful, something unforgivable.

She couldn't take the boy to Mr Harkness again. Not only did the memory of that scene in his office the day before make her shudder, but a repeated visit would be an admission that after thirty-eight years of teaching she was not up to the mark as a disciplinarian.

But for her sake, if for nothing else, Robert had to be put in his place. With a gesture, Miss Gildea order the rest of the class to their seats and turned to Robert who remained standing.

'Robert,' said Miss Gildea, 'I want an apology for what has just happened.'

'I'm sorry, Miss Gildea,' Robert said, and it looked as if his eyes would be brimming with tears in another moment.

Miss Gildea hardened her heart to this. '*I apologise, Miss Gildea, and it will not happen again,*' she prompted.

Miraculously, Robert contained his tears. 'I apologise, Miss Gildea, and it will not happen again,' he muttered and dropped limply into his seat.

ROBERT

'Well!' said Miss Gildea, drawing a deep breath as she looked around at the hushed class. 'Perhaps that will be a lesson to us all.'

The classroom work did not go well after that, but, as Miss Gildea told herself, there were only a few days left to the end of term, and after that, praise be, there was the garden, the comfortable front porch of the old house to share with neighbours in the summer evenings, and then next term a new set of faces in the classroom, with Robert's not among them.

Later, closing the windows of the room after the class had left, Miss Gildea was brought up short by the sight of a large group gathered on the sidewalk near the parked buses. It was Robert, she saw, surrounded by most of the Sixth Grade, and obviously the centre of interest. He was nodding emphatically when she put her face to the window, and she drew back quickly at the sight, moved by some queer sense of guilt.

Only a child, she assured herself, *he's only a child*, but that thought did not in any way dissolve the anger against him that stuck like a lump in her throat.

That was on Thursday. By Tuesday of the next week, the final week of the term, Miss Gildea was acutely conscious of the oppressive atmosphere lying over the classroom. Ordinarily, the awareness of impending vacation acted on the class like a violent agent dropped into some inert liquid. There would be ferment and seething beneath the surface, manifested by uncontrollable giggling and whispering, and this would grow more and more turbulent until all restraint and discipline was swept away in the general upheaval of excitement and good spirits.

That, Miss Gildea thought, was the way it always had been, but it was strangely different now. The Sixth Grade, down to the most irrepressible spirits in it, acted as if it had been turned to a set of robots before her startled eyes. Hands tightly clasped on desks, eyes turned toward her with an almost frightening intensity, the class responded to her mildest requests as if they were shouted commands. And when she walked down the aisles between them, one and all seemed to have adopted Robert's manner of shrinking away fearfully at her approach.

Miss Gildea did not like to think of what all this might mean, but valiantly forced herself to do so. Can it mean, she asked herself, that all think as Robert does, are choosing this way of showing it? And, if they knew how cruel it was, would they do it?

Other teachers, Miss Gildea knew, sometimes took problems such as this to the Teachers' Room where they could be studied and answered by those who saw them in an objective light. It might be that the curious state of the Sixth Grade was being duplicated in other classes. Perhaps, she herself was imagining the whole thing, or, frightening thought, looking back, as people will when they grow old, on the sort of past that never really did exist. Why, in that case – and Miss Gildea had to laugh at herself with a faint merriment – she would just find herself reminiscing about her thirty-eight years of teaching to some bored young woman who didn't have the fraction of experience she did.

But underneath the current of these thoughts, Miss Gildea knew there was one honest reason for not going to the Teachers' Room this last week of the term. She had received no gifts, not one. And the spoils from each grade heaped high in a series of pyramids against the wall. The boxes of fractured cookies, the clumsily wrapped jars of preserves, the scarves, the stockings, the handkerchiefs, infinite, endless boxes of handkerchiefs, all were there to mark the triumph of each teacher. And Miss Gildea, who in all her years at District School Number Three had been blushingly proud of the way her pyramid was highest at the end of each term, had not yet received a single gift from the Sixth Grade class.

After the class was dismissed that afternoon, however the spell was broken. Only a few of her pupils still loitered in the hallway near the door, Miss Gildea noticed, but Robert remained in his seat. Then, as she gathered together her belongings Robert approached her with a box outheld in his hand. It was, from its shape, a box of candy, and, as Miss Gildea could tell from the wrapping, expensive candy. Automatically, she reached a hand out, then stopped herself short. He'll never make-up to me for what he's done, she told herself furiously; I'll never let him.

'Yes, Robert?' she said coolly.

'It's a present for you, Miss Gildea,' Robert said, and then as Miss Gildea watched in fascination he began to strip the wrappings from it. He laid the paper neatly on the desk and lifted the cover of the box to display the chocolates within. 'My mother said that's the biggest box they had,' he said wistfully. 'Don't you even want them, Miss Gildea?'

Miss Gildea weakened despite herself. 'Did you think I would, after what's happened, Robert?' she asked.

Robert reflected a moment. 'Well,' he said at last, 'if you want me to, I'll eat one right in front of you, Miss Gildea.'

Miss Gildea recoiled as if at a faraway warning. *Don't let him say any more*, something inside her cried; *he's only playing a trick, another horrible trick*, and then she was saying, 'Why would I want you to do that, Robert?'

'So you'll see they're not poison or anything, Miss Gildea,' Robert said. 'Then you'll believe it, won't you, Miss Gildea?'

She had been prepared. Even before he said the words, she had felt her body drawing itself tighter and tighter against what she knew was coming. But the sound of the words themselves only served to release her like a spring coiled too tightly.

'You little monster!' sobbed Miss Gildea and struck wildly at the proffered box which flew almost to the far wall, while chocolates cascaded stickily around the room. 'How dare you!' she cried. 'How dare you!' and her small bony fists beat at Robert's cowering shoulders and back as he tried to retreat.

He half turned in the aisle, slipped on a piece of chocolate, and went down to his knees, but before he could recover himself Miss Gildea was on him again, her lips drawn back, her fists pummelling him as if they were a pair of tireless mallets. Robert had started to scream at the top of his lungs from the first blow, but it was no more than a remote buzzing in Miss Gildea's ears.

'Miss Gildea!'

That was Mr Harkness's voice, she knew, and those must be Mr Harkness's hands which pulled her away so roughly that she had to keep herself from falling by clutching at her desk. She stood there weakly, feeling the wild fluttering of her heart, feeling the sick churning of shame and anguish in her while she tried to bring the room into focus again. There was the knot of small excited faces peering through the open doorway, they must have called Mr Harkness, and Mr Harkness himself listening to Robert who talked and wept alternately, and there was a mess everywhere. Of course, thought Miss Gildea dazedly, those must be chocolate stains. Chocolate stains all over my lovely clean room.

Then Robert was gone, the faces at the door were gone, and the door itself was closed behind them. Only Mr Harkness remained, and Miss Gildea watched him as he removed his glasses, cleaned them carefully, and then held them up at arm's length and studied them before settling them once more on his nose.

'Well, Miss Gildea,' said Mr Harkness as if he were speaking to the glasses rather than to her, 'this is a serious business.'

Miss Gildea nodded.

'I am sick,' Mr Harkness said quietly, 'really sick at the thought that somewhere in this school, where I tried to introduce decent pedagogical standards, corporal punishment is still being practised.'

'That's not fair at all, Mr Harkness,' Miss Gildea said shakily. 'I hit the boy, that's true, and I know I was wrong to do it, but that is the first time in all my life I raised a finger against any child. And if you knew my feelings—'

'Ah,' said Mr Harkness, 'that's exactly what I would like to know, Miss Gildea.' He nodded to her chair, and she sat down weakly. 'Now, just go ahead and explain everything as you saw it.'

It was a difficult task, made even more difficult by the fact that Mr Harkness chose to stand facing the window. Forced to address his back this way, Miss Gildea found that she had the sensation of speaking in a vacuum, but she mustered the facts as well as she could, presented them with strong emotion, and then sank back in the chair quite exhausted.

Mr Harkness remained silent for a long while, then slowly turned to face Miss Gildea. 'I am not a practising psychiatrist,' he said at last, 'although as an educator I have, of course, taken a considerable interest in that field. But I do not think it needs a practitioner to tell what a clearcut and obvious case I am facing here. Nor,' he added sympathetically, 'what a tragic one.'

'It might simply be,' suggested Miss Gildea, 'that Robert—'

'I am not speaking about Robert,' said Mr Harkness soberly, quietly.

It took an instant for this to penetrate, and then Miss Gildea felt the blood run cold in her.

'Do you think I'm lying about all this?' she cried increduously. 'Can you possibly—'

'I am sure,' Mr Harkness replied soothingly, 'that you were describing things exactly as you saw them, Miss Gildea. But – have you ever heard the phrase "persecution complex"? Do you think you could recognise the symptoms of that condition if they were presented objectively? I can, Miss Gildea. I assure you, I can.'

Miss Gildea struggled to speak, but the words seemed to choke her. 'No,' she managed to say, 'you couldn't! Because some mischievous boy chooses to make trouble—'

'Miss Gildea, no child of eleven, however mischievous, could draw the experiences Robert has described to me out of his imagination. He has discussed these experiences with me at length; now I have heard your side of the case. And the conclusions to be drawn, I must say, are practically forced on me.'

The room started to slip out of focus again, and Miss Gildea frantically tried to hold it steady.

'But that just means you're taking his word against mine!' she said fiercely.

'Unfortunately, Miss Gildea, not his word alone. Last weekend, a delegation of parents met the School Board and made it quite plain that they were worried because of what their children told them of your recent actions. A dozen children in your class described graphically at that meeting how you had accused them of trying to poison your drinking water, and how you had threatened them because of this. And Robert, it may interest you to know, was not even one of them.

'The School Board voted your dismissal then and there, Miss Gildea, but in view of your long years of service it was left for me to override that decision if I wished to on my sole responsibility. After this episode, however, I cannot see that I have any choice, I must do what is best.'

'Dismissal?' said Miss Gildea vaguely. 'But they can't. I only have two more years to go. They can't do that, Mr Harkness; all they're trying to do is trick me out of my pension!'

'Believe me,' said Mr Harkness gently, 'they're not trying to do anything of the sort, Miss Gildea. Nobody in the world is trying to hurt you. I give you my solemn word that the only thing which has entered into consideration of this case from first to last has been the welfare of the children.'

The room swam in sunlight, but under it Miss Gildea's face was grey and lifeless. She reached forward to fill her glass with water, stopped short, and seemed to gather herself together with a sudden brittle determination. 'I'll just have to speak to the Board myself,' she said in a high breathless voice. 'That's the only thing to do, go there and explain the whole thing to them!'

'That would not help,' said Mr Harkness pityingly. 'Believe me, Miss Gildea, it would not.'

Miss Gildea left her chair and came to him, her eyes wide and frightened. She laid a trembling hand on his arm and spoke eagerly, quickly, trying to make him understand. 'You see,' she said, 'that means I won't get my pension. I must have two more years for that, don't you see? There's the payment on the house, the garden – no, the garden is part of the house, really – but without the pension—'

She was pulling furiously at his arm with every phrase as if she could drag him bodily into a comprehension of her words, but he stood unyielding and only shook his head pityingly. 'You must control yourself, Miss Gildea,' he pleaded. 'You're not yourself, and it's impossible—'

'No!' she cried in a strange voice. 'No!'

When she pulled away he knew almost simultaneously what she intended to do, but the thought froze him to the spot, and when he moved it was too late. He burst into the corridor through the door she had flung open, and almost threw himself down the stairway to the main hall. The door to the street was just swinging shut and he ran toward it, one hand holding the rim of his glasses, a sharp little pain digging into his side, but before he could reach the door he heard the screech of brakes, the single agonised scream, and the horrified shout of a hundred shrill voices.

He put his hand on the door, but could not find the strength to open it. A few minutes later, a cleaning women had to sidle around him to get outside and see what all the excitement was about.

Miss Reardon, the substitute, took the Sixth Grade the next day, and, everything considered, handled it very well. The single ripple in the even current of the session came at its very start when Miss Reardon explained her presence by referring to the 'sad accident that happened to dear Miss Gildea'. The mild hubbub which followed this contained several voices, notably in the back of the room, which protested plaintively, 'It was *not* an accident, Miss Reardon; she ran right in front of that bus,' but Miss Reardon quickly brought order to the room with a few sharp raps of her ruler, and after that, classwork was carried on in a pleasant and orderly fashion.

Robert walked home slowly that afternoon, swinging his schoolbag placidly at his side, savouring the June warmth soaking into him, the fresh green smell in the air, the memory of Miss Reardon's understanding face so often turned toward his in eager and friendly interest. His home was identical with all the others on the block, square white boxes with small lawns before them, and its only distinction was that all its blinds were drawn down. After he had closed the front door very quietly behind him, he set his schoolbag down in the hallway, and went into the stuffy half-darkness of the living room.

Robert's father sat in the big armchair in his bathrobe, the way he always did, and Robert's mother was bent over him holding a glass of water.

'No!' Robert's father said. 'You just want to get rid of me, but I won't let you! I know what you put into it, and I won't drink it! I'll die before I drink it!'

'Please,' Robert's mother said, 'please take it. I swear it's only water. I'll drink some myself if you don't believe me.' But when she drank a little and then held the glass to his lips, Robert's father only tossed his head from side to side.

Robert stood there watching the scene with fascination, his lips moving in silent mimicry of the familiar words. Then he cleared his throat.

'I'm home, mama,' Robert said softly. 'Can I have some milk and cookies, please?'

Stanley Ellin

The Question

I am an electrocutioner . . . I prefer this word to executioner; I think words make a difference. When I was a boy, people who buried the dead were undertakers, and then somewhere along the way they became morticians and are better off for it.

Take the one who used to be the undertaker in my town. He was a decent, respectable man, very friendly if you'd let him be, but hardly anybody would let him be. Today, his son – who now runs the business – is not an undertaker but a mortician, and is welcome everywhere. As a matter of fact, he's an officer in my Lodge and is one of the most popular members we have. And all it took to do that was changing one word to another. The job's the same but the word is different, and people somehow will always go by words rather than meanings.

So, as I said, I am an electrocutioner – which is the proper professional word for it in my state where the electric chair is the means of execution.

Not that this is my profession. Actually, it's a sideline, as it is for most of us who perform executions. My real business is running an electrical supply and repair shop just as my father did before him. When he died I inherited not only the business from him, but also the position of state's electrocutioner.

We established a tradition, my father and I. He was running the shop profitably even before the turn of the century when electricity was a comparatively new thing, and he was the first man to perform a successful electrocution for the state. It was not the state's first electrocution, however. That one was an experiment and was badly bungled by the engineer who installed the chair in the state prison. My father, who had helped install the chair, was the assistant at the electrocution, and he told me that everything that could go wrong that day did go wrong.

The current was eccentric, his boss froze on the switch, and the man in the chair was alive and kicking at the same time he was being burned to a crisp. The next time, my father offered to do the job himself, rewired the chair, and handled the switch so well that he was offered the job of official electrocutioner.

I followed in his footsteps, which is how a tradition is made, but I am afraid this one ends with me. I have a son, and what I said to him and what he said to me is the crux of the matter. He asked me a question – well, in my opinion, it was the kind of question that's at the bottom of most of the world's troubles today. There are some sleeping dogs that should be left to lie; there are some questions that should not be asked.

To understand all this, I think you have to understand me, and nothing could be easier. I'm sixty, just beginning to look my age, a little over-weight, suffer sometimes from arthritis when the weather is damp. I'm a good citizen, complain about my taxes but pay them on schedule, vote for the right party, and run my business well enough to make a comfortable living from it.

I've been married thirty-five years and never looked at another woman in all that time. Well, looked maybe, but no more than that. I have a married daughter and a grand-daughter almost a year old, and the prettiest, smilingest baby in town. I spoil her and don't apologise for it, because in my opinion that is what grandfathers were made for – to spoil their grandchildren. Let mama and papa attend to the business; grandpa is there for the fun.

And beyond all that I have a son who asks questions. The kind that shouldn't be asked.

Put the picture together, and what you get is someone like yourself. I might be your next-door neighbour, I might be your old friend, I might be the uncle you meet whenever the family gets together at a wedding or a funeral. I'm like you.

Naturally, we all look different on the outside but we can still recognise each other on sight as the same kind of people. Deep down inside where it matters we have the same feelings, and we know that without any questions being asked about them.

'But,' you might say, 'there is a difference between us. You're the one who performs the executions, and I'm the one who reads about them in the papers, and that's a big difference, no matter how you look at it.'

Is it? Well, look at it without prejudice, look at it with absolute honesty, and you'll have to admit that you're being unfair,

Let's face the facts, we're all in this together. If an old friend of yours happens to serve on a jury that finds a murderer guilty, you don't lock the door against him, do you? More than that: if you could get an introduction to the judge who sentences that murderer to the electric chair, you'd be proud of it, wouldn't you? You'd be honoured to have him sit at your table, and you'd be quick enough to let the world know about it.

And since you're so willing to be friendly with the jury that convicts and the judge that sentences, what about the man who has to pull the switch? He's finished the job you wanted done, he's made the world a better place for it. Why must he go hide away in a dark corner until the next time he's needed?

There's no use denying that nearly everybody feels he should, and there's less use denying that it's a cruel thing for anyone in my position to face. If you don't mind some strong language, it's a damned outrage to hire a man for an unpleasant job, and then despise him for it. Sometimes it's hard to abide such righteousness.

How do I get along in the face of it? The only way possible – by keeping my secret locked up tight and never being tempted to give it away. I don't like it that way, but I'm no fool about it.

The trouble is that I'm naturally easygoing and friendly. I'm the sociable kind. I like people, and I want them to like me. At Lodge meetings or in the clubhouse down at the golf course I'm always the centre of the crowd. And I know what would happen if at any such time I ever opened my mouth and let that secret out. A five-minute sensation, and after that the slow chill setting in. It would mean the end of my whole life then and there, the kind of life I want to live, and no man in his right mind throws away sixty years of his life for a five-minute sensation.

You can see I've given the matter a lot of thought. More than that, it hasn't been idle thought. I don't pretend to be an educated man, but I'm willing to read books on any subject that interests me, and execution has been one of my main interests ever since I got into the line. I have the books sent to the shop where nobody takes notice of another piece of mail, and I keep them locked in a bin in my office so that I can read them in private.

There's a nasty smell about having to do it this way – at my age you hate to feel like a kid hiding himself away to read a dirty magazine – but I have no choice. There isn't a soul on earth outside of the warden at the state's prison and a couple of picked guards there who know I'm the one pulling the switch at an execution, and I intend it to remain that way.

Oh, yes, my son knows now. Well, he's difficult in some ways, but he's no fool. If I wasn't sure he would keep his mouth shut about what I told him, I wouldn't have told it to him in the first place.

Have I learned anything from those books? At least enough to take a pride in what I'm doing for the state and the way I do it. As far back in history as you want to go there have always been executioners. The day that men first made laws to help keep peace among themselves was the day the first executioner was born. There have always been law-breakers; there must always be a way of punishing them. It's as simple as that.

The trouble is that nowadays there are too many people who don't want it to be as simple as that. I'm no hypocrite, I'm not one of those narrow-minded fools who thinks that every time a man comes up with a generous impulse he's some kind of crackpot. But he can be mistaken. I'd put most of the people who are against capital punishment in that class. They are fine, high-minded citizens who've never in their lives been close enough to a murderer or rapist to smell the evil in him. In fact, they're so fine and high-minded that they can't imagine anyone in the world not being like themselves. In that case, they say anybody who commits murder or rape is just a plain, ordinary human being who's had a bad spell. He's no criminal, they say, he's just sick. He doesn't need the electric chair; all he needs is a kindly old doctor to examine his head and straighten out the kinks in his brain.

In fact, they say there is no such thing as a criminal at all. There are only well people and sick people, and the ones who deserve all your worry and consideration are the sick ones. If they happen to murder or rape a few of the well ones now and then, why, just run for the doctor.

This is the argument from beginning to end, and I'd be the last one to deny that it's built on honest charity and good intentions. But it's a mistaken argument. It omits the one fact that matters. When anyone commits murder or rape he is no longer in the human race. A man has a human brain and a God-given soul to control his animal nature. When the animal in him takes control he's not a human being any more. Then he has to be exterminated the way any animal must be if it goes wild in the middle of helpless people. And my duty is to be the exterminator.

It could be that people just don't understand the meaning of the word *duty* any more. I don't want to sound old-fashioned, God forbid, but when I was a boy things were more straight-forward and clear-cut. You learned to tell right from wrong, you learned to do what had to be done, and you didn't ask questions every step of the way. Or if you had to ask any questions, the ones that mattered were *how* and *when*.

Then along came psychology, along came the professors, and the main question was always *why*. Ask yourself *why, why, why* about everything you do, and you'll end up doing nothing. Let a couple of generations go along that way, and you'll finally have a breed of people who sit around in trees like monkeys, scratching their heads.

Does this sound far-fetched? Well, it isn't. Life is a complicated thing to live. All his life a man finds himself facing one situation after another, and the way to handle them is to live by the rules. Ask yourself *why* once too often, and you can find yourself so tangled up that you go under. The show must go on. Why? Women and children first. Why? My country, right or wrong. Why? Never mind your duty. Just keep asking *why* until it's too late to do anything about it.

Around the time I first started going to school my father gave me a dog, a collie pup named Rex. A few years after Rex suddenly became unfriendly, the way a dog will sometimes, and then vicious, and then one day he bit my mother when she reached down to pat him.

The day after that I saw my father leaving the house with his hunting rifle under his arm and with Rex on a leash. It wasn't the hunting season, so I knew what was going to happen to Rex and I knew why. But it's forgivable in a boy to ask things that a man should be smart enough not to ask.

'Where are you taking Rex?' I asked my father. 'What are you going to do with him?'

'I'm taking him out back of town,' my father said. 'I'm going to shoot him.'

'But why?' I said, and that was when my father let me see that there is only one answer to such a question.

'Because it has to be done,' he said.

I never forgot that lesson. It came hard; for a while I hated my father for it, but as I grew up I came to see how right he was. We both knew why the dog had to be killed. Beyond that, all questions would lead nowhere. Why the dog had become vicious, why God had put a dog on earth to be killed this way – these are the questions that you can talk out to the end of time, and while you're talking about them you still have a vicious dog on your hands.

It is strange to look back and realise now that when the business of the dog happened, and long before it and long after it, my father was an electrocutioner, and I never knew it. Nobody knew it, not even my mother. A few times a year my father would pack his bag and a few tools and go away for a couple of days, but that was all any of us knew. If you asked him where he was going he would simply say he had a job to do out of town. He was not a man you'd ever suspect of philandering or going off on a solitary drunk, so nobody gave it a second thought.

It worked the same way in my case. I found out how well it worked when I finally told my son what I had been doing on those jobs out of town, and that I had gotten the warden's permission to take him on as an assistant and train him to handle the chair himself when I retired. I could tell from the way he took it that he was as thunderstruck at this as I had been thirty years before when my father had taken me into his confidence.

'Electrocutioner?' said my son. 'An *electrocutioner?*'

'Well, there's no disgrace to it,' I said. 'And since it's got to be done, and somebody has to do it, why not keep it in the family? If you knew anything about it, you'd know it's a profession that's often passed down in a family from generation to generation. What's wrong with a good, sound tradition? If more people believed in tradition you wouldn't have so many troubles in the world today.'

It was the kind of argument that would have been more than enough to convince me when I was his age. What I hadn't taken into account was that my son wasn't like me, much as I wanted him to be. He was a grown man in his own right, but a grown man who had never settled down to his responsibilities. I had always kept closing my eyes to that. I had always seen him the way I wanted to and not the way he was.

When he left college after a year, I said, all right, there are some people who aren't made for college, I never went there, so what difference does it make. When he went out with one girl after another and could never make up his mind to marrying any of them, I said, well, he's young, he's sowing his wild oats, the time will come soon enough when he's ready to take care of a home and family. When he sat day-dreaming in the shop instead of tending to business I never made a fuss about it. I knew when he put his mind to it he was as good an electrician as you could ask for, and in these soft times people are allowed to do a lot more dreaming and a lot less working than they used to.

The truth was that the only thing that mattered to me was being his friend. For all his faults he was a fine-looking boy with a good mind. He wasn't much for mixing with people, but if he wanted to he could win anyone over. And in the back of my mind all the while he was growing up was the thought that he was the only one who would learn my secret some day, and would share it with me, and make it easier to bear. I'm not secretive by nature. A man like me needs a thought like that to sustain him.

So when the time came to tell him he shook his head and said no. I felt that my legs had been kicked out from under me. I argued with him and he still said no, and I lost my temper.

'Are you against capital punishment?' I asked him. 'You don't have to apologise if you are. I'd think all the more of you, if that's your only reason.'

'I don't know if it is,' he said.

'Well, you ought to make up your mind one way or the other,' I told him. 'I'd hate to think you were like every other hypocrite around who says it's all right to condemn a man to the electric chair and all wrong to pull the switch.'

'Do I have to be the one to pull it?' he said. 'Do you?'

'Somebody has to do it. Somebody always has to do the dirty work for the rest of us. It's not like the Old Testament days when everybody did it for himself. Do you know how they executed a man in those days? They laid him on the ground tied hand and foot, and everybody around had to heave rocks on him until he was crushed to death. They didn't invite anybody to stand around and watch. You wouldn't have had much choice then, would you?'

'I don't know,' he said. And then because he was as smart as they come and knew how to turn your words against you, he said, 'After all, I'm not without sin.'

'Don't talk like a child,' I said. 'You're without the sin of murder on you or any kind of sin that calls for execution. And if you're so sure the Bible has all the answers, you might remember that you're supposed to render unto Caesar the things that are Caesar's.'

'Well,' he said, 'in this case I'll let you do the rendering.'

I knew then and there from the way he said it and the way he looked at me that it was no use trying to argue with him. The worst of it was knowing that we had somehow moved far apart from each other and would never really be close again. I should have had sense enough to let it go at that. I should have just told him to forget the whole thing and keep his mouth shut about it.

Maybe if I had ever considered the possibility of his saying no, I would have done it. But because I hadn't considered any such possibility I was caught off balance. I was too much upset to think straight. I will admit it now. It was my own fault that I made an issue of things and led him to ask the one question he should never have asked.

'I see,' I told him. 'It's the same old story, isn't it? Let somebody else do it. But if they pull your number out of a hat and you have to serve on a jury and send a man to the chair, that's all right with you. At least, it's all right as long as there's somebody else to do the job that you and the judge and every decent citizen wants done. Let's face the facts, boy, you don't have the guts. I'd hate to think of you even walking by the death house. The shop is where you belong. You can be nice and cosy there, wiring up fixtures and ringing the cash register. I can handle my duties without your help.'

It hurt me to say it. I had never talked like that to him before, and it hurt. The strange thing was that he didn't seem angry about it; he only looked at me puzzled.

'Is that all it is to you?' he said. 'A duty?'

'Yes.'

'But you get paid for it, don't you?'

'I get paid little enough for it.'

He kept looking at me that way. 'Only a duty?' he said, and never took his eyes off me. 'But you enjoy it, don't you?'

That was the question he asked.

You enjoy it, don't you? You stand there looking through a peephole in the wall at the chair. In thirty years I have stood there more than a hundred times looking at that chair. The guards bring somebody in. Usually he is in a daze; sometimes he screams, throws himself around and fights. Sometimes it is a woman, and a woman can be as hard to handle as a man when she is led to the chair. Sooner or later, whoever it is is strapped down and the black hood is dropped over his head. Now your hand is on the switch.

The warden signals, and you pull the switch. The current hits the body like a tremendous rush of air suddenly filling it. The body leaps out of the chair with only the straps holding it back. The head jerks, and a curl of smoke comes from it. You release the switch and the body falls back again.

You do it once more, do it a third time to make sure. And whenever your hand presses the switch you can see in your mind what the current is doing to that body and what the face under the hood must look like.

Enjoy it?

That was the question my son asked me. That was what he said to me, as if I didn't have the same feelings deep down in me that we all have.

Enjoy it?

But, my God, how could anyone *not* enjoy it!

Patricia Highsmith

The Terrapin

Victor heard the elevator door open, his mother's quick footsteps in the hall, and he flipped his book shut. He shoved it under the sofa pillow out of sight, and winced as he heard it slip between sofa and wall and fall to the floor with a thud. Her key was in the lock.

'Hello, Vee-ector-r!' she cried, raising one arm in the air. Her other arm circled a big brown paper bag, her hand held a cluster of little bags. 'I have been to my publisher and to the market and also to the fish market,' she told him. 'Why aren't you out playing? It's a lovely, lovely day!'

'I was out,' he said. 'For a little while. I got cold.'

'Ugh!' She was unloading the grocery bag in the tiny kitchen off the foyer. 'You are seeck, you know that? In the month of October, you are cold? I see all kinds of children playing on the sidewalk. Even, I think, that boy you like. What's his name?'

'I don't know,' Victor said. His mother wasn't really listening, anyway. He pushed his hands into the pockets of his short, too small shorts, making them tighter than ever, and walked aimlessly around the living-room, looking down at his heavy, scuffed shoes. At least his mother had to buy him shoes that fit him, and he rather liked these shoes, because they had the thickest soles of any he had ever owned, and they had heavy toes that rose up a little, like mountain climbers' shoes. Victor paused at the window and looked straight out at a toast-coloured apartment building across Third Avenue. He and his mother lived on the eighteenth floor, next to the top floor where the penthouses were. The building across the street was even taller than this one. Victor had liked their Riverside Drive apartment better. He had liked the school he had gone to there better. Here they laughed at his clothes. In the other school, they had finally got tired of laughing at them.

'You don't want to go out?' asked his mother, coming into the living-room, wiping her hands briskly on a paper bag. She sniffed her palms. 'Ugh! That stee-enk!'

'No, Mama,' Victor said patiently.

'Today is Saturday.'

'I know.'

'Can you say the days of the week?'

'Of course.'

'Say them.'

'I don't want to say them. I know them.' His eyes began to sting around the edges with tears. 'I've known them for years. Years and years. Kids five years old can say the days of the week.'

But his mother was not listening. She was bending over the drawing-table in the corner of the room. She had worked late on something last night. On his sofa bed in the opposite corner of the room, Victor had not been able to sleep until two in the morning, when his mother had gone to bed on the studio couch.

'Come here, Veector. Did you see this?'

Victor came on dragging feet, hands still in his pockets. No, he hadn't even glanced at her drawing-board this morning, hadn't wanted to.

'This is Pedro, the little donkey. I invented him last night. What do you think? And this is Miguel, the little Mexican boy who rides him. They ride and ride all over Mexico, and Miguel thinks they are lost, but Pedro knows the way home all the time, and . . .'

Victor did not listen. He deliberately shut his ears in a way he had learned to do from many years of practice, but boredom, frustration – he knew the word frustration, had read all about it – clamped his shoulders, weighed like a stone in his body, pressed hatred and tears up to his eyes, as if a volcano were churning in him. He had hoped his mother might take a hint from his saying that he was cold in his silly short shorts. He had hoped his mother might remember what he had told her, that the fellow he had wanted to get acquainted with downstairs, a fellow who looked about his own age, eleven, had laughed at his short pants on Monday afternoon. *They make you wear your kid brother's pants or something?* Victor had drifted away, mortified. What if the fellow knew he didn't even own any longer pants, not even a pair of knickers, much less *long* pants, even blue jeans! His mother, for some cock-eyed reason, wanted him to look 'French', and made him wear short shorts and stockings that came to just below his knees, and dopey shirts with round collars. His mother wanted him to stay about six years old, for ever, all his life. She liked to test out her drawings on him. *Veector is my sounding board,* she sometimes said to her friends. *I show my drawings to Veector and I know if children will like them.* Often Victor said he liked stories that he did not like, or drawings that he was indifferent to, because he felt sorry for his mother and because it put her in a better mood if he said he liked them. He was quite tired now of children's book illustrations, if he had ever in his life liked them – he really couldn't remember – and now he had two favourites: Howard Pyle's illustrations in some of Robert Louis Stevenson's books and Cruikshank's in Dickens. It was too bad, Victor thought, that he was absolutely the last person of whom his mother should have asked an opinion, because he simply *hated* children's illustrations. And it was a wonder his mother didn't see this, because she hadn't sold any illustrations for books for years and years, not since *Wimple-Dimple*, a book whose jacket was all torn and turning yellow now from age, which sat in the centre of the bookshelf in a little cleared spot, propped up against the back of the bookcase so everyone could see it. Victor had been seven years old when that book was printed. His mother liked to tell people and remind him, too, that he had told her what he wanted to see her draw, had watched her make every drawing, had shown his opinion by laughing or not, and that she had been absolutely guided by him. Victor doubted this very much, because first of all the story was somebody else's and had been written before his mother did the drawings, and her drawings had had to follow the story, naturally. Since then, his mother had done only a few illustrations now and then for magazines for children, how to make paper pumpkins and black paper cats for Hallowe'en and things like that, though she took her portfolio around to publishers all the time. Their income came from his father, who was a wealthy businessman in France, an exporter of perfumes. His mother said he was very wealthy and very handsome. But he had married again, he never wrote, and Victor had no interest in him, didn't even care if he never saw a picture of him, and he never had. His father was French with some Polish, and his mother was Hungarian with some French. The word Hungarian made Victor think of gypsies, but when he had asked his mother once, she had said emphatically that she hadn't any gypsy blood, and she had been annoyed that Victor brought the question up.

And now she was sounding him out again, poking him in the ribs to make him wake up, as she repeated:

'Listen to me! Which do you like better, Veector? "In all Mexico there was no bur-r-ro as wise as Miguel's Pedro," or "Miguel's Pedro was the wisest bur-r-ro in all Mexico."?'

'I think – I like it the first way better.'

'Which way is that?' demanded his mother, thumping her palm down on the illustration.

Victor tried to remember the wording, but realised he was only staring at the pencil smudges, the thumbprints on the edges of his mother's illustration board. The coloured drawing in the centre did not interest him at all. He was not-thinking. This was a frequent, familiar sensation to him now, there was something exciting and important about not-thinking, Victor felt, and he thought one day he would find something about it – perhaps under another name – in the Public Library or in the psychology books around the house that he browsed in when his mother was out.

'Veec-tor! What are you doing?'

'Nothing, Mama!'

'That is exactly it! Nothing! Can you not even *think*?'

A warm shame spread through him. It was as if his mother read his thoughts about not-thinking. 'I am thinking,' he protested. 'I'm thinking about *not*-thinking.' His tone was defiant. What could she do about it, after all?

'About what?' Her black, curly head tilted, her mascaraed eyes narrowed at him.

'Not-thinking.'

His mother put her jewelled hands on her hips. 'Do you know, Veec-tor, you are a little bit strange in the head?' She nodded. 'You are seeck. Psychologically seeck. And retarded, do you know that? You have the behaviour of a leetle boy five years old,' she said slowly and weightily. 'It is just as well you spend your Saturdays indoors. Who knows if you would not walk in front of a car, eh? But that is why I love you, little Veector.' She put her arm around his shoulders, pulled him against her and for an instant Victor's nose pressed into her large, soft bosom. She was wearing her flesh-coloured dress, the one you could see through a little where her breast stretched it out.

Victor jerked his head away in a confusion of emotions. He did not know if he wanted to laugh or cry.

His mother was laughing gaily, her head back. 'Seeck you are! Look at you! My lee-tle boy still, lee-tle short pants – Ha! Ha!'

Now the tears showed in his eyes, he supposed, and his mother acted as if she were enjoying it! Victor turned his head away so she would not see his eyes. Then suddenly he faced her. 'Do you think I like these pants? *You* like them, not me, so why do you have to make fun of them?'

'A lee-tle boy who's crying!' she went on, laughing.

Victor made a dash for the bathroom, then swerved away and dived onto the sofa, his face towards the pillows. He shut his eyes tight and opened his mouth, crying but not-crying in a way he had learned through practice also. With his mouth open, his throat tight, not breathing for nearly a minute, he could somehow get the satisfaction of crying, screaming even, without anybody knowing it. He pushed his nose, his open mouth, his teeth, against the tomato-red sofa pillow, and though his mother's voice went on in a lazily mocking tone, and her laughter went on, he imagined that it was getting fainter and more distant from him. He imagined, rigid in every muscle, that he was suffering the absolute worst that any human being could suffer. He imagined that he was dying. But he did not think of death as an escape, only as a concentrated and painful incident. This was the climax of his not-crying. Then he breathed again, and his mother's voice intruded:

'Did you hear me? – *Did you hear me?* Mrs Badzerkian is coming for tea. I want you to wash your face and put on a clean shirt. I want you to recite something for her. Now what are you going to recite?'

'In winter when I go to bed,' said Victor. She was making him memorise every poem in *A Child's Garden of Verses.* He had said the first one that came into his head, and now there was an argument, because he had recited that one the last time. 'I said it, because I couldn't think of any other one right off the bat!' Victor shouted.

'Don't yell at me!' his mother cried, storming across the room at him. She slapped his face before he knew what was happening.

He was up on one elbow on the sofa, on his back, his long, knobby-kneed legs splayed out in front of him. All right, he thought, if that's the way it is, that's the way it is. He looked at her with loathing. He would not show the slap had hurt, that it still stung. No more tears for today, he swore, no more even not-crying. He would finish the day, go through the tea, like a stone, like a soldier, not wincing. His mother paced around the room, turning one of her rings round and round, glancing at him from time to time, looking quickly away from him. But his eyes were steady on her. He was not afraid. She could even slap him again and he wouldn't care.

At last, she announced that she was going to wash her hair, and she went into the bathroom.

Victor got up from the sofa and wandered across the room. He wished he had a room of his own to go to. In the apartment on Riverside Drive, there had been three rooms, a living-room and his and his mother's rooms. When she was in the living-room, he had been able to go into his bedroom and vice versa, but here . . . They were going to tear down the old building they had lived in on Riverside Drive. It was not a pleasant thing for Victor to think about. Suddenly remembering the book that had fallen, he pulled out the sofa and reached for it. It was Menninger's *The Human Mind,* full of fascinating case histories of people. Victor put it back on the bookshelf between an astrology book and *How to Draw.* His mother did not like him to read psychology books, but Victor loved them, especially ones with case histories in them. The people in the case histories did what they wanted to do. They were natural. Nobody bossed them. At the local branch library, he spent hours browsing through the psychology shelves. They were in the adults' section, but the librarian did not mind his sitting at the tables there, because he was quiet.

Victor went into the kitchen and got a glass of water. As he was standing there drinking it, he heard a scratching noise coming from one of the paper bags on the counter. A mouse, he thought, but when he moved a couple of the bags, he didn't see any mouse. The scratching was coming from inside one of the bags. Gingerly, he opened the bag with his fingers, and waited for something to jump out. Looking in, he saw a white paper carton. He pulled it out slowly. Its bottom was damp. It opened like a pastry box. Victor jumped in surprise. It was a turtle on its back, a live turtle. It was wriggling its legs in the air, trying to turn over. Victor moistened his lips, and frowning with concentration, took the turtle by its sides with both hands, turned him over and let him down gently into the box again. The turtle drew in its feet then, and its head stretched up a little and it looked straight at him. Victor smiled. Why hadn't his mother told him she'd brought him a present? A live turtle. Victor's eyes glazed with anticipation as he thought of taking the turtle down, maybe with a leash around its neck, to show the fellow who'd laughed at his short pants. He might change his mind about being friends with him, if he found he owned a turtle.

'Hey, Mama! Mama!' Victor yelled at the bathroom door. 'You brought me a tur-rtle?'

'A what?' The water shut off.

'A turtle! In the kitchen!' Victor had been jumping up and down in the hall. He stopped.

His mother had hesitated, too. The water came on again, and she said in a shrill tone, 'C'est une terrapène! Pour un ragoût!'

Victor understood, and a small chill went over him because his mother had spoken in French. His mother addressed him in French when she was giving an order that had to be obeyed, or when she anticipated resistance from him. So the terrapin was for a stew. Victor nodded to himself with a stunned resignation, and went back to the kitchen. For a stew. Well, the terrapin was not long for this world, as they say. What did a terrapin like to eat? Lettuce? Raw bacon? Boiled potato? Victor peered into the refrigerator.

He held a piece of lettuce near the terrapin's horny mouth. The terrapin did not open its mouth, but it looked at him. Victor held the lettuce near the two little dots of its nostrils, but if the terrapin smelled it, it showed no interest. Victor looked under the sink and pulled out a large wash pan. He put two inches of water into it. Then he gently dumped the terrapin into the pan. The terrapin paddled for a few seconds, as if it had to swim, then finding that its stomach sat on the bottom of the pan, it stopped, and drew its feet in. Victor got down on his knees and studied the terrapin's face. Its upper lip overhung the lower, giving it a rather stubborn and unfriendly expression, but its eyes – they were bright and shining. Victor smiled when he looked hard at them.

'Okay, monsieur terrapène,' he said, 'just tell me what you'd like to eat and we'll get it for you! – Maybe some tuna?'

They had had tuna fish salad yesterday for dinner, and there was a small bowl of it left over. Victor got a little chunk of it in his fingers and presented it to the terrapin. The terrapin was not interested. Victor looked around the kitchen, wondering, then seeing the sunlight on the floor of the living-room, he picked up the pan and carried it to the living-room and set it down so the sunlight would fall on the terrapin's back. All turtles liked sunlight, Victor thought. He lay down on the floor on his side, propped up on an elbow. The terrapin stared at him for a moment, then very slowly and with an air of forethought and caution, put out its legs and advanced, found the circular boundary of the pan, and moved to the right, half its body out of the shallow water. It wanted out, and Victor took it in one hand, by the sides, and said:

'You can come out and have a little walk.'

He smiled as the terrapin started to disappear under the sofa. He caught it easily, because it moved so slowly. When he put it down on the carpet, it was quite still, as if it had withdrawn a little to think what it should do next, where it should go. It was a brownish green. Looking at it, Victor thought of river bottoms, of river water flowing. Or maybe oceans. Where did terrapins come from? He jumped up and went to the dictionary on the bookshelf. The dictionary had a picture of a terrapin, but it was a dull, black and white drawing, not so pretty as the live one. He learned nothing except that the name was of Algonquian origin, that the terrapin lived in fresh or brackish water, and that it was edible. Edible. Well, that was bad luck, Victor thought. But he was not going to eat any terrapène tonight. It would be all for his mother, that ragoût, and even if she slapped him and made him learn an extra two or three poems, he would not eat any terrapin tonight.

His mother came out of the bathroom. 'What are you doing there? – Veector?'

Victor put the dictionary back on the shelf. His mother had seen the pan. 'I'm looking at the terrapin,' he said, then realised the terrapin had disappeared. He got down on hands and knees and looked under the sofa.

'Don't put him on the furniture. He makes spots,' said his mother. She was standing in the foyer, rubbing her hair vigorously with a towel.

Victor found the terrapin between the wastebasket and the wall. He put him back in the pan.

'Have you changed your shirt?' asked his mother.

Victor changed his shirt, and then at his mother's order sat down on the sofa with *A Child's Garden of Verses* and tackled another poem, a brand new one for Mrs Badzerkian. He learned two lines at a time, reading it aloud in a soft voice to himself, then repeating it, then putting two, four and six lines together, until he had the whole thing. He recited it to the terrapin. Then Victor asked his mother if he could play with the terrapin in the bathtub.

'No! And get your shirt all splashed?'

'I can put on my other shirt.'

'No! It's nearly four o'clock now. Get that pan out of the living-room!'

Victor carried the pan back to the kitchen. His mother took the terrapin quite fearlessly out of the pan, put it back into the white paper box, closed its lid, and stuck the box in the refrigerator. Victor jumped a little as the refrigerator door slammed. It would be awfully cold in there for the terrapin. But then, he supposed, fresh or brackish water was cold now and then, too.

'Veector, cut the lemon,' said his mother. She was preparing the big round tray with cups and saucers. The water was boiling in the kettle.

Mrs Badzerkian was prompt as usual, and his mother poured the tea as soon as she had deposited her coat and pocketbook on the foyer chair and sat down. Mrs Badzerkian smelled of cloves. She had a small, straight mouth and a thin moustache on her upper lip which fascinated Victor, as he had never seen one on a woman before, not one at such short range, anyway. He never had mentioned Mrs Badzerkian's moustache to his mother, knowing it was considered ugly, but in a strange way, her moustache was the thing he liked best about her. The rest of her was dull, uninteresting, and vaguely unfriendly. She always pretended to listen carefully to his poetry recitals, but he felt that she fidgeted, thought of other things while he spoke, and was glad when it was over. Today, Victor recited very well and without any hesitation, standing in the middle of the living-room floor and facing the two women, who were then having their second cups of tea.

'Très bien,' said his mother. 'Now you may have a cookie.'

Victor chose from the plate a small round cookie with a drop of orange goo in its centre. He kept his knees close together when he sat down. He always felt Mrs Badzerkian looked at his knees and with distaste. He often wished she would make some remark to his mother about his being old enough for long pants, but she never had, at least not within his hearing. Victor learned from his mother's conversation with Mrs Badzerkian that the Lorentzes were coming for dinner tomorrow evening. It was probably for them that the terrapin stew was going to be made. Victor was glad that he would have the terrapin one more day to play with. Tomorrow morning, he thought, he would ask his mother if he could take the terrapin down on the sidewalk for a while, either on a leash or in the paper box, if his mother insisted.

'—like a chi-ild!' his mother was saying, laughing, with a glance at him, and Mrs Badzerkian smiled shrewdly at him with her small, tight mouth.

Victor had been excused, and was sitting across the room with a book on the studio couch. His mother was telling Mrs Badzerkian how he had played with the terrapin. Victor frowned down at his book, pretending not to hear. His mother did not like him to open his mouth to her or her guests once he had been excused. But now she was calling him her 'lee-tle ba-aby Veec-tor . . .'

He stood up with his finger in the place in his book. 'I don't see why it's childish to look at a terrapin!' he said, flushing with sudden anger. 'They are very interesting animals, they—'

His mother interrupted him with a laugh, but at once the laugh disappeared and she said sternly, 'Veector, I thought I had excused you. Isn't that correct?'

He hesitated, seeing in a flash the scene that was going to take place when Mrs Badzerkian had left. 'Yes, Mama. I'm sorry,' he said. Then he sat down and bent over his book again.

Twenty minutes later, Mrs Badzerkian left. His mother scolded him for being rude, but it was not a five- or ten-minute scolding of the kind he had expected. It lasted hardly two minutes. She had forgotten to buy heavy cream, and she wanted Victor to go downstairs and get some. Victor put on his grey woollen jacket and went out. He always felt embarrassed and conspicuous in the jacket, because it came just a little bit below his short pants, and he looked as if he had nothing on underneath the coat.

Victor looked around for Frank on the sidewalk, but he didn't see him. He crossed Third Avenue and went to a delicatessen in the big building that he could see from the living-room window. On his way back, he saw Frank walking along the sidewalk, bouncing a ball. Now Victor went right up to him.

'Hey,' Victor said. 'I've got a terrapin upstairs.'

'A what?' Frank caught the ball and stopped.

'A terrapin. You know, like a turtle. I'll bring him down tomorrow morning and show you, if you're around. He's pretty big.'

'Yeah? – Why don't you bring him down now?'

'Because we're gonna eat now,' said Victor. 'See you.' He went into his building. He felt he had achieved something. Frank had looked really interested. Victor wished he could bring the terrapin down now, but his mother never liked him to go out after dark, and it was practically dark now.

When Victor got upstairs, his mother was still in the kitchen. Eggs were boiling and she had put a big pot of water on a back burner. 'You took him out again!' Victor said, seeing the terrapin's box on the counter.

'Yes, I prepare the stew tonight,' said his mother. 'That is why I need the cream.'

Victor looked at her. 'You're going to – You have to kill it tonight?'

'Yes, my little one. Tonight.' She jiggled the pot of eggs.

'Mama, can I take him downstairs to show Frank?' Victor asked quickly. 'Just for five minutes, Mama. Frank's down there now.'

'Who is Frank?'

'He's that fellow you asked me about today. The blond fellow we always see. Please, Mama.'

His mother's black eyebrows frowned. 'Take the terrapène downstairs? Certainly not. Don't be absurd, my baby! The terrapène is not a toy!'

Victor tried to think of some other lever of persuasion. He had not removed his coat. 'You wanted me to get acquainted with Frank—'

'Yes. What has that got to do with a terrapin?'

The water on the back burner began to boil.

'You see, I promised him I'd—' Victor watched his mother lift the terrapin from the box, and as she dropped it into the boiling water, his mouth fell open. '*Mama!*'

'What is this? What is this noise?'

Victor, open-mouthed, stared at the terrapin whose legs were now racing against the steep sides of the pot. The terrapin's mouth opened, its eyes looked directly at Victor for an instant, its head arched back in torture, the open mouth sank beneath the seething water – and that was the end. Victor blinked. It was dead. He came closer, saw the four legs and the tail stretched out in the water, its head. He looked at his mother.

She was drying her hands on a towel. She glanced at him, then said, 'Ugh!' She smelled her hands, then hung the towel back.

'Did you have to kill him like that?'

'How else? The same way you kill a lobster. Don't you know that? It doesn't hurt them.'

He stared at her. When she started to touch him, he stepped back. He thought of the terrapin's wide open mouth, and his eyes suddenly flooded with tears. Maybe the terrapin had been screaming and it hadn't been heard over the bubbling of the water. The terrapin had looked at him, wanting him to pull him out, and he hadn't moved to help him. His mother had tricked him, done it so fast, he couldn't save him. He stepped back again. 'No, don't touch me!'

His mother slapped his face, hard and quickly.

Victor set his jaw. Then he about-faced and went to the closet and threw his jacket onto a hanger and hung it up. He went into the living-room and fell down on the sofa. He was not crying now, but his mouth opened against the sofa pillow. Then he remembered the terrapin's mouth and he closed his lips. The terrapin had suffered, otherwise it would not have moved its legs so terribly fast to get out. Then he wept, soundlessly as the terrapin, his mouth open. He put both hands over his face, so as not to wet the sofa. After a long while, he got up. In the kitchen, his mother was humming, and every few minutes he heard her quick, firm steps as she went about her work. Victor had set his teeth again. He walked slowly to the kitchen doorway.

The terrapin was out on the wooden chopping board, and his mother, after a glance at him, still humming, took a knife and bore down on its blade, cutting off the terrapin's little nails. Victor half closed his eyes, but he watched steadily. The nails, with bits of skin attached to them, his mother scooped off the board into her palm and dumped into the garbage bag. Then she turned the terrapin onto its back and with the same sharp, pointed knife, she began to cut away the pale bottom shell. The terrapin's neck was bent sideways. Victor wanted to look away, but still he stared. Now the terrapin's insides were all exposed, red and white and greenish. Victor did not listen to what his mother was saying, about cooking terrapins in Europe, before he was born. Her voice was gentle and soothing, not at all like what she was doing.

'All right, don't look at me like that!' she suddenly threw at him, stomping her foot. 'What's the matter with you? Are you crazy? Yes, I think so! You are seeck, you know that?'

Victor could not touch any of his supper, and his mother could not force him to, even though she shook him by the shoulders and threatened to slap him. They had creamed chipped beef on toast. Victor did not say a word. He felt very remote from his mother, even when she screamed right into his face. He felt very odd, the way he did sometimes when he was sick at his stomach, but he was not sick at his stomach. When they went to bed, he felt afraid of the dark. He saw the terrapin's face very large, its mouth open, its eyes wide and full of pain. Victor wished he could walk out the window and float, go anywhere he wanted to, disappear, yet be everywhere. He imagined his mother's hands on his shoulders, jerking him back, if he tried to step out the window. He hated his mother.

He got up and went quietly into the kitchen. The kitchen was absolutely dark, as there was no window, but he put his hand accurately on the knife rack and felt gently for the knife he wanted. He thought of the terrapin, in little pieces now, all mixed up in the sauce of cream and egg yolks and sherry in the pot in the refrigerator.

His mother's cry was not silent; it seemed to tear his ears off. His second blow was in her body, and then he stabbed her throat again.

Only tiredness made him stop, and by then people were trying to bump the door in. Victor at last walked to the door, pulled the chain bolt back, and opened it for them.

He was taken to a large, old building full of nurses and doctors. Victor was very quiet and did everything he was asked to do, and answered the questions they put to him, but only those questions, and since they didn't ask him anything about a terrapin, he did not bring it up.

Daphne du Maurier

Not after Midnight

I am a schoolmaster by profession. Or was. I handed in my resignation
to the Head before the end of the summer term in order to forestall inevitable dismissal. The reason I gave was true enough – ill-health, caused
by a wretched bug picked up on holiday in Crete, which might necessitate a stay in hospital of several weeks, various injections, etc. I did not
specify the nature of the bug. He knew, though, and so did the rest of
the staff. And the boys. My complaint is universal, and has been so
through the ages, an excuse for jest and hilarious laughter from earliest
times, until one of us oversteps the mark and becomes a menace to
society. Then we are given the boot. The passer-by averts his gaze, and
we are left to crawl out of the ditch alone, or stay there and die.

If I am bitter, it is because the bug I caught was picked up in all
innocence. Fellow-sufferers of my complaint can plead predisposition,
poor heredity, family trouble, excess of the good life, and, throwing
themselves on a psychoanalyst's couch, spill out the rotten beans within
and so effect a cure. I can do none of this. The doctor to whom I endeavoured to explain what had happened listened with a superior smile,
and then murmured something about emotionally destructive identifica-
tion coupled with repressed guilt, and put me on a course of pills. They
might have helped me if I had taken them. Instead I threw them down
the drain and became more deeply imbued with the poison that seeped
through me, made worse of course by the fatal recognition of my condition by the youngsters I had believed to be my friends, who nudged
one another when I came into class, or, with stifled laughter, bent their
loathsome little heads over their desks – until the moment arrived when
I knew I could not continue, and took the decision to knock on the
headmaster's door.

Well, that's over, done with, finished. Before I take myself to hospital or alternatively, blot out memory, which is a second possibility, I want to establish what happened in the first place. So that, whatever becomes of me, this paper will be found, and the reader can make up his mind whether, as the doctor suggested, some want of inner balance made me an easy victim of superstitious fear, or whether, as I myself believe, my downfall was caused by an age-old magic, insidious, evil, its origins lost in the dawn of history. Suffice to say that he who first made the magic deemed himself immortal, and with unholy joy infected others, sowing in his heirs, throughout the world and down the centuries, the seeds of self-destruction.

To return to the present. The time was April, the Easter holidays. I had been to Greece twice before, but never Crete. I taught classics to the boys at the preparatory school, but my reason for visiting Crete was not to explore the sites of Knossos or Phaestus but to indulge a personal hobby. I have a minor talent for painting in oils, and this I find all-absorbing, whether on free days or in the school holidays. My work has been praised by one or two friends in the art world, and my ambition was to collect enough paintings to give a small exhibition. Even if none of them sold, the holding of a private show would be a happy achievement.

Here, briefly, a word about my personal life. I am a bachelor. Age forty-nine. Parents dead. Educated at Sherborne and Brasenose, Oxford. Profession, as you already know, schoolmaster. I play cricket and golf, badminton, and rather poor bridge. Interests, apart from teaching, art, as I have already said, and occasional travel, when I can afford it. Vices, up to the present, literally none. Which is not being self-complacent, but the truth is that my life has been uneventful by any standard. Nor has this bothered me. I am probably a dull man. Emotionally I have had no complications. I was engaged to a pretty girl, a neighbour, when I was twenty-five, but she married somebody else. It hurt at the time, but the wound healed in less than a year. One fault, if fault it is, I have always had, which perhaps accounts for my hitherto monotonous life. This is an aversion to becoming involved with people. Friends I possess, but at a distance. Once involved, trouble occurs, and too often disaster follows.

I set out for Crete in the Easter holidays with no encumbrance but a fair-sized suitcase and my painting gear. A travel agent had recommended a hotel overlooking the Gulf of Mirabello on the eastern coast, after I had told him I was not interested in archaeological sights but wanted to paint. I was shown a brochure which seemed to meet my requirements. A pleasantly situated hotel close to the sea, and chalets by the water's edge where one slept and breakfasted. Clientele well-to-do, and although I count myself no snob I cannot abide paper-bags and orange-peel. A couple of pictures painted the previous winter – a view of St Paul's Cathedral under snow, and another one of Hampstead Heath, both sold to an obliging female cousin – would pay for my journey, and I permitted myself an added indulgence, though it was really a necessity the hiring of a small Volkswagen on arrival at the airport of Herakleion.

The flight, with an overnight stop in Athens, was pleasant and un-eventful, the forty-odd miles' drive to my destination somewhat tedious, for being a cautious driver I took it slowly, and the twisting road, once I reached the hills, was decidedly hazardous. Cars passed me, or swerved towards me, hooting loudly. Also, it was very hot, and I was hungry. The sight of the blue Gulf of Mirabello and the splendid mountains to the east acted as a spur to sagging spirits, and once I arrived at the hotel, set delightfully in its own grounds, with lunch served to me on the terrace despite the fact that it was after two in the afternoon – how different from England! – I was ready to relax and inspect my quarters. Disappoint-ment followed. The young porter led me down a garden path flagged on either side by brilliant geraniums to a small chalet bunched in by neigh-bours on either side, and overlooking, not the sea, but a part of the garden laid out for mini-golf. My next-door neighbours, an obviously English mother and her brood, smiled in welcome from their balcony, which was strewn with bathing-suits drying under the sun. Two middle-aged men were engaged in mini-golf. I might have been in Maidenhead.

'This won't do,' I said, turning to my escort. 'I have come here to paint. I must have a view of the sea.'

He shrugged his shoulders, murmuring something about the chalets beside the sea being fully booked. It was not his fault, of course. I made him trek back to the hotel with me, and addressed myself to the clerk at the reception desk.

'There has been some mistake,' I said. 'I asked for a chalet overlooking the sea, and privacy above all.'

The clerk smiled, apologised, began ruffling papers, and the inevitable excuses followed. My travel agent had not specifically booked a chalet overlooking the sea. These were in great demand, and were fully booked. Perhaps in a few days there might be some cancellations, one never could tell, in the meantime he was sure I should be very comfortable in the chalet that had been allotted to me. All the furnishings were the same, my breakfast would be served me, etc., etc.

I was adamant. I would not be fobbed off with the English family and the mini-golf. Now having flown all those miles at considerable expense. I was bored by the whole affair, tired, and considerably annoyed.

'I am a professor of art,' I told the clerk. 'I have been commissioned to execute several paintings while I am here, and it is essential that I should have a view of the sea, and neighbours who will not disturb me.'

(My passport states my occupation as professor. It sounds better than schoolmaster or teacher, and usually arouses respect in the attitude of reception clerks.)

The clerk seemed genuinely concerned, and repeated his apologies. He turned again to the sheaf of papers before him. Exasperated, I strode across the spacious hall and looked out of the door on to the terrace down to the sea.

'I cannot believe,' I said, 'that every chalet is taken. It's too early in the season. In summer, perhaps, but not now.' I waved my hand towards the western side of the bay. 'That group over there,' I said, 'down by the water's edge. Do you mean to say every single one of them is booked?'

He shook his head and smiled. 'We do not usually open those until mid-season. Also, they are more expensive. They have a bath as well as a shower.'

'How much more expensive?' I hedged.

He told me. I made a quick calculation. I could afford it if I cut down on all other expenses. Had my evening meal in the hotel, and went without lunch. No extras in the bar, not even mineral water.

'Then there is no problem,' I said grandly. 'I will willingly pay more for privacy. And, if you have no objection, I should like to choose the chalet which would suit me best. I'll walk down to the sea now and then come back for the key, and your porter can bring my things.'

I gave him no time to reply, but turned on my heel and went out on to the terrace. It paid to be firm. One moment's hesitation, and he would have fobbed me off with the stuffy chalet overlooking the mini-golf. I could imagine the consequences. The chattering children on the balcony next door, the possibly effusive mother, and the middle-aged golfers urging me to have a game. I could not have borne it.

I walked down through the garden to the sea, and as I did so my spirits rose. For this, of course, was what had been so highly coloured on the agent's brochure, and why I had flown so many miles. No exaggeration, either. Little white-washed dwellings, discreetly set apart from one another, the sea washing the rocks below. There was a beach, from which doubtless people swam in high season, but no one was on it now, and, even if they should intrude, the chalets themselves were well to the left, inviolate, private. I peered at each in turn, mounting the steps, standing on the balconies. The clerk must have been telling the truth about none of them being let before full season, for all had their windows shuttered. All except one. And directly I mounted the steps and stood on the balcony I knew that it must be mine. This was the view I had imagined. The sea beneath me, lapping the rocks, the bay widening into the gulf itself, and beyond the mountains. It was perfect. The chalets to the east of the hotel, which was out of sight anyway, could be ignored.

NOT AFTER MIDNIGHT

One, close to a neck of land, stood on its own like a solitary outpost with a landing-stage below, but this would only enhance my picture when I came to paint it. The rest were mercifully hidden by rising ground. I turned, and looked through the open windows to the bedroom within. Plain white-washed walls, a stone floor, a comfortable divan bed with rugs upon it. A bedside table with a lamp and telephone. But for these last it had all the simplicity of a monk's cell, and I wished for nothing more.

I wondered why this chalet, and none of its neighbours, was un-shuttered, and stepping inside I heard from the bathroom beyond the sound of running water. Not further disappointment, and the place booked after all? I put my head round the open door, and saw that it was a little Greek maid swabbing the bathroom floor. She seemed startled at the sight of me. I gestured, pointed, said, 'Is this taken?' She did not understand, but answered me in Greek. Then she seized her cloth and pail and, plainly terrified, brushed past me to the entrance, leaving her work unfinished.

I went back into the bedroom and picked up the telephone, and in a moment the smooth voice of the reception clerk answered.

'This is Mr Grey,' I told him, 'Mr Timothy Grey. I was speaking to you just now about changing my chalet.'

'Yes, Mr Grey,' he replied. He sounded puzzled. 'Where are you speaking from?'

'Hold on a minute,' I said. I put down the receiver and crossed the room to the balcony. The number was above the open door. It was 62. I went back to the telephone. 'I'm speaking from the chalet I have chosen,' I said. 'It happened to be open – one of the maids was cleaning the bathroom, and I'm afraid I scared her away. This chalet is ideal for my purpose. It is No. 62.'

He did not answer immediately, and when he did he sounded doubt-ful. 'No. 62?' he repeated. And then, after a moment's hesitation, 'I am not sure if it is available.'

'Oh, for heaven's sake . . .' I began, exasperated, and I heard him talking in Greek to someone beside him at the desk. The conversation went back and forth between them; there was obviously some difficulty, which made me all the more determined.

'Are you there?' I said. 'What's the trouble?'

More hurried whispers, and then he spoke to me again. 'No trouble, Mr Grey. It is just that we feel you might be more comfortable in No. 57, which is a little nearer to the hotel.'

'Nonsense,' I said, 'I prefer the view from here. What's wrong with No. 62? Doesn't the plumbing work?'

'Certainly the plumbing works,' he assured me, while the whispering started again. 'There is nothing wrong with the chalet. If you have made up your mind I will send down the porter with your luggage and the key.'

He rang off, possibly to finish his discussion with the whisperer at his side. Perhaps they were going to step up the price. If they did, I would have further argument. The chalet was no different from its empty neighbours, but the position, dead centre to sea and mountains, was all I had dreamed and more. I stood on the balcony, looking out across the sea and smiling. What a prospect, what a place! I would unpack and have a swim, then put up my easel and do a preliminary sketch before starting serious work in the morning.

I heard voices, and saw the little maid staring at me from half-way up the garden path, cloth and pail still in hand. Then, as the young porter advanced downhill bearing my suitcase and painting gear, she must have realised that I was to be the occupant of No. 62, for she stopped him mid-way, and another whispered conversation began. I had evidently caused a break in the smooth routine of the hotel. A few moments later they climbed the steps to the chalet together, the porter to set down my luggage, the maid doubtless to finish her swabbing of the bathroom floor. I had no desire to be on awkward terms with either of them, and, smiling cheerfully, placed coins in both their hands.

'Lovely view,' I said loudly, pointing to the sea. 'Must go for a swim,' and made breast-stroke gestures to show my intent, hoping for the ready smile of the native Greek, usually so responsive to goodwill.

The porter evaded my eyes and bowed gravely, accepting my tip nevertheless. As for the little maid, distress was evident in her face, and forgetting about the bathroom floor she hurried after him. I could hear them talking as they walked up the garden path together to the hotel.

Well, it was not my problem. Staff and management must sort out their troubles between them. I had got what I wanted, and that was all that concerned me. I unpacked and made myself at home. Then slipping on bathing trunks, I stepped down to the ledge of rock beneath the balcony, and ventured a toe into the water. It was surprisingly chill, despite the hot sun that had been upon it all day. Never mind. I must prove my mettle, if only to myself. I took the plunge and gasped, and being a cautious swimmer at the best of times, especially in strange waters, swam round and round in circles rather like a sea-lion pup in a zoological pool.

Refreshing, undoubtedly, but a few minutes were enough, and as I climbed out again on to the rocks I saw that the porter and the little maid had been watching me all the time from behind a flowering bush up the garden path. I hoped I had not lost face. And anyway, why the interest? People must be swimming every day from the other chalets.

NOT AFTER MIDNIGHT

The bathing-suits on the various balconies proved it. I dried myself on the balcony, observing how the sun, now in the western sky behind my chalet, made dappled patterns on the water. Fishing-boats were return-ing to the little harbour port a few miles distant, the chug-chug engines making a pleasing sound.

I dressed, taking the precaution of having a hot bath, for the first swim of the year is always numbing, and then set up my easel and instantly became absorbed. This was why I was here, and nothing else mattered. I worked for a couple of hours, and as the light failed, and the colour of the sea deepened and the mountains turned a softer purple blue, I rejoiced to think that tomorrow I should be able to seize this after-glow in paint instead of charcoal, and the picture would begin to come alive.

It was time to stop. I stacked away my gear, and before changing for dinner and drawing the shutters – doubtless there were mosquitoes, and I had no wish to be bitten – watched a motor-boat with gently purring engine draw in softly to the eastward point with the landing-stage away to my right. Three people aboard, fishing enthusiasts no doubt, a woman amongst them. One man, a local, probably, made the boat fast, and stepped on the landing-stage to help the woman ashore. Then all three stared in my direction, and the second man, who had been standing in the stern, put up a pair of binoculars and fixed them on me. He held them steady for several minutes, focusing, no doubt, on every detail of my personal appearance, which is unremarkable enough, heaven knows, and would have continued had I not suddenly become annoyed and withdrawn into the bedroom, slamming the shutters to. How rude can you get, I asked myself? Then I remembered that these western chalets were all unoccupied, and mine was the first to open for the season. Possibly this was the reason for the intense interest I appeared to cause, beginning with members of the hotel staff and now embracing guests as well. Interest would soon fade. I was neither pop star nor millionaire. And my painting efforts, however pleasing to myself, were hardly like to draw a fascinated crowd.

Punctually at eight o'clock I walked up the garden path to the hotel and presented myself in the dining-room for dinner. It was moderately full and I was allotted a table in the corner, suitable to my single status, close to the screen dividing the service entrance from the kitchens. Never mind. I preferred this position to the centre of the room, where I could tell immediately that the hotel clientele were on what my mother used to describe as an 'all fellows to football' basis.

I enjoyed my dinner, treated myself – despite my de luxe chalet – to half a bottle of domestica wine, and was peeling an orange when an almighty crash from the far end of the room disturbed us all. Waiters hurried to the scene. Heads turned, mine amongst them. A hoarse American voice, hailing from the deep South, called loudly, 'For God's sake clear up this Goddarn mess!' It came from a square-shouldered man of middle age, whose face was so swollen and blistered by exposure to the sun that he looked as if he had been stung by a million bees. His eyes were sunk into his head, which was bald on top, with a grizzled thatch on either side, and the pink crown had the appearance of being tightly stretched, like the skin of a sausage about to burst. A pair of enormous ears the size of clams gave further distortion to his appearance, while a drooping wisp of moustache did nothing to hide the protruding underlip, thick as blubber and about as moist. I have seldom set eyes on a more unattractive individual. A woman, I suppose his wife, sat beside him, stiff and bolt upright, apparently unmoved by the debris on the floor, which appeared to consist chiefly of bottles. She was likewise middle-aged, with a mop of tow-coloured hair turning white, and a face as sunburnt as her husband's, but mahogany brown instead of red.

'Let's get the hell out of here and go to the bar!' The hoarse strains echoed across the room. The guests at the other tables turned discreetly back to their own dinner, and I must have been the only one to watch the unsteady exit of the bee-stung spouse and his wife – I could see the deaf-aid in her ear, hence possibly her husband's rasping tones – as he literally rolled past me to the bar, a lurching vessel in the wake of his steady partner. I silently commended the efficiency of the hotel staff, who made short work of clearing the wreckage.

The dining-room emptied. 'Coffee in the bar, sir,' murmured my waiter. Fearing a crush and loud chatter I hesitated before entering, for the camaraderie of hotel bars has always bored me, but I hate going without my after-dinner coffee. I need not have worried. The bar was empty, apart from the white-coated server behind the bar, and the American sitting at a table with his wife. Neither of them was speaking. There were three empty beer bottles already on the table before him. Greek music played softly from some lair behind the bar. I sat myself on a stool and ordered coffee.

The bar-tender, who spoke excellent English, asked if I had spent a pleasant day. I told him yes, I had had a good flight, found the road from Herakleion hazardous, and my first swim rather cold. He explained that it was still early in the year. 'In any case,' I told him, 'I have come to paint, and swimming will take second place. I have a chalet right on the water-front, No. 62, and the view from the balcony is perfect.'

Rather odd. He was polishing a glass, and his expression changed. He seemed about to say something, then evidently thought better of it, and continued with his work.

'Turn that God-damn record off!'

The hoarse, imperious summons filled the empty room. The bar-man made at once for the gramophone in the corner and adjusted the switch. A moment later the summons rang forth again.

'Bring me another bottle of beer!'

Now, had I been the bar-tender I should have turned to the man and, like a parent to a child, insisted that he said please. Instead, the brute was promptly served, and I was just downing my coffee when the voice from the table echoed through the room once more.

'Hi, you there, chalet No. 62. You're not superstitious?'

I turned on my stool. He was staring at me, glass in hand. His wife looked straight in front of her. Perhaps she had removed her deaf-aid. Remembering the maxim that one must humour madmen and drunks, I replied courteously enough.

'No,' I said, 'I'm not superstitious. Should I be?'

He began to laugh, his scarlet face creasing into a hundred lines.

'Well, God darn it, I would be,' he answered. 'The fellow from that chalet was drowned only two weeks ago. Missing for two days, and then his body brought up in a net by a local fisherman, half-eaten by octo-puses.'

He began to shake with laughter, slapping his hand on his knee. I turned away in disgust, and raised my eyebrows in enquiry to the bar-tender.

'An unfortunate accident,' he murmured. 'Mr Gordon such a nice gentleman. Interested in archaeology. It was very warm the night he disappeared, and he must have gone swimming after dinner. Of course the police were called. We were all most distressed here at the hotel. You understand, sir, we don't talk about it much. It would be bad for business. But I do assure you that bathing is perfectly safe. This is the first accident we have ever had.'

'Oh, quite,' I said.

Nevertheless . . . It was rather off-putting, the fact that the poor chap had been the last to use my chalet. However, it was not as though he had died in the bed. And I was not superstitious. I understood now why the staff had been reluctant to let the chalet again so soon, and why the little maid had been upset.

'I tell you one thing,' boomed the revolting voice. 'Don't go swimming after midnight, or the octopuses will get you too.' This statement was followed by another outburst of laughter. Then he said, 'Come on, Maud. We're for bed,' and he noisily shoved the table aside.

I breathed more easily when the room was clear and we were alone.

'What an impossible man,' I said. 'Can't the management get rid of him?'

The bar-tender shrugged. 'Business is business. What can they do?

The Stolls have plenty of money. This is their second season here, and they arrived when we opened in March. They seem to be crazy about the place. It's only this year, though, that Mr Stoll has become such a heavy drinker. He'll kill himself if he goes on at this rate. It's always like this, night after night. Yet his day must be healthy enough. Out at sea fishing from early morning until sundown.'

'I dare say more bottles go over the side than he catches fish,' I observed.

'Could be,' the bar-tender agreed. 'He never brings his fish to the hotel. The boatman takes them home, I dare say.'

'I feel sorry for the wife.'

The bar-tender shrugged. 'She's the one with the money,' he replied sotto voce, for a couple of guests had just entered the bar, 'and I don't think Mr Stoll has it all his own way. Being deaf may be convenient to her at times. But she never leaves his side, I'll grant her that. Goes fishing with him every day. Yes, gentlemen, what can I get for you?'

He turned to his new customers, and I made my escape. The cliché that it takes all sorts to make a world passed through my head. Thank heaven it was not my world, and Mr Stoll and his deaf wife could burn themselves black under the sun all day at sea as far as I was concerned, and break beer bottles every evening into the bargain. In any event, they were not neighbours. No. 62 may have had the unfortunate victim of a drowning accident for its last occupant, but at least this had insured privacy for its present tenant.

I walked down the garden path to my abode. It was a clear starlit night. The air was balmy, and sweet with the scent of the flowering shrubs planted thickly in the red earth. Standing on my balcony I looked out across the sea towards the distant shrouded mountains and the harbour lights from the little fishing port. To my right winked the lights of the other chalets, giving a pleasing, almost fairy impression, like a clever backcloth on a stage. Truly a wonderful spot, and I blessed the travel agent who had recommended it.

I let myself in through my shuttered doorway and turned on the bed-side lamp. The room looked welcoming and snug; I could not have been better housed. I undressed, and before getting into bed remembered I had left a book I wanted to glance at on the balcony. I opened the shutters and picked it up from the deck-chair where I had thrown it, and once more, before turning in, glanced out at the open sea. Most of the fairy lights had been extinguished, but the chalet that stood on its own on the extreme point still had its light burning on the balcony. The boat, tied to the landing-stage, bore a riding-light. Seconds later I saw something moving close to my rocks. It was the snorkel of an underwater swimmer. I could see the narrow pipe, like a minute periscope, move steadily across the still, dark surface of the sea. Then it disappeared to the far left out of sight. I drew my shutters and went inside.

I don't know why it was, but the sight of that moving object was somehow disconcerting. It made me think of the unfortunate man who had been drowned during a midnight swim. My predecessor. He too, perhaps, had sallied forth one balmy evening such as this, intent on under-water exploration, and by so doing lost his life. One would imagine the unhappy accident would scare off other hotel visitors from swimming alone at night. I made a firm decision never to bathe except in broad daylight, and – chicken-hearted, maybe – well within my depth.

I read a few pages of my book, then, feeling ready for sleep, turned to switch out my light. In doing so I clumsily bumped the telephone, which fell to the floor. I bent over, picked it up, luckily no damage done, and saw that the small drawer that was part of the fixture had fallen open. It contained a scrap of paper, or rather card, with the name Charles Gordon upon it, and an address in Bloomsbury. Surely Gordon had been the name of my predecessor? The little maid, when she cleaned the room, had not thought to open the drawer. I turned the card over. There was something scrawled on the other side, the words 'Not after midnight'. And then, maybe as an afterthought, the figure 38. I replaced the card in the drawer and switched off the light. Perhaps I was over-tired after the journey, but it was well past two before I finally got off to sleep. I lay awake for no rhyme or reason, listening to the water lapping against the rocks beneath my balcony.

I painted solidly for three days, never quitting my chalet except for the morning swim and my evening meal at the hotel. Nobody bothered me. An obliging waiter brought my breakfast, from which I saved rolls for midday lunch, the little maid made my bed and did her chores without disturbing me, and when I had finished my impressionistic scene on the afternoon of the third day I felt quite certain it was one of the best things I had ever done. It would take pride of place in the planned exhibition of my work. Well satisfied, I could now relax, and I determined to explore along the coast the following day, and discover another view to whip up inspiration. The weather was glorious. Warm as a good English June. And the best thing about the whole site was the total absence of neighbours. The other guests kept to their side of the domain, and, apart from bows and nods from adjoining tables as one entered the dining-room for dinner, no one attempted to strike up acquaintance. I took good care to drink my coffee in the bar before the obnoxious Mr Stoll had left his table.

I realised now that it was his boat which lay anchored off the point.

They were away too early in the morning for me to watch their departure, but I used to spot them returning in the late afternoon; his square, hunched form was easily recognisable, and the occasional hoarse shout to the man in charge of the boat as they came to the landing-stage. Theirs, too, was the isolated chalet on the point, and I wondered if he had picked it purposely in order to soak himself into oblivion out of sight and earshot of his nearest neighbours. Well, good luck to him, as long as he did not obtrude his offensive presence upon me.

Feeling the need of gentle exercise, I decided to spend the rest of the afternoon taking a stroll to the eastern side of the hotel grounds. Once again I congratulated myself on having escaped the cluster of chalets in this populated quarter. Mini-golf and tennis were in full swing, and the little beach was crowded with sprawling bodies on every available patch of sand. But soon the murmur of the world was behind me, and screened and safe behind the flowering shrubs I found myself on the point to the landing-stage. The boat was not yet at its mooring, nor even in sight out in the gulf.

A sudden temptation to peep at the unpleasant Mr Stoll's chalet swept upon me. I crept up the little path, feeling as furtive as a burglar on the prowl, and stared up at the shuttered windows. It was no different from its fellows, or mine for that matter, except for a tell-tale heap of bottles lying in a corner of the balcony. Brute . . . Then something else caught my eye. A pair of frog-feet, and a snorkel. Surely, with all that liquor inside him, he did not venture his carcass under water? Perhaps he sent the local Greek whom he employed as crew to seek for crabs. I remembered the snorkel on my first evening, close to the rocks, and the riding-light in the boat.

I moved away, for I thought I could hear someone coming down the path and did not want to be caught prying, but before doing so I glanced up at the number of the chalet. It was 38. The figure had no particular significance for me then, but later on, changing for dinner, I picked up the tie-pin I had placed on my bedside table, and on sudden impulse opened the drawer beneath the telephone to look at my predecessor's card again. Yes, I thought so. The scrawled figure *was* 38. Pure coincidence, of course, and yet . . . 'Not after midnight'. The words suddenly had meaning. Stoll had warned me about swimming late on my first evening. Had he warned Gordon too? And Gordon had jotted down the warning on his card with Stoll's chalet-number underneath? It made sense, but obviously poor Gordon had disregarded the advice. And so, apparently, did one of the occupants of Chalet 38.

I finished changing, and instead of replacing the card in the telephone drawer put it in my wallet. I had an uneasy feeling that it was my duty to hand it in to the reception desk in case it threw any light on my unfortunate predecessor's demise. I toyed with the thought through dinner, but came to no decision. The point was, I might become involved, questioned by the police. And as far as I knew the case was closed. There was little point in my suddenly coming forward with a calling-card lying forgotten in a drawer that probably had no significance at all.

It so happened that the people seated to the right of me in the dining-room appeared to have gone, and the Stoll's table in the corner now came into view without my being obliged to turn my head. I could watch them without making it too obvious, and I was struck by the fact that he never once addressed a word to her. They made an odd contrast. She stiff as a ramrod, prim-looking, austere, forking her food to her mouth like a Sunday school teacher on an outing, and he, more scarlet than ever, like a great swollen sausage, pushing aside most of what the waiter placed before him after the first mouthful, and reaching out a pudgy, hairy hand to an ever-emptying glass.

I finished my dinner and went through to the bar to drink my coffee. I was early, and had the place to myself. The bar-tender and I exchanged the usual pleasantries and then, after an allusion to the weather, I jerked my head in the direction of the dining-room.

'I noticed our friend Mr Stoll and his lady spent the whole day at sea as usual,' I said.

The bar-tender shrugged. 'Day after day, it never varies,' he replied, 'and mostly in the same direction, westward out of the bay into the gulf. It can be squally, too, at times, but they don't seem to care.'

'I don't know how she puts up with him,' I said. 'I watched them at dinner – he didn't speak to her at all. I wonder what the other guests make of him.'

'They keep well clear, sir. You saw how it was for yourself. If he ever does open his mouth it's only to be rude. And the same goes for the staff. The girls dare not go in to clean the chalet until he's out of the way. And the smell!' He grimaced, and leant forward confidentially. 'The girls say he brews his own beer. He lights the fire in the chimney, and has a pot standing, filled with rotting grain, like some sort of pig swill! Oh, yes, he drinks it right enough. Imagine the state of his liver, after what he consumes at dinner and afterwards here in the bar!'

'I suppose,' I said, 'that's why he keeps his balcony light on so late at night. Drinking pig-swill until the small hours. Tell me, which of the hotel visitors is it who goes under-water swimming?'

The bar-tender looked surprised. 'No one, to my knowledge. Not since the accident, anyway. Poor Mr Gordon liked a night swim, at least so we supposed. He was one of the few visitors who ever talked to Mr Stoll, now I think of it. They had quite a conversation here one evening in the bar.'

'Indeed?'

'Not about swimming, though, or fishing either. They were discussing antiquities. There's a fine little museum here in the village, you know, but it's closed at present for repairs. Mr Gordon had some connection with the British Museum in London.'

'I wouldn't have thought,' I said, 'that would interest friend Stoll.'

'Ah,' said the bar-tender, 'you'd be surprised. Mr Stoll is no fool. Last year he and Mrs Stoll used to take the car and visit all the famous sites, Knossos, Mallia, and other places not so well known. This year it's quite different. It's the boat and fishing every day.'

'And Mr Gordon,' I pursued, 'did he ever go fishing with them?'

'No, sir. Not to my knowledge. He hired a car, like you, and explored the district. He was writing a book, he told me, on archaeological finds in eastern Crete, and their connection with Greek mythology.'

'Mythology?'

'Yes, I understood him to tell Mr Stoll it was mythology, but it was all above my head, you can imagine, nor did I hear much of the conversation – we were busy that evening in the bar. Mr Gordon was a quiet sort of gentleman, rather after your own style, if you'll excuse me, sir, seeming very interested in what they were discussing, all to do with the old gods. They were at it for over an hour.'

H'm . . . I thought of the card in my wallet. Should I, or should I not, hand it over to the reception clerk at the desk? I said goodnight to the bar-tender and went back through the dining-room to the hall. The Stolls had just left their table and were walking ahead of me. I hung back until the way was clear, surprised that they had turned their backs upon the bar and were making for the hall. I stood by the rack of post-cards, to give myself an excuse for loitering, but out of their range of vision, and watched Mrs Stoll take her coat from a hook in the lobby near the entrance, while her unpleasant husband visited the cloakroom, and then the pair of them walked out of the front door which led direct to the car park. They must be going for a drive. With Stoll at the wheel in his condition?

I hesitated. The reception clerk was on the telephone. It wasn't the moment to hand over the card. Some impulse, like that of a small boy playing detective, made me walk to my own car, and when Stoll's tail-light was out of sight – he was driving a Mercedes – I followed in his wake. There was only the one road, and he was heading east towards the village and the harbour lights. I lost him, inevitably, on reaching the little port, for, instinctively making for the quayside opposite what appeared to be a main café, I thought he must have done the same. I parked the Volkswagen, and looked around me. No sign of the Mercedes. Just a sprinkling of other tourists like myself, and local inhabitants, strolling, or drinking in front of the café.

Oh well, forget it, I'd sit and enjoy the scene, have a lemonade. I must have sat there for over half-an-hour, savouring what is known as 'local colour', amused by the passing crowd, Greek families taking the air, pretty, self-conscious girls eyeing the youths, who appeared to stick together, practising a form of segregation, a bearded Orthodox priest who smoked incessantly at the table next to me, playing some game of dice with a couple of very old men, and of course the familiar bunch of hippies from my own country, considerably longer-haired than anybody else, dirtier, and making far more noise. When they switched on a transistor and squatted on the cobbled stones behind me, I felt it was time to move.

I paid for my lemonade, and strolled to the end of the quay and back – the line upon line of fishing-boats would be colourful by day, and possibly the scene worth painting – and then I crossed the street, my eye caught by a glint of water inland, where a side-road appeared to end in a cul-de-sac. This must be the feature mentioned in the guidebook as the Bottomless Pool, much frequented and photographed by tourists in the high season. It was larger than I had expected, quite a sizeable lake, the water full of scum and floating debris, and I did not envy those who had the temerity to use the diving-board at the further end of it by day.

Then I saw the Mercedes. It was drawn up opposite a dimly-lit café, and there was no mistaking the hunched figure at the table, beer-bottles before him, the upright lady at his side, but to my surprise, and I may add disgust, he was not imbibing alone but appeared to be sharing his after-dinner carousal with a crowd of raucous fishermen at the adjoining table.

Clamour and laughter filled the air. They were evidently mocking him, Greek courtesy forgotten in their cups, while strains of song burst forth from some younger member of the clan, and suddenly he put out his hand and swept the empty bottles from his table on to the pavement, with the inevitable crash of broken glass and the accompanying cheers of his companions. I expected the local police to appear at any moment and break up the party, but there was no sign of authority. I did not care what happened to Stoll – a night in gaol might sober him up – but it was a wretched business for his wife. However, it wasn't my affair, and I was turning to go back to the quay when he staggered to his feet, applauded by the fishermen, and, lifting the remaining bottle from his table, swung it over his head. Then, with amazing dexterity for one in his condition, he pitched it like a discus-thrower into the lake. It must have missed me by a couple of feet, and he saw me duck. This was too much. I advanced towards him, livid with rage.

'What the hell are you playing at?' I shouted.

He stood before me, swaying on his feet. The laughter from the café ceased as his cronies watched with interest. I expected a flood of abuse, but Stoll's swollen face creased into a grin, and he lurched forward and patted me on the arm.

'Know something?' he said. 'If you hadn't been in the way I could have lobbed it into the centre of the God-damn pool. Which is more than any of those fellows could. Not a pure-blooded Cretan amongst them. They're all of them God-damn Turks.'

I tried to shake him off, but he clung on to me with the effusive affection of the habitual drunkard who has suddenly found, or imagines he has found, a life-long friend.

'You're from the hotel, aren't you?' he hiccoughed. 'Don't deny it, buddy boy, I've got a good eye for faces. You're the fellow who paints all day on his God-damn porch. Well, I admire you for it. Know a bit about art myself. I might even buy your picture.'

His bonhomie was offensive, his attempt at patronage intolerable.

'I'm sorry,' I said stiffly, 'the picture is not for sale.'

'Oh, come off it,' he retorted. 'You artists are all the same. Play hard to get until someone offers 'em a darn good price. Take Charlie Gordon now . . .' He broke off, peering slyly into my face. 'Hang on, you didn't meet Charlie Gordon, did you?'

'No,' I said shortly, 'he was before my time.'

'That's right, that's right,' he agreed, 'poor fellow's dead. Drowned in the bay there right under your rocks. At least, that's where they found him.'

His slit eyes were practically closed in his swollen face, but I knew he was watching for my reaction.

'Yes,' I said, 'so I understand. He wasn't an artist.'

'An artist?' Stoll repeated the word after me, then burst into a guffaw of laughter. 'No, he was a connoisseur, and I guess that means the same God-damn thing to a chap like me. Charlie Gordon, connoisseur. Well, it didn't do him much good in the end, did it?'

'No,' I said, 'obviously not.'

He was making an effort to pull himself together, and still rocking on his feet he fumbled for a packet of cigarettes and a lighter. He lit one for himself, then offered me the packet. I shook my head, telling him I did not smoke. Then, greatly daring, I observed, 'I don't drink either.'

'Good for you,' he answered astonishingly, 'neither do I. The beer they sell you here is all piss anyway, and the wine is poison.' He looked over his shoulder to the group at the café and with a conspiratorial wink dragged me to the wall beside the pool.

'I told you all those bastards are Turks, and so they are,' he said, 'wine-drinking, coffee-drinking Turks. They haven't brewed the right stuff here for over five thousand years. They knew how to do it then.'

I remembered what the bar-tender had told me about the pig-swill in his chalet. 'Is that so?' I enquired.

He winked again, and then his slit eyes widened, and I noticed that they were naturally bulbous and protuberant, a discoloured muddy brown with the whites red-flecked. 'Know something?' he whispered hoarsely. 'The scholars have got it all wrong. It was beer the Cretans drank here in the mountains, brewed from spruce and ivy, long before wine. Wine was discovered centuries later by the God-damn Greeks.'

He steadied himself, one hand on the wall, the other on my arm. Then he leant forward and was sick into the pool. I was very nearly sick myself.

'That's better,' he said, 'gets rid of the poison. Doesn't do to have poison in the system. Tell you what, we'll go back to the hotel and you shall come along and have a night-cap at our chalet. I've taken a fancy to you, Mr What's-your-Name. You've got the right ideas. Don't drink, don't smoke, and you paint pictures. What's your job?'

It was impossible to shake myself clear, and I was forced to let him tow me across the road. Luckily the group at the café had now dispersed, disappointed, no doubt, because we had not come to blows, and Mrs Stoll had climbed into the Mercedes and was sitting in the passenger seat in front.

'Don't take any notice of her,' he said. 'She's stone-deaf unless you bawl at her. Plenty of room at the back.'

'Thank you,' I said, 'I've got my own car on the quay.'

'Suit yourself,' he answered. 'Well, come on, tell me, Mr Artist, what's your job? An academician?'

I could have left it at that, but some pompous strain in me made me tell the truth, in the foolish hope that he would then consider me too dull to cultivate.

'I'm a teacher,' I said, 'in a boys' preparatory school.'

He stopped in his tracks, his wet mouth open wide in a delighted grin. 'Oh, my God,' he shouted, 'that's rich, that's really rich. A God-damn tutor, a nurse to babes and sucklings. You're one of us, my buddy, you're one of us. And you've the nerve to tell me you've never brewed spruce and ivy!'

He was raving mad, of course, but at least this sudden burst of hilarity had made him free my arm, and he went on ahead of me to his car, shaking his head from side to side, his legs bearing his cumbersome body in a curious jog-trot, one-two . . . one-two . . . like a clumsy horse.

I watched him climb into the car beside his wife, and then I moved swiftly away to make for the safety of the quayside, but he had turned his car with surprising agility, and had caught up with me before I reached the corner of the street. He thrust his head out of the window, smiling still.

'Come and call on us, Mr Tutor, any time you like. You'll always find a welcome. Tell him so, Maud. Can't you see the fellow's shy?'

His bawling word of command echoed through the street. Strolling passers-by looked in our direction. The stiff, impassive face of Mrs Stoll peered over her husband's shoulder. She seemed quite unperturbed, as if nothing was wrong, as if driving in a foreign village beside a drunken husband was the most usual pastime in the world.

'Good evening,' she said in a voice without any expression. 'Pleased to meet you, Mr Tutor. Do call on us. Not after midnight. Chalet 38 . . .'

Stoll waved his hand, and the car went roaring up the street to cover the few kilometres to the hotel, while I followed behind, telling myself that this was one invitation I should never accept if my life depended on it.

It would not be true to say the encounter cast a blight on my holiday and put me off the place. A half-truth, perhaps. I was angry and disgusted, but only with the Stolls. I awoke refreshed after a good night's sleep to another brilliant day, and nothing seems so bad in the morning. I had only the one problem, which was to avoid Stoll and his equally half-witted wife. They were out in their boat all day, so this was easy. By dining early I could escape them in the dining-room. They never walked about the grounds, and meeting them face to face in the garden was not likely. If I happened to be on my balcony when they returned from fishing in the evening, and he turned his field-glasses in my direction, I would promptly disappear inside my chalet. In any event, with luck, he might have forgotten my existence, or, if that was too much to hope for, the memory of our evening's conversation might have passed from his mind. The episode had been unpleasant, even, in a curious sense, alarming, but I was not going to let it spoil the days that remained to me.

The boat had left its landing-stage by the time I came on to my balcony to have breakfast, and I intended to carry out my plan of exploring the coast with my painting gear, and, once absorbed in my hobby, could forget all about them. And I would not pass on to the management poor Gordon's scribbled card. I guessed now what had happened. The poor devil, without realising where his conversation in the bar would lead him, had been intrigued by Stoll's smattering of mythology and nonsense about ancient Crete, and, as an archaeologist, had thought further conversation might prove fruitful. He had accepted an invitation to visit Chalet 38 – the uncanny similarity of the words on the card and those spoken by Mrs Stoll still haunted me – though why he had chosen to swim across the bay instead of walking the slightly longer way by the rock path was a mystery. A touch of bravado, perhaps? Who knows? Once in Stoll's chalet he had been induced, poor victim, to drink some of the hell-brew offered by his host, which must have knocked all sense and judgement out of him, and when he took to the water once again, the carousal over, what followed was bound to happen. I only hoped he had been too far gone to panic, and sank instantly. Stoll had never come forward to give the facts, and that was that. Indeed, my theory of what had happened was based on intuition alone, coincidental scraps that appeared to fit, and prejudice. It was time to dismiss the whole thing from my mind and concentrate on the day ahead.

Or rather, days. My exploration along the coast westward, in the opposite direction from the harbour, proved even more successful than I had anticipated. I followed the winding road to the left of the hotel, and having climbed for several kilometres descended again from the hills to sea level, where the land on my right suddenly flattened out to what seemed to be a great stretch of dried marsh, sun-baked, putty-coloured, the dazzling blue sea affording a splendid contrast as it lapped the stretch of land on either side. Driving closer I saw that it was not marsh at all but salt flats, with narrow causeways running between them, the flats themselves contained by walls intersected by dykes to allow the sea-water to drain, leaving the salt behind. Here and there were the ruins of abandoned windmills, their rounded walls like castle keeps, and in a rough patch of ground a few hundred yards distant, and close to the sea, was a small church – I could see the minute cross on the roof shining in the sun. Then the salt flats ended abruptly, and the land rose once more to form the long, narrow isthmus of Spinalongha beyond.

I bumped the Volkswagen down to the track leading to the flats. The place was quite deserted. This, I decided, after viewing the scene from every angle, would be my pitch for the next few days. The ruined church in the foreground, the abandoned windmills beyond, the salt-flats on the left, and blue water rippling to the shore of the isthmus on my right.

I set up my easel, planted my battered felt hat on my head, and forgot everything but the scene before me. Those three days on the salt-flats – for I repeated the expedition on successive days – were the high-spot of my holiday. Solitude and peace were absolute. I never saw a single soul. The occasional car wound its way along the coast road in the distance and then vanished. I broke off for sandwiches and lemonade, which I'd brought with me, and then, when the sun was hottest, rested by the ruined windmill. I returned to the hotel in the cool of the evening, had an early dinner, and then retired to my chalet to read until bedtime. A hermit at his prayers could not have wished for greater seclusion.

The fourth day, having completed two separate paintings from different angles, yet loath to leave my chosen territory, which had now become a personal stamping ground, I stacked my gear in the car and struck off on foot to the rising terrain of the isthmus, with the idea of choosing a new site for the following day. Height might give an added advantage. I toiled up the hill, fanning myself with my hat, for it was extremely hot, and was surprised when I reached the summit to find how narrow was the isthmus, no more than a long neck of land with the sea immediately below me. Not the calm water that washed the salt-flats I had left behind, but the curling crests of the outer gulf itself, whipped by a northerly wind that nearly blew my hat out of my hand. A genius might have caught those varying shades on canvas – turquoise blending into Aegean blue with wine-deep shadows beneath – but not an amateur like myself. Besides, I could hardly stand upright. Canvas and easel would have instantly blown away.

I climbed downwards towards a clump of broom affording shelter, where I could rest for a few minutes and watch that curling sea, and it was then that I saw the boat. It was moored close to a small inlet where the land curved and the water was comparatively smooth. There was no mistaking the craft: it was theirs all right. The Greek they employed as crew was seated in the bows, with a fishing-line over the side, but from his lounging attitude the fishing did not seem to be serious, and I judged he was taking his siesta. He was the only occupant of the boat. I glanced directly beneath me to the spit of sand along the shore, and saw there was a rough stone building, more or less ruined, built against the cliff-face, possibly used at one time as a shelter for sheep or goats. There was a haversack and a picnic-basket lying by the entrance, and a coat. The Stolls must have landed earlier from the boat, although nosing the bows of the craft on to the shore must have been hazardous in the running sea, and were now taking their ease out of the wind. Perhaps Stoll was even brewing his peculiar mixture of spruce and ivy, with some goat-dung added for good measure, and this lonely spot on the isthmus of Spina-longha was his 'still'.

Suddenly the fellow in the boat sat up, and winding in his line he moved to the stern and stood there, watching the water. I saw something move, a form beneath the surface, and then the form itself emerged, head-piece, goggles, rubber suiting, aqualung and all. Then it was hidden from me by the Greek bending to assist the swimmer to remove his top-gear, and my attention was diverted to the ruined shelter on the shore. Something was standing in the entrance. I say 'something' because doubtless owing to a trick of light, it had at first the shaggy appearance of a colt standing on its hind legs. Legs and even rump were covered with hair, and then I realised that it was Stoll himself, naked, his arms and chest as hairy as the rest of him. Only his swollen scarlet face pro-claimed him for the man he was, with the enormous ears like saucers standing out from either side of his bald head. I had never in all my life seen a more revolting sight. He came out into the sunlight and looked towards the boat, and then, as if well pleased with himself and his world, strutted forward, pacing up and down the spit of sand before the ruined shelter with that curious movement I had noticed earlier in the village, not the rolling gait of a drunken man but a stumping jog-trot, arms akimbo, his chest thrust forward, his backside prominent behind him.

The swimmer, having discarded goggles and aqualung, was now coming into the beach with long leisurely strokes, still wearing flippers – I could see them thrash the surface like a giant fish. Then, flippers cast aside on the sand, the swimmer stood up, and despite the disguise of the rubber suiting I saw, with astonishment, that it was Mrs Stoll. She was carrying some sort of bag around her neck, and advancing up the sand to meet her strutting husband she lifted it over her head and gave it to him. I did not hear them exchange a word, and they went together to the hut and disappeared inside. As for the Greek, he had gone once more to the bows of the boat to resume his idle fishing.

I lay down under cover of the broom and waited. I would give them twenty minutes, half-an-hour, perhaps, then make my way back to the salt-flats and my car. As it happened, I did not have to wait so long. It was barely ten minutes before I heard a shout below me on the beach, and peering through the broom I saw that they were both standing on the spit of sand, haversack, picnic-basket and flippers in hand. The Greek was already starting the engine, and immediately afterwards he began to pull up the anchor. Then he steered the boat slowly inshore, touching it beside a ledge of rock where the Stolls had installed themselves. They climbed aboard, and in another moment the Greek had turned the boat, and it was heading out to sea away from the sheltered inlet and into the gulf. Then it rounded the point and was out of my sight.

Curiosity was too much for me. I scrambled down the cliff on to the sand and made straight for the ruined shelter. As I thought, it had been a haven for goats; the muddied floor reeked, and their droppings were everywhere. In a corner, though, a clearing had been made, and there were planks of wood, forming a sort of shelf. The inevitable beer bottles were stacked beneath this, but whether they had contained the local brew or Stoll's own poison I could not tell. The shelf itself held odds and ends of pottery, as though someone had been digging in a rubbish dump and had turned up broken pieces of discarded household junk. There was no earth upon them, though; they were scaled with barnacles, and some of them were damp, and it suddenly occurred to me that these were what archaeologists call 'sherds', and came from the sea-bed. Mrs Stoll had been exploring, and exploring underwater, whether for shells or for

something of greater interest I did not know, and these pieces scattered
here were throwouts, of no use, and so neither she nor her husband had
bothered to remove them. I am no judge of these things, and after looking
around me, and finding nothing of further interest, I left the ruin.

The move was a fatal one. As I turned to climb the cliff I heard the
throb of an engine, and the boat had returned once more, to cruise along
the shore, so I judged from its position. All three heads were turned in my
direction, and inevitably the squat figure in the stern had field-glasses
poised. He would have no difficulty, I feared, in distinguishing who it was
that had just left the ruined shelter and was struggling up the cliff to the
hill above.

I did not look back but went on climbing, my hat pulled down well
over my brows in the vain hope that it might afford some sort of concealment. After all, I might have been any tourist who had happened to be
at that particular spot at that particular time. Nevertheless, I feared
recognition was inevitable. I tramped back to the car on the salt-flats,
tired, breathless and thoroughly irritated. I wished I had never decided
to explore the further side of the peninsula. The Stolls would think I had
been spying upon them, which indeed was true. My pleasure in the day
was spoilt. I decided to pack it in and go back to the hotel. Luck was
against me, though, for I had hardly turned on to the track leading from
the marsh to the road when I noticed that one of my tyres was flat. By
the time I had put on the spare wheel – for I am ham-fisted at all
mechanical jobs – forty minutes had gone by.

My disgruntled mood did not improve, when at last I reached the
hotel, to see that the Stolls had beaten me to it. Their boat was already
at its moorings beside the landing-stage, and Stoll himself was sitting on
his balcony with field-glasses trained upon my chalet. I stumped up the
steps feeling as self-conscious as someone under a television camera and
went into my quarters, closing the shutters behind me. I was taking a
bath when the telephone rang.

'Yes?' Towel round the middle, dripping hands, it could not have rung
at a more inconvenient moment.

'That you, Mr Tutor-boy?'

The rasping, wheezing voice was unmistakable. He did not sound
drunk, though.

'This is Timothy Grey,' I replied stiffly.

'Grey or Black, it's all the same to me,' he said. His tone was unpleasant, hostile. 'You were out on Spinalongha this afternoon. Correct?'

'I was walking on the peninsula,' I told him. 'I don't know why you
should be interested.'

'Oh, stuff it up,' he answered, 'you can't fool me. You're just like the
other fellow. You're nothing but a God-damn spy. Well, let me tell you

this. The wreck was clean-picked centuries ago.'

'I don't know what you're talking about,' I said. 'What wreck?'

There was a moment's pause. He muttered something under his breath, whether to himself or to his wife I could not tell, but when he resumed speaking his tone had moderated, something of pseudo-bonhomie had returned.

'O.K. . . . O.K. Tutor-boy,' he said. 'We won't argue the point. Let us say you and I share an interest. Schoolmasters, university professors, college lecturers, we're all alike under the skin, and above it too sometimes.' His low chuckle was offensive. 'Don't panic, I won't give you away,' he continued. 'I've taken a fancy to you, as I told you the other night. You want something for your God-darn school museum, correct? Something you can show the pretty lads and your colleagues, too? Fine. Agreed. I've got just the thing. You call round here later this evening, and I'll make you a present of it. I don't want your God-damn money . . .' He broke off, chuckling again, and Mrs Stoll must have made some remark, for he added, 'That's right, that's right. We'll have a cosy little party, just the three of us. My wife's taken quite a fancy to you too.'

The towel round my middle slipped to the floor, leaving me naked. I felt vulnerable for no reason at all. And the patronising, insinuating voice infuriated me.

'Mr Stoll,' I said, 'I'm not a collector for schools, colleges or museums. I'm not interested in antiquities. I am here on holiday to paint, for my own pleasure, and quite frankly I have no intention of calling upon you or any other visitor at the hotel. Good evening.'

I slammed down the receiver and went back to the bathroom. Infernal impudence. Loathsome man. The question was, would he now leave me alone, or would he keep his glasses trained on my balcony until he saw me go up to the hotel for dinner, and then follow me, wife in tow, to the dining-room? Surely he would not dare to resume the conversation in front of waiters and guests? If I guessed his intentions aright, he wanted to buy my silence by fobbing me off with some gift. Those day-long fishing expeditions of his were a mask for under-water exploration – hence his allusion to a wreck – during which he hoped to find, possibly had found already, objects of value that he intended to smuggle out of Crete. Doubtless he had succeeded in doing this the preceding year, and the Greek boatman would be well paid for holding his tongue.

This season, however, it had not worked to plan. My unfortunate predecessor at Chalet 62, Charles Gordon, himself an expert in antiquities, had grown suspicious. Stoll's allusion, 'You're like the other fellow. Nothing but a God-damn spy', made this plain. What if Gordon had received an invitation to Chalet 38, not to drink the spurious beer but to inspect Stoll's collection and be offered a bribe for keeping silent? Had he refused, threatening to expose Stoll? Did he really drown accidentally, or had Stoll's wife followed him down into the water in her rubber-suit and mask and flippers, and then, once beneath the surface . . .?

My imagination was running away with me. I had no proof of anything. All I knew was that nothing in the world would get me to Stoll's chalet, and indeed, if he attempted to pester me again, I should have to tell the whole story to the management.

I changed for dinner, then opened my shutters a fraction and stood behind them, looking out towards his chalet. The light shone on his balcony, for it was already dusk, but he himself had disappeared. I stepped outside, locking the shutters behind me, and walked up the garden to the hotel.

I was just about to go through to the reception hall from the terrace when I saw Stoll and his wife sitting on a couple of chairs inside, guarding, as it were, the passage-way to lounge and dining-room. If I wanted to eat I had to pass them. Right, I thought. You can sit there all evening waiting. I went back along the terrace, and circling the hotel by the kitchens went round to the car park and got into the Volkswagen. I would have dinner down in the village, and damn the extra expense. I drove off in a fury, found an obscure taverna well away from the harbour itself, and instead of the three-course hotel meal I had been looking forward to on my en pension terms – for I was hungry after my day in the open and meagre sandwiches on the salt-flats – I was obliged to content myself with an omelette, an orange and a cup of coffee.

It was after ten when I arrived back in the hotel. I parked the car, and skirting the kitchen quarters once again made my way furtively down the garden path to my chalet, letting myself in through the shutters like a thief. The light was still shining on Stoll's balcony, and by this time he was doubtless deep in his cups. If there was any trouble with him the next day I would definitely go to the management.

I undressed and lay reading in bed until after midnight, then, feeling sleepy, switched out my light and went across the room to open the shutters, for the air felt stuffy and close. I stood for a moment looking out across the bay. The chalet lights were all extinguished except for one. Stoll's of course. His balcony light cast a yellow streak on the water beside his landing-stage. The water rippled, yet there was no wind. Then I saw it. I mean, the snorkel. The little pipe was caught an instant in the yellow gleam, but before I lost it I knew that it was heading in a direct course for the rocks beneath my chalet. I waited. Nothing happened, there was no sound, no further ripple on the water. Perhaps she did this every evening. Perhaps it was routine, and while I was lying on my bed reading, oblivious of the world outside, she had been treading water close to the rocks. The thought was discomforting, to say the least of it, that regularly after midnight she left her besotted husband asleep over his hell-brew of spruce and ivy and came herself, his under-water-partner, in her black-seal rubber suit, her mask, her flippers, to spy upon Chalet 62. And on this night in particular, after the telephone conversation and my refusal to visit them, coupled with my new theory as to the fate of my predecessor, her presence in my immediate vicinity was more than ominous, it was threatening.

Suddenly, out of the dark stillness to my right, the snorkel-pipe was caught in a finger-thread of light from my own balcony. Now it was almost immediately below me. I panicked, turned, and fled inside my room, closing the shutters fast. I switched off the balcony light and stood against the wall between my bedroom and bathroom, listening. The soft air filtered through the shutters beside me. It seemed an eternity before the sound I expected, dreaded, came to my ears. A kind of swishing movement from the balcony, a fumbling of hands, and heavy breathing. I could see nothing from where I stood against the wall, but the sounds came through the chinks in the shutters, and I knew she was there. I knew she was holding on to the hasp, and the water was dripping from the skin-tight rubber suit, and that even if I shouted, 'What do you want?' she would not hear. No deaf-aids under water, no mechanical device for soundless ears. Whatever she did by night must be done by sight, by touch.

She began to rattle on the shutters. I took no notice. She rattled again. Then she found the bell, and the shrill summons pierced the air above my head with all the intensity of a dentist's drill upon a nerve. She rang three times. Then silence. No more rattling of the shutters. No more breathing. She might yet be crouching on the balcony, the water dripping from the black rubber suit, waiting for me to lose patience, to emerge.

I crept away from the wall and sat down on the bed. There was not a sound from the balcony. Boldly I switched on my bedside light, half expecting the rattling of the shutters to begin again, or the sharp ping of the bell. Nothing happened, though. I looked at my watch. It was half-past twelve. I sat there hunched on my bed, my mind that had been so heavy with sleep now horribly awake, full of foreboding, my dread of that sleek black figure increasing minute by minute so that all sense and reason seemed to desert me, and my dread was the more intense and irrational because the figure in the rubber suit was female. What did she want?

I sat there for an hour or more until reason took possession once again. She must have gone. I got up from the bed and went to the shutters and listened. There wasn't a sound. Only the lapping of water beneath the rocks. Gently, very gently, I opened the hasp and peered through the shutters. Nobody was there. I opened them wider and stepped on to the balcony. I looked out across the bay, and there was no longer any light shining from the balcony of No. 38. The little pool of water beneath my shutters was evidence enough of the figure that had stood there an hour ago, and the wet footmarks leading down the steps towards the rocks suggested she had gone the way she came. I breathed a sigh of relief. Now I could sleep in peace.

It was only then that I saw the object at my feet, lying close to the shutter's base. I bent and picked it up. It was a small package, wrapped in some sort of waterproof cloth. I took it inside and examined it, sitting on the bed. Foolish suspicions of plastic bombs came to my mind, but surely a journey underwater would neutralise the lethal effect? The package was sewn about with twine, criss-crossed. It felt quite light. I remembered the old classical proverb, 'Beware of the Greeks when they bear gifts'. But the Stolls were not Greeks, and, whatever lost Atlantis they might have plundered, explosives did not form part of the treasure-trove of that vanished continent.

I cut the twine with a pair of nail-scissors, then unthreaded it piece by piece and unfolded the waterproof wrapping. A layer of finely-meshed net concealed the object within, and, this unravelled, the final token itself lay in my open hand. It was a small jug, reddish in colour, with a handle on either side for safe holding. I had seen this sort of object before – the correct name, I believe, is rhyton – displayed behind glass cases in museums. The body of the jug had been shaped cunningly and brilliantly into a man's face, with upstanding ears like scallop-shells, while pro-truding eyes and bulbous nose stood out above the leering, open mouth, the moustache drooping to the rounded beard that formed the base. At the top, between the handles, were the upright figures of three strutting men, their faces similar to that upon the jug, but here human resemblance ended, for they had neither hands nor feet but hooves, and from each of their hairy rumps extended a horse's tail.

I turned the object over. The same face leered at me from the other side. The same three figures strutted at the top. There was no crack, no blemish that I could see, except a faint mark on the lip. I looked inside the jug and saw a note lying on the bottom. The opening was too small for my hand, so I shook it out. The note was a plain white card, with words typed upon it. It read: 'Silenos, earth-born satyr, half-horse, half-man, who, unable to distinguish truth from falsehood, reared Dionysus, god of intoxication, as a girl in a Cretan cave, then became his drunken tutor and companion.'

That was all. Nothing more. I put the note back inside the jug, and the jug on the table at the far end of the room. Even then the lewd mocking face leered back at me, and the three strutting figures of the horsemen stood out in bold relief across the top. I was too weary to wrap it up again. I covered it with my jacket and climbed back into bed. In the morning I would cope with the laborious task of packing it up and getting my waiter to take it across to Chalet 38. Stoll could keep his rhyton – heaven knew what the value might be – and good luck to him. I wanted no part of it.

Exhausted, I fell asleep, but, oh God, to no oblivion. The dreams which came, and from which I struggled to awaken, but in vain, belonged to some other unknown world horribly intermingled with my own. Term had started, but the school in which I taught was on a mountain top hemmed in by forest, though the school buildings were the same and the classroom was my own. My boys, all of them familiar faces, lads I knew, wore vine-leaves in their hair, and had a strange, unearthly beauty both endearing and corrupt. They ran towards me, smiling, and I put my arms about them, and the pleasure they gave me was insidious and sweet, never before experienced, never before imagined, the man who pranced in their midst and played with them was not myself, not the self I knew, but a demon shadow emerging from a jug, strutting in his conceit as Stoll had done upon the spit of sand at Spinalongha.

I awoke after what seemed like centuries of time, and indeed broad daylight seeped through the shutters, and it was a quarter to ten. My head was throbbing. I felt sick, exhausted. I rang for coffee, and looked out across the bay. The boat was at its moorings. The Stolls had not gone fishing. Usually they were away by nine. I took the jug from under my coat, and with fumbling hands began to wrap it up in the net and waterproof packing. I had made a botched job of it when the waiter came on to the balcony with my breakfast tray. He wished me good morning with his usual smile.

'I wonder,' I said, 'if you would do me a favour.'

'You are welcome, sir,' he replied.

'It concerns Mr Stoll,' I went on. 'I believe he has Chalet 38 across the bay. He usually goes fishing every day, but I see his boat is still at the landing-stage.'

'That is not surprising,' the waiter smiled. 'Mr and Mrs Stoll left this morning by car.'

'I see. Do you know when they will be back?'

'They will not be back, sir. They have left for good. They are driving to the airport en route for Athens. The boat is probably vacant now if you wish to hire it.'

He went down the steps into the garden, and the jar in its waterproof packing was still lying beside the breakfast tray.

The sun was already fierce upon my balcony. It was going to be a scorching day, too hot to paint. And anyway, I wasn't in the mood. The events of the night before had left me tired, jaded, with a curious sapped feeling due not so much to the intruder beyond my shutters as to those interminable dreams. I might be free of the Stolls themselves, but not of their legacy.

I unwrapped it once again and turned it over in my hands. The leering, mocking face repelled me; its resemblance to the human Stoll was not pure fancy but compelling, sinister, doubtless his very reason for palming it off on me – I remembered the chuckle down the telephone – and if he possessed treasures of equal value to this rhyton, or even greater, then one object the less would not bother him. He would have a problem getting them through Customs, especially in Athens. The penalties were enormous for this sort of thing. Doubtless he had his contacts, knew what to do.

I stared at the dancing figures near the top of the jar, and once more I was struck by their likeness to the strutting Stoll on the shore of Spinalongha, his naked, hairy form, his protruding rump. Part man, part horse, a satyr . . . 'Silenos, drunken tutor to the god Dionysus.'

The jar was horrible, evil. Small wonder that my dreams had been distorted, utterly foreign to my nature. But not perhaps to Stoll's? Could it be that he too had realised its bestiality, but not until too late? The bar-tender had told me that it was only this year he had gone to pieces, taken to drink. There must be some link between his alcoholism and the finding of the jar. One thing was very evident, I must get rid of it – but how? If I took it to the management questions would be asked. They might not believe my story about its being dumped on my balcony the night before; they might suspect that I had taken it from some archaeological site, and then had second thoughts about trying to smuggle it out of the country or dispose of it somewhere on the island. So what? Drive along the coast and chuck it away, a rhyton centuries old and possibly priceless?

I wrapped it carefully, put it in my jacket pocket and walked up the garden to the hotel. The bar was empty, the bar-tender behind his counter polishing glasses. I sat down on a stool in front of him and ordered a mineral water.

'No expedition today, sir?' he enquired.

'Not yet,' I said. 'I may go out later.'

'A cool dip in the sea and a siesta on the balcony,' he suggested, 'and by the way, sir, I have something for you.'

He bent down and brought out a small screw-topped bottle filled with what appeared to be bitter lemon.

'Left here last evening with Mr Stoll's compliments,' he said. 'He waited for you in the bar until nearly midnight, but you never came.

So I promised to hand it over when you did.'

I looked at it suspiciously. 'What is it?' I asked.

The bar-tender smiled. 'Some of his chalet home-brew,' he said. 'It's quite harmless, he gave me a bottle for myself and my wife. She says it's nothing but lemonade. The real smelling stuff must have been thrown away. Try it.' He had poured some into my mineral water before I could stop him.

Hesitant, wary, I dipped my finger into the glass and tasted it. It was like the barley-water my mother used to make when I was a child. And equally tasteless. And yet . . . it left a sort of aftermath on the palate and the tongue. Not as sweet as honey nor as sharp as grapes, but pleasant, like the smell of raisins under the sun, curiously blended with the ears of ripening corn.

'Oh well,' I said, 'here's to the improved health of Mr Stoll,' and I drank my medicine like a man.

'I know one thing,' said the bar-tender, 'I've lost my best customer. They were away early this morning.'

'Yes,' I said, 'so my waiter informed me.'

'The best thing Mrs Stoll could do would be to get him into hospital,' the bar-tender continued. 'Her husband's a sick man, and it's not just the drink.'

'What do you mean?'

He tapped his forehead. 'Something wrong up here,' he said. 'You could see for yourself how he acted. Something on his mind. Some sort of obsession. I rather doubt we shall see them again next year.'

I sipped my mineral water, which was undoubtedly improved by the barley taste.

'What was his profession?' I asked.

'Mr Stoll? Well, he told me he had been professor of classics in some American university, but you never could tell if he was speaking the truth or not. Mrs Stoll paid the bills here, hired the boatman, arranged everything. Though he swore at her in public he seemed to depend on her. I sometimes wondered, though . . .'

He broke off.

'Wondered what?' I enquired.

'Well . . . She had a lot to put up with. I've seen her look at him some-times, and it wasn't with love. Women of her age must seek some sort of satisfaction out of life. Perhaps she found it on the side while he indulged his passion for liquor and antiques. He had picked up quite a few items in Greece, and around the islands and here in Crete. It's not too difficult if you know the ropes.'

He winked. I nodded, and ordered another mineral water. The warm atmosphere in the bar had given me a thirst.

'Are there any lesser known sites along the coast?' I asked. 'I mean, places they might have gone ashore to from the boat?'

It may have been my fancy, but I thought he avoided my eye.

'I hardly know, sir,' he said. 'I dare say there are, but they would have custodians of some sort. I doubt if there are any places the authorities don't know about.'

'What about wrecks?' I pursued. 'Vessels that might have been sunk centuries ago, and are now lying on the sea bottom?'

He shrugged his shoulders. 'There are always local rumours,' he said casually, 'stories that get handed down through generations. But it's mostly superstition. I've never believed in them myself, and I don't know anybody with education who does.'

He was silent for a moment, polishing a glass. I wondered if I had said too much. 'We all know small objects are discovered from time to time,' he murmured, 'and they can be of great value. They get smuggled out of the country, or if too much risk is involved they can be disposed of locally to experts and a good price paid. I have a cousin in the village connected with the local museum. He owns the café opposite the Bottomless Pool. Mr Stoll used to patronise him. Papitos is the name. As a matter of fact, the boat hired by Mr Stoll belongs to my cousin; he lets it out on hire to the visitors here at the hotel.'

'I see.'

'But there . . . You are not a collector, sir, and you're not interested in antiques.'

'No,' I said, 'I am not a collector.'

I got up from the stool and bade him good morning. I wondered if the small package in my pocket made a bulge.

I went out of the bar and strolled on to the terrace. Nagging curiosity made me wander down to the landing-stage below the Stolls' chalet. The chalet itself had evidently been swept and tidied, the balcony cleared, the shutters closed. No trace remained of the last occupants. Before the day was over, in all probability, it would be opened for some English family who would strew the place with bathing-suits.

The boat was at its moorings, and the Greek hand was swabbing down the sides. I looked out across the bay to my own chalet on the opposite side and saw it, for the first time, from Stoll's viewpoint. As he stood there, peering through his field-glasses, it seemed clearer to me than ever before that he must have taken me for an interloper, a spy – possibly, even someone sent out from England to enquire into the true circumstances of Charles Gordon's death. Was the gift of the jar, the night before departure, a gesture of defiance? A bribe? Or a curse?

Then the Greek fellow on the boat stood up and faced towards me. It was not the regular boatman, but another one. I had not realised this before when his back was turned. The man who used to accompany the Stolls had been younger, dark, and this was an older chap altogether. I remembered what the bar-tender had told me about the boat belonging to his cousin, Papitos, who owned the café in the village by the Bottomless Pool.

'Excuse me,' I called, 'are you the owner of the boat?'

The man climbed on to the landing-stage and stood before me.

'Nicolai Papitos is my brother,' he said. 'You want to go for trip round the bay? Plenty good fish outside. No wind today. Sea very calm.'

'I don't want to fish,' I told him. 'I wouldn't mind an outing for an hour or so. How much does it cost?'

He gave me the sum in drachmae, and I did a quick reckoning and made it out to be not more than two pounds for the hour, though it would doubtless be double that sum to round the point and go along the coast as far as that spit of sand on the isthmus of Spinalongha. I took out my wallet to see if I had the necessary notes or whether I should have to return to the reception desk and cash a traveller's cheque.

'You charge to hotel,' he said quickly, evidently reading my thoughts. 'The cost go on your bill.'

This decided me. Damn it all, my extras had been moderate to date.

'Very well,' I said, 'I'll hire the boat for a couple of hours.'

It was a curious sensation to be chug-chugging across the bay as the Stolls had done so many times, the line of chalets in my wake, the harbour astern on my right and the blue waters of the open gulf ahead. I had no clear plan in mind. It was just that, for some inexplicable reason, I felt myself drawn towards that inlet near the shore where the boat had been anchored on the previous day. 'The wreck was picked clean centuries ago . . .' Those had been Stoll's words. Was he lying? Or could it be that day after day, through the past weeks, that particular spot had been his hunting-ground, and his wife, diving, had brought the dripping treasure from its sea-bed to his grasping hands? We rounded the point, and inevitably, away from the sheltering arm that had hitherto encompassed us, the breeze appeared to freshen, the boat became more lively as the bows struck the short curling seas.

The long isthmus of Spinalongha lay ahead of us to the left, and I had some difficulty in explaining to my helmsman that I did not want him to steer into the comparative tranquillity of the waters bordering the salt-flats, but to continue along the more exposed outward shores of the isthmus bordering the open sea.

'You want to fish?' he shouted above the roar of the engine. 'You find very good fish in there,' pointing to my flats of yesterday.

'No, no,' I shouted back, 'further on along the coast.'

He shrugged. He couldn't believe I had no desire to fish, and I wondered, when we reached our destination, what possible excuse I could make for heading the boat inshore and anchoring, unless – and this seemed plausible enough – I pleaded that the motion of the boat was proving too much for me.

The hills I had climbed yesterday swung into sight above the bows, and then, rounding a neck of land, the inlet itself, the ruined shepherd's hut close to the shore.

'In there,' I pointed. 'Anchor close to the shore.'

He stared at me, puzzled, and shook his head. 'No good,' he shouted, 'too many rocks.'

'Nonsense,' I yelled. 'I saw some people from the hotel anchored here yesterday.'

Suddenly he slowed the engine, so that my voice rang out foolishly on the air. The boat danced up and down in the troughs of the short seas.

'Not a good place to anchor,' he repeated doggedly. 'Wreck there, fouling the ground.'

So there was a wreck. . . . I felt a mounting excitement, and I was not to be put off.

'I don't know anything about that,' I replied, with equal determination, 'but this boat did anchor here, just by the inlet, I saw it myself.'

He muttered something to himself, and made the sign of the cross.

'And if I lose the anchor?' he said. 'What do I say to my brother Nicolai?'

He was nosing the boat gently, very gently, towards the inlet, and then, cursing under his breath, he went forward to the bows and threw the anchor overboard. He waited until it held, then returned and switched off the engine.

'If you want to go in close, you must take the dinghy,' he said sulkily. 'I blow it up for you, yes?'

He went forward once again, and dragged out one of those inflatable rubber affairs they use on air-sea rescue craft.

'Very well,' I said, 'I'll take the dinghy.'

In point of fact, it suited my purpose better. I could paddle close inshore, and would not have him breathing over my shoulder. At the same time, I couldn't forbear a slight prick to his pride.

'The man in charge of the boat yesterday anchored further in without mishap,' I told him.

My helmsman paused in the act of inflating the dinghy.

'If he like to risk my brother's boat that is his affair,' he said shortly. 'I have charge of it today. Other fellow not turn up for work this morning, so he lose his job. I do not want to lose mine.'

I made no reply. If the other fellow had lost his job it was probably because he had pocketed too many tips from Stoll.

The dinghy inflated and in the water, I climbed into it gingerly and began to paddle myself towards the shore. Luckily there was no run upon the spit of sand, and I was able to land successfully and pull the dinghy after me. I noticed that my helmsman was watching me with some interest from his safe anchorage, then, once he perceived that the dinghy was unlikely to come to harm, he turned his back and squatted in the bows of the boat, shoulders humped in protest, meditating no doubt, upon the folly of English visitors.

My reason for landing was that I wanted to judge, from the shore, the exact spot where the boat had anchored yesterday. It was as I thought. Perhaps a hundred yards to the left of where we had anchored today, and closer inshore. The sea was smooth enough, I could navigate it perfectly in the rubber dinghy. I glanced towards the shepherd's hut, and saw my footprints of the day before. There were other footprints too. Fresh ones. The sand in front of the hut had been disturbed. It was as though something had lain there, and then been dragged to the water's edge where I stood now. The goatherd himself perhaps, had visited the place with his flock earlier that morning.

I crossed over to the hut and looked inside. Curious . . . The little pile of rubble, odds and ends of pottery, had gone. The empty bottles still stood in the far corner, and three more had been added to their number, one of them half-full. It was warm inside the hut, and I was sweating. The sun had been beating down on my bare head for nearly an hour – like a fool I had left my hat back in the chalet, not having prepared myself for this expedition – and I was seized with an intolerable thirst. I had acted on impulse, and was paying for it now. It was, in retrospect, an idiotic thing to have done. I might become completely dehydrated, pass out with heat-stroke. The half-bottle of beer would be better than nothing.

I did not fancy drinking from it after the goatherd, if it was indeed he who had brought it here; these fellows were none too clean. Then I remembered the jar in my pocket. Well, it would at least serve a purpose. I pulled the package out of its wrappings and poured the beer into it. It was only after I had swallowed the first draught that I realised it wasn't beer at all. It was barley-water. It was the same home-brewed stuff that Stoll had left for me in the bar. Did the locals, then, drink it too? It was innocuous enough, I knew that; the bar-tender had tasted it himself, and so had his wife.

When I had finished the bottle I examined the jar once again. I don't know how it was, but somehow the leering face no longer seemed so lewd. It had a certain dignity that had escaped me before. The beard, for instance. The beard was shaped to perfection around the base – whoever had fashioned it was a master of his craft. I wondered whether

Socrates had looked thus when he strolled in the Athenian agora with his pupils and discoursed on life. He could have done. And his pupils may not necessarily have been the young men whom Plato said they were, but of a tenderer age, like my lads at school, like those youngsters of eleven and twelve who had smiled upon me in my dreams last night.

I felt the scalloped ears, the rounded nose, the full soft lips of the tutor Silenos upon the jar, the eyes no longer protruding but questioning, appealing, and even the naked horsemen on the top had grown in grace. It seemed to me now they were not strutting in conceit but dancing with linked hands, filled with a gay abandon, a pleasing, wanton joy. It must have been my fear of the midnight intruder that had made me look upon the jar with such distaste.

I put it back in my pocket, and walked out of the hut and down the spit of beach to the rubber dinghy. Supposing I went to the fellow Papitos who had connections with the local museum, and asked him to value the jar? Supposing it was worth hundreds, thousands, and he could dispose of it for me, or tell me of a contact in London? Stoll must be doing this all the time, and getting away with it. Or so the bar-tender had hinted. . . . I climbed into the dinghy and began to paddle away from the shore, thinking of the difference between a man like Stoll, with all his wealth, and myself. There he was, a brute with a skin so thick you couldn't pierce it with a spear, and his shelves back at home in the States loaded with loot. Whereas I . . . Teaching small boys on an inadequate salary, and all for what? Moralists said that money made no difference to happiness, but they were wrong. If I had a quarter of the Stolls' wealth I could retire, live abroad, on a Greek island, perhaps, and winter in some studio in Athens or Rome. A whole new way of life would open up, and just at the right moment too, before I touched middle-age.

I pulled out from the shore and made for the spot where I judged the boat to have anchored the day before. Then I let the dinghy rest, pulled in my paddles and stared down into the water. The colour was pale green, translucent, yet surely fathoms deep, for, as I looked down to the golden sands beneath, the sea-bed had all the tranquillity of another world, remote from the one I knew. A shoal of fish, silver-bright and gleaming, wriggled their way towards a tress of coral hair that might have graced Aphrodite, but was seaweed moving gently in whatever currents lapped the shore. Pebbles that on land would have been no more than rounded stones were brilliant here as jewels. The breeze that rippled the gulf beyond the anchored boat would never touch these depths, but only the surface of the water, and as the dinghy floated on, circling slowly without pull of wind or tide, I wondered whether it was the motion in itself that had drawn the unhearing Mrs Stoll to underwater swimming. Treasure was the excuse, to satisfy her husband's greed, but down there, in the depths, she would escape from a way of life that must have been unbearable.

Then I looked up at the hills above the retreating spit of sand, and I saw something flash. It was a ray of sunlight upon glass, and the glass moved. Someone was watching me through field-glasses. I rested upon my paddles and stared. Two figures moved stealthily away over the brow of the hill, but I recognised them instantly. One was Mrs Stoll, the other the Greek fellow who had acted as their crew. I glanced over my shoulder to the anchored boat. My helmsman was still staring out to sea. He had seen nothing.

The footsteps outside the hut were now explained. Mrs Stoll, the boatman in tow, had paid a final visit to the hut to clear the rubble, and now, their mission accomplished, they would drive on to the airport to catch the afternoon 'plane to Athens, their journey made several miles longer by the detour along the coast-road. And Stoll himself? Asleep, no doubt, at the back of the car upon the salt-flats, awaiting their return.

The sight of that woman once again gave me a profound distaste for my expedition. I wished I had not come. And my helmsman had spoken the truth; the dinghy was now floating above rock. A ridge must run out here from the shore in a single reef. The sand had darkened, changed in texture, become grey. I peered closer into the water, cupping my eyes with my hands, and suddenly I saw the vast encrusted anchor, the shells and barnacles of centuries upon its spikes, and as the dinghy drifted on the bones of the long-buried craft itself appeared, broken, sparless, her decks, if decks there had been, long since dismembered or destroyed.

Stoll had been right: her bones had been picked clean. Nothing of any value could now remain upon that skeleton. No pitchers, no jars, no gleaming coins. A momentary breeze rippled the water, and when it became clear again and all was still I saw the second anchor by the skeleton bows, and a body, arms outstretched, legs imprisoned in the anchor's jaws. The motion of the water gave the body life, as though, in some desperate fashion, it still struggled for release, but, trapped as it was, escape would never come. The days and nights would follow, months and years, and slowly the flesh would dissolve, leaving the frame impaled upon the spikes.

The body was Stoll's, head, trunk, limbs grotesque, inhuman, as they swayed backwards and forwards at the bidding of the current.

I looked up once more to the crest of the hill, but the two figures had long since vanished, and in an appalling flash of intuition a picture of what had happened became vivid: Stoll strutting on the spit of sand, the half-bottle raised to his lips, and then they struck him down and dragged him to the water's edge, and it was his wife who towed him, drowning, to his final resting-place beneath the surface, there below me, impaled on the crusted anchor. I was sole witness to his fate, and no matter what lies she told to account for his disappearance I would remain silent; it was not my responsibility; guilt might increasingly haunt me, but I must never become involved.

I heard the sound of something choking beside me – I realise now it was myself, in horror and in fear – and I struck at the water with my paddles and started pulling away from the wreck back to the boat. As I did so my arm brushed against the jar in my pocket, and in sudden panic I dragged it forth and flung it overboard. Even as I did so, I knew the gesture was in vain. It did not sink immediately but remained bobbing on the surface, then slowly filled with that green translucent sea, pale as the barley liquid laced with spruce and ivy. Not innocuous but evil, stifling conscience, dulling intellect, the hell-brew of the smiling god Dionysus, which turned his followers into drunken sots, would claim another victim before long. The eyes in the swollen face stared up at me, and they were not only those of Silenos the satyr tutor, and of the drowned Stoll, but my own as well, as I should see them soon reflected in a mirror. They seemed to hold all knowledge in their depths, and all despair.

David Fletcher

Corabella

It was about the middle of June when Michael first acknowledged that the children were becoming an insuperable problem. If he hadn't loved Janice so much, if he hadn't been so determined to make up to her for all the misery she must have suffered, he would have thrown in the towel there and then. But that would have caused unhappiness to both of them. In fact, it would have broken his heart. So far he had avoided making any criticism of the children because he knew how much she loved them and how they had kept her going during the worst period of her marriage and its final breakdown. And it couldn't have been easy for them, he reminded himself. No wonder they were difficult, resentful of another man entering their young lives. If their father was the only model they had to judge him by . . . But these arguments had begun to take on a hollow ring, to sound like the convenient quotes from textbooks they actually were. He had to talk to Janice about the children, even at the risk of hurting, perhaps even alienating her. He had kept quiet too long.

It was the brutal, winding kick in the stomach from Paul that finally decided it. There was a park a short walk from the small garden flat Janice had rented in South London, and Michael had taken the children there one hot, Saturday afternoon. Paul was too old, or considered himself too old to hold Michael's hand. Therefore, Melinda did so reluctantly. Michael could feel the hostility in her stiff little hand as they walked, as usual, in silence. Once in the park she broke free of him and ran after her brother.

The purpose of these outings, of course, was to give Michael and the children a chance to get to know each other. In fact, all that happened was that Michael spent his time pursuing them, trying to make sure that they came to no harm. In any open space they ran from him and quickly became absorbed in their own world. On bus rides or river trips they sat ostentatiously together and, if possible, several seats away from him. At the cinema once, they had moved seats while he was using the lavatory. Michael had tried everything to get close to them, to amuse and entertain but by that Saturday afternoon he had given up. Having located Melinda's red dress beside the paddling pool, he lay down on the dry grass and kept half an eye on them. He knew that Janice did not like them to paddle in the pool and equally that were he to cross the grass and forbid it he would certainly be greeted by open defiance. Perhaps if he didn't put the idea into their heads . . . They did not go into the water. They stayed close together, apparently deep in some game of their own. Then they turned as one and came steadily across the grass to where he lay, propped on his side.

'Hello,' he smiled at Melinda, working on the principle that being the younger and female he might make some headway with her. Besides, she hung back a little, watching him pensively. Paul stood close, however, and Michael remembered thinking, afterwards, as he had turned towards the boy that his stout shoes were quite unsuitable for this weather. The boy drew back his right leg and kicked Michael, as hard as he could, in the stomach.

By the time Michael was able to speak he had realised the futility of remonstrating with Paul. The children waited for him at the gates and, still holding his stomach which felt as though it contained a jagged rock, he joined them and led them silently home. Or rather to the corner of their road whereupon Melinda broke free of his hand and chased after her brother, leaving him to follow them in.

He spent the rest of the day with them and they were, as always in their mother's presence, polite and well-behaved to him. There was no chance to speak to Janice about them until bedtime, at which point they came to him and quietly thanked him for having taken them to the park. Paul extended his hand and Michael duly shook it. He even managed to lay his hand briefly on Melinda's flaxen head. Smiling, Janice led them out of the room.

The flat was small, all she could afford since she steadfastly refused to let Michael help her until they were married. He understood, but was frustrated by her independence. The small, square sitting room opened, by way of french doors, straight into a walled handkerchief of garden. The bedrooms were situated next to this room and the children's window faced onto the garden. He heard Janice adjusting it and the quiet murmur of her voice as she settled them.

'Janice,' he began as soon as she came back into the room. 'I must talk to you about the children. Paul kicked me in the stomach today. It's just not working.'

'Oh yes, he told me about that. I'm sorry, I hadn't realised it was anything that bothered you.'

'What do you mean, he told you?'

'About the wrestling match. He was so impressed with you, but rather afraid that his kicking you like that might mean you wouldn't do it again.'

Michael felt as though he had stepped into a nightmare, and the feeling grew as Janice steadfastly refused to believe him.

'Michael, they have never lied to me in their lives. I mean you can't expect me to believe that Paul deliberately kicked you, in cold blood.'

'But that is just what he did do. There is no way it could have been an accident, Janice. And besides, that's only the latest in a long line of incidents.'

Michael heard his voice as he recounted the catalogue of things the children had done and knew that it sounded querulous and his complaints trivial. Indeed, calmly recited in the context of their exemplary behaviour in Janice's presence, the incidents did sound trivial, and unbelievable.

'Mike,' she said gently when, out of sheer embarrassment, he had let his voice tail away. 'Perhaps the real trouble is that you aren't used to children. Even I sometimes think they are a different species. You learn to make allowances, to understand. It will be all right but, darling, you've got to get used to them as children every bit as much as they have to accept you as a step-father.'

She made it all sound so rational, so easy. He was an only child. He knew nothing about children except what he had read in books. It was very difficult for a man to take on two growing children with definite, formed personalities of their own. Janice thought the experts minimised, even ignored the vast amount a potential step-parent had to learn before he could feel at ease with children.

'I'm sorry,' he said, taking her hand. 'I suppose I have been expecting too much, and over-reacting.'

'You should have told me before.'

'I didn't want to worry you. I suppose I didn't want you to know that I'd failed with them. I so want to make a success of it.'

'You haven't failed. And you will make a success of it. You all will, all three.'

At the open window of their room Melinda smiled at Paul who grinned back.

Michael felt better, felt reassured and was determined to make greater efforts with the children. In the middle of the following week he went to dinner, played chess with Paul and snakes and ladders with Melinda. It crossed his mind that perhaps Janice had spoken to them about their behaviour for he sensed a new relaxation in them, an absence of hostility, even when he was alone with Paul while Janice was supervising Melinda's bath. Perhaps he had made the breakthrough. Perhaps that kick had been the end, the necessary, final expression of antagonism. Or perhaps the kick had been a test, a challenge to see if Michael was like their father, a man who responded violently to anything that crossed him. And when Melinda demanded that he should put her to bed and tuck her in, he knew that he had succeeded.

She slept in the lower bunk and Michael carefully arranged the single sheet over her, tucking the ends firmly in. She looked at him with her mother's frank grey eyes. He stooped to kiss her. She twisted away from him.

'Oh, I forgot to say good-night to Corabella,' she announced, jumping out of bed. Michael was so relieved that her reaction was not a violent rejection of him that he smiled and followed her across the room. Then his blood froze. He felt sick, a ringing in his ears and felt the cold sweat break out all over his body. He backed away, staring in disgusted fascination at the glass tank on the window ledge which he had not previously noticed. Melinda stood on tip-toe and peered into the case.

'Good-night, Corabella,' she said and then turned back towards the bed. Her eyes widened at the sight of Michael's face. He tried to pull himself together, but it was impossible.

'What's the matter?' she asked.

'That... thing...' he stammered, for he could not bring himself even to say the word. Melinda looked puzzled. He nodded desperately towards the glass case.

'That's not a thing. That's Corabella. She's the biggest and most beautiful spider in the whole world,' Melinda said proudly and trotted back to bed. Somehow, Michael managed to tuck her in again but his eagerness to get out of the room, away from that creature, prevented him even trying to kiss her.

He was shaking and knew that his face would be grey with fear. Janice thought he was ill. In her anxiety she forgot Paul, who stood in the doorway, knotting the cord of his pyjamas.

'Do you know that they've got a spider in there? An enormous one.'

Janice looked at him in disbelief, then threw back her head and laughed.

'You don't mean to tell me that you're afraid of spiders? Oh Mike, that's too ridiculous.'

'It's a phobia,' he said. 'I'm not afraid but literally terrified. Janice, you've got to get rid of that thing. I mean people don't keep them. Please, you must kill it straight away.'

CORABELLA

'No,'

Janice shot him an angry glance and hurried to Paul who looked every bit as upset as Michael.

'Don't be silly, darling,' she said, encircling his shoulders with her arm. 'Mike wasn't serious. Nobody's going to hurt Corabella.'

'I was serious,' Michael shouted. 'Don't you understand? I can't bear the things. They terrify me. Just knowing it's there . . .'

'I hate you,' Paul shouted, and bolted from the comfort of his mother's arms into his room, slamming the door behind him.

'Now look what you've done,' Janice said, and hurried after Paul.

Michael knew that he had lost all the ground he had made that evening. He knew, too, that it was ridiculous. But he had to go and stand as far as possible from that door while his eyes searched every inch of the room for other spiders. It was always this way. Once he even suspected the presence of one he was unable to relax or even behave naturally. Summer and winter he always kept the plug in the bath and the washbasin. Throughout the warm months he sprayed his flat daily with an insecticide which killed them. It was no accident that his flat was on the top floor of a brand new building which stood in a wasteland of concrete which, Michael liked to believe, no spider would willingly enter.

When Janice returned she was too angry to say much and Michael was too frightened to stay. He fled from the flat and spent more than an hour minutely inspecting his own. He sprayed until he coughed with the scent of the insecticide and could not get to sleep for hours. Every time he closed his eyes he saw Corabella's eight horribly poised legs.

Janice tried to reason with him the next day in a long telephone call. She had, as always, taken a thoroughly practical approach to the problem. She gave him details of various cures about which she had read. Michael had read about them, too, and shuddered to think even of the first step.

'All you have to do is sit in a room with a therapist, and they have a dead spider in a sealed glass jar right on the other side of the room and . . .'

'No,' he said. 'Please, I don't even want to talk about it.'

In his turn he tried to persuade her to make the children put the creature back into the garden. No need to kill it, just get it out of the flat.

'No.' Janice was adamant. 'I've brought them up to be free of these irrational fears. Nearly all children are frightened of spiders because of the bad example of adults. I'm proud that mine are not. Besides, it's educational.'

Eventually, they agreed not to talk about it and Michael contrived not to go to the flat. He didn't ask about Corabella, nor did he allow himself to consider whether Janice realised that his sudden insistence that he should take her out, or that he should meet them all at the National Gallery, or outside the cinema was because he did not dare to go into the flat. If she did understand, she said nothing. And gradually the fear began to fade as it always did if he were not reminded of it.

And then Janice rang him at the office and, to his surprise and delight, said Melinda wanted to ask him something.

'Please will you take Paul and me to the fun fair?'

'Yes, of course. I'd love to. When would you like to go?'

Janice came back on the line full of apologies. He didn't have to take them, he wasn't to feel pressurised. It was just that she got sick on the rides.

'I love them all,' Michael told her, 'And I'd love to take the kids. I'll pick them up tomorrow.'

The whole spider incident, he felt, was behind them. He would go into the flat, collect the children and have a marvellous time. The fact that Melinda had asked touched him. He knew that Janice had been right about his having to make allowances and about letting the relationship develop at the children's speed. He felt accepted. And it was true, he did love fun fairs.

That night the children stood solemnly together in front of the glass case. Corabella had made herself a handsome, strong web, and she stood poised in its centre, her legs spread out, waiting. Paul had explained to Melinda that it might be necessary to sacrifice Corabella. She understood. In fact, she didn't mind at all. Paul did, a little, but he kept his fingers crossed. Perhaps it would not be necessary.

It transpired that the children, by some quirk of conditioning, shared between them their mother's delicate stomach at fairgrounds. Firmly they explained that Melinda got sick if she whizzed around on the whirly things, and Paul got sick if he went up high. So much, Michael thought, for Janice's claims to have brought them up without irrational fears. They must have learned these from her for such reactions were, he knew, entirely psychosomatic. However, he complimented them on their good sense in telling him and confessed himself delighted that he would get to ride on everything. He decreed a rota system. They would take it turn and turn about. He and Melinda on the helter-skelter, he and Paul on the Waltzer and so on. Neither of them wanted to go on the boating lake.

And in this way, though Michael did not realise it, Corabella was preserved from the possibly deleterious effects of any unusual motion. Paul and Melinda simply slipped her carefully prepared box to one another so that she always remained in the safe keeping of the child who waited, smiling and patient, while Michael and the other rode.

CORABELLA

That is until the Big Wheel.

This was to be the climax of Melinda's afternoon. She insisted that they get right to the head of the queue so that they were the first to take their place in the swinging, mounting cars. That way they got a longer ride. Michael admired the logic of this and readily agreed. They got on and the bar was fastened across in front of them. Melinda was glad to see that there was plenty of room on the seat and shifted along to the end, leaving a good space between Michael and herself. Their car slowly mounted backwards with a longish pause between each jerking movement while the next car was occupied. The fun fair was busy that afternoon and they made one complete revolution of the wheel before the ride proper started. While the last car was loading, Melinda took the box out of her pocket but kept it out of sight, pressed against the wall of the bar. The timing, she knew, was all-important. Slowly the wheel turned. Michael called and waved to Paul who waved back. Melinda allowed one complete revolution to take place and the second to begin before she removed the lid of the box and deftly covered it with her hand. Corabella was anxious to get out. She could tell from the tickling against her imprisoning palm.

'Look, Michael,' she said simply as their car approached the crest of the ride, and tipped the box up on the seat between them. Probably, she thought, Corabella was confused for she paused a moment before scuttling fast towards Michael.

It is not always so that people freeze with fear. Michael didn't. He jumped to his feet, his legs trapped by the safety bar, his arms flailing, but the impetus of the car's sudden descent was made lethal by the violent rocking his sudden movement had caused. He seemed to hang for a moment, looking at Corabella, before plunging down.

Melinda hung on tight. She was far too busy to watch what happened. In fact, her car still swung sickeningly, but she was not afraid. The wheel made another one and a half revolutions before the machinery was halted. During that time Melinda retrieved Corabella, who curled up, a fat, satisfying blob in her hand. Melinda placed her gently on the floor of the car and squashed her with her foot. Then, working swiftly, she flattened the carboard box and threw it under the seat where other unremarkable litter already lay.

The rest of that day passed in a blur for the children. Everyone said they must be in a state of delayed shock. Melinda answered their questions as best she could, but there was no reason why Michael should have jumped from the car. She hadn't even been looking, and then the car swung so frighteningly . . . A doctor was called to give them both a mild sedative. Janice needed a stronger one and before she fell asleep she remembered that she had not told the children that Corabella was missing. She hoped they wouldn't be too upset.

'Paul?' Melinda whispered from the lower bunk.

'What?'

'Did his head go splat like you said it would?'

Paul giggled.

'Yes. Splat.'

'I wish I'd seen that,' Melinda said enviously, and drowsily.

'Mm. Pity about poor Corabella, though,' Paul said.

Melinda giggled in her turn. She hadn't told Paul about Corabella.

'I made her go splat,' she said proudly. 'With my foot.'

Paul felt sick.

'But that's murder,' he said.

'No. She was sacrificed. Like you said. Besides,' she added, turning over sleepily, 'she might have talked.'

Paul did not go to sleep. Ridiculous though he kept telling himself it was, he was afraid of Melinda.

ACKNOWLEDGEMENTS

The Publishers wish to thank the following for permission to reprint previously published material. Every effort has been made to locate all persons having any rights in the stories appearing in this book but appropriate acknowledgement has been omitted in some cases through lack of information. Such omissions will be corrected in future printings of the book upon written notification to the Publishers.

Victor Gollancz and David Higham Associates Ltd for 'Suspicion' from *In the Teeth of the Evidence* by Dorothy L. Sayers. Copyright © 1939 Dorothy L. Sayers.

A.M. Heath & Company Ltd and the Estate of the late Geoffrey Household for 'Taboo' by Geoffrey Household.

The Carnell Literary Agency for 'The Words of Guru' by C.M. Kornbluth. Copyright © 1941 by Street and Smith Publications Inc.

Robert Bloch, A.M. Heath & Company Ltd and The Scott Meredith Literary Agency, Inc. for 'Yours Truly, Jack the Ripper' by Robert Bloch.

The Peters Fraser and Dunlop Group Ltd and Don Congdon Associates, Inc. for 'The Veld' from *The Golden Apples of the Sun* by Ray Bradbury. Copyright © 1950 by Ray Bradbury; © 1978 renewed by Ray Bradbury.

The Peters Fraser and Dunlop Group Ltd for 'Evening Primrose' from *The John Collier Reader* by John Collier.

A.M. Heath & Company Ltd and Ralph M. Vicinanza Ltd, New York, New York, for 'Back From the Grave' by Robert Silverberg. Copyright © 1958, 1986 by Agberg Ltd.

Random House Inc., the Estate of William Faulkner and Curtis Brown Ltd for 'A Rose for Emily' from *Collected Stories of William Faulkner* by William Faulkner. Copyright © 1930 and renewed 1958 by William Faulkner.

Sterling Lord Literistic, Inc. and The Peters Fraser and Dunlop Group Ltd for 'The Comforts of Home' by Flannery O'Connor.

Roald Dahl, Penguin Books Ltd, Murray Pollinger and Alfred Knopf Inc. for 'Pig' from *Kiss, Kiss* by Roald Dahl. Copyright © 1959 by Roald Dahl.

Stanely Ellin and Curtis Brown Ltd for 'Robert' and 'The Question' by Stanley Ellin.

Patricia Highsmith, William Heinemann and The Atlantic Monthly Press for 'The Terrapin' from *Eleven* by Patricia Highsmith.

The Estate of Dame Daphne du Maurier and Curtis Brown Ltd for 'Not After Midnight' by Daphne du Maurier. Copyright © 1971 Daphne du Maurier.

Anthony Sheil Associates Ltd for 'Corabella' by David Fletcher.